REBORN

BOOK I OF THE EVOLUTION GENE

AARON HODGES

Edited by Genevieve Lerner
Proofread by Sara Houston
Illustration by Christian Bentulan
Typography by Nikko Marie

ABOUT THE AUTHOR

 Aaron Hodges was born in 1989 in the small town of Whakatane, New Zealand. He studied for five years at the University of Auckland, completing a Bachelors of Science in Biology and Geography, and a Masters of Environmental Engineering. After working as an environmental consultant for two years, he grew tired of office work and decided to quit his job in 2014 and see the world. One year later, he published his first novel - Stormwielder.

For the child inside us all.
Let them soar.

PART ONE

ONE

CHRIS LET OUT A SIGH AS HE SETTLED INTO THE WORN-OUT sofa, then cursed as a broken spring stabbed at his backside. Wriggling sideways to avoid it, he leaned back and reached for the remote, only to realise it had been left beside the television. Muttering under his breath, he climbed back to his feet, retrieved the remote and flicked on the television, then collapsed back into the chair. This time he was careful to avoid the broken springs.

He closed his eyes as the blue glow of the television lit the room. The shriek of the adverts quickly followed, but he barely had the energy to be annoyed. He was still studying full-time, but now his afternoons were taken up by long hours at the construction site. Even then, they were struggling. His only hope was winning a place at the California State University. Otherwise, he would have little choice but to accept the apprenticeship his supervisor was offering.

"Another attack was reported today from the rural town of Julian," a reporter's voice broke through the stream of adverts, announcing the start of the six o'clock news.

Chris's ears perked up and he opened his eyes to look at the television. Images flashed across the screen of an old mining town, its dusty dirt roads and rundown buildings looking like they had not been touched since the 1900s. A row of horse-drawn carriages lined the street, their owners standing beside them.

The sight was a common one in the rural counties of the Western Allied States. In the thirty years since the states of California, Oregon and Washington had declared their independence, the divide between urban and rural communities had grown exponentially. Today there were few citizens in the countryside who could afford luxuries such as cars and televisions.

"We're just receiving word the police have arrived on the scene," the reporter continued.

On the television, a black van with the letters SWAT painted on the side had just pulled up. The rear doors swung open, and a squad of black-garbed riot-police leapt out. They gathered around the van and then moved on past the carriages. Dust swirled around them, but they moved without hesitation, the camera following them at a distance.

The image changed as the police moved around a corner into an empty street. The new camera angle looked down at the police from the rooftop of a nearby building. It followed the SWAT unit as they split into two groups and spread out along the street, moving quickly, their rifles at the ready.

Then the camera panned down the street and refocused on the broken window of a grocery store. The image grew as the camera zoomed, revealing the nightmare inside the store.

Chris swallowed as images straight from a horror movie flashed across the screen. The remnants of the store lay scattered across the linoleum floor, the contents of broken cans and bottles staining the ground red. Amongst the wreckage, a dozen people lay motionless, face down in the dark red liquid.

The camera tilted and zoomed again, bringing the figures into sharper focus. Chris's stomach twisted and he forced himself to look away. But even the brief glimpse had been enough to see the people in the store were dead. Their pale faces stared blankly into space, the blood drained away, their skin marked by jagged streaks of red and patches of purple. Few, if any of the victims were whole. Pieces of humanity lay scattered across the floor, the broken limbs still dripping blood.

Finally turning back to the television, Chris swallowed as the camera panned in on the sole survivor of the carnage. The man stood amidst the wreckage of the store, blood streaking his face and arms, stained his shirt red. His head was bowed, and the only sign of life was the rhythmic rise and fall of his shoulders. As the camera zoomed on his face, his cold grey eyes were revealed. They stared at the ground, blank and lifeless.

Standing, Chris looked away, struggling to contain the meagre contents of his stomach.

"The *Chead* is thought to have awakened around sixteen hundred hours," the reporter started to speak again, drawing Chris back to the screen. "Special forces have cleared the immediate area and are now preparing to engage with the creature."

"Two hours." Chris jumped as a woman's voice came from behind him.

Spinning on his heel, he let out a long breath as his mother walked in from the kitchen. "I thought you had a night class!" he gasped, his heart racing.

His mother shook her head, a slight smile touching her face. "We finished early." She shrugged, then waved at the television. "They've been standing around for two hours. Watching that thing. Some of those people were still alive when it all started. They could have been saved. Would have, if they'd been somebody important."

Chris pulled himself off the couch and moved across to embrace his mother. Wrapping his arms around her, he kissed her cheek. She returned the gesture, and then they both turned to watch the SWAT team approach the grocery store. The men in black moved with military precision, jogging down the dirt road, sticking close to the buildings. If the *Chead* came out of its trance, no one wanted to be caught in the open. While the creatures looked human, they possessed a terrifying speed, and had the strength to tear full-grown men limb from limb.

As the scene inside the grocery store demonstrated.

Absently, Chris clutched his mother's arm tighter. The *Chead* were almost legend throughout the Western Allied States, a dark shadow left over from the days of the American War.

The first whispers of the creatures were believed to have started in 2030, not long after the United States had fallen.

At first they had been dismissed as rumour by a country eager to move on from the decade-long conflict of the American War. The attacks had been blamed on resistance fighters in rural communities, who had never fully supported their severance from the United States. So the government had imposed curfews over rural communities and sent in the military to quell the problem.

Meanwhile, the rest of the young nation had moved forward, and prospered. The pacific coast had boomed as migrants arrived from the allied nations of Mexico and Canada, replacing the thousands of lives lost in the American War.

But through the years, reports of attacks continued, and accounts by survivors eventually filtered through to the media. Each claimed the slaughter had been carried out by one or two individuals – often someone well known in the community. One day, they would be an ordinary neighbour, mother, father, child. The next, they would become the monster now standing in the grocery store.

It was not until one of the creatures was captured, that the government had admitted its mistake. By then, rural communities had suffered almost a decade of terror at the hands of the monstrosities. Newsrooms and government agencies had been beside themselves with the discovery, with blame pointed in every direction from poor rural police-reporting, to secret operations by the Texans to destabilise the Western Allied States.

The government had extended curfews across the entire country and increased military patrols, but the measures had done little to slow the spread of attacks. Last year, in 2050, the first *Chead* sighting had been reported in Los Angeles, and was quickly followed by attacks in Portland and Seattle. Fortunately, they had yet to reach the streets of San Francisco. Even so, a perpetual State of Emergency had been put into effect.

On the television, the SWAT team had reached the grocery store and were now gathering outside, their rifles trained on the entrance. One lowered his rifle and stepped towards it, the others covering him from behind. Reaching the door, he stretched out an arm and began to pull it open.

The *Chead* did not make a sound as it tore through the store windows and barrelled into the man. A screech came through the old television speakers as the men scattered before the *Chead's* ferocity. With one hand, it grabbed its victim by the throat and hurled him across the street. The thud as he struck the ground was audible over the reporter's microphone.

The crunch of their companion's untimely demise seemed to snap the other members of the squadron into action. The first bangs of gunfire echoed over the television speakers, but the *Chead* was already moving. It tore across the dirt road as bullets raised dust-clouds around it, and smashed into another squad member. A scream echoed up from the street as man and *Chead* went down, disappearing into a cloud of dust.

Despite the risk of hitting their comrade, the rest of the SWAT team did not stop firing. The chance of survival once a *Chead* had its hands on you was zero to none, and no one wanted to take the chance it might escape.

With a roar, the *Chead* reared up from the dust, then spun as a bullet struck it in the shoulder. Blood blossomed from the wound as it staggered backwards, its grey eyes wide, flickering with surprise. It reached up and touched a finger to the hole left by the bullet, its brow creasing with confusion.

Then the rest of the men opened fire, and the battle was over.

TWO

ANGELA FALLOW SQUINTED THROUGH THE RAIN-STREAKED windshield, struggling to make out details in the lengthening gloom. A few minutes ago the streetlights had flickered into life, but despite their yellowed light, shadows still hung around the house across the street. Tall hedges marked the boundary with the neighbouring properties, while a white picket fence stood between her car and the old cottage.

Leaning closer to the window, Angela held her breath to keep the glass from fogging, and willed her eyes to pierce the twilight. But beyond the brightly-lit sidewalk, there was no sign of movement. Letting out a long sigh, she sat back in her seat and smiled with quiet satisfaction. There was no sign of anyone outside the house, no silent shadows slipping closer to the warm light streaming from the windows.

At least, none that could be seen.

Berating herself for her nerves, Angela turned her attention to the touchscreen on her dashboard. Its soft glow brightened as she tapped its screen, making her glad for the tinted windows. No one in the house would be able to see the car was occupied.

Angela pursed her lips, studying the charts on the screen one last time. It displayed the driver's license of a young woman in her early forties. Auburn hair hung around her shoulders and she wore the faintest hint of a smile on her red lips. The smile spread to her cheeks, crinkling the skin around her olive-green eyes.

Margaret Sanders

Beneath the picture was a description of the woman: her height, weight, license number, last known address, school and work history, her current occupation as a college teacher, and marital status. The last was listed as widowed with a single child. Her husband had succumbed to cancer almost a decade previously.

Shaking her head, Angela looked again at the woman's eyes, wondering what could have driven her to this end. She had a house, a son, solid employment as a teacher. Why would she throw it all away, when she had so much to lose?

Idly, she wondered whether Mrs Sanders would have done things differently if given another chance. The smile lines around her eyes were those of a kind soul, and her alleged support for the resistance fighters seemed out of character. It was a shame the government did not give second chances – especially not with traitors of the state.

Now both mother and son would suffer for her actions.

Tapping the screen, Angela pulled up the son's file. Christopher Sanders, at eighteen, was the reason she had come tonight. The assault team would handle the mother and any of her associates who might be on the property, but the son had been selected for the Praegressus project. That meant he had to be taken alive and unharmed.

His profile described him as five-foot-eleven, with a weight of 150 pounds – not large by any measure. Her only concern was the black belt listed beneath his credentials, though Angela knew such accomplishments usually meant little in reality. Particularly when the target was unarmed, unsuspecting and outnumbered.

A picture of her target popped onto the screen with another tap, and a flicker of discomfort spread through her stomach. His brunette hair showed traces of his mother's auburn locks, while the hazel eyes must have descended from a dominant *bey2* allele in his father's chromosome. A hint of light-brown facial hair traced the edges of his jaw, mingling with the last traces of teenage acne. Despite his small size, he had the broad, muscular shoulders of an athlete, and there was little sign of fat on his youthful face.

Sucking in a breath, Angela flicked off the screen. This was not her first assignment, though she hoped it might be her last. For months now she had overseen the collection of subjects for the Praegressus project, and the task had never gotten easier. The faces of the children she had taken haunted her, staring at her when she closed her eyes. Her only consolation was that without her, those children would have suffered the same fate as their parents. At least the research facility gave them a fighting chance.

And looking into the boy's eyes, she knew he was a fighter.

Angela closed her eyes, shoving aside her doubt, and reached out and pressed a button on the car's console.

"Are you in position?" she spoke to the empty car.

"Ready when you are, Fallow," a man replied.

Nodding her head, Fallow reached beneath her seat and retrieved a steel briefcase. Unclipping its restraints, she lifted out a jet injector and held it up to the light. The stainless-steel instrument appeared more like a gun than a piece of medical equipment, but it served its purpose well enough. Once her team had Chris restrained, it would be a simple matter to use the jet injector to anesthetise the young man for transport.

Removing a vial of etorphine from the case, she screwed it into place and pressed a button on the side. A short *hiss* confirmed it was pressurised. She eyed the clear liquid, hoping the details in the boy's file were correct. She had prepared the dosage of etorphine earlier for Chris's age and weight, but a miscalculation could prove fatal.

"Fallow, still waiting on your signal?" the voice came again.

Fallow bit her lip and closed her eyes. Taking a deep breath, she shivered in the cold of the car.

If not you, then someone else.

She opened her eyes. "Go."

THREE

THE SCREEN OF THE OLD CRT TELEVISION FLICKERED TO
black as Chris's mother moved across and switched it off.
Her face was pale when she turned towards him, and a
shiver ran through her as she closed her eyes.

"Your Grandfather would be ashamed, Chris," she said,
shaking her head. "He went to war against the United
States because he believed in our freedom. He fought to
keep us free, not to spend decades haunted by the ghosts of
the past."

Chris shivered. He'd never met his grandfather, but his
mother and grandmother talked of him enough that Chris
felt he knew him. When the United States had refused to
accept the independence of the Western Allied States, his
grandfather had accepted the call to defend their young
nation. He had enlisted in the WAS Marines and had
shipped off to war. The conflict had quickly expanded to
engulf the whole of North America. Only the aid of
Canada and Mexico had given the WAS the strength to

survive, and eventually prevail against the aggression of the United States.

Unfortunately, his grandfather had not survived to see the world change. He had learned of Chris's birth while stationed in New Mexico, but had never returned to see his grandson grow. So Chris knew him only from photos, and the stories of his mother and grandmother.

"Things will change soon." Chris shook his head. "Surely?"

His mother crinkled her nose. "I've been saying that for ten years," she said as she moved towards the kitchen, ruffling Chris's hair as she passed him, "but things only ever seem to get worse."

Chris moved after her and pulled out a chair at the wooden table. The kitchen was small, barely big enough for the two of them, but it was all they needed. His mother was already standing at the stove, stirring a pot of stew he recognised as leftovers from the beef shanks of the night before.

"Most don't seem to care, as long as the attacks are confined to the countryside," Chris commented.

"Exactly." His mother turned, emphatically waving the wooden spoon. "They think it doesn't matter, that our wealth will protect us. Well, it won't stay that way forever."

"No." Chris shook his head. "That one in Seattle..." he shuddered. Over fifty people had been killed by a single *Chead* in a shopping mall. Police had arrived within ten minutes, but that was all the time it had needed.

Impulsively, he reached up and felt the pocket watch he wore around his neck. His mother had given it to him ten years ago, at his father's funeral. It held a picture of his parents, smiling on the shore of Lake Washington in Seattle, where they had met. His heart gave a painful throb as he thought of the terror engulfing the city.

Noticing the gesture, his mother abandoned the pot and pulled him into a hug. "It's okay, Chris. We'll survive this. We're a strong people. They'll come up with a solution, even if we have to march up to parliament's gates and demand it."

Chris nodded and was about to speak when a crash came from somewhere in the house. They pushed apart and spun towards the kitchen doorway. Though they lived in the city, when Chris's father had passed away they had been forced to move closer to the city's edge. It was not the safest neighbourhood, and it was well past the seven o'clock curfew now. Whoever, or whatever, had made the noise was not likely to be friendly.

Sucking in a breath, Chris moved into the doorway and risked a glance into the lounge. The single incandescent bulb cast shadows across the room, leaving dark patches behind the couch and television. He stared hard into the darkness, searching for signs of movement, and then retreated to the kitchen.

Silently, his mother handed him a kitchen knife. He took it after only a second's hesitation. She held a second blade in a practiced grip. Looking at her face, Chris swallowed hard. Her eyes were hard, her brow creased in a scowl, but he did not miss the fear there. Together they faced the door, and waited.

The squeak of the loose floorboard in the hall sounded as loud as a gunshot in the silent house. Chris glanced at his mother, and she nodded back. There was no doubt now.

A crash came from the lounge, then the thud of heavy boots as the intruder gave up all pretence of stealth. Chris tensed, his knuckles turning white as he gripped the knife handle. He spread his feet into a forward stance, readying himself.

The crack of breaking glass came from their right as the kitchen window exploded inwards, and a black-suited figure tumbled into the room. The man bowled into his mother, sending her tumbling to the ground before she could swing the knife. Chris sprang to the side as another man charged through the doorway to the lounge, then drew back and hurled the knife.

Without pausing to see whether the knife struck home, Chris twisted and leapt, driving his shoulder into the midriff of the intruder standing over his mother. But the man was ready for him, and with his greater bulk brushed Chris off with little effort. Stumbling sideways, Chris clenched his fists and charged again.

The man grinned, raising his arms to catch him. With his attention diverted, Chris's mother rose up behind him, knife still in hand, and drove the blade deep into the attacker's hamstring.

Their black-garbed attacker barely had time to scream before Chris's fist slammed into his windpipe His face paled and his hands went to his neck. He staggered backwards, strangled noises gurgling from his throat, and toppled over the kitchen table.

Chris offered his mother a hand, but before she could take it a creak came from the floorboards behind him. The man from the lounge loomed up, grabbing Chris by the shoulder before he could leap to safety. Still on the ground, his mother rolled away as Chris twisted around, fighting to break the man's hold. Cursing, he aimed an elbow at the man's gut, but his arm struck solid body armour and bounced off.

That explains the knife, the thought raced through his mind, before another crash from the window chased it away.

Beside him, his mother surged to her feet as a third man came through the window. Still holding the bloodied knife, she screamed and charged the man. Straining his arms, Chris bucked against his captor's grip, but there was no breaking the man's iron hold. Stomach clenched, he watched his mother attack the heavily-armed assailant.

The fresh intruder carried a long steel baton in one hand, and as she swung her knife it flashed out and caught her wrist. His mother screamed and dropped the knife, then retreated across the room cradling her arm. A fourth man appeared through the door to the lounge. Before Chris could shout a warning, he grabbed her from behind.

His mother shrieked and threw back her head, trying to catch the man in the chin, but her blows bounced off his body armour. Her eyes widened as his arm went around her neck, cutting off her breath. Heart hammering in his chest, Chris twisted and kicked at his opponent's shins, desperate to aid his mother, but the man showed no sign of relenting.

"*Mum!*" He screamed as her eyes drooped closed.

"Fallow, situation under control. You're up." The man from the window spoke into his cuff. He moved across to his fallen comrade, whose face was turning purple. "Hold on, soldier. Medical's on its way."

"Who are you?" Chris gasped.

The man ignored him. Instead, he went to work on the fallen man. Removing his belt, he bound it around the man's leg. The injured man groaned as the speaker worked, his eyes closed and his teeth clenched. A pang of guilt touched Chris, but he crushed it down.

"What the hell happened?" Chris looked up as a woman appeared in the doorway.

The woman was dark-skinned, but the colour rapidly fled her face as her gaze swept over the kitchen. She raised a hand to her mouth, her eyes lingering on the blood, then flicking between the men and their captives. Shock showed in their amber depths, but already it was fading as she reasserted control. Lowering her hand to her side, she pursed her red lips. Her gaze settled on Chris.

A chill went through Chris as he noticed the red emblazoned bear on the front of her black jacket. The symbol marked her as a government employee. These were not random thugs in the night – they were police, and they were here for Chris and his mother.

Taking a breath, the woman nodded to herself, then reached inside her jacket and drew something into the light. The breath went from Chris's chest as he glimpsed the steel contraption in her hand. For a second he thought it was a pistol, but as she drew closer he realised his mistake. It was some sort of hypodermic gun, some medical contraption he had seen in movies, though in real life it looked far more threatening, more deadly.

"Who are you?" Chris croaked as she paused in front of him.

Her eyes drifted to Chris's face, but she only shook her head and looked away. She studied the liquid in the vial attached to the gun's barrel, then at Chris, as though weighing him up.

"Hold him," she said at last.

"What?" Chris gasped as his captor's hands pulled his arms behind his back. "What are you doing? Please, you're making some mistake, we haven't done anything wrong!"

The woman did not answer as she raised the gun to his neck. Chris struggled to move, but the man only pulled his arms harder, sending a bolt of pain through his shoulders. Biting back a scream, Chris looked up at the woman. Their eyes met, and he thought he saw a flicker of regret in the woman's eyes.

Then the cold steel of the hypodermic gun touched his neck, followed by a hiss of gas as she pressed the trigger. Metal pinched at Chris's neck for a second, before the woman stepped back. Holding his breath, Chris stared at the woman, his eyes never leaving hers.

Within seconds the first touch of weariness began to seep through Chris's body. He blinked as shadows spread around the edges of his vision. Idly, he struggled to free his arms, so he might chase the shadows away. But the man still held him fast. Sucking in a mouthful of air, Chris fought against the exhaustion. Blinking hard, he stared at the woman, willing himself to resist the pull of sleep.

But there was no stopping the warmth spreading through his limbs. His head bobbed and his arms went limp, until the only thing keeping him upright was the strength of his captor.

The woman's face was the last thing Chris saw as he slipped into the darkness.

FOUR

Liz shivered as the air conditioner whirred, sending a blast of icy air in her direction. Wrapping her arms around herself, she closed her eyes and waited for it to pass. The scent of chlorine drifted on the air, its chemical reek setting her head to pounding. Her teeth chattered and she shuddered as the whir of fans died away. Groaning, Liz opened her eyes and returned to studying her surroundings.

Ten minutes ago, she had woken in this thirty-foot room, enclosed by the plain, unadorned concrete walls and floor. A door stood on the opposite wall, a small glass panel revealing a bright hallway beyond. It offered the only escape from the little room, but it might as well have been half a world away. Between Liz and the door stood the wire mesh of her little steel cage.

Shaking, she gripped the wire tight in her fingers and placed her head against it. Silently, she searched the vaults of her memories, struggling to find a cause for her current predicament. But she had no memory of how she had come to be there, lying shivering on the concrete floor of a cage.

She cursed as the blast of the air conditioner returned. Her thin clothes were little better than rags, fine in the warm Californian climate, but completely inadequate for the freezing temperatures the central heating system had apparently been set too. To make matters worse, her boots were gone, along with the blade she kept tucked inside them. Without it she felt naked, exposed inside the tiny cage.

At least I'm not alone, she thought wryly, looking through the wire into the cage beside her.

A young man somewhere around her own eighteen years lay there, still dozing on the concrete floor. His clothes were better kept than her own, though there was a bloodstain on one sleeve. From the quality of the shirt he wore, she guessed he was from the city. His short-cropped brown hair and white skin only served to confirm her suspicions.

With a low groan, the boy began to stir. Idly, she wondered what he would make of the nightmare he was about to awake too.

Liz shivered, not from the cold now, but dread. She cast her eyes around the room one last time, desperate for something, *anything*, that might offer escape. As a child, her parents had often warned her of what happened to those who drew the government's ire. Though they were never reported, disappearances had been common in her village. Adults, children, even entire families were known to simply disappear overnight. Though few were brave enough to voice their suspicions out loud, everyone knew who had taken them.

It seemed that after two years on the run, those same people had finally caught up with Liz.

The clang of the door as it opened tore Liz from her musings. Looking up, she saw two men push their way past the heavy steel door. They wore matching uniforms of black pants and green shirts, along with the gold-and-red embossed badges of bears that marked them as soldiers. Both carried a rifle slung over one shoulder, and moved with the casual ease of professional killers.

Liz straightened as the men's eyes drifted over to her cage, refusing to show her fear. Even so, she had to suppress a shudder as wide grins split their faces. Scowling, she crossed her arms and stared them down.

"Feisty one, ain't she?" the first said in a strong Californian accent. Shaking his head, he moved past the cages to a panel in the wall.

"Looks like the boy's still asleep," the other commented as he joined the first. "Gonna be a nasty wake-up call."

Together, they pulled open the panel and retrieved a hose. Thick nylon strings encased the outer layer of the hose, and a large steel nozzle was fitted to its end. Dragging it across the room, they pointed it at the sleeping boy and flipped a lever on the nozzle.

Water gushed from the hose and through the wire of the cage to engulf the unconscious young man. A blood-curdling scream echoed off the walls as he seemed to levitate off the floor, and began to thrash against the torrent of water.

Liz bit back laughter as another scream came, half gurgled by the water. The men with the hose showed no such restraint, and their laughter rang through the room. They ignored the young man's strangled cries, holding the water steady until it seemed he could not help but drown in the torrent.

When they finally shut off the water, the boy collapsed to the floor of his cage, gasping for breath. He shuddered, spitting up water, but the men were already moving towards Liz, and she had no more time to consider his predicament.

She raised her hands as the men stopped in front of her cage. "No need for that, boys. I'm already clean, see?" She did a little turn, her cheeks warming as she sensed their eyes on her again.

The men chuckled, but shook their heads. "Sorry girl, boss's orders."

They pulled the lever before Liz could offer any further argument.

Liz gave a strangled shriek as the ice-cold water drove her back against the wire of the cage. She lifted her hands in front of her face, fighting to hold back the water, but it made little difference against the rush. Gasping, she choked as water flooded her throat, and sank to her knees. An icy hand gripped her chest as she inhaled again, turning her back to protect her face. The power of the water forced her up against the wire, and she gripped it hard with her fingers, struggling to hold herself upright.

When the torrent finally ceased, Liz found herself crouched on the ground with her back to the men. She did not turn as a coughing fit shook her body. An awful cold seeped through her bones as she struggled for breath. Water filled her ears and nose, muffling the words of the men until she shook her head to clear it.

Tightening her hold on the wire, Liz used it to pull herself to her feet. Head down, she gave a final cough and faced the room.

The men were already returning the hose to its panel in the wall. They spoke quietly amongst themselves, but fell silent as the hinges of the door squeaked again. Liz looked up as a group of men and women entered the room. There were five in total, three men and two women, and each wore a white lab coat with black pants. Four of them carried electronic tablets, their heads bent over the little screens, while the fifth approached the guards. They straightened as he drew up in front of them, their grins fading.

"Are our latest subjects ready for processing?" the man asked, his voice cool.

One of the guards nodded. "Yes, Doctor Halt. We've just finished hosing them down."

A smile twitched at Halt's lips. "Very good," he dismissed the men with a flick of his hand and turned to face the cages.

Pursing his thin lips, Halt moved closer, pacing around Liz's cage in a slow circle. His eyes did not leave her as he moved, and eventually she was forced to look away. He moved like a predator, his grey eyes studying her like prey, eyeing up which piece of flesh to taste first. Wrapping her arms around herself, Liz fixed her eyes to the concrete and tried to ignore him.

When Liz looked up again, Halt had moved on to studying the young man in the other cage. But her fellow captive was ignoring him. Instead, he stared at the group of doctors, his brow creased with confusion, as though struggling to recall a distant memory.

"*You!*" the boy shouted suddenly, slamming his hands against the wire. "You were at my house! What am I doing here? *What have you done with my mother?*" His last words came out as a shriek.

Halt glanced back at the group of doctors. "Doctor Fallow, would you care to explain why the subject knows your face?"

The woman at the head of the group turned beet red. Biting her lip, she replied. "There were complications during his extraction, Halt," her voice came out soft, but Liz sensed her defiance behind them. "I had to enter before the subject was unconscious, or we risked casualties amongst the extraction team."

Halt eyed her for a moment, apparently weighing up her words before he nodded. "Very well." He turned back to the cages. "No matter. Elizabeth Flores, Christopher Sanders, welcome to the Praegressus Facility."

Cold fingers gripped Liz by the throat, silencing her voice. They knew her last name. That meant they knew who she was, where she came from. The last trickle of hope slipped from her heart. It was no mistake she had found herself here.

Christopher was not so easily quelled. "What am I doing here? You can't hold us like his, I know my rights—"

Halt raised a hand and her neighbour fell silent. Moving across, Halt stood outside Christopher's cage and stared through the wire. "Your mother has been charged with treason."

Colour fled the boy's face, turning his white skin a sickly yellow. He swallowed and opened his mouth, but no words came out. Tears crystallised at the corner of his eyes, but he blinked them back before they could fall.

Biting her tongue, Liz watched the two stare at one another. She was impressed by Christopher's resilience. He might speak with an urban accent, but it seemed he possessed more courage than half the boys she'd once known in her boarding school. If his mother had been convicted of treason, it meant death for her and her immediate family. A pass was given for the elderly, but there was no such exception for children…

Swallowing, Liz eyed the group still lingering behind Halt. If that was the reason Christopher was here, she didn't like her chances. She had always guessed the authorities might come after her and had done her best to avoid detection. With cameras on every street corner, she had been forced to keep to the countryside she knew so well. Even then, she had always known it would only be a matter of time before someone found her.

Even so, she wanted to find out how much they really knew about her.

FIVE

"What about me?" Liz croaked. "My parents are gone. I've done nothing wrong."

Halt's eyes turned towards her and his scowl deepened. "Elizabeth Flores." He paused, looking her up and down with a sneer. "Vagrant, beggar, fugitive. You have escaped justice for long enough. After what your parents did, did you really think we would not come for you? That we would not hunt you to the ends of the earth?"

White-hot fire lit Liz's chest, but she forced herself to take a deep breath and swallow the screams building in her throat. She wanted to deny the accusations, to curse him and the others, but she knew there was no point. She had tried that once before, when they had first come for her. But one look at her ragged clothes, at the curly black hair and olive skin, and they had dismissed her words as lies.

Her shoulders slumped as Halt looked away. Wrapping her arms around herself, she staggered to the back of the cage and sank to the floor. She wasn't giving up, not yet, but she knew when silence offered the better course of action.

Unlike her fellow prisoner.

"What is this place?" Christopher's voice was soft, as though if he whispered, the answer might offer some sort of mercy.

Liz glanced across at him, and watched as he lost his battle with the tears. Despite herself, a pang of sympathy twitched in her chest. She knew what it was like, to lose her parents. She would not wish it on anyone.

"This is your redemption." Halt spread his arms, including them both in the gesture. "This is your chance to redress the crimes of your parents, to contribute to the betterment of our nation. The government has seen fit to offer you both a reprieve."

"How generous of them," Liz muttered from the floor.

She shivered as Halt's eyes found hers. They flashed with anger, offering a silent warning against further interruptions. Pursing her lips, she gripped the wire tighter. It cut into her fingers as she willed herself to contain her anger.

"My mother was not a traitor," came Christopher's response. "How dare you–"

Halt waved a hand and the guards who still waited at the rear of the room came to life. They marched past the silent group of doctors and approached Chris's cage. One produced a key and a second later they had the door open. Moving inside, there was a brief scuffle as they tried to get their hands on the boy. One staggered back from a blow to the face, before the other managed to use his bulk to pin Christopher to the wire.

When they both had a firm grip on him, they hauled him out and forced him to his knees in front of Halt. The doctor loomed over the boy, his arms folded. He contemplated Chris with eyes empty of compassion, like a spider studying a fly trapped in its web. Liz watched on in silence, hardly daring to breathe as Halt nodded to the guards.

The one on the left drew back his boot and slammed it into Christopher's stomach. He collapsed without a sound, his mouth wide, gasping like a fish out of water. A low wheeze came from his throat as he rolled onto his back and strained for breath. It came in a sudden rush, before the boot crashed into his side, almost lifting him off the ground.

A scream tore from the young man's throat as he rolled into a ball. But the other guard only grabbed him by the back of the shirt and hauled him back to his knees. The two of them looked back at Halt then, waiting for further instruction.

Smiling, Halt approached, one finger tapping idly against his elbow. Softly, he continued as though nothing had changed. "As I was saying, you have been given a reprieve, but the crimes of your parents still stand, as does the sentence on your lives. That makes you dead in the eyes of the state. You are no one, nothing but what we permit you to be. If you're lucky, you might find yourselves worthy of our work here at the Praegressus Facility." Liz shivered at the name. It sounded Latin, though she had no idea what it might mean. "More likely though, you will die. But know at least your deaths will have advanced the interests of our fine nation."

Chris still knelt on the ground between the guards, his breath coming in ragged gasps. Halt eyed him, as though weighing whether his words had sunk in, before continuing.

"In the meantime, you will come to respect and obey your betters," Halt spoke. "Soon, you will be shown to your new accommodation. But first, I want to be sure you understand the gravity of your situations. Christopher Sanders, why are you here?"

On the ground, Chris looked up at the doctor. His eyes shone, but no tears fell. Turning his head to the side, he spat on the concrete and scowled. "She's a terrible cook," he coughed, then continued, "but I'd hardly say that makes her a traitor–"

The guard's fist caught him on the side of the head and sent him crashing to the floor. A boot followed, and for the next thirty seconds the room rang with the thud of hard leather boots on flesh, interspersed with Christopher's muffled cries. When the guards finally pulled back, the young man lay still, a low groan the only sign of life.

"Get him up," Halt commanded.

Together the guards hauled the boy back to his knees. This time Halt leaned down, until the two of them were face to face. "Well?"

Christopher's shoulders sagged and his head bowed. A soft sob came from his mouth, and for a second she thought he would not speak. Then he nodded, and a whisper followed. "Okay," he croaked, "okay... My mother… was a traitor." He looked up as he finished, a spark of flame still burning in his eyes. "*Does that make you happy?*"

The doctor eyed him for a long while, as though measuring up his admission with the show of defiance. Finally he nodded, and the guards grabbed Christopher by the shoulders and muscled him back into the cage.

The clang as the door closed sent a thrill of ice down Liz's spine. She stared down at the floor, sensing the eyes of the room on her, and waited for Halt to address her.

"Ah, Elizabeth Flores," his voice snaked its way around her, raising the hackles on her neck. "You have run for so long. Surely you at least must admit to your parents' crimes?"

Looking up, Liz found the cold grey eyes of the doctor watching her. She suppressed a shudder and quickly looked away. Taking slow, measured breaths, she beat down the rage burning in her chest. She took one step, then another, until she reached the front of her cage. Leaning against the wire, she looked down at the doctor and raised an eyebrow.

"What would you like me to admit too?" she whispered.

Halt took a step back from the cage, but she did not miss the way his eyes lingered on her. She gave a little smirk as he growled. "Disgusting girl," he spat. "Admit that your parents were monsters - that you aided them, that for years you have run from the law, hiding from justice."

A tremble of rage raced through Liz. She bit her lip. Closing her eyes, she sent out a silent prayer for the souls of her parents. Their faces drifted through her mind – smiling, happy, at peace. They had been kind and sweet, only ever wanting for her to be happy, to have a better life than the one they'd lived. For years they had scraped and saved their every penny, so they could send her to boarding school. The day she'd been accepted, she had never seen them so happy. And for three years, she had suffered the taunts of her peers in that school to keep them that way.

But they were long gone now; they did not care what was said about them. There was no need for Liz to suffer now, to bleed for their memory. Not now, when there was no hope of escape. But silently she made a vow to herself, to bide her time and conserve her strength, until an opportunity showed itself.

When she opened her eyes again, she found the cold grey eyes of Halt looking back, and smirked.

"Fine, I admit it. My parents were monsters. What of it?"

She almost laughed as the doctor's face darkened, an angry red flushing across his cheeks. He clenched his fists and made to approach the cage before stopping himself. Flashing a glance over his shoulder at their audience, he shook his head and smiled.

"Very good," he eyed the two of them. "So, we understand one another."

SIX

CHRIS GRIPPED THE WIRE OF HIS CAGE AS HALT EYED THE two of them. Clamping his mouth shut, he ignored the voice in his head that screamed for answers. His jaw and back ached where the guards had struck him, and he was not eager to repeat the experience. The ugly thugs were grinning at him now, as though daring him to give them another chance. Instead, he bit his tongue and waited to see what came next.

His mind was still reeling, struggling to put together the pieces of his scattered memories. Images from the night flashed through his mind – the *Chead* on the television, the men in his house, his mother falling.

Ice wrapped around his throat as Halt's words twisted in his mind.

Traitor.

A tremor ran through him and he suppressed a sob. The sentence for treason was death. Often just the accusation of such a crime was enough. And now his mother had been taken, stolen away by the woman in the white coat.

Holding his breath, Chris struggled with his fear, his terror that she might already be gone. That he might now be alone, an orphan in a harsh, unforgiving world.

With a low moan, Chris took a great, shuddering breath and shook his head. That was the least of his problems. Whatever his mother's fate, he could do nothing for her now, trapped in this cage.

Opening his eyes, he looked across as Halt spoke. "Now that we have an understanding, we must prepare you for the project." A thin smile spread across his lips. "Take off your clothes."

A chill spread through Chris's chest as Halt folded his arms. Behind him, the guards shifted, edging close, wide grins splitting their faces. A sharp intake of breath came from the other cage, but otherwise the girl did not move.

Chris shrank back from the wire. "Why?"

Halt took a step forward. "Now, Christopher, I had hoped we had moved past this. The dog does not question his master when he is told to sit."

Clenching his fists, Chris shook his head. His eyes travelled past Halt, to the audience of doctors. They lingered on the face of the woman, the doctor called Fallow. "This isn't right," he breathed.

Letting out a long sigh, Halt waved the guards forward. They approached the cage, shoulders hunched, moving with a cold proficiency. Chris hesitated as they reached the door and fumbled with the latch. Then he began to unbutton his shirt, his cheeks flushing with embarrassment.

Outside the guards paused, looking back at Halt in question. The doctor nodded curtly, and they retreated to their positions behind him.

In the cage, Chris quickly stripped off his clothing piece by piece, shivering as the icy breath of the air conditioner brushed across his skin. The hairs stood up on the back of his neck as he pulled off his last strip of clothing and tossed it to the floor. Turning sideways, he bowed his head, struggling to cover himself.

Then, reaching up he unclipped the chain that still hung around his neck. It came away easily, the little pocket watch falling into his hand. He clenched it in his fist, a tremble of grief washing through him. Flicking open the metal catch, he looked at the faces of his mother and father, at their kind smiles, and then closed it again.

Struggling to hold back his tears, he placed the pocket watch gently, reverently on his pile of clothes.

Standing, he felt the eyes of the doctors roaming over his naked flesh, examining him, seeking out his every secret. A deep sense of helplessness rose in his chest, threatening to overwhelm him. Cheeks flushed, he stared hard at the ground, fighting to ignore the world.

"Very good, Christopher," Halt's voice was patronising, and Chris almost choked on the shame that rose in his throat, "and you, Elizabeth?"

Out of the corner of his eye, Chris caught movement from the other cage. Turning his head, he watched as Elizabeth approach the front of the cage. Her lips were pulled into a smirk, but her blue eyes flashed with a barely concealed anger. She pressed herself against the wire and stared across at Halt.

"Come and get me," she growled, her voice threatening.

Chris's eyes widened. After her earlier acquiescence, he had not expected her to resist.

In front of the cages, Halt gave a slow shake of his head. "Bring her," he hissed.

The guards marched passed him and yanked the door to the cage open. Elizabeth retreated from the door, watching as the first of the men pushed their way inside. Then, with a wild shriek, she leapt. At maybe one hundred and twenty-five pounds, she was dwarfed by the guard. Even so, her sudden attack caught him by surprise and sent him tumbling backwards into his comrade.

As the two of them went down in a heap, Elizabeth leapt for the door. She made it over the threshold before the first guard managed to stagger upright. His arm swung out, catching her by the leg, and she slammed into the concrete outside the cage. With another screech, she kicked out with her free leg, catching the guard in the face. He gave a muffled curse, but held on.

In seconds the other guard was up. He strode across to where Elizabeth fought to free herself, reached down, and wrapped one meaty hand around her hair. The girl gave a pained cry as he lifted her up and held her off the ground. She kicked feebly at empty air, her hands batting at his chest. Her mouth gaped as the colour fled her face.

With a contemptuous flick of his arm, the guard tossed her aside. Elizabeth crashed hard into the concrete. She struggled to regain her composure, but a heavy boot drove down onto her back, sending her face first into the floor.

Halt walked across and knelt beside the girl, a cold smile on his snakelike lips.

"Elizabeth," Halt's voice was laced now with honey, "be a good girl now. You cannot join the project with those reminders of your old life. Remove your clothes."

Chris shuddered as the man stood, his grey eyes flashing as he watched the girl lift herself to her hands and knees. One trembling hand reached for the buttons of her shirt and began to pluck them open. Closing his eyes, Chris looked away, unwilling to participate in her shaming.

He glanced back up a few minutes later as the sound of metal striking concrete rang through the room. His eyes were drawn to the object now lying on the ground between Halt and the shivering girl. The thick steel links of a chain lay between them like a snake, the silver metal shining in the fluorescent lights. For an instant, he wondered where it had come from, but his thoughts quickly turned to what it was.

A collar.

SEVEN

"PUT IT ON," HALT'S VOICE SLIVERED THROUGH THE ROOM, cold, commanding.

Elizabeth flinched away from him, but the guard's hand flashed out and caught her by the hair. Dragging her forward, he shoved her back to her knees in front of the collar. A tremble went through the girl as she glared up at Halt, her eyes flashing. For a second, Chris thought she would resist, but then with a trembling hand she reached out and picked up the collar.

Elizabeth's mouth twisted with disgust as she held the steel linked chain in front of her. Her eyes closed, her nostrils flaring as she sucked in a breath. Chris waited, his own breath held, aware his turn would come soon.

"This is what you want, you disgusting—" the girl broke off as the guard's fist sent her reeling.

A low groan came from her lips, but she straightened on the ground, the collar still in hand. She looked at Halt, and then away again. With trembling hands, she lifted the collar to her throat. The *click* it made as it fastened echoed loudly in the concrete room.

Halt smiled and clapped his hands. The guards grabbed Elizabeth by each arm and hauled her back up. With a few shoves they had her back in the cage, and the steel door swung shut behind her. Then Halt's grey eyes turned towards Chris, where he still waited naked inside his own cage.

"I suppose it's my turn then?" He asked with false bravado.

Halt stared him down, the grey eyes piercing him through. Horror curled its way up Chris's throat as he felt his cheeks warming. His eyes drifted towards the other doctors, who still stood in silence. Outside, the guards approached his cage. Watching them, he saw that one carried a bundle of orange clothing, the other a steel link collar identical to the one Elizabeth now wore.

"Move to the back of the cage," one guard ordered.

Clenching his fists, Chris stumbled back from the door as the guard flicked the latch and pushed it open. His body ached from his beating, and in the narrow space he didn't like his chances of besting the two men. He had already watched the girl take that approach and fail. He would have to wait, bide his time until an opportunity arose.

Inside the cage, the first of the guards collected his clothes and replaced them with the orange bundle. The collar was placed on top of the pile, and then the two men retreated, swinging the door shut behind them.

Chris looked across at Halt, waiting for an order. When none was forthcoming, he moved across to the pile and picked up the collar. Raising an eyebrow, he tried and failed to suppress his sarcasm. "What are we? Your pets now?"

Halt smirked. "Would you like another lesson, Christopher?"

Letting out a long breath, Chris shook his head. He squeezed his fingers, letting the cold metal of the collar dig into his flesh. His heart pounded hard in his chest, screaming a warning, that if he obeyed now there would be no going back.

Dimly, he remembered a story his father had told him when he was younger. It had been almost ten years since the cancer had taken him, but he could still recall his father's voice with crystal clarity. His rough baritone drifted up from Chris's memories, as he described how the *Mahouts* in Thailand had once tamed their elephants.

The *Mahouts* had placed chains around the legs of young elephants and attached them to heavy pegs in the ground. Whenever the elephants tried to escape, the chain would contract, cutting into the elephant's leg, making it bleed. Eventually the elephant would realise the futility of trying to escape.

As adults, the same chain and peg were used to restrain the giant creatures. And though they then possessed the strength to escape the peg and chain, they never tried.

There had been a point to his father's tale, but for the life of him, Chris could not recall its meaning now. Instead, he stared down at the collar, wondering if he was about to take the first step into his own captivity.

But he had no choice but to obey.

With deliberate slowness, Chris raised the collar to his neck. A tingle ran through his skin as the metal touched the flesh of his throat, and a terrifying dread rose within him. A voice screamed for him to run, to hurl the collar away from him.

Instead, he closed his eyes and pulled the collar closed around his neck. The steel links slid across his flesh like the coils of a python, icy to the touch, and came together with a loud click.

Struggling to breathe, Chris sank to his knees and fumbled for the pile of clothes. A sudden, desperate shame at his nakedness took him. He felt exposed, as though his nudity highlighted his new bondage, relegating him to little better than an animal.

Scrambling into the bright orange uniform, he sank back to his knees. A sick despair rose in his throat, but he pushed it down, struggling to keep a flicker of hope above the rising waters. The collar's icy grip tightened around his throat, stealing away his breath. A claustrophobic scream grew in his throat as he coughed for air.

Halt only gave a satisfied nod and stepped back from the cage.

Glancing across at the other cage, he saw Elizabeth had managed to pull on an orange jumpsuit of her own. The heavy fabric clung to her lithe frame, and Chris couldn't help but think of what he had glimpsed of her earlier. A dark bruise showed on her forehead as her clear blue eyes flickered in his direction. His cheeks warmed as she raised an eyebrow and brushed a lock of hair from her face. The wild black curls hung around her shoulders, the ends jagged and split, as though they had been cut by a knife.

Taking a breath, the girl pulled herself to her feet. The collar flashed around her neck, an all too vivid reminder of their captivity. Her fists clenched and her lips drew back in a snarl, but otherwise she remained quiet.

In front of the cages, Halt gave a satisfied smirk. "Very good. I'm pleased to see you are both fast learners. Perhaps you will surprise me." Chris flinched as Halt clapped his hands again. "Now, before you are taken to your new accommodations, I must warn you, I have little patience for agitators. Dissent will not be tolerated. Those collars around your necks are more than they appear. Do not attempt to remove them. Any effort to tamper with them without the correct key will trigger a small explosive discharge, which will have… unpleasant results."

Chris swallowed hard. A trick of sweat ran down his neck and he tasted bile in his throat. Clenching his teeth, he sucked in a breath and fought to keep himself from throwing up whatever remained in his stomach. In the opposite cage, Elizabeth showed no sign she had heard Halt's words. She stood with eyes closed, one arm against the cage wall, as though that was the only thing keeping her upright.

When neither of them spoke, Halt continued. "As we have no wish to risk our guards every time our subjects step out of line, the collars are used as a disciplinary tool."

Leaning against the wall of his cage, Chris stifled a fake yawn, unwilling to show his fear. "Seems a little harsh, blowing off someone's head for a bit of back talk."

The doctor glared at him, then gave a slow shake of his head. "Perhaps you are not as quick to learn as I thought," he raised his arm and pulled down his sleeve.

He wore a sleek black watch around his wrist, all shining metal and glass. As he tapped its surface, the screen glowed bright blue. Another tap and a loud beep came from Chris's collar. The hairs on his neck stood up as Halt looked back at him.

"Your collars are capable of delivering an electric shock of five hundred volts and up to one hundred milliamps. They are activated remotely by these watches, which you will find all personnel within the facility are equipped with." A slow grin spread across Halt's face. "A simple tap of the screen, by any doctor or guard, and all collars within a twenty-foot radius are activated. Or an individual subject's collar may be chosen at our discretion. Perhaps you would like a demonstration?"

Holding his breath, Chris shook his head. From the corner of his eye, he saw the girl make the same gesture.

Halt eyed the two of them, his eyes lit with a strange light. "You don't seem too enthusiastic," he laughed. "Too bad." Before anyone could move he pressed a thumb to the watch.

Chris opened his mouth to scream as the collar around his neck gave a loud beep. Before a sound could escape him, fingers of fire wrapped around his throat, cutting off his cry. His jaw locked hard as electricity surged through his body. His back arched with sudden agony, and the strength went from his legs, sending him toppling to the concrete. A burning cramp tore through his muscles as he thrashed against the ground. Damp water · still pooling on the concrete soaked through his new clothes, but he barely noticed.

A loud buzzing filled his ears, but through it, he could hear Halt's voice. "This is twenty milliamps. Enough to deliver a painful shock, even freeze your motor functions. Not enough to kill – or at least, not over short periods of time."

Another beep sounded and the flow of electricity ceased. Chris slumped to the ground, eyes closed, a low moan crackling up from his chest. The sudden absence of pain was a sweet relief, He sucked in an eager breath, the cold air burning in his throat.

As the last twitch in his muscles faded away, he cracked open his eyes and looked through the wire mesh. He had fallen on his side and now found himself looking through the wire at Elizabeth. She was on the ground as well, her tangled hair covering her face, her limbs splayed out across the concrete. Her forehead sported a nasty cut where she must have struck the ground.

Halt stood between the cages, the same dark grin twisting his face. His eyes found Chris's, and the smile spread.

"Welcome to the Praegressus Project."

EIGHT

ANGELA FALLOW WAITED UNTIL THE DOOR CLOSED BEHIND her before allowing her mask to crack. A sharp sob cut the air as she stumbled across the room and collapsed onto the bed. The soft duvet cushioned her fall, but it did nothing for the burden weighing on her soul. Burying her head in a pillow, she finally allowed the tears to flow.

What have I done?

For years she had worked in government laboratories, studying the creatures that had come to be known as the *Chead,* examining their genetic composition and identifying chromosomal alterations within their DNA. While the more superstitious citizens of the Western Allied States regarded the *Chead* as some paranormal phenomenon, she had dedicated her life to dissecting the mysteries of the creatures.

She had been the first to discover the link between the *Chead* awakenings across the country. A short sequence of nucleic acids discovered in one of the samples put her on the trail, and within days she had confirmed her suspicion. Whether the *Chead* had woken in rural Washington or downtown Los Angeles, the same virus was present in the genome of every known *Chead*.

Porcine Endogenous Retrovirus, or PERV, a well-known retrovirus amongst the scientific community. Since the turn of the twentieth century, the virus had been used to exchange DNA between pig and human cells. PERV was a provirus – meaning it fully integrated into the host genome. This led to its use in the modification of genes within the organs of pigs, to increase their receptivity when transplanted into human subjects.

But Angela had checked the records of every *Chead*, and none had ever been a candidate for xenotransplantation.

Normally, the presence of the virus alone would have meant little. There was not a person alive whose chromosome did not contain some viral elements. In fact, many scientists speculated the alterations caused by proviruses played a significant role in evolution, altering genes and alleles at a rate far faster than ordinary mutation.

However, once the link had been discovered, it had not taken Angela long to piece out other discrepancies in the *Chead* chromosomes. Alongside the PERV recombinations, she identified genome markers with foundations in everything from primates to canines, eagles to rabbits. Even genes from rare animals such as the Philippine Tarsier and the Western Australian Taipan had featured in the genetic puzzle presented by the *Chead*.

In the end, the evidence all pointed to a single, undeniable conclusion.

The *Chead* were no accident. Someone had created them, designed a virus and released it into the world.

The question of who remained unanswered, though the government had quickly pointed the blame on that old enemy – the United States. Or at least the scattered remnant states remaining of the once-great-nation.

But that was not Angela's concern. Now knowing the cause, she had applied herself to countering its spread. Fortunately, the virus did not appear to be contagious. No cases had been reported of friends or family contracting the virus from awakened *Chead*, though the government still rounded them up as a precaution.

That left the question of how the victims were infected. She suspected an outside source was at work there, though again, it was up to others to solve that puzzle.

As for those already infected by the virus, Angela had quickly ruled out a cure. Ordinary viruses incorporated themselves into the host DNA, much as the *Chead* virus had done. However, the similarities ended there. Symptoms of an ordinary viral infection arose when a virus began self-replication, eventually leading to cell rupture and the spread of virons to other cells. Sickness showed as human cells were hijacked by the virons and used for further self-replication.

Instead of following this route, the *Chead* virus remained latent within the cells. It appeared to be almost perfectly incorporated into the human chromosomes of the *Chead* subjects. The alterations exhibited by the *Chead* were the result of gene expression in the cells themselves – the first symptoms only showing once those genes activated. This was similar to how many babies possessed blue eyes for their first few weeks, until genes for brown eyes were activated.

In other words, the virus was a part of the *Chead* now. There was no reversing the process.

Upon learning of Angela's discovery, the government had decided to take her research in a new direction.

Now she was close to an answer – closer than they'd ever been before. Initial trials on bovine subjects had proven successful, but Halt and his government overseers wanted more. They were desperate for an answer, for a beacon of hope to hold up to the people. Even the usually ice cold Halt had appeared flustered in recent weeks, and she sensed far more than her career rested on what happened over the next few weeks and months.

Shivering, Angela wrapped her arms tight around herself. Not for the first time, she wondered what her life would have been like, had she taken a different path. Deep in her soul, she still longed for the wild open space of the country-side, the endless stars and unmarked horizons. Her family's ranch had been remote, far from the bustling hives of the cities – though of course, they did not really own it. They had worked the land, harvested the crops, while the landowner in the city took the profits.

As a young girl, she had resented that fact, and the limita-tions of rural life. So she had studied and schemed, and won a place in a scholarship programme in Los Angeles. She had grasped the opportunity with both hands, and run off to find her place in the big wide world.

Funny how things changed, with thirty-five years' worth of wisdom.

The world was a wild place too, but in the city, life was far less forgiving than the country.

Angela shuddered as she heard again the awful screams, watched as the girl writhed on the floor of the cage. In the silence of her mind, Angela imagined the girl's blue eyes seeking her out, begging for help.

Another sob tore from Angela's throat. Those eyes, that face; they were so like her own. In those youthful features, she saw her past, saw the girl she had once been reflected back.

What have I done?

The question came again, persistent. She had never thought it would come to this. When Halt had told her their plan to gather candidates for human trials, it had seemed simple. Family members convicted of treason were destined to suffer the same fate as the accused. So why not make use of those lives?

Young, healthy candidates were needed for the trials to maximise the chances of success. The children of traitors seemed the perfect answer to their needs.

Only now she faced the reality of that decision, it was more awful than she could ever have imagined. Halt might see them as a means to an end, but Angela could not look past the humanity in their eyes. Halt was a monster, seeming to delight in the breaking of each new candidate, but for Angela, the guilt ate at her soul.

On the bed, she heard again the crunch of fists on flesh. Her stomach swirled and it was all she could do not to throw up.

"What have I done?" she whispered.

The plain walls of her private quarters offered no answers, only their silent judgement. This was her life, this little white room, the empty double bed, the white dresser and coat rack beside the door. Her wool fleece hung on the rack, untouched for weeks now.

Staring at it, Angela was taken by an impulse to escape, to leave this place and walk out into the wilderness beyond the facilities walls. Standing, she strode across and tore the coat from the rack. Swinging it around her shoulders, she fastened the buttons and pushed open the door.

The corridor outside ran left and right. Left led deeper into the facility, where her laboratory and the prison rooms waited. She turned right, moving past the closed doors of the other living quarters. It was well past midnight, and the other staff would have retired long ago. Only the night guards would be awake now.

It only took a few minutes to reach the outer door – a fire exit, but from past excursions she knew there was no alarm attached. The heavy steel door watched her approach, unmoved by her sorrow. Placing her shoulder to it, she gave a hard shove and pulled at the latch.

A long screech echoed down the corridor, followed by a blast of cold wind.

Clenching her teeth, Angela pushed it wider and slipped out into the darkness. She pulled the cloak tighter around herself as a tendril of ice slid down her back, and listened as the door clicked shut behind her. She wasn't concerned – there were no locks on the outer doors. Out here, break-ins were the least of their worries.

Angela sucked in a long breath of the mountain air and looked up at the sky. A thousand pinpricks of light dotted the darkness, the full scope of the Milky Way laid bare before her. The pale sliver of a crescent moon cast dim shadows across the rocky ground, where a thin layer of snow dotted the stones. Beyond the light coming from the building behind her, the night beckoned.

Shivering, Angela watched her breath mist in the freezing air. It was eerie, staring out into the absolute black. Other than the sky, not a pinprick of light showed beyond the facility. They were far from civilisation here, miles into the mountains, as remote as one could be within the Western Allied State. Or the WAS, as it had come to be known.

Staring at the stars, Angela could almost imagine herself a child again. A desperate yearning rose within her, to return to the simplicity of life then, to the warmth of her family ranch.

Sucking in another breath, Angela watched the darkness, imagining the long curves of the hidden mountains. The first snow had arrived a few days ago, heralding the onset of winter. Climatologists were predicting a strong *El Nino* though, which would mean a mild winter.

Standing there in the darkness, with the icy wind biting at her skin, Angela could not help but disagree. This winter would be long and savage, and few at the facility would survive its coming. Only the strongest would endure.

She hoped the candidates would prove up to the challenge. They had only one chance, one opportunity. Fail now, and the government would end it all.

Bowing her head, Angela turned back to the fire door. She pushed it open and returned to the warm light of the corridor. Once back inside, she leaned back against the door and slid to the floor.

Just a little longer, she clung to the thought.

Just a little longer, and she could rest, could put this all behind her.

Just a little longer, and she would save the world.

NINE

CLANG.

Liz flinched as the cell door swung closed behind her, the harsh sound slashing through her self-control. She clenched her fists, fighting to control the shiver running through her body. Every fibre of her being screamed for her to panic, to run and hide, but she sucked in a breath instead, calming her trembling nerves. Cold steel pressed against her throat, a constant reminder of her captivity.

A sharp pain came from her palms as her nails dug into flesh. With a great effort, she unclenched her fists. The breath caught in her throat, but she swallowed and sucked in another, refusing to give into her panic. The heavy threads of the orange uniform rubbed against her skin, though in truth its quality was better than anything she'd scavenged in the past two years.

Staring ahead, Liz cast her eyes over her new home. The plain concrete walls matched what she'd glimpsed of the rest of the facility on the short trip from cage to prison cell. The journey had taken less than five minutes, a quick march down long corridors, past open doors and strange rooms filled with glass tubes and steel contraptions. Some she recognised from her boarding school: Bunsen burners and beakers, test tubes and cylinders. But the rest was far beyond her understanding – plastic boxes that hummed and whirred, steel cubes of unknown purpose, containers filled with a strange, gel-like substance.

The guards ushered them past each room with quick efficiency, leaving no time for questions. Only once had Liz paused, when they'd passed a room apparently used as a canteen. The smell of coffee and burnt toast wafted out, and she'd seen a dozen people sitting around a table, talking quietly. Before Liz could speak, a guard had jabbed the butt of his rifle into the small of her back.

A little gasp burst from her lips, and several people inside had glanced up. Their eyes took her in for a moment, then they looked away, returning to their conversation. Seeing their indifference, Liz had felt the last drops of hope curdle in her chest.

From there they'd been led through a thick iron door, into the grim corridor of a prison block. Faces lined the cells on either side of the corridor as they marched past. Wide eyes stared at them, their owners no more than children, ranging from around thirteen to twenty years of age.

Now Liz stood in a tiny concrete cell, the iron bars at her back locking her in, sealing her off from the outside world. Two sets of bunk beds had been pushed against the walls on her left and right, while at the rear a toilet and sink were bolted into the floor. Curtains dangled down beside the toilet, presumably to offer some small semblance of privacy.

And between the bunks stood her new roommates.

The boy and girl stared back at Liz and Christopher. The boy stood well over six feet, his muscled shoulders and arms dwarfing the girl beside him. His skin was a dark hue of Native American descent, except where a long white scar stretched down his right arm. Long black hair hung around his razor-sharp face, and hawkish brown eyes studied her with detached curiosity.

Beside him, the girl could not have provided a greater contrast. Her pale white skin shone in the bright overhead lights, unmarked by so much as a freckle, and at around five foot three, she barely came up to the boy's chest. She stood with arms folded, her posture defensive, though with her thin frame Liz guessed she'd struggle to fend off a toddler. Long hair hung down to her waist, the scarlet locks well-trimmed but unwashed. At first glance, Liz thought she might have just walked off a photoshoot.

But with closer reflection, Liz noticed the faint marks of bruises on her arms, the traces of purple on her cheeks and the dark circles beneath her tawny yellow eyes. Cuts and old scars marked her knuckles, and several of her once-long nails were broken.

Maybe not so harmless after all, Liz mused.

The boy from the cages, Christopher, stood beside her, making them a party of four. Although it wasn't much of a party. So far they'd gone a full minute without speaking.

Outside, the last thud of boots ceased and the crash of the outer doors closing heralded the departure of their escort.

Between the bunks, the boy came to life. "Welcome to hell," he spoke in a Washington accent as he offered a hand, "I'm Sam, I'll be your captain today. Ashley here will be your air hostess."

Beside him, Ashley rolled her eyes and pursed her lips, but did not speak.

Liz winced as she recognised the urban twang. She had already dismissed the possibility of the girl being rural, but she had held up hope for the boy at least… A lonely sorrow rose within her as she wrapped her arms around herself. It seemed not only was she to be locked away, but her roommates were going to be a bunch of kids straight out of prep school.

Closing her eyes, she recognised Christopher's voice as he spoke. "Ah…" the boy sounded confused by their new roommate's banter. "My name's Chris, and ah… this is Elizabeth, I guess."

Her ears twitched as she heard the shuffling of feet, no doubt the sound of the two shaking hands. Shivering, she blinked back the sudden tears that sprang to her eyes, determined to keep her weakness to herself. Her head throbbed where the guards had struck her, and a dull ache came from the small of her back.

The tremor came again, the cold air of the room eating at her resistance. Her eyes snapped open, her gaze sweeping her surroundings, finding three sets of eyes studying her closely. A frown creased Sam's forehead and his mouth opened, as though to ask a question, but she looked away before he could speak. A sudden yearning to be alone took her, a need for the peaceful quiet of the country. The concrete walls seemed to be closing on her, the still air suffocating.

Her eyes found the beds, taking in the unmade beds on the bottom. Above them, the sheets of the top bunks were pulled tight, untouched by sleep.

Without a word, she stumbled past Sam and Ashley and grasped at the ladder. Arms shaking, she pulled herself up and rolled onto the hard mattress of her new bed.

"Your girlfriend's a friendly one, Chris," Sam's voice carried up to her, but Liz only closed her eyes, and willed away the sounds. Her breath came in ragged gasps as she tried to still her racing heart.

"She's just scared," was Chris's uncertain reply.

You're wrong, she thought.

She was angry, horrified, frustrated, and more than anything in the world she just wanted to curl up in a corner and cry. But instead, she found herself trapped in a tiny cell with three teenagers from the city – two young men and a girl who would never understand her, her past.

"She should be," Sam's voice took on a bitter tone, "you two haven't even seen the worst of it yet."

Sam's voice put Liz on edge, dragging her back from the peace she sought, but she kept her mouth shut. Scuffling came from below as the three moved, then the bunk shifted beneath her as someone sat on the bed below. Cracking open one eye, Liz saw the two boys still standing, and guessed Ashley had retreated to her bed.

"I don't plan on sticking around to find out," Chris spoke in a hoarse whisper. "I have to get out of here."

Soft laughter followed his statement. "Don't we all, kid," Sam replied jokingly. "But it's kind of a one-way ticket."

"I don't care," Chris's voice smouldered with anger. "Fallow… That woman, she took my mother. I can't, I can't let anything happen to her."

"Tough luck, kid. Wherever she is, she's going to have to cope without you. The only way out of here is in a body bag. Just be glad it wasn't our pal Doctor Halt who grabbed her – although I'm sure he could arrange a reunion if you asked him nicely."

Below, Chris swore. "How can you joke?" he snarled, his voice rising. "Don't you understand? There's been some mistake. My mother hasn't done anything wrong. Her father died in the American War; she would never betray the WAS --"

"And you think our families are any different?" the larger boy snapped back, the humour falling from his voice. "You think we all conspired against the government? Don't be a fool. There's no going back, no changing things now. Not for any of us."

Silence fell over the cell, the only noise the soft breath of those below. A grin tugged at Liz's lips as she embraced the quiet, taking the opportunity to calm her roiling thoughts. The lights were bright overhead, burning through her eyelids, but at least the assault on her ears had ceased. Thinking of the other three, she felt a pang of empathy for them, a sadness for their loss. They were orphans now too, same as her.

Perhaps she was not so alone, after all.

"It doesn't matter," Chris's voice came as a whisper now, "I'll find a way."

Sam chuckled. "You and what army? Even if you could remove that collar, could break out of this cell, where would you go? Who would help you, Chris? You're the son of a traitor, a fugitive without rights."

A rustling came from below, followed by a yelp. Glancing down, her eyes widened as she saw Chris pushing Sam up against the wall.

"She's not a traitor," Chris grated out the words. "And like I said, it doesn't matter. I'm not going to sit here and give up. I'm not going to let them win."

There was no humour in Sam's face now. Scowling, he reached up and with deliberate slowness gripped Chris's hands and removed them from his shirt.

"Listen, *kid*," his voice was threatening now. "You still don't get it, do you? We mean *nothing* to these people. You'll find that out tomorrow, how *little* your life means. They'll kill you the second you cross them."

"Let them try," Chris snapped.

Sam's face darkened, and then it was his turn to grab Chris by the shirt. Without apparent effort, he lifted Chris off the ground, leaving the smaller boy kicking feebly at empty air.

"Believe me, I couldn't care less if you get yourself killed," Sam snapped. "But since we're trapped in here with you, chances are your stupidity will get us *all* executed—"

Sam broke off as Chris twisted in his grasp and drove a foot into the larger boy's stomach. Air exploded between Sam's teeth as he staggered backwards, dropping Chris unceremoniously to the ground. Chris landed lightly on his feet and straightened, eying Sam across the cell.

Liz raised an eyebrow as the two faced each other, their faces twisted with anger.

"*Enough*!" A girl's sharp voice cut the air.

The two boys practically jumped out of their skins as Ashley stood between them. Moving with a cat-like grace, she moved across to Sam and placed a hand on his chest. Her eyes flickered from Sam to Chris, a gentle smile warming her lips.

"Enough," she said again, softly this time. Even so, there was strength in her words.

Liz watched with surprise as Sam's shoulders slumped, the tension fleeing at Ashley's touch. Chris stared, his eyes hesitant, before he lowered his fists. The smile still on her lips, Ashley gave a quick nod.

"We can't fight amongst ourselves," she chided, like a teacher reprimanding her students. "Sam, you know that better than anyone. We need each other."

She turned towards Chris then, her eyes soft. "Chris, I know you're afraid, that you're terrified for your mother. I know it's awful, that you're confused. But you must calm yourself. Your mother would not want you to throw your life away."

Liz blinked, shocked by the calm manner with which Ashley had taken control of the situation. With surprising insight, she had cut straight to the heart of the matter and found a way to quench Chris's rising anger. Despite her reservations, Liz found herself warming to the girl.

Below, Ashley turned back to Sam. "Sam, you can't hide behind that charade. Not from me," she paused, her tawny eyes watching him, "not after everything we've been through."

Sam bowed his head. "You caught me, as usual," he said with a shrug. Pushing past her, he threw himself on his own bed. "I still don't want him getting us all killed though!"

Ashley nodded. Her eyes swept the room, lingering for a second as they caught Liz watching her, before turning to Chris. She moved across to him and placed a hand on his shoulder.

"You are not alone, Chris," she whispered. "Wherever you came from before, we are in this together now. We're family, you and I. All of us," Ashley spoke with words rich in emotion. "And you're right. We can't just give up. We *will* find a way out of here, together. Whoever these people are, they are only human. They're not perfect. Eventually they'll make a mistake, leave some hole in their defences. And when they do, we'll be ready for them, we'll take our chance."

Liz's heart lurched as the yellow eyes flickered back to her. "That goes for you too, Elizabeth."

Warmth spread to Liz's cheeks as the other girl watched her. She nodded slowly, struggling to cover her embarrassment. Listening to Ashley's words, she could almost feel a flicker of hope stir inside her. Maybe the girl was right, maybe she wasn't alone after all. Whatever their differences, Ashley was right. They were in this together now.

Sitting up, Liz placed her hands beneath her and propelled herself off the side of the bed. She landed lightly, her bare feet slapping against the concrete, and straightened in front of Ashley. A smile, genuine now, tugged at her lips, but she tried to maintain a stoic expression. She didn't want to get too far ahead of herself – they were still from the city, after all.

Liz took a deep breath and offered Ashley her hand.

"You can call me Liz."

TEN

CHRIS EXHALED HARD AS HE ROUNDED THE FINAL BEND IN
the track, his lungs burning with the exertion. Pain tore
through his calves and his stomach gave a sickening lurch,
but he pressed on. The dirt track gripped easily beneath his
bare feet, propelling him on towards the finish line. From
behind came the ragged breath of the others, some hot on
his tail, others fallen far behind.

Allowing himself a smile, Chris glanced to the side, and
almost tripped when he saw Liz draw alongside him. The
black-haired girl had her head down, her eyes fixed to the
path, and was picking up pace. Panting hard, Chris followed
suit, and side by side, the two of them raced down the final
straight.

For the last few feet, Chris's feet barely touched the ground.
In the corners of his vision, he saw shadows pressing in,
exhaustion threatening. Through the darkness, he glimpsed
Liz pulling ahead, saw the wild grin spread across her face
as she crossed the line a second before him.

Drawing to a stop behind her, Chris shook his head, his mouth unable to form words. Bending in two, he sucked in a mouthful of air. He felt strangely light-headed, his lungs aflame. It took him a full minute to truly catch his breath. By then the others had pulled up nearby.

Lowering himself to the ground, Chris blinked sweat from his eyes. Using one large orange sleeve, he wiped his forehead clear and shook his head at Liz.

"You're fast," he croaked.

It was the second day since their awakening, and since then the two of them had barely spoken. Despite her reluctant greeting in the cell, Liz remained withdrawn. She had been quiet when they spoke in the cell, and said little of her past.

Liz only shrugged. Two blue eyes glanced at him, and then away. "It's the air," she breathed. "We're in the mountains – I can taste it. You're probably not used to the altitude."

Chris nodded, and stars danced across his vision. A groan built in his throat as he saw Liz straighten, but he pushed it down and lifted himself to his feet. Ignoring the ache in his muscles, they moved across to join the others.

Sam and Ashley stood with their hands on their hips, looking like they had barely broken a sweat. Chris cursed himself for exerting so much energy. Who knew what else the day had in store for them.

Yesterday, they had been taken into a laboratory and put through a series of tests. The doctors had worked with a cool efficiency, asking questions, giving instructions, taking measurements, all the while steadfastly refusing to engage with the captives. Behind the doctors, the guards remained colder still, their hard eyes following the prisoners' every movement.

The tests had been easy, little more than a thorough examination by the local GP. But now it seemed the easy part was over. That morning they had been roused in the early hours by the shriek of a buzzer and the sudden brilliance of the overhead lights. For a few seconds Chris had tried to resist, exhausted after a long night spent tossing and turning, unable to sleep. But Sam and Ashley had been insistent, dragging them from their beds to stand for inspection.

Within minutes, the guards marched past. A doctor accompanied them, pausing outside each cell to make notes on his electronic tablet. Chris shivered as the man's eyes fell on him. There had been a mindless look to him, a mechanical way in which he took the roster, as though this was no more than an inventory check at the grocery store.

When the doctor left, the guards returned with a trolley. The hallway rang with the sound of bowls sliding through metal grates. Chris had stared for a long moment at the oatmeal congealing in his bowl, before the rumbling of his stomach won him over. Resigning himself, he'd taken up his spoon and eaten all he could.

Then their escort of doctors and guards had arrived, taking them from the quiet of their cell and marching them through the facility to this field – if it could be called that. The open space was the size of a football field, but there was not a blade of grass in sight.

Instead, a fine dust covered the ground, spreading out across the oval like snow. A running track ran around its circumference, edged by tall, imposing walls that hemmed them in on all sides. The cold grey concrete stretched up almost thirty feet, interspersed with the metal railings of observation decks. A guard stood at each deck, rifles held in ready arms.

Above the walls, the sun beat down from the cloudless blue sky. The world outside was hidden by the walls, and whether Liz's mountains existed beyond remained a mystery.

Other than the doctors and their escort of guards, the field was empty. The doctors had made quick notes on their ever-present tablets, before nodding to the guards. Orders were barked, and the four of them had set off running.

Now they stood together in a little circle, panting softly as they waited for the next command. The doctors hovered nearby, their eyes fixed on their tablets, talking quietly amongst themselves. The guards still stood beside them, their dark eyes fixed on the prisoners.

Beyond the little group of overseers, a red light started to flash above the door they'd entered through. A buzzer sounded, short and sharp. Beside the doctors, the guards straightened, turning to face the entrance. The door gave a loud click and swung inwards.

Another group of doctors entered, followed by four prisoners in matching orange uniforms. Chris scanned the faces of the doctors, searching for Fallow, but there was no sign of her. His shoulders slumped and he clenched his fists, struggling to contain his disappointment. The woman was his only remaining link to his mother, but she had been conspicuously absent since their initiation.

As the group moved towards them, Chris sensed movement beside him. Glancing at the others, he was surprised to see Sam's face harden, the easy smile slipping from his lips. The older boy reached out and grasped Ashley by the wrist, then nodded in the direction of the newcomers. Ashley's face paled when she saw the group of orange prisoners, and she stumbled sideways a step before Sam caught her.

"What?" Chris hissed.

The two glanced at each other and then shook their heads. "Nothing," Sam muttered.

Before Chris could say anything more, the new group of inmates pulled up across from them. They hovered a few paces away, three boys and a girl, their eyes studying Chris and the others with suspicion. Chris stared back, wondering at the reaction of Sam and Ashley.

Clearing his throat, one of the doctors stepped between the two groups. He glanced at his tablet, then left and right. "Ashley and Samuel. Richard and Jasmine. You have already qualified for the next round of analysis. You are here to ensure your health does not deteriorate."

Chris watched a flicker of discomfort cross the faces of a boy and girl in the opposite group, and guessed they were the ones the man was addressing. Richard sported short blond hair and angry green eyes that did not waver from Ashley and Sam. He was almost a foot shorter than Sam, but more than matched the larger boy for muscle. He kept his arms crossed tight, his stocky shoulders hunched, and a scowl fixed on his face.

The girl, who he guessed was Jasmine, stood head to head beside Richard, a matching glare twisting her red lips. Her hair floated in the breeze, the black locks brushing across her face. The skin around her brown eyes pinched as she turned towards Chris, and caught him staring. Air had hissed between her teeth as she raised one jet-black eyebrow.

Chris quickly looked away, his heart beginning to race. Between them, the doctor had turned his attention on them.

"Elizabeth and Christopher, today we will test your fitness and athleticism, to assess your suitability for the next stage of the program. William and Joshua will be joining you. I suggest you get acquainted."

Chris's eyes drifted over to the other boys, and found them staring back. Their eyes did not hold the same animosity as Jasmine and Richard, just a wary distrust. The one on the left was a scrawny stickman of a figure, his long arms and legs little more than bone. Sharp cheekbones stood out on his face, and his jade-green eyes held more than a hint of fear. The other was larger, his arms well-muscled, but he did not match Richard or Sam for sheer bulk. He stood several inches above Chris's five-foot-eleven, and had long blond hair that hung down around his shoulders.

Seeing neither of the two were about to introduce themselves, Chris made to step towards them. Sam's hand flashed out, catching him by the shoulder. Chris glanced at the larger boy, raising an eyebrow in question, but Sam only shook his head. Settling back in line, Chris glanced at Liz and saw his own confusion reflected in her eyes. Ashley's hand clenched around her wrist, holding her back.

The doctor glanced between the two groups, and with a shrug, pressed on. "Very well," he cleared his throat, "All of you, line up," he paused as the eight of them moved hesitantly to stand in one line, and then nodded. "Today–"

The doctor broke off, his brow creasing as the buzzer by the entrance sounded again. As one, the group turned towards the door. Chris shuddered as he glimpsed the face of the newcomer. Unconsciously he took a step back. A shiver ran through him, raising goose bumps down his arms and neck.

ELEVEN

CHRIS SHIVERED AS DOCTOR HALT STRODE TOWARDS THEM, his eyes surveying the group as he approached. His arms swung casually at his sides, as though this were no more than a casual Sunday stroll for him. A smile played across his thin lips. He drew to a stop alongside the doctor that had been addressing them.

"Doctor Radly," his voice was like honey. "How goes training day?"

"Good," Radly spoke with hesitation. He was obviously surprised to see Halt. "How can I help you, sir?"

A soft laughter whispered from Halt's lips. "I thought I might assist," his eyes slid across the group of prisoners. "We need to advance our schedule – the directors are demanding results."

Radly bit his lips, eying them uncertainly. "We have four candidates ready in this unit. We still need time to assess the remaining four. Most of the other units are the same."

Shaking his head, Halt strode down the line, his eyes sweeping over each of them in turn. As Halt passed him, Chris risked a glance at the others. Sam and Ashley stared straight ahead, steadfastly ignoring the presence of Richard and Jasmine beside them. A hint of perspiration shimmered from Sam's brow, but otherwise the two of them seemed untouched by the run. On his other side, Liz stood with arms folded, while beyond the two newcomers wore uncertain frowns on their faces.

The crunch of gravel warned Chris of Halt's return, and he quickly turned to face straight ahead again. The man's eyes stared hard at Chris as he passed, and then moved on to Liz. The thud of his boots continued down the line as he went on to examine Joshua and William, before returning.

Scowling, Halt stood beside Doctor Radly. Raising an arm, he pointed at Liz, then to the lanky boy from the other group. "Those two," he scowled. "Pitiful creatures if ever I saw them. They won't last long."

Radly opened his mouth, then closed it. Glancing at his e-tablet, he shook his head and looked back at Halt. "Sir, we have a framework in place…" he trailed off as Halt stared at him.

Silence fell across the group of doctors. Chris glanced sideways at Liz, his heart beating hard against his chest. The girl stood staring straight ahead, her brow creased, fists clenched at her side. Though she did not move an inch, Chris could sense the tension building in her tiny frame, like a cat preparing to spring.

"Well, let's see," Halt's voice came again. A second later he strode past and stopped in front of Liz. "Elizabeth Flores," he looked her up and down. "How good to see you again."

Liz didn't move, just stood staring straight ahead. Nodding, Halt moved onto his next victim. "William Beth, a sorry looking excuse for a man, if ever I saw one."

A tremor went through the boy as he stepped back and raised his arms. "Please, sir, please, I'll do whatever you say."

Halt took another step forward, and the boy stumbled backwards. His feet slipped in the dust and he crashed to the ground. Towering over him, Halt sneered. "Pathetic," he spat. "Get up."

William nodded. He scrambled to his feet, eyes wide with terror. "Please–"

His plea was cut off as Halt's hand flashed out and caught him by the throat. Without apparent effort, the doctor hoisted the boy into the air. William gave a half-choked scream, his face darkening. His hands batted at Halt's arm, his legs kicking feebly in the air, but Halt did not waver. His cold grey eyes watched as the boy's struggles slowly grew weaker.

Chris watched in horror, his mouth open in a silent scream. A voice in his head screamed for him to help, but as he shifted an iron hand shot out and caught him by the wrist. He glanced back, opening his mouth to argue, but looking at Sam's face, the words died on his tongue. There was a cold despair in Sam's brown eyes, a haggard look to his face. Slowly, he shook his head.

Turning back, Chris watched as Halt tossed William to the ground. A low groan came from the boy as he struck, his legs collapsing beneath him. Dust billowed out around him. Gasping for breath, he struggled to his hands and knees and tried to crawl away.

Halt followed him at a casual stroll. Without taking his eyes from the boy, he began to speak. "You are all here at my pleasure. But I have no use for the weak," apparently losing patience with his victim, he lifted a foot and drove his boot into the small of his back. William collapsed face first into the ground.

Lifting his boot, Halt stared down at the boy. "Get up."

Arms shaking, William managed to lift himself to his hands and knees. His beet-red face looked up at Halt, eyes watering. He swayed where he crouched and a tremor went through him, but he made no move to stand.

Shaking his head, Halt growled. "Wretched specimen. Well, if you're too lazy to stand, I will give you one last chance to prove your merit. How many pushups can you do?"

A confused look came over the boy's face. "Push... pushups?"

"Yes." Halt took a step closer, his face darkening.

William shook his head. "I... I don't know…"

Halt sucked in a breath. He turned to face the other doctors. "He doesn't know." He gave a soft laugh and turned back to the boy. "Well, shall we find out then?"

He stared down at the boy, waiting for a reply, but William had gone quiet. The eyes of every doctor and prisoner were on him. Chris held his breath, sensing the trap in Halt's tone, but not knowing how it would be sprung.

"Well, get to it then," Halt snapped. He looked up at the doctor hovering nearby. "Radly, you can call the count for us."

At Halt's feet, a sharp sob came from William. Slowly, he lowered his hands to the ground and spread his legs. As Radly shouted out the count, William lowered himself to within an inch of the ground and then straightened his arms again.

Chris and the others watched on, faces grim, as Radly continued to count. Beside him, Liz's expression was unreadable, though there was a slight sheen to her eyes, hinting at tears.

As Radly reached fifteen, William's arms began to tremble. His breath came in ragged gasps and his face flushed red. A shudder ran through his bony body, and with a sob he collapsed to the ground. A triumphant grin spread across Halt's face as he folded his arms.

"Sixteen," Radly repeated the call.

"Please," William coughed, lying with limbs splayed across the ground, "please, please I can't!"

"Keep going," Halt snarled.

He tried, Chris had to give him that. Veins popping in his forehead, teeth clenched, arms shaking with the effort, the boy managed half a pushup before he collapsed back to the ground. This time he didn't bother to beg, just lay staring up at Halt, a haunted look in his eyes.

Shaking his head, Halt looked across at them. "In case you were wondering, this is what 'weak' looks like." Cold eyes still watching them, Halt reached down and tapped the sleek black glass of his watch.

Chris flinched as an awful scream came from the ground. He stumbled backwards, turning to face the source, raising his fists to defend himself. But there was no threat – just William, thrashing on the ground, his half-gasped screams clawing their way up from his throat. Eyes wide and staring, William's head slammed back against the ground. His fingers bent into claws, scrambling at the steel collar around his neck, even as another convulsion tore through him.

Panic gripped Chris and he stepped towards the boy. Sam's iron grasp stopped him again, pulling him back. Chris swore, struggling to break free, unable to stand by and watch the torture any longer. He looked at Sam, fighting to break free, but Sam only stared passed him, eyes never leaving the convulsing boy. Behind him, Ashley stood as still as a statue, her eyes fixed on William, her face expression-less. Her scarlet hair blew across her face, but she did not so much as raise a hand to brush it away.

The fight went from Chris in a rush. Shuddering with horror, he turned back.

"Such a shame, to see our people come to this," Halt's words slithered through the air, filled with contempt. "Once upon a time we were proud, strong. Our forefathers marched to war with joy in their hearts and sent the cowards of the United States scurrying. Even then they did not stop. They followed the enemy back to their holes, and left a smoking crater in the heart of their so-called democracy."

Chris gritted his teeth. Beside Halt, William's struggles were weakening, his eyes closing as the veins on his neck stood taught. Agony swept across his features, contorting his face into a twisted scowl.

Still Halt spoke. "How your ancestors would turn in their graves to know of your treachery, of your betrayal of the nation they fought to create."

Forcing his eyes closed, Chris sucked in a breath. The hand on his shoulder gave a gentle squeeze, but otherwise Sam stayed silent. Through the strangled screams, Halt's words twisted their way through Chris's ears. The wrinkled, smiling face of his grandmother drifted through his mind, telling of how her husband had fought and died in the American war. In 2020, a conglomerate of Washington, Oregon and California had unilaterally ceded from the United States. Arizona and New Mexico had quickly joined them, as support poured in from Canada and Mexico.

For a few years, a tense peace had hovered between the newly formed Western Allied States and the USA. However, talks had quickly descended to threats, as the USA demanded their return to the union. Within a few years, war was declared, and chaos had engulfed North America. A decade of conflict followed, leaving thousands dead on both sides.

Then, as the war was coming to a head, the Western Allied States had made one last, desperate gamble. In one decisive strike, Washington, DC was left in ruins, the leadership of the United States demolished in a single blow. The remnants of the union quickly crumbled then, leaving a scattering of independent states who either signed for peace, or were overrun.

Many scholars argued the values and beliefs of both nations had been lost the day Washington, DC fell. The Western Allied States had been left tainted, their ideals corrupted by that one act of evil. Watching Halt torture the helpless boy, Chris could not help but agree.

"Perhaps some of you may prove worthy, may one day live up to the memories of your ancestors." Halt's eyes flashed as he watched them.

Biting back a scream, Chris tensed his fists. More than anything he wanted to wipe the smirk from the doctor's face. Only Sam's firm hand on his shoulder stopped him.

Halt stared down at the boy, arms folded. The light on William's collar still flashed red, though his twitching had slowed to little jerks of his arms and legs. He let out a long sigh. "I will give the boy this, he does not die easily," he reached for his watch.

"*Halt*," Halt froze as a woman's voice carried across the dirt.

The group turned as one, staring as Doctor Fallow strode through the entrance. Chris blinked. So engrossed had he been in William and Halt, he had not heard the buzz of her entrance. Now, as she marched across the dusty ground, Fallow tapped at the watch on her wrist. Beside Halt, William's convulsions came to a sudden stop.

For a moment, Chris thought the boy had finally succumbed to the collar. Then a low groan came from his twisted body, and Chris let out a sigh of relief. He looked across as Fallow drew to a stop in front of Halt, her eyes flashing with anger.

"What the *hell* do you think you're doing?" Fallow growled.

TWELVE

"WHAT THE *HELL* DO YOU THINK YOU'RE DOING?" ANGELA Fallow growled, her heart pounding as Halt turned to face her.

"My job." Halt's eyes flashed, and Angela took an involuntary step backwards.

Shaking her head at her weakness, Angela drew herself up. "Your job is to oversee this facility, Halt. Mine is to ensure we have the candidates needed for the project." Her eyes flickered to the boy lying at Halt's feet, and her stomach swirled.

The boy lay unconscious on the ground, an angry red spreading around his throat like a rash. He gave the odd twitch as his muscles spasmed, but otherwise he was still, the only sign of life the dull rattling of his breath. It looked like she had arrived just in time. One of the doctors had alerted her to Halt's interference with his tablet, but she had been on the other side of the facility.

Halt took a step towards her, his fists clenched. "Need I remind you, Fallow, you answer to me."

This time Angela did not back down. She lifted her head, facing the taller doctor. "Not in this, Halt. The Praegressus project is *mine* to oversee. Its framework was designed by all of us; we *all* agreed to follow it while vetting the candidates," she twisted her lips. "However distasteful some of us may consider the methods."

Taking another step, Halt towered over her. His eyes burned with rage, and for a long moment, he did not speak. She stared him down, unwilling to break, to give in. Halt had gone too far, stepped a mile past the lines of human decency here. Whoever their prisoners were, they did not deserve to be treated like this.

The breath went from Halt in a sudden rush. Nodding he waved a hand and turned away. "Very well, Fallow," he said the words lightly, but she did not miss the warning beneath them. He turned towards the watching doctors. "We shall do things *your* way. But we cannot wait. I want the new round of trials started tomorrow. The final batch of candidates will be needed by the week's end."

Swallowing, Angela glanced at her co-workers. They hovered in a group, a mixture of fear and disdain in their eyes. She knew some would support her, eager to do things by the book. But others she was not so sure on. They were more willing to take risks, to press on without concern for the candidates brought to the facility. Or they were just plain terrified of Halt.

In truth, she could not blame them. While she had once regarded the man with respect, since his elevation to head doctor, he had revealed a darker side. Doctors who crossed him were terminated without cause, safety procedures had been cut, and with the subjects, there were no limits to his cruelty.

She eyed him now, silently calculating the population of subjects still to be vetted. There were two hundred prisoners in the facility, with roughly half of them still needing to confront the parameters of the framework. That left a hundred candidates to vet – of which fifty would hopefully survive to begin the experiment.

And that wasn't even accounting for the final touches she needed to make on the formula.

"A week's not enough time," she said.

Halt shrugged. "I'm sorry, Fallow. That's out of my hands. The directors want results. The people are growing restless, they need answers, and if the government doesn't provide them…" he trailed off.

Angela sucked in a breath, her eyes travelling over the group of prisoners in their orange jumpsuits. She shivered as she met the boy's eyes. Christopher stared back at her, eyes wide, the unspoken question written across his face.

She quickly looked away, hearing again the screams of the boy's mother. Biting her lip, she faced Halt. "We'll have to skip the resting period. It may result in sub-optimal outcomes."

Halt waved a hand. He was already moving towards the doorway, leaving his tortured victim lying face down in the dust. "You will find a solution, Fallow," their eyes met, "I know you will."

Angela's breath caught in her throat, but she held his gaze until he turned away. She shuddered as he disappeared through the iron doors, the resistance falling from her like water. A half-muffled groan slipped from her lips, but she bit it back and turned towards the gathered doctors.

They stared back at her, awaiting instruction.

Angela straightened. "Okay, you heard Halt. We need to get these candidates classified. You know the drill." She clapped her hands and smiled as the other doctors broke from their silent reverie.

One by one, the doctors moved away, each taking one of the orange-garbed candidates with them. She saw Radly take the boy, Christopher, by the arm, saw his hazel eyes turn in her direction. Looking away, she studied a cloud drifting through the sky. Her mind drifted for a moment, remembering again the way Margaret Sanders had fought. The woman had downed a highly-trained Marine, almost killed him in fact.

A mother's love.

Idly, she remembered her own mother, the way she had fussed over their little family. Despite the wide expanse of the property, they had always struggled, making do with the rations the landowner left for them. But her mother had suffered their poverty with good grace, stewing rabbit bones and baking hard bread in the coal stove.

She imagined Margaret Sanders possessed a similar resolve, a determination to do what was best for her children.

So why, then, had she been so foolish. Her treason against the government had doomed her son, and only by the grace of the government had he not been tossed into an interrogation cell alongside her. She shuddered, thinking of those dark places, imagining the woman's pretty face bruised and beaten.

Out on the field, Chris had begun to run, as Doctor Radly studied readings on his tablet. The collars transmitted a constant stream of data to the tablets: heartbeat, blood pressure, oxygen levels, and a range of other readings. That information would be used to rank them later.

Watching the candidates, Angela turned her thoughts to what lay ahead for them. She shuddered as a darkness settled on her soul. Again, she reminded herself what was at stake, of the necessity of the Praegressus project. Again, she could not quite convince herself.

THIRTEEN

LIZ LAY IN THE DARKNESS, EYES OPEN, STARING OUT INTO empty space. Somewhere above was the concrete ceiling, but in the pitch-black she imagined the sky stretched overhead, infinite in its expanse. Only there were no stars, no moon or drifting satellites, and in her heart, she could not convince herself of the illusion.

In her heart, she remained trapped, locked away within the soulless walls of the facility.

She could still feel the boy's eyes watching her, begging for help, for an end to the torture. A shudder ran through her as she remembered the way Halt had looked at her, the piercing grey of his eyes as he considered her worth. It had been so close, a simple coin toss, and he might have chosen her…

Biting back a sob, Liz closed her eyes, though it made no difference in the darkness. She had wanted to go to him; only Ashley's hand had stopped her. Instead, she had stood in silence, hand in hand with the girl from the city, as William slid towards death.

In the cell, Liz shivered, a scream building in her throat. She bit it back, and drew the thin cover closer. Goosebumps pricked at her skin as she rolled onto her side. Her body ached and a constant thud came from her temples. The doctors had subjected them to eight hours of torturous exercise, until the sun had finally dropped below the towering walls. By then her body had been little more than a series of bruises. A measly meal of broiled stew had followed in their cell, though in truth it was better than most of what she'd scavenged on the streets. Then the lights had clanked off, plunging them into the darkness.

"You okay, Liz?" Ashley whispered from the darkness.

Liz suppressed a shudder.

Am I okay? She turned the question over in her mind. Silently, she wondered whether she would ever be okay again. At the thought, a yearning rose within her, a need for companionship, for comfort.

"I'm alive," she replied, then. "What about you?"

Out on the field, Ashley had barely moved while William lay writhing in the dirt. Her face had remained impassive, the only sign anything was amiss was her iron-like grip around Liz's hand. Afterwards, Ashley had moved through the drills and tasks set by the doctors with an eerie calm, as though her mind were far away, detached from the horrors around her.

There was a long pause before Ashley replied. "I'm alive too." Her breath quickened. "That's saying a lot."

"How long… how long have you and Sam been here?"

Another pause. "Weeks, a month. I've lost count of the days."

"And… And you've seen things like that, like today with William?"

Below, Ashley gave a sharp snort. "That, and worse." She shifted in the bed, causing the bunk to rock. "It only gets worse, Liz."

Liz shivered, thinking of the icy glances that had passed between Ashley and Sam, and the couple in the other group. "What about the two in the other group, Richard and Jasmine and the rest."

"What about them?" Ashley's response was abrupt, her voice sharp.

"You knew them," Liz whispered softly, aware she was treading on dangerous ground. "Or at least, you knew Richard and Jasmine."

"You'll find out soon enough, Liz. Best you not worry about it."

Liz swallowed. Ashley's reply brooked no argument, and an uneasy silence fell between them. For a while, Liz lay still, staring into space, wondering at the truth behind Ashley's words. Below, Sam gave a snort and rolled in his bed. Liz stifled a groan as a rumble came from the boy's chest and he started to snore.

"The boys don't seem to be having any trouble sleeping," she whispered, hoping Ashley was still awake.

"You know what boys are like," came Ashley's reply. She could almost hear the girl smiling. "Emotional capacity of a brick and all…" her voice trailed off for a moment. "Sam… he closes it off I think, buries it deep. It comes out in other ways though, his frustration. Like how he reacted to Chris when you arrived."

"And you?" Liz couldn't help but dig deeper. Through the heat and torture, the agonising exercise and the hard-faced stares of the doctors, Ashley had not missed a beat. She had smiled through each new challenge, as though privy to some secret joke, and moved with that same fluid grace Liz had first seen displayed in this cell.

When the girl did not answer, Liz pressed on. "You looked so calm, even when…" she trailed off as William's agonised face flashed through her thoughts.

Ashley had remained impassive throughout it all, only moving once Doctor Fallow arrived to intervene. Her calm had been… frightening.

"I was?" Ashley sounded surprised. Sheets rustled in the darkness. "I wasn't. Inside I was screaming, but I've learned when to keep things to myself, when not to draw attention. Even before this place, it was a skill I'd mastered."

Liz sat up at that. "What do you mean?"

Soft laughter came from below. "I've had a lot of practice, Liz. My parents worked for the government."

An icy hand slid its way down Liz's throat and wrapped its fingers around her heart. Her breath stuttered, the cold steel pressing against her throat. She grasped at the covers, fingers tearing at the cheap fabric.

Below, Ashley was still talking. "They worked in Media Relations, of all things. No one important, nothing to do with the President and his people. Just a couple of analysts in a tiny department of our fine administration," her last sentence rang with sarcasm. "But even two lowly analysts quickly discovered there's no such thing as free speech these days. *Especially* for those close to power. They had to learn to wear masks, to hide their true beliefs about the goings-on of the government. By the time my older sister and I came along, they were masters at it. So I guess you could say, I learned from the best."

"Why would they stay?" Liz tried to hide it, but the question came out harsh, accusing.

A ruffle of blankets came from below her. "Why?" Ashley's voice trailed off, as though considering the question. "For us, I guess. To give us a better life. They may not have agreed with everything the government did, but they knew leaving was not really an option. Their careers would have been destroyed. They didn't want to raise their daughters on the streets."

"Yes, it's not much of a life," Liz all but growled.

Ashley fell silent, and for a long while it seemed she would not reply. Guilt welled in Liz's chest, but she pushed it down. Anger wound its way around her throat, but before she could reply, Ashley spoke.

"Didn't really matter in the end though, did it? They sacrificed their beliefs, their integrity, so we could live, but it didn't make any difference. They were found out, and here I am."

Liz's anger dwindled with Ashley's words. It was not the girl's fault she had been born into wealth, while Liz had been condemned to the poverty-stricken regions. Even so, she could not quite set aside the anger, could not quite let it go.

"Sorry," she offered at last, her tone still harsh. "It's just, for as long as I can remember, the government has been the enemy. Even as a child, they were the people who came and took our food, the landowners who held our lives in the palm of their hands. Then, when I was older, after my parents… after they passed…" She shook her head, angry images flashing through her mind.

"I understand," Ashley's whisper came from below. "But none of that matters now, does it? Whatever our parents were, whatever we've been through, we've arrived at the same destiny. We're both trapped in the same nightmare. You'll learn that, soon enough."

"It gets worse?" Liz spoke the words without emotion. Her energy was spent, and she could hardly bring herself to care about whatever new trials the morning might hold.

"Only if you're human," Ashley replied.

The words rang with finality and Liz sensed the conversation had come to an end. Shivering, she hugged the covers tight around her. Suddenly she longed to be wrapped in another's arms, felt the need for human touch. An image of her mother drifted through her thoughts, a warm smile on her lips, eyes dancing with humour.

Biting back a sob, Liz buried her head in the pillow, anxious to hide her sorrow. As she cried, another thought drifted through her thoughts, a question that demanded an answer.

One she should have asked. Silently, she cursed her selfish grief.

"Ashley," she breathed. "What happened to your sister?"

Silence hung over the darkness, and long minutes passed, until Liz was sure the girl had already fallen asleep.

"She's dead." The answer came just as Liz was preparing to give up.

The girl's soft sobs carried up from below, carrying with them the pain of loss.

"I'm sorry," Liz whispered, the words hollow, even to her.

Ashley did not reply, and Liz lay back on her bed, listening as the girl's sobs faded away.

It was a long time before sleep found Liz.

FOURTEEN

Liz stumbled as she entered the room, the sudden, brilliant light blinding her. Stars danced across her vision as the door slammed closed behind her. She jumped at the sound, and almost tripped, before she managed to right herself. Straightening, she blinked again and looked around the room.

Overhead, fluorescent bulbs lined the ceiling, filling the room with their distant whine. Otherwise, the room was unlike anything she'd seen so far. Three walls were covered by white padding, while the third shone with silver glass, its surface reflecting her tangled hair and shadowed eyes. She shivered, seeing the exhaustion in her eyes, the bruises marking her cheeks.

For three days, the doctors had taken them to the outdoor field, and driven them through an endless series of tests and exercise. Unused to the constant strain, Liz had quickly learned that failure meant pain. So she had dug deep within herself, to stores of strength she had not known she possessed, and survived. But now things had changed again.

She took another step into the room, the soft floor yielding beneath her feet. Turning from the one-way mirror, she shifted to face the boy in the centre of the room. His long blond hair hung in dirty clumps around his face, where purple bruises matched Liz's own. Biting his lip, his eyes flickered around the room, uncertainty writ in his every movement. Behind him was another door, its surface padded like the one she had entered through.

Joshua, she recalled his name from their first day on the training field.

His eyes turned on her as she thought his name. "What's going on?" he croaked.

Liz shrugged and shook her head. "I don't know, Joshua."

They had not spoken since that first day on the field. Ashley and Sam had been insistent, refusing to even acknowledge the other group of inmates. Somehow, Liz did not think their rule applied now.

Before either of them could speak further, a loud squeal interrupted. Liz winced, the hairs on her neck standing up, before the sound died away. A voice quickly followed.

"Welcome," the voice began, coming from somewhere in the ceiling. "Congratulations on surviving the framework. As you know, only the strongest are needed for the final stages of the Praegressus project."

Liz crossed her arms and turned to face the mirror. Raising an eyebrow, she rolled her eyes so those behind could see. She was sick of listening to these people, to them acting like they owned her. Collar or no, she refused to be treated like an animal any longer, to bend to their will.

The voice ignored her display of insolence and continued. "Unfortunately, time constraints require us to press on. This phase of the project must be completed by week's end. This means omitting the standard rest period for new subjects such as yourselves."

"Hardly seems fair," Liz muttered under her breath, flashing a quick grin at Joshua.

Joshua shrugged and cast another uncertain look at the glass. They stood in silence for a moment, waiting for the voice to continue. "Regretfully, we must cull our population of candidates for the next phase of the Praegressus project. Only those with the strongest constitutions would survive the final process regardless, and we do not have resources to waste on failed specimens. Thus, today only the best will survive."

Liz shuddered at the way the voice described cold-blooded murder. She recalled the faces lining the corridor outside their cell. Some of those boys and girls could have been as young as thirteen, the oldest maybe twenty. Their whole lives were ahead of them. And these people wished to snuff them out, to cull them like they were no more than field mice beneath their boots.

Joshua seemed a little younger than her, maybe seventeen at a stretch. He was a little taller too, and bulkier, with the broad shoulders of a swimmer. His amber eyes were watching her now, his fear shining out like a beacon.

"Only one of you will leave that room alive. You must decide for yourselves, whether you possess the will to live. To the victor, goes life."

Liz clenched her fists, eyes flickering from the mirror to Joshua. She sought out some sign of the watchers beyond, but the glass was too thick, showing only the horror on her face. And the boy's wide eyes, the hardening of his brow, his fists clenching as he faced her.

Whatever her own thoughts, Joshua had clearly already made up his mind.

Only if you're human, Ashley's words from their midnight conversation returned to her.

They weighed on her soul as she watched Joshua, saw his muscles tensing. And she knew in her heart, she too would do whatever was necessary to survive.

The fear had already fallen from Joshua's face. His eyes swept over her, weighing her up. A smile spread across his lips as he realised his chances of victory were high. There was no question who the doctors expected to survive.

Straightening, he stepped towards her.

Liz quickly retreated. She studied him as they began to circle, searching for an advantage. It was easy to see she was no match for his strength, but she was light on her feet and hoped he might prove over-confident. After two years on the streets, wandering between towns and cities, Liz was no stranger to a fight.

Yet with the padded walls ringing her in, there was no room for mistakes. If he caught her in his long arms, she would be finished. Though she was yet to see how determined he was about his capacity for murder, she didn't want to test his mercy.

She certainly would not be giving him any second chances.

Joshua gave a sudden shout and leapt towards her, eating up the space between them in a single stride. Liz twisted as he came for her, jumping backwards to avoid his flailing arms, and smiled as he staggered past. Despite his size advantage, the boy was no fighter.

Maybe she stood a chance after all.

Joshua came to a stop near the wall and spun to face her. A wicked scowl twisted his face. Liz swallowed hard and braced herself.

Raising her fists, she nodded. "Let's get this over with then."

A low growl came from Joshua as he started towards her again, his footsteps controlled now, each movement carefully measured. Liz spread her feet wide and slid one foot backwards, readying herself. She had no intention of letting him get close enough to grab her, but he needed to be a *little* closer yet.

As Joshua took another step, Liz gave a low growl and hurled herself forward. His eyes widened as she closed in on him, but close as they were, there was no time to react. Liz slammed her fist into the centre of his chest, aiming for the solar plexus.

Air exploded between the boy's teeth and he staggered backwards, a half-choked groan rattling from his throat. The colour fled his face as he clutched his stomach, mouth wide and gasping.

Watching his distress, Liz hesitated, guilt welling up within her. Joshua had not been expecting her to fight back, certainly not with such sudden violence. But as he bent in two, wheezing in the cold air, she knew she could not spare him. If she allowed him to recover, he would not fall for the same trick again.

Bent in two, Joshua's head provided the perfect target. Stepping in, Liz clasped her hands together and brought them down on the back of his head.

Joshua's legs buckled and he slumped to the ground without a sound. His arms splayed out on either side of him and a muffled groan came from his mouth. Relief swept through Liz at the sound – at least she hadn't killed him. Maybe they would spare him. After all, they couldn't have expected her to win this matchup.

Turning to the one-way mirror, she raised an eyebrow in question. As she did, Joshua's hand shot out and grabbed her by the leg.

Liz screamed as fingers like steel closed around her ankle and tugged, sending her crashing to the ground. The shock of the fall sent the breath rushing from her, and she gasped, struggling to breathe. Pain shot through her ankle as the fingers squeezed. Screaming a curse, she kicked out with her foot, but Joshua surged forward and caught it in his other hand.

Panic clenched Liz's stomach as she fought to break his grip. Sucking in a lungful of air, she tried to roll away, but his hands held her like iron shackles. However hard she strained, he held her tighter, teeth flashing as his lips drew back in a grin.

In a sudden rush, he dragged her across the floor, pulling himself up as he did so. For a second the hands released her, but before she could squirm free, Joshua's weight crashed down on her chest, pinning her down.

Hands fumbled at her throat, fingernails tearing at her skin.

Tendrils of horror wrapped around Liz and she lashed out with a fist, catching Joshua in the side of the head. He reeled sideways, but his weight did not shift and she failed to break free.

Recovering his balance, Joshua snarled and raised a fist. Flinching, Liz raised her arm, then screamed as his blow glanced off her forearm and into her shoulder. She swung at his face again, but there was no strength in the blow this time, and it bounced weakly off his chin.

Liz was not so lucky.

Stars exploded across her vision as Joshua's fist connected with her forehead. Her head thudded back into the soft ground. Distantly she thought how kind it was for the doctors to have provided a padded floor while they murdered each other. Then another blow thudded into her jaw, and the fight went from her in a sudden rush. Darkness spun at the edges of her vision.

Cold fear spread through her stomach as an almost tentative hand wrapped around her neck. She sucked in a breath as pressure closed around her throat. Panic caught her as she stared up at Joshua, silently pleading for mercy.

Joshua stared back, eyes hard, lips drawn back in a snarl. His teeth clenched with rage – whoever he'd been before entering this room, that Joshua was now long gone. He had been burned away, the innocence of the boy replaced by anger, by bitter hatred, and the desperation to live.

Fire grew in Liz's chest, willing her to action. She kicked feebly, struggling to manoeuvre herself into a position to attack. But his weight was far beyond her strength to lift, and before she could struggle further he lifted her head and slammed it back into the ground. Despite the spongy surface, Liz's head spun.

She opened her mouth, gasping in desperation, but the pressure did not relent. Darkness filled the edges of her vision as every muscle in her body began to scream. Bit by bit her strength slipped away, replaced by the endless burning of suffocation.

On top of her, Joshua leaned closer, eyes wide with vicious intent.

In that moment, Liz saw her chance.

He was so close, just inches away. She could not miss. With the last of her strength, she clenched her fist and drove it up into Joshua's throat. The steel rim of the collar bit into her knuckles, but behind it, she felt something give, something fracture with the force of her blow.

The pressure around her throat vanished as Joshua toppled backwards. A low gurgling echoed off the walls as he gasped, his hands going to his own neck, his legs thrashing against the soft floor.

Liz sucked in a long gasp of icy air, her throat burning as air flooded her lungs. A wave of agony swept through her, but she struggled to her hands and knees, still coughing and wheezing. Her head swirled and the room spun, but she dug her nails into the spongy floor and willed herself to remain conscious.

Get up, Liz!

Summoning the last of her strength, Liz pulled herself to her feet and stood swaying in the centre of the room. The white lights burned in her eyes, blinding her, but she clenched her fists, and by sheer will stayed upright.

She looked down at Joshua, bracing herself, and her stomach lurched.

Joshua no longer moved, no longer thrashed, no longer breathed. His mouth hung open, his eyes wide and staring, but the boy was gone. His face was a mottled white and purple, the veins of his neck bulging, and a black bruise was already spreading from beneath his collar.

Joshua lay dead at her feet, his life fled.

Tears ran from Liz's eyes as she sank to the ground.

The darkness came rushing up to meet her.

FIFTEEN

CHRIS WATCHED AS WILLIAM STAGGERED UPRIGHT, HIS HEART sinking at the thought of another round. But to his relief, the boy's feet slipped from beneath him and he toppled forward, landing with an undignified thud on the padded floor.

Closing his eyes, Chris let out a long sigh.

It's over.

The thought offered scant comfort. In truth, it had not been much of a fight. While William was tall and had long arms, there was not a scrap of muscle on the boy. And he had never quite recovered from the first day on the field. Young and inexperienced, he had still been the first to attack, but it was clear his heart was not in it. Chris had easily deflected his clumsy blows and retreated across the room.

Crossing his arms, he had looked at the glass, and shaken his head in refusal.

A loud beep had come from his collar followed by a bolt of electricity that sent him to his knees. Gasping, he reached for the steel collar, but the shock had already ceased.

The voice had come again as Chris climbed back to his feet.

"That was your only warning. Engage with your opponent, or forfeit your life."

That had been five minutes ago, and despite his reluctance, Chris had had no choice but to obey.

Now guilt ate at his stomach, curdling the measly remnants of his breakfast. William crouched on the floor, his breath coming in ragged gasps as he struggled to regain his feet.

Despite the voice's command, Chris had still held back, pulling his blows where he could. But as the fight progressed, the boy had grown more desperate, and Chris had been forced to act.

A kick to William's head had sent him reeling, and he had never recovered.

Now Chris waited, staring into the mirrored glass, struggling to pierce the reflection and find the faces of his captors. Whoever they were, he hated them with a violence he had not thought himself capable of.

The door behind the boy opened with a squeal of old hinges. Chris looked up as two guards entered, followed by a woman in a white lab coat. His heart lurched, before he realised the woman was not Fallow. One of the guards moved across to check on William, while the other approached Chris, gesturing him back against the wall.

Once she was satisfied both prisoners were secure, the woman strode across the room, her lips pursed, eyes fixed on the fallen boy. A wireless headset curled around her left ear, half hidden by the curls of her auburn hair. She spoke as she moved, transmitting observations to whoever was on the other end. In one hand, she carried a sleek steel instrument.

Chris shivered as he recognised the gun-shaped jet injector, identical to the one Fallow had used on him the night he was taken.

The woman who was not Fallow crouched beside William, still talking into her headset. William was on his hands and knees, struggling to find his balance. Reaching out, the woman laid a hand on his shoulder.

"Subject is still conscious. He appears to be suffering from concussion," her words carried across to Chris. "Assessment?"

A low groan came from William as he turned towards the woman's voice. "Wha… what happened?"

Chris closed his eyes, guilt welling up within him. He had seen these same symptoms in his Dojang, when younger fighters failed to wear their head guards. Still, he didn't think he'd hit William too hard, just enough to take the fight out of him.

The doctor was nodding to the voice in her ear. "Affirmative. There would be no purpose in resuming the fight. Administering the injection."

Before Chris could react to the announcement, the woman leaned down and pressed the jet injector to William's neck.

The hiss of gas followed as the vial attached to the gun emptied. Quickly, she withdrew the gun, stood, and retreated across the room.

On the ground, William raised a hand to his neck, his face tightening.

The woman looked on, face impassive, arms crossed and fingers tapping against her elbow.

Whatever had been in the injection did not take long to act. Chris stood frozen as William began to cough. Then, without warning his eyes rolled back in his skull. A violent shudder went through him as his breathing stopped, then began again with a desperate gasp, as though he were sucking air through a straw. He bent over, groaning, his mouth moving as he tried to speak. Wild eyes flickered around the room, pleading for help.

As William's desperate eyes found Chris, the spell broke. He started forward, but the outstretched arm of a guard barred his way. Before he could slip past, the guard grasped him by the shirt and tossed him back against the wall. The pads broke the impact, but he staggered as he landed and barely kept his feet.

He looked up in time to see William pitch face first into the ground, a low moan marking his final exhalation of breath. His feet kicked for a second, then lay still. Silence fell across the room as the guard stepped back from Chris and faced the doctor.

The woman walked across the room and crouched beside William. Reaching out, she felt his neck. After a few seconds, she gave a curt nod.

"Subject has expired. Subject Christopher Sanders has passed the framework," her voice was cold.

"*Why?*" Chris screamed.

The woman looked up quickly, her eyes widening. Beside her, the guards edged forwards, placing themselves between Chris and the doctor.

"Why?" Chris grated again, taking a step forward.

The woman's surprise had already faded, though her eyes flicked to the guards before she addressed him. "He was weak. He would not have survived phase two. This was the humane option."

"*Humane?*" Chris clenched his fists. "He was helpless!"

"With the concussion, he would have passed without pain," the doctor spoke with a calm efficiency, as though explaining something to a child.

A wild anger took Chris then, an impossible rage that swept away all caution. Without thinking, he leapt forward, fingers reaching for the woman's throat. The guards stepped forward to meet him, but Chris never made it that far.

Agony tore through his neck, spreading in an instant through every fibre of his being, taking his feet out from under him. He gasped as he struck the ground, his arms locking, every muscle screaming as a thousand needles stabbed them. A convulsion rippled through him and his limbs flailed wildly. His head thumped hard against the ground, as the reek of burning reached his nostrils. His back arched and he opened his mouth to unleash a silent scream.

When the agony finally ceased, he found himself staring up at the ceiling. The bright light sent a bolt of agony through his head, and he quickly closed his eyes again.

Movement came from nearby, followed by a voice. "Do that again, and we will find someone else to fill your place."

Chris opened his eyes to find the woman crouched beside him. She held a finger over her watch, a ready smile twisting her lips.

He nodded, swallowing hard as the collar pressed against his throat.

"This is for the greater good, Christopher," the doctor continued. "Without us, you would all be in the same place as this boy. At least here, we have given you a fighting chance. Trust me, when I say the government interrogators are not nearly as humane."

She stood then, waving a hand at the guards. "Get him up."

Rough hands grasped Chris beneath his shoulders and hauled him to his feet. He stumbled as they held him, struggling to control his legs. They jerked and twitched, refusing to obey, but eventually he got them firmly on the ground. Even so, the guards did not release him, perhaps knowing from experience how unstable he was.

"Bring him," the woman said as she turned and opened the door.

Chris's eyes lingered on the dead boy as the guards dragged him from the room. William still lay where he had fallen, still and silent, eyes wide and staring from the lifeless husk of his body.

Then they were outside, marching down long white corridors. Distantly, Chris thought they were heading for the cells, but he paid no attention to his surroundings. His mind was elsewhere, locked away in the room with William, his dead eyes still staring.

It's your fault, the thought ate at him.

William had never stood a chance. The minute they'd entered the room, the boy's life had been forfeit. These people had known it, had wanted it to happen.

Doors slammed as they moved deeper into the facility. He knew where they were heading now, that he would soon find himself back in the tiny cell. The others would be waiting for him. And they would know, would see the truth in his eyes.

That he was a killer.

SIXTEEN

THE STEEL DOOR TO THE PRISON BLOCK APPEARED AHEAD, the guards already moving to open it. In a blink, they were through, marching down the long corridor of the prison block. The cells were almost empty now, only a few faces remaining to press against the bars and watch Chris's return.

When he first saw their cell, he thought it was empty. But as the guards drew the door open, he glimpsed movement from Liz's bed, saw her haggard face poke into view. She watched in grim silence as the guards propelled Chris inside.

Steel screeched behind him, followed by the clang of the locking mechanism. Footsteps retreated down the corridor, fading until another clang announced their departure.

Reaching out, Chris gripped the metal bar of his bunk. His legs shook, threating to give way. He closed his eyes, waiting for Liz to speak, to hurl her accusations.

You killed him.

The words whispered in his mind, but Liz remained silent. Only the distant tread of the guard in the corridor could be heard. He took a deep breath, tasting the bleach in the air, the blood from a cut on his lip.

"Are you okay?" He jumped as Liz finally spoke.

He looked up then, finding Liz's big eyes watching him, and saw his own pain reflected in their sapphire depths. She sat in her bunk, knuckles wide as she gripped the metal sidebar. Her eyes watered and a single tear streaked down her cheek.

"No." Chris's shoulders slumped. "You?"

She shook her head, looked away, but he had seen the flash of guilt in her eyes. The truth hung over the room like a blanket, smothering them.

They were alive.

Taking a better grip of his bunk, Chris hauled himself up. Dragging himself across the sagging mattress, he collapsed into his pillow. Then he turned and saw Liz still watching him. Her lips trembled. There was no sign of the proud, defiant girl he'd first seen in the cages. The last few days, last few hours, had broken her.

Broken us both, a voice reminded him.

Pushing himself up, Chris twisted to face Liz. "Did they…" his voice trailed off. He couldn't finish the question.

Her crystal blue eyes found his, shining in the glow of the overhead lights. "No," she whispered. "I did."

A chill went through Chris at her words. He stared at her, noticing now the purple bruise on her cheek, the dried blood on her lip. His eyes travelled lower and found the swollen black skin beneath her collar. He shuddered. Her struggle had been far more real than his. He remembered the boy Joshua, guessed he was the one…

"What happened?" he murmured.

Liz closed her eyes. "I didn't mean…" She sucked in a breath, and her eyes flashed open. "I didn't *want* to," she finished with a growl.

Chris nodded, leaning back against the concrete wall. "You did what you had to, Liz," he offered.

"He would have killed me," she continued as though he had not spoken. "I had to do it. He left me no choice…"

Chris felt a sudden urge to wrap his arms around the girl, to hold her until the pain left her. This was a side of her he had not seen, the vulnerability beneath the armour she'd worn from the first moment he'd laid eyes on her. Gone was the hardness, the distant air of superiority. The foulness of this place had eaten the rest, had reduced them both to shadows of their former selves.

He could almost feel his humanity fading away, slipping through his fingers like grains of rice. With each fresh atrocity he witnessed, with every awful thing they forced him to do, he could feel his soul slipping away, feel himself becoming the animal they thought him to be. One way or another, soon he would cease to exist, and nothing would remain of the boy his mother had raised.

"It doesn't matter." Liz looked up at that. He continued, his voice breaking. "Whether you killed him or not, only one of you was ever walking out of that room. After my… after William fell, the doctors came. He couldn't stand, couldn't defend himself. They executed him."

A sharp hiss of breath came from Liz, but it was a long time before she replied. "Who are these people?"

Monsters. Chris thought, but did not speak the word.

Across from him, Liz started to cough. A long, drawn out series of wheezes and gasps rattled from her chest, going on and on, until her face was flushed red and her brow creased with pain.

Finally, she leaned back against the wall, panting for breath.

"Are you okay?" Chris whispered

Liz opened her eyes and stared at him. "Of course, city boy. I can take a beating."

Chris winced. His own anger rose but he bit back a curt reply. There was no point taking offence. He could see her pain, knew where the anger came from. He had not missed the coldness with which she addressed them at times, her hesitation to join their conversations.

Another rattle came from her chest as she laid her head back against the wall.

"We're not all bad, you know," he said at last. "Not all rich, either. There are a lot of people who disagree with the government now, even in the cities. There have been protests…"

"Protests?" Liz coughed, her voice wry. "Well, nice to hear you're getting out."

Chris sighed. "I understand–"

"I don't think you do," Liz cut him off. "You think you do, but you don't. While you lived in your cosy home in the city, I was forced onto the streets. Not because I wanted to, not because I had a choice, but because everyone I knew was dead. Slaughtered."

Shivering, Chris opened his mouth to reply, then closed it, unable to find the words.

Liz eyed him for a moment and then continued. "I had nowhere to go, no one left to turn to. I thought the government would help when they arrived, that they would protect me. But when they came, they looked at me like I was nothing, like I was an inconvenience to them. They would have arrested me, thrown me in some place like this if I hadn't run."

Chris looked away from the pain in Liz's eyes. He stared at his hands, the bruises on his knuckles, his stomach clenched with guilt.

"I'm sorry," he whispered at last, looking up. "You shouldn't have been treated that way. It's not right," he paused. "Was it a *Chead*?"

Liz flinched at the word. When she did not reply, Chris went on. "Mum always said something needed to be done, that her father would have been ashamed by how things have changed since the war. We should never have let the inequality between the cities and the countryside grow so bad," he paused for breath, "But that does not change what

I said. We're not all evil, Liz. Some of us want to fix things, want the government to be held to account."

"So I should just give you all the benefit of the doubt?" Liz snapped.

"No," Chris replied in a soft tone. "You should judge us by our own actions, not those of others," he breathed out. "A long time ago, I might have hated you too, Liz. Feared you for being different, for speaking with a rural accent."

"But not now?"

He shook his head. "No," he trailed off, remembering a time long ago. "When I was younger, I was running late getting home from class. It was getting dark, and we don't live in a good neighbourhood. When I was nearly home, a man stepped from the shadows. He had a knife."

"Let me guess, he was from the country too?"

Chris laughed softly. "No, he spoke like a normal person." He couldn't help but tease her for the assumption. Shaking his head, he continued, "But I think he was an addict of some sort – his eyes were wild and his hands shook. Before I had a chance to reach for my bag, he swung the knife at me, and caught me in the shoulder. I still have the scar…"

Liz nodded. "I saw."

Chris glanced across at her, his cheeks warming. He remembered his embarrassment when they had been forced to remove their clothes. Apparently, Liz had allowed her eyes to roam more than his own.

"What does this have to do with anything, Chris?"

With a shrug, Chris continued. "I think he would have killed me if someone else hadn't come along." He paused, looking across at Liz. "I don't know where he came from, but suddenly there was a man standing between us. *He* spoke with a rural accent, told the mugger to leave. When the man didn't listen, my rescuer took his knife away and sent him running."

"And this suddenly changed your mind about us?"

Chris shrugged. "Not overnight, no. But the man walked me home, right to my front door. He even told mum what to do with my cut. He didn't have to help me, could have left me to die, dismissed me as some spoiled city boy who deserved it. But he chose to help me instead. Since then, I've tried to do the same. To give people a chance, whoever they are."

Liz let out a long sigh. "And you want the same from me now?" she asked. "Because some man from the country saved you from a mugger?"

Chuckling, Chris nodded his head. "It would be nice to have a clean slate."

Liz shook her head. "After today, I'm not sure a clean slate exists for us, Chris. Joshua's blood is on my hands…"

"No," Chris replied firmly. "It's on theirs."

Liz nodded, but they both knew the words meant little. They might not have had a choice, but that did not lessen the burden.

"We're all in this together now, aren't we?" Liz repeated Ashley's words from all those days ago, on the day they had arrived.

Chris's gut clenched as he realised the two still had not returned.

On the other bed, Liz continued, her voice hesitant. "Okay, Chris," she whispered. "I'll give you a chance."

"Thank you," he said after a while.

Silence settled around them again then. Chris stared up at the ceiling, struggling to resolve the conflict of emotion battling within him. William's face drifted through his thoughts, eyes wide and staring, but the guilt felt a little less now. Liz had faced the same question, given the same answer.

Somehow, that made things just a little easier to bear.

Long hours ticked past. Still the others did not return. Chris and Liz waited in the hushed stillness of the cell, listening to the thump of the guard's boots outside, the whisper of voices from other cells. Liz's breath grew more ragged.

Finally, the bang of the outer door announced someone's approach. The soft tread of footsteps followed, moving down the corridor. Metal screeched as cell doors opened, while other footsteps continued on towards them.

Chris sat up as shadows fell across the bars of their cell. Relief touched his chest as he looked out, and saw Ashley and Sam standing outside. Hinges squeaked as the door opened and they stumbled inside. Sad smiles touched their faces as they looked up at Chris and Liz.

"So," Sam breathed. "You're alive."

SEVENTEEN

WITHOUT PAUSING TO KNOCK, ANGELA SHOVED THE DOOR to Halt's office open and strode inside. She glimpsed surprise on the harsh lines of his face as he looked up, though it had vanished by the time the door slammed shut behind her. Anger replaced it as he half-rose from his chair, fists clenched hard on his desk.

"What—"

"You have no right!" Angela cut him off.

Halt straightened. "I have every right," his voice was low, dangerous.

Hands trembling, Angela approached his desk. "It's not ready, Halt," she hissed. "You can't start those trials tomorrow. I need more time."

Rising, Halt walked around his desk, until he stood towering over her. Angela stared back, defiant, anger feeding her strength. She had just learned Halt planned to initiate the next phase of the Praegressus project tomorrow. The same project she had dedicated the last ten years of her life too.

"The directors want results, Doctor Fallow," Halt bit out the words, "and you've been stalling."

Angela refused to back down. "I've been doing my job," she snapped. "And I'm telling you, *the virus is not ready!*"

Halt smiled. "I've looked over your work, Fallow," Angela shivered at his tone. "And I say it's ready. After all, *fortune favours the bold*."

The words of the old Latin proverb curled around Angela's mind as she stepped back. They reminded her of Halt in those first days. The government had sent him after her discovery with the *Chead*, bringing her their new directive.

The Praegressus Project.

Praegressus – Latin for evolution, the adaptation of species down the countless millennia.

Shivering, Angela drew in a breath to steady herself. "There are still problems with the uptake," she ground out. "You could kill them all with your recklessness."

"The alternations will work—"

"Of course they will," Angela interrupted. "Animal trials have shown us as much. It's their immune response that concerns me. Their bodies will tear themselves apart fighting the virus."

Halt waved a hand as he moved back behind his desk. "Should that eventuate, we will administer immunosuppressants until the chromosomal changes have set," he sat back at his desk, eyebrow raised. "Is that all?"

"Immunosuppressants?" Angela pressed her palms against the desk and leaned in. "We'll have to move them to the clean room, watch them around the clock. They wouldn't last a day in the cells."

"Whatever it takes, Fallow." Halt stared her down. "We can't wait any longer. The government wants answers. We'll be shut down if we don't provide a solution soon. The attacks are growing worse. The authorities are desperate."

"What?" Angela questioned.

Halt leaned back in his chair. "The fools underestimated the *Chead* for too long. They should have given us the funding we needed for this years ago. There was an attack in San Francisco yesterday. They've reached the capital, Fallow. The President himself is demanding answers."

Angela shook her head, doubt gnawing at her chest. "You really think this is the answer?"

"Of course." Halt's cold eyes regarded her with a detached curiosity. "Do not lose focus now, Doctor Fallow. Not when we're so close. The Praegressus project will change everything. When it succeeds, the Western Allied States will herald in a new era of human evolution. The *Chead* will be hunted down and eradicated, our enemies at home and abroad consigned to the pages of history."

Looking into her superior's eyes, Angela shuddered. Naked greed lurked in their grey depths. For the first time, she allowed herself to look around, to take in the grisly display lining the walls of Halt's office. The sight she had been doing her best to ignore.

All around, animal eyes stared back at her. Halt's office was lined with shelves, each holding a collection of jars filled with clear fluids. Suspended within hung a silent host of animals of every shape and size. Birds and lizards, cats and snakes and what looked like a platypus stared down at her, their eyes blank and dead. An opossum curled around its ringed tail on the shelf behind Halt's head, while beside it a baby chimpanzee hugged its chest. With its eyes closed, it could have been sleeping.

Angela looked away, struggling to hide her disgust from Halt.

"Soon they will all be obsolete," Halt commented, noticing her discomfort.

"Yes," she almost choked on the word.

But at what cost? She added silently.

Halt eyed her closely and raised one eyebrow. "Was there anything else, Doctor Fallow?"

Angela shook her head. She knew when she was defeated. Turning, she all but ran from the room. She closed the door carefully behind her, her anger spent. Once outside, she placed a hand against the wall, shivering with sudden fear. Events were accelerating now, slipping beyond her control, and it was all she could do to keep up.

In her mind, she saw images of San Francisco, the steep roads teaming with life. She imagined the devastation a *Chead* would cause in such a place, the mindless slaughter. Bodies would line the streets as police struggled to reach the scene through the traffic-clogged streets. How long might the *Chead* have run rampant?

Straightening, Angela turned from Halt's door and moved away. Tomorrow, if they succeeded, the world would change. Humanity's evolution would take one giant leap forward, and one way or another, there would be no going back.

A sudden doubt rose within her, a fear for what was to come. What if they were wrong? What if they failed, and it was all for nought?

And what if they succeeded? What then?

Her skin tingled as she remembered Halt's words, heard again his triumphant declaration.

Our enemies, at home and abroad, will be consigned to the pages of history.

EIGHTEEN

A cold breeze blew across Liz's neck, rustling the branches above her head. Sucking in a breath, she picked up the pace, eying the lengthening shadows beneath the trees. She was close to home now, the path familiar beneath her feet, but it was a steep climb and she had no wish to make it in the dark.

Around her, the forest was eerily silent, the usual evening chorus of birds and insects mute. It put her on edge, eyes flicking over the scraggly trees neighbouring the path. Their dense branches shifted with the wind, but otherwise there was no sign of movement.

She moved on.

Behind her the path wound down through the forest. The mountain on which their homestead perched stood alone amidst the Californian flood-plains, looking out across their broad expanse. All around the rock were the lands of the Flores family – or at least the lands they managed. Once they had been theirs, but no longer.

Liz smiled as she approached the final bend in the track. The house was only a short thirty-minute walk up the mountain, but she was still glad to see the end of it. It had been a long journey from San Francisco.

Around her the trees opened out, revealing the homestead sitting at the trail's end. Glancing around, Liz listened for the first shouts of welcome. Her family employed a dozen labourers on the property, and most were like family to her.

Silence.

A shiver went through Liz as she closed on the homestead. Her eyes flickered around the collection of buildings, searching for movement, for signs of life.

It was only then she saw the bodies.

They lay strewn across the homestead, torn and broken, their faces grey and dead. Blood splattered the walls nearby, streaked across the peeling paint. Her eyes swept over the bodies, lingering on their faces. There was Nancy, the old woman who had helped raise her, who had cooked meals while her mother helped in the fields. And there, Henry, the man her father thought of as a brother.

Standing amidst the carnage, Liz's eyes drifted up to the building she called home. Without thinking, she found herself moving towards it. Her movements were jerky, her breath coming as desperate sobs. Reaching the old wooden door, she pushed it open.

It swung inwards without resistance, revealing the wreckage within. Swallowing a scream, Liz staggered inside, eyes sweeping the shattered plaster walls, the torn-up floorboards. Dust and rubble lay strewn across the floor, mingling with the blood pooling at the end of the corridor.

Barely daring to breathe, Liz stepped inside the house. With cautious footsteps, she slid down the corridor, eyes fixed on the blood. She winced at each soft tread of her boots, the sound impossibly loud in the silent house.

The corner neared. In a sudden rush, Liz darted forward, eyes wide, desperate to see…

Liz screamed and threw up her arms, tearing herself from the nightmare. Her eyes snapped open, but absolute darkness stretched out around her and she screamed again, thrashing against the tangle of covers wrapped around her. The bed creaked as she rolled. The safety bar creaked as she slammed into it, then gave way. She found herself falling, plummeting through empty air, a final scream tearing from her throat.

Thud.

A bolt of agony lanced through her arms as she struck the concrete. The last tendrils of the dream fell away, plunging her back into reality – and the pain that went with it. She groaned, her throat burning as it pressed against the cold steel of her collar.

"What?" somewhere in the darkness, a voice shouted.

"Who's there?" someone else yelled.

"Liz?" She recognised Chris's voice.

Above her, his bunk rattled as he moved. Then hands were reaching for her, grasping her shoulder, pulling her up.

"Are you alright?" Chris's voice came again.

Half in shock, Liz couldn't manage more than a nod. Distantly, she was surprised at the tenderness in his words, his sudden concern. A second later, she realised he could not see her nod. Opening her mouth, she managed a croak. "Yes."

As sanity slowly returned, a wave of embarrassment swept through Liz. She closed her eyes, silently berating herself for her panic. It had been so long since she'd had the dream – months, maybe even a year. Why had it returned now, after all this time?

"What happened?" Sam's voice was heavy with sleep.

"Sorry," Liz murmured, heart still racing. "Was just a bad dream."

"Some bad dream," Ashley's hand settled on her shoulder. "Go back to bed, Sam. You need your beauty sleep."

A string of inaudible mumbling came from Sam's bed, quickly followed by a soft snore.

Arms shaking, Liz pulled herself up, helped by Chris on one side, Ashley on the other.

"It's okay," she murmured and then suppressed a groan.

Her throat was aflame, throbbing with each beat of her heart. She tried to swallow, but it only made the pain worse. The steel collar dug into her swollen throat. Gasping, she fought for breath.

"What's wrong?" Chris asked in the darkness, taking her weight beneath his shoulder.

"My throat," Liz gasped.

"Water." Somehow Chris understood. "Ashley, help me get her to the sink."

A sharp pain twisted through Liz's shin where she'd landed as she tried to take her weight. With a silent moan, she collapsed back against them. To her right, Ashley swore as the shift in weight sent her stumbling into the bed. Then she straightened, shifted her body beneath Liz's shoulder, and helped her the few steps to the sink.

Liz slumped to the ground as Ashley released her. The sound of water followed as Chris helped her to sit comfortably.

"Here," Ashley whispered. "Open your mouth, Liz. The water will help."

Liz obeyed as Ashley's hands fumbled at her face. She almost lost an eye before Ashley finally found her lips. Then cool water dripped into her mouth, trickling from the palm of the girl's hands. Swallowing slowly, Liz let out a long sigh as the cold spread down her throat.

They repeated the procedure three more times before Liz's breathing began to ease. At last she croaked for them to stop, and they settled back down together on Ashley's bed.

"How are you feeling now?" Ashley whispered.

In the other bed, Sam was still snoring. Listening in the darkness, Liz found herself jealous of the boy's ability to sleep through anything. She desperately needed the release of sleep, to escape the pain of her beaten body. But she knew it would not come now, not after the dream.

"I'm okay," she breathed. "You should go back to sleep."

A soft chuckle came from the girl. "My bed's a little crowded now. It's okay, I think the lights will turn on soon."

Her words were met by a distant clang, followed by a low buzzing in the ceiling. Liz blinked as white light flooded the room, then raised an eyebrow at Ashley. She sat beside Liz, her yellow eyes ringed by shadow, the scarlet locks of her tangled with sleep. A smile tugged at her lips.

A groan came from the opposite bed as Sam rolled over and pulled the pillow over his head.

"God," Chris's voice came from her other side.

Liz turned to face him. "What?"

He blinked and shook his head. "Your neck, no wonder you couldn't breathe. It's a rather attractive shade of purple."

Liz lifted a hand and touched a finger to her throat, but flinched back as the muscles spasmed. She bit her lip, swallowing the pain. "I've had worse."

Chris shivered, but said nothing.

For the next few minutes they sat in silence, listening to the growing crescendo of Sam's snores. Finally, Ashley stood and moved across to his bed. Taking a hold of his blanket, she tore it away, exposing his half-naked body to the cold. His curses echoed from the walls as Ashley retreated to her bed, bringing Sam's cover with her.

Liz chuckled as Ashley spread the cover over them, trying to ignore the burning from her throat. "Thanks, I was getting cold," she grinned at the other girl.

"Hey!" Sam was sitting up now, blinking hard in the fluorescent light. Lifting his pillow, he tossed it across the room. Chris caught it easily and placed it behind his head.

Liz smiled as a little of the weight lifted from her heart. Wriggling her backside, she snuggled in beneath the blanket, and basked in the warmth from either side of her. Together, they grinned as Sam found the shirt he'd discarded the night before and pulled it over his broad shoulders. Liz watched with a tinge of disappointment as he covered himself.

"Hey, my eyes are up here, ladies," Sam laughed.

Liz snorted. "Like I'd be interested in a city slugger like you, Sam."

Ashley giggled and Chris chuckled while Sam rolled his eyes. Then the clang of the outer door echoed down the corridor, plunging the room into silence. The smiles fell from their faces as they shared sad glances, the weight of yesterday's guilt returning.

"What happens next?" Chris murmured.

Sam's eyes flickered towards Ashley. "After we… survived, you two showed up," Sam replied with a shrug. "You know the rest."

Beside her, Ashley shifted on the bed. "Yesterday, on the training field, the doctors were talking," the girl spoke in a low voice. "I overheard a bit. They were talking about things moving ahead. So who knows what comes next."

The bed shifted again as Chris pulled himself up. A pang of sadness touched Liz as his warmth left her side. He moved to the bars and glanced down the corridor. "Well, whatever comes next, at least breakfast is on its way," his words were spoken with a false lightness, failing to hide the strain beneath, but Liz appreciated his attempt to brighten the gloomy discussion.

Sam groaned. "Don't suppose it's something other than that gruel they call oatmeal?"

"Sure, what's your order? I'll give them a shout." Chris laughed.

"I'll take some eggs with a side of bacon. Maybe some hash browns. Oh, and a burger. You got all that?"

"How about a television while you're at it, Chris?" Ashley put in.

Shaking his head, Chris returned to the bed and slid in beside Liz. "Ah, bacon. I can't even remember the last time we had that at home."

As his warmth touched Liz she found herself sliding closer, until her side pressed up against him. A tingle ran up her arm at the touch, and she held her breath, waiting for him to pull away. When he did not move, she smiled, only then recalling his words. Her grin spread. While the food on the ranch had not technically been theirs to eat, her family had made an art of pilfering extra supplies whenever they were available. Bacon had been just one of the many luxury food items she'd enjoyed.

"Oh, I don't know, back on the farm we had bacon and eggs for breakfast most days. It gets a little old."

She chuckled as the three of them turned to stare at her. Unfortunately, the laughter was too much for her throat, and she broke into a coughing fit. It was a few minutes before she found her voice again.

"Country secret," she croaked at last, and the others groaned.

The screeching wheels of the breakfast cart came to a sudden halt outside their cell. The guard banged his rifle against the bars while the other opened the grate through which they passed the food.

"Come and get it." The guard with the gun laughed. "Big day for you I hear."

Chris retrieved the four bowls of oatmeal, much to Sam's chagrin, and they sat down to their meal.

Afterwards the four of them sat back and waited, listening for the sound of the outer door. Closing her eyes, Liz did her best to ignore the agony that was her neck. Her good mood quickly fell away as the pain beat down on her. Silently, she cursed the doctors, the guards and their guns, even Joshua for his vicious attack.

"What do you think he meant?" Sam asked after an hour, addressing the room at large.

"Nothing good," Chris offered unhelpfully.

"Well, they need us alive for something," Ashley put in. She had joined Sam on the other bed now, surrendering her bed to Liz and Chris. "Whatever this place is, its top secret. My parents weren't the most connected of individuals in the government, but most things reached the rumour mill at some point. I don't think this place was ever mentioned. As far as the media are concerned, the children of traitors were…" her voice trailed off, and Liz felt a pang of sadness for the girl.

Without speaking, Sam reached up and placed an arm around Ashley, drawing her into a hug. Watching them, Liz's sadness grew, rising from some lonely chasm inside her. The last two years had been long and hard, and more than once she had found herself craving the touch of another human being. Licking her lips, she glanced at Chris, then gave herself a silent shake. Drawing up her knees, she hugged them to her chest.

Movement came from beside her, but it was just Chris rearranging himself on the bed. He spoke into the uncomfortable silence. "Maybe it's the same with our families then. Maybe they've been taken someplace else," there was no mistaking the tremor of hope in his voice.

As the others nodded, Liz closed her eyes. The others might still cling to the hope their families were alive, but hers were gone.

"Wouldn't that be nice?" Sam replied with false cheer. "We can all have a reunion someday, share torture stories around the campfire—"

"Shut up, Sam." Ashley pushed him away and looked at Chris. "We can only hope, Chris. Although my sister…" she bowed her head, eyes shining. "She got in the way. They never gave her a chance."

Before any of them could respond, a loud clang echoed down the corridor.

The four of them exchanged a long glance.

"Showtime," Sam whispered.

NINETEEN

THE SOFT SCREECH OF IRON ROLLERS CARRIED DOWN THE corridor as the door to a cell slid open. Together, the four of them jumped from their beds and pressed themselves up against the bars. Head hard against the cold steel, Liz peered out into the corridor, straining to see what was happening. The faces of their fellow inmates appeared behind the bars of the other cells, eyes wide and staring.

At the very limits of her viewpoint, Liz could just make a group of doctors clustered around the cell at the end of the corridor, talking quietly amongst themselves. Beside them, guards were shouting at the occupants of the cell. They carried steel batons now, instead of the familiar rifles of the past few days.

As Liz watched, the guards disappeared into the cell. The raised voices of the prisoners carried to them, followed by the muffled thud of steel on flesh.

Retreating from the bars, Liz looked at the others. Sam and Chris stared back, their eyes wide, uncertainty written across their faces. Ashley only pursed her lips, her eyes roaming the cell.

Liz turned back to the bars as a girl's scream carried down the corridor. Looking along the rows of cells, she watched the doctors gathering around a steel trolley. One of the doctors was leaning over an open drawer on the side of the cart. Reaching inside, he drew out a packet of syringes. Vials of a clear liquid quickly followed, as he handed them out to the other doctors. Together, they turned and followed the guards into the cell. Another shriek echoed down the corridor, a boy's this time.

"What's going on?" Chris asked from behind her.

Liz glanced back at the others. "It's some sort of injection. They've got syringes and a trolley loaded with God knows what else."

As she finished speaking, a long, drawn out screeched erupted from the cell at the end of the corridor. Liz flinched, pressing her face hard against the bars, straining to see. It was the girl again. Distantly she remembered the faces of the two captives: a young girl with blonde hair, a boy with black dreadlocks.

The girl's scream slowly died away, but before it ceased the boy's voice joined in, carrying the awful notes of agony to the four of them in their little cell. Liz shuddered, fighting the urge to cover her ears. The shrieks rose and fell, twisting and cracking, almost inhuman in their anguish.

Turning, she saw the blood draining from the other's faces, felt her own cheeks grow cold with an awful fear.

Slowly the screams died away, leaving only silence.

And the screech of trolley wheels on concrete as the doctors made their way to the next cell.

"What do we do?" Chris repeated his question from earlier.

"We fight," came Ashley's reply.

Liz turned and stared at the girl, heart thudding hard in her chest. "*What?*" from down the corridor came the rattle of another cell opening. "What about the collars–" she broke off as a cough tore at her throat.

Staggering past the others, she fumbled at the sink and turned the faucet. As she drank, Ashley continued to speak.

"Those batons, why do they need them?" her voice sounded calm, as though they were discussing the weather. "They haven't used them before now."

"It's like you said before," Sam mused. "They don't want us dead. They've been saving us for something. For *this.*"

"Really?" Chris snapped. He waved a hand. "Because I'm pretty sure they just killed those two."

"They're not using the collars," Liz croaked as she re-joined them. The realisation had come as she pressed her mouth to the faucet, making the collar dig into her neck. "No guns *or* collars."

Sam grinned and cracked his knuckles. "In that case, I agree with Ashley."

Liz leaned against the pole of her bunk bed, drawing reassurance from its icy touch. She looked at the others, fear fluttering in her stomach. Sam looked more alive than she'd ever seen him, his eyes alight with a frightening rage. Chris stood beside him, tense and ready, one eye on the door to the cell.

And Ashley… just looked like Ashley – cool, calm, collected.

She pushed past the boys as another scream rattled the walls. As they took up station near the door, she crouched between the beds, and lifted a piece of railing which lay wedged against the wall. Liz blinked, realising it was the safety railing for her bed, the one that had given way and sent her crashing to the concrete.

Ashley moved across to Sam and offered him the bar. Teeth flashing, he took it and held it up to the light. The three parts of the rail formed a distorted U-shape, with two short piece of steel jutting from the longer centre piece.

"Work at the joints, see if you can break them apart."

As Sam set to work trying to separate the bars, Ashley moved to the front of the cell and resumed her watch. Liz joined her, and together they followed the doctors slow progress through the prison.

"They're done with us," Chris whispered behind them.

Outside the screams continued, at times slowly fading, only to resume as the doctors reached the next cell.

"No," Ashley whispered. Her eyes took on a haunted look. "I think they're only just getting started."

"Here." Liz turned and Sam offered her one of the smaller bars. He grinned. "Just pretend they're city sluggers like me."

Liz smiled back. Silently she reached out and squeezed his arm. He nodded and moved across to Ashley and Chris, offering them the other two bars. Ashley took one, but Chris shook his head. His eyes did not leave the corridor, but he spoke from the side of his mouth.

"I'd prefer to keep my hands free, thanks."

Outside, the doctors had reached the cell directly across from them. Its only occupant stood at the bars, watching as the doctors drew to a halt. His eyes were bloodshot and tears streamed down his face.

"Please, I never did anything wrong," his voice was feeble, barely a whisper.

He retreated into his cell as the guards slid the door open. Before he could so much as raise his fists they were on him, batons flashing in the fluorescent lights. A few seconds later they had him pinned to the bed. Without preamble, the doctors entered the cell. As the guards held the boy down, one doctor pulled down his pants, while another prepared the needle. The injection was given, then the doctors and guards retreated from the cell, slamming the door closed behind them.

Liz flinched as the boy screamed and began to writhe. Then the guards moved between them and the other cell, and there was no more time to consider their neighbour's plight.

Gripping the bars of their cell tight in her hands, Liz watched as the guards gathered near the door. The pain in her throat had strangely faded away, leaving only a dull ache. Blood pounded in her ears as she tensed, readying herself.

"Stand back, drop those," one of the guards ordered, eying their makeshift batons.

When they didn't move, he turned to look at the doctors.

"What are you waiting for?" Doctor Radly's voice carried into the cell. "Get in there and take those off them. You know we can't use the collars. We can't have any interference with their nervous system."

The guard nodded and reached out to unlock the door. The others gathered behind him, seven in total, their batons held ready.

A strange calm settled over Liz as the door slid open, the terror of the past few days falling away. Whatever Ashley thought, this was it. This was their only chance. If they failed, she knew in her heart they would be lost.

As the first of the guards moved into the cell, movement came from beside her. She turned in time to see Chris lunge forward. The guard grinned and raised his baton, but Chris was faster still. Leaping lightly from the concrete floor, he twisted in the air to avoid the man's blow, and drove a kick into the side of the guard's head.

Liz gaped as the man's eyes rolled up in his skull and he collapsed to the ground

Chris landed lightly in the doorway and retreated back to re-join them.

"Six to go," he grinned, his smile infectious.

Shaking her head, Liz gripped the metal bar tighter and tried to hide her shock.

Outside, the remaining guards grabbed their fallen comrade by the feet and dragged his unconscious body out into the corridor. One of the doctors crouched beside him and placed a stethoscope to his chest. Radly glanced down at the man, then back at the guards. Each of them dwarfed even Sam's large frame, but still they stood hesitating in the hallway. The fate of their comrade had given them pause.

"Well?" he snapped. "What are we paying you for? Get in there!"

The guards shared a glance, then approached together. Pushing the sliding door wide open, they entered as a group this time. They paused for a second in the entrance-way, hefting their batons, then came forward in a sudden rush.

Liz tensed as the first guard came for her, his steel baton flashing for her face. Ducking back, the hackles on her neck tingled as it swept over her head. Then she lifted her own weapon and drove it into the man's midriff.

The blow caught him as he was moving forward, and his own weight drove the air from his lungs. As he staggered to a halt, Liz lifted her bar to strike him again, then threw herself to the side as another guard swung at her. Steel rang out as the baton left a dent in the bunk bed behind her.

Recovering, she turned and found the first guard already straightening. Now the two of them bore down on her, forcing her away from the others.

Liz gripped her makeshift weapon tight, knowing she was hopelessly outmatched. Snarling, she threw herself forward anyway. They grinned, raised their batons. Then a body stumbled backwards into them, sending them stumbling forward. Seeing her chance, Liz swung her pole into the face of the nearest guard.

As the man staggered sideways, she leapt for the gap he'd left, eager to re-join the others. But as she moved, the other recovered and stepped in to block her, baton already in motion. The blow caught her in the stomach, knocking the breath from her lungs and sending her staggering backwards into the wall.

Groaning, she tried to straighten, but a fist caught her in the side of the face. Her feet crumpled beneath the force of the blow, and she slid sideways into the crook between the wall and the bunk. Coughing up blood, she tried to regain her feet, but a heavy boot crashed into her back, pinning her to the ground.

Head ringing, Liz twisted on the ground, desperate for a glimpse of the others. But the fight was already over, the guards' weight and numbers making short work of the four prisoners in the narrow confines of the cell. Sam lay immobilised on his own bed, a guard's knee pressed between his shoulder blades. Ashley was similarly restrained on the floor nearby, while Chris still stood, his arms held by a man on either side of him. The last guard was just getting to his feet, a nasty bruise on his forehead.

"About time," Radly's sarcastic voice came from somewhere out of view. "Would you like something easier next time. Maybe some toddlers?"

The guards were silent as the doctors filed in, carrying their assortment of vials and syringes. As the doctors prepared themselves, Radly looked around the room. His eyes settled on Liz. "Get her up."

Tears stung Liz's eyes as a rough hand grasped a handful of her hair and pulled. Screaming, she drove a fist into the man's side, but the blow hardly seemed to faze him. A tearing pain came from her scalp as he pulled again. Kicking and screaming, Liz found herself hauled to her feet.

"This one's feisty," the guard commented as he tossed her onto Ashley's bed.

Before Liz could free herself, the weight of the guard landed on her back. An awful helplessness welled in her as she tried and failed to shift his weight. Pain lanced from her scalp again as the guard yanked her head back, forcing her to look at them.

"Stay still," the guard growled in her ear.

"Please don't do this," Ashley pleaded from the floor.

The thud of a boot striking flesh silenced her desperate words. A low groan followed. Liz twisted again, trying to get a glimpse of her friend, but the white coat of a doctor moved to block her view. Looking up, she saw Doctor Radly staring down at her.

"Enough," Radly's tone brooked no argument.

Unlike Halt, Radly did not appear to take any joy in their pain. Rather, he didn't seem to care about their comfort one way or another. He moved around the cell with a cold efficiency, retrieving the stoppered vial from the hands of another doctor. Lifting a nasty looking syringe, he eyed the thick needle for a second before driving it through the vial's rubber stopper. Then he drew back the plunger, watching as the liquid disappeared into the syringe.

"Doctor Faulks," Radly addressed someone standing just outside of Liz's view. "This is the PERV-A strain?"

"Yes," a woman's reply came quickly. "We've already finished with the B strain. The rest are marked down for PERV-A."

Nodding, Radly turned back to Liz. "Hold her," Liz shuddered as the guard shifted, taking a firmer hold of her shoulders.

From the corner of her eye, she watched Radly approach, his gloved hands holding the syringe in a gentle grip. Then he disappeared from her line of vision. Seconds later firm hands tugged at her pants, and a cold breeze blew across her backside. She tensed, pushing back against her assailant's relentless strength.

A sigh came from behind her. "This will go easier for you if you relax, Ms Flores."

Hearing her last name sent a bolt of shock through Liz. For a second she hesitated, then bit off a string a profanity that would have made her father blush.

Another sigh, then a cold cloth pressed against her buttcheek. A shiver raced up her spine, more shock from the violation than from the cold. A low, guttural growl built in her throat, and the guard's knee pressed harder into the small of her back. But she no longer cared. A desperate horror was growing within her, an awful fear, a need to break free.

She screamed again, writhing and bucking beneath the guard, straining to shift his weight.

A sudden pinch came from her naked backside, followed by a cool pressure that spread quickly across her cheek. It was gentle at first, a cold numbness that tingled as it went. But it quickly warmed, like a fire gathering heat, until her muscles were aflame from its touch. The tingle raced outwards, spreading the numbing sensation to her legs and arms.

Liz gasped, fighting back against the pain, desperate to fend it off. She gritted her teeth, tensing against its relentless spread. The pressure on her back vanished as the guard released her, but by then she barely noticed. Her attention was elsewhere, her focus fixed on the waves of sensation rippling through her body.

Then as though a switch had been flicked, the muscles down the length of her back locked in a sudden cramp. Pain unlike any she'd experienced closed around her, walling her off from the world, trapping her in the iron arms of its cage. Her eyes snapped open, but all she saw were stars, whirling through her vision, blinding in their brilliance. In the distance she heard a scream, a girl's voice tearing at the blackness of her mind, but she could do nothing to help her now.

Agony engulfed her body, her mind, her very soul.

TWENTY

COLD.

The thought filtered through the thick sludge of Chris's mind, parting the darkness like a curtain. Then it was all around him, wrapping his body in an icy blanket, turning his breath to ragged gasps. A shiver caught him, rippling down his body, throwing off the last dredges of sleep.

Frozen air burned his nostrils as he inhaled, bringing with it the familiar tang of bleach. But there was more to the scent now, an underlying stench of rot and decay that made his stomach swirl. Opening his mouth, he tasted the metallic reek of blood and vomit on the air.

Sound quickly followed the return of his taste and smell. His ears tingled, catching the murmur of a breath, the creak of metal joints moving beneath restless bodies, the hiss of an air conditioner. From somewhere in the room came the rattle of chains, the familiar whine of the overhead lights.

I'm alive, the words whispered in Chris's mind, though he couldn't quite recall why that surprised him.

Keeping his eyes closed, Chris sucked in another breath, struggling to restore the shattered pieces of his consciousness. Dimly he remembered the fire burning up his spine, spreading to his chest, filling his lungs. But there was no pain now, only the dull ache of his muscles, as though they had lain unused for countless days.

How long? His brow creased.

How long had he lain there, unconscious, in the clutches of whatever drug the doctors had given him?

Sounds echoed from all around him, growing louder as he lay there, echoing as though from a wide expanse. Chains rattled as he moved his arms, and he felt the cold touch of steel restraining his wrists. Without opening his eyes, he realised he had been handcuffed to the bed.

Apparently they were still taking no chances with their patients.

Memories drifted through the darkness of his thoughts, rising as though from a fog. Images of the fight flashed by, the crack as Sam fell to a baton, the thud of Ashley hitting the floor. He had not seen what happened to Liz, not until the guards had overwhelmed him, and he'd found her curled up in the corner.

Helpless, he had watched as Liz was lifted onto the bed and injected. Her screams had been instant and horrifying, so deafening even the guards had retreated from her. Her agony tore at his soul, begged for him to save her from the monsters. But he had been powerless against the raw strength of the men on either side of him.

His heart beat harder as thoughts of the girl rose in his mind. A sense of urgency took him, and he shifted his arms, testing the movement allowed by the handcuffs. The links rattled as he ran a hand along the chain, and found where the handcuffs attached to a guard rail running horizontally along the side of his bed.

Other sounds came to him now: the beeping of a nearby machine, the whir of a pump, the hiss of air escaping tubes. Listening, he heard the steady beeps accelerating, matching the racing of his heart.

Somewhere in the room, a door banged. Chris froze, his fingers still clenched around the metal bar. The soft tread of footsteps moved through the room, followed by voices.

"Has the danger passed?" Halt's voice came from Chris's right.

"We think so." He recognised Fallow, though her voice was strained, exhausted. "It was a close thing though. I told you it wasn't ready."

"Perhaps," Halt replied. "But we expected losses. Despite our best efforts, some of the candidates were simply too weak to withstand the morphological alterations."

"We lost forty percent!" Chris winced as Fallow's voice cracked. He heard a long inhalation of breath, before she continued in a calmer voice. "I expected mortality to be less than fifteen. As it is, we barely have a viable population… If we'd had more time…"

"More time?" Halt laughed. "That is the cry of a coward, Fallow! More time, more money, always more *something!*" he took a breath. "As Archimedes once said: 'Give me a lever and a place to stand, and I will move the earth.' But we only have the time and resources the government has provided us with. And our time is up."

"The *government* will not be satisfied with a forty percent mortality rate, Halt," Fallow growled.

"No," came the head doctor's swift reply. "But if the survivors show promise, you will have won the time you need to find perfection, Fallow."

Silence followed. Slowly their footsteps came closer. Listening to the beep of the machine beside him, Chris held his breath, struggling to slow his racing heart.

"And have we succeeded, Fallow?" Halt's voice was eager.

It was a while before the woman replied. "The results are mixed. Tissue samples taken over the last few weeks have shown steady integration between the host chromosomes and the viral DNA. Candidates who received the PERV-B strain have advanced more rapidly than PERV-A, and now show complete integration. However, we are yet to determine whether the altered genomes are expressing correctly."

"Excellent," there was unmasked glee in Halt's voice. "When do you expect them to be ready to test genome expression?"

"We've taken them off the immunosuppressants, and so far, they have shown no adverse reactions. We expect them to begin waking from their comas over the next few days. Once they're conscious, we can begin testing their basic motor skills and cognitive function, to determine whether the virus had any degenerative effects…" Fallow trailed off as Halt snorted.

"We don't have time to waste on your procedures, Fallow. We need *results*."

"I don't see how–" Fallow began.

"Don't give me that, Fallow," Halt snapped. "You know very well there is no need for those tests. As far as the directors are concerned, we have either succeeded or failed. There is only one test the candidates need to pass to show that."

There was a long pause before Fallow replied. "Halt…" her voice was entreating now. "That's simply not possible. They've been unconscious for weeks. The recovery time alone… They're in no condition–"

"If the experiment succeeded, recovery time should not be an issue," Halt's voice sounded like he was just a few feet away. "Look, this one appears to be conscious."

On the bed, a tingle raced up Chris's spine. Silently he held his breath, fighting the instinct to leap from the bed and flee. His arms prickled as goose bumps spread along his skin.

"You're right," Fallow's murmur seemed to come from directly overhead. "Her heartbeat has recovered to normal levels.

A girl's cry tore the air, followed by the angry rattle of chains. Chris cracked his eye open a fraction, desperate to see what was happening. Pain shot through his skull as white light streamed between his eyelids, momentary blinding him. Then the light faded and the room clicked into sudden focus. Beyond the rails of his bed, rows of beds stretched out across a wide room, each occupied by an unconscious patient dressed in green scrubs. A tangle of tubes and wires wrapped around each body like a spider web spun around a fly. From the brief glimpse he caught, Chris guessed there were some thirty beds, though many were empty.

The girl Halt and Fallow were discussing was sitting up in the hospital bed directly across from Chris. Her back was turned to him, and she had both arms chained to the bed. Curly black hair tumbled down the back of her scrubs, and with a shiver of recognition, Chris realised it was Liz.

She's alive!

Chris struggled to muffle his sharp intake of breath. Beside him, the beep of the machine started to race. Silently he clenched the sidebar of his bed until his palms hurt. Through the shadows of his eyelashes, he watched Halt move to stand over Liz.

"Incredible." Halt was studying the machine beside Liz's bed. Lines and numbers flashed across the screen, he guessed providing readings from the long tubes and wire that covered Liz. "Look at her vitals."

Fallow stood in silence beside him, shadows ringing her eyes, her lips pursed tight.

Halt shook his head and looked at her. "I would say she is fully recovered, wouldn't you, Doctor Fallow."

Reluctantly Fallow nodded, a look of resignation coming over her face.

"Excellent, then I see no reason to delay. Get her ready."

Blood pounded in Chris's head as a sudden rage swept through him. He didn't know what Halt had planned for Liz, what fresh horror he had in store, but he refused to lie quietly while she faced it alone. Whatever happened, they were still in this together. For all he knew, Sam and Ashley might already be gone, but Liz still lived. He would not lose her now.

"Leave her alone," he growled, sitting up in the bed.

On the other bed, Liz turned towards him, her eyes widening with shock. Behind her, Fallow's face seemed to crumple, while a grin spread slowly across Halt's face. In that instant, Chris felt a pit open in his stomach; a sudden realisation he had made a terrible mistake.

Still, it was worth it to see the relief sweep across Liz's face.

"Excellent." Halt clapped his hands. "Bring him too. It may even the odds."

TWENTY-ONE

LIZ SHIVERED AS FALLOW UNLOCKED THE CUFFS AROUND HER wrists. Blinking, she stared at the woman's face. Her features faded in and out of focus, and a bolt of nausea swept through her stomach. She wrapped a hand around the sidebar to steady herself and blinked again.

"Are you okay?" Liz flinched as a hand touched her shoulder.

"*Don't!*" she growled, leaning back.

Closing her eyes, Liz willed her stomach to settle, then opened them again. To her relief, the features of Fallow's face finally snapped into place. She blinked again, surprised to see the dark rings beneath the woman's eyes, the patchwork of tiny cracks across the skin of her cheeks, the thin red capillaries threading her eyes. Her head swam; she had never noticed such detail in someone's face before.

"I'm sorry." Liz's ears twitched at the sound, before a harsh shriek cut through the words.

She recoiled and slapped her hands over her ears. Distantly she heard the doctor's voice over the ringing. A hand reached for her, but she twisted, falling sideways on the bed. Fallow paused, staring down at her, and then retreated a step.

Slowly the ringing died away, and Liz finally removed her hands from her ears.

"I'm sorry," Fallow's voice was a whisper now, but she heard it with perfect clarity, "How do you feel?"

Grating her teeth, Liz shook her head and looked across at Chris. As their eyes met her heart gave a lurch, and she felt again the relief that had swept through her when he'd sat up.

He's alive!

Despite the apparent odds against them, somehow the two of them had survived whatever demented experiment the doctors had performed on them. Beside her, Fallow had busied herself removing the various tubes and wires that had been hooked up to the machine. Swallowing the surge of hate clogging her throat, Liz faced her.

"Why are you doing this?" Liz could not keep the resignation from her voice.

Fallow sighed, her eyes closing a moment before she looked at Liz. "You'll find out soon enough, Elizabeth."

Liz stared at the grief shining from Fallow's eyes. Despite herself, Liz felt pity for the woman. Even so, the doctor's words triggered a sense of foreboding within her, and she pressed on, desperate to exploit the woman's weakness.

"You don't have to do this," she whispered. "Halt's gone. You could let us go, unlock these collars."

A faint smile twitched at Fallow's lips. "A tempting proposition," she shook her head. "They'd kill you both before you even reached the front door. Then they would come for me." Her amber eyes locked on Liz. She stared back in silent appeal. But Fallow only smiled and continued on with false humour. "Besides, you are the culmination of my life's work."

"What about *our* lives?" Chris's snarl came from behind Liz. "What right—"

He broke off as Fallow raised a hand. She shook her head again, her smile fading. "You know the law, Christopher. Your mother was found guilty of treason. In due time, she will answer for those crimes. As her son, you would have faced the same fate."

Even to Liz, Fallow's words sounded hollow, spoken like they left a bad taste in her mouth. Even so, after that the woman ignored their pleas. Moving across to Chris, she removed the cuffs and wires. Within a few minutes she had them on their feet and staggering around the room like senior citizens.

Liz's legs trembled with each step, refusing to obey the simplest instructions. A dull ache was quickly spreading up her hamstrings, and several times she had to grab at neighbouring beds to steady herself. Chris was no better; managing to knock over a series of machines within two steps of leaving his bed, after which he promptly crashed to the linoleum floor.

From the corner of her eyes, Liz caught movement from several of the beds, but the doctor was too preoccupied with Chris to notice. Steadying herself, she took a moment to search the room for Ashley and Sam. But as the fluorescent light caught in her eyes she found their focus shifting again, and the room began to blur. By the time her vision cleared, Fallow was already shepherding them towards the doorway.

Outside, Liz's legs finally began to obey, though they remained stiff and sore. Chris was steadily improving too, but he still needed her shoulder to keep moving down the narrow corridor. Two guards stood on either side of the door to the room, but they made no move to follow them. Fallow kept pace several feet behind them though, no doubt ready to use the collars should they place a foot out of line.

Step by faltering step, they made their way through the facility, obeying Fallow's direction whenever they came to an intersection of corridors. After a few turns, Chris could walk unaided, though it was a while before he managed more than a slow stumble. Fortunately for him, the doctor did not seem to be in any hurry.

But despite their slow pace, the journey could not last forever, and far too little time had passed before they found themselves outside a familiar white door. Liz shivered as she recognised it, memories of her fight with Joshua spiralling through her mind.

She turned as Fallow spoke from behind them. "Go in."

Wordlessly, Liz shook her head. Dread wrapped around her stomach as she reached out and took Chris's hand. Together they faced the doctor, standing straight now, the strength slowly returning to their limbs.

"We won't," Liz drew herself up and stepped towards Fallow. "I won't."

Fallow retreated a step. She lifted her arm, the watch on her wrist flashing in warning. "Won't what?" Fallow asked.

"I won't fight her." Chris coughed, stepping up beside Liz. "I'd rather die."

Fallow's shoulders slumped and she gave a little shake of her head. "That's not… no," she gestured with a hand. "Just go."

Liz and Chris shared a glance, still hesitating. Despite Fallow's strange reassurance, fear gnawed at Liz's stomach; a dread she could not shake. The last time she had entered this room, an innocent boy had lost his life. And she had almost lost her own. Her hand drifted to her throat, but there was no pain now, only the cold reminder of the collar nestled beneath her chin.

How long were we asleep?

"Don't make me use the collars." Fallow lifted her finger to her watch.

They went.

As the door clicked shut behind her, Liz found herself standing again in the padded room, blinking in the brilliant light. An awful smell wafted through the air, a sickly sweet that caught in her throat. As her vision cleared, and the room came into focus, she realised with a sharp breath they were not alone.

A boy stood in the centre of the room. He wore the same plain orange jumpsuit they had sported in the cells, though she had never seen him there. His head was bowed, and his breath came in ragged gasps, his shoulders trembling with each violent exhalation. He held his hands clenched at his side, and though his eyes were open, he did not seem to have noticed them. Black hair dangled in front of his face, obscuring the rest of his features.

Liz edged towards him, her heart beating hard in her chest. Behind her, Chris gasped, and she felt his hand on her shoulder. But she twisted free, her panic rising. Gripped by a desperate need to see, to know for sure, she slid closer.

Leaning down, she peered into the boy's eyes.

Hard grey eyes stared back, their surface glazed with sleep, unseeing.

But as she stared, they blinked, the life behind them stirring.

And Liz screamed.

TWENTY-TWO

Chris recognised it the instant they stepped into the room. Though outwardly it looked no different than any other boy, a strangeness hung about his hunched figure. The stench of him was strong in the room, a sickly sweetness that clung to the air.

He didn't need to see the grey eyes to know what it was.

Chead.

He had tried to stop Liz as she stepped towards it, but she only shook herself free and crept closer. Clenching his fists, he tested his strength, feeling it quickly returning. Silently, he watched as Liz bent to peer into the boy's face.

Then she was staggering backwards, her screams reverberating around the room. The *Chead's* features contorted, the ripple of awakening sweeping across its face, and then Chris was retreating too, fumbling at the door, shouting for help, knowing it would not come.

Beside him, Liz screamed again and staggered sideways. His hand flashed out, catching her by her scrubs, dragging her back to him as she began to thrash. Her panic swept over him, waking him from his stupor, and he shoved her behind him.

When he looked up, he caught the iron-grey eyes of the *Chead* staring at him. A smile spread across its face, and sent pure terror screaming through every fibre of his being. Another shriek came from behind him as Liz pounded on the padded door.

Taking a breath, Chris took a step towards the *Chead,* an eerie calm coming over him. He placed himself squarely between Liz and the creature, ignoring the urge to turn and shake her, to pull the girl back from the depths of her terror. But her words were still fresh in his mind, and he heard again the agony in her voice as she told him of her parents' death.

He could not blame her for panicking.

Staring into the eyes of the *Chead,* Chris searched for a sign of life, for a hint of the human it had once been.

In the centre of the room, the *Chead* raised an eyebrow. "Welcome," the word sounded strange, almost metallic, as though speech did not come easily to it.

For a second all Chris could do was stand and gape. He blinked, moving his mouth, struggling to find the words. "Wha– what?" he finally managed.

Grey eyes flickered from Chris to Liz. Then with deliberate slowness, the *Chead* turned and began to pace. It walked towards the mirror first, pausing as the boy's image rose up before it, a snarl twisting its lips. Then is spun, moving back past Chris and Liz until it reached the far wall, where it turned to make another pass. Metal shone around its neck, and for the first time Chris realised it wore a collar around its neck.

"What. Am. I?" The creature ground out the words. It paused and looked straight at Chris. "You already know that…"

Chris did not reply. His mind was still reeling, struggling to comprehend one irresolvable fact: it spoke. The *Chead* could speak – not just that, it could understand him. No newspaper, no television channel had ever mentioned a *Chead* speaking, never mind being self-aware. As far as the public were concerned, the *Chead* were monsters – uncontrollable, terrible, killing machines.

They did not think.

They did not speak.

"How?" Chris croaked.

By the door, he could sense Liz slowly regaining her composure. The thuds on the door had ceased, her screams dying to soft gasps. Movement came from beside him and on trembling legs Liz re-joined him. Out of the corner of his eye he watched a shiver run through her and reached out an arm. Their hands touched, their fingers entwining. He gave her hand a quick squeeze and turned back to the *Chead*.

It had stopped its pacing and stood again in the centre of the room, its grey eyes watching them. Its nostrils flared as it inhaled.

"You… smell different," it grated, then. "How do I speak?" it finished Chris's question.

Chris nodded his confirmation.

A smile spread across the *Chead's* face. "I learnt," it nodded, its head leaning to the side. "I remembered…"

A tremor ran through Liz's hand, but when he looked at the girl her eyes remained fixed straight ahead, her lips pressed tight together.

The *Chead's* head twisted strangely again, as though in curiosity. "You are different," it said again, its smile spreading, though there was no humour in the grey eyes. "Like me."

Chris's stomach clenched at its words.

What does it mean?

"What did you mean, you remembered?" Liz interrupted his thoughts.

The *Chead's* eyes flickered in her direction. "I remembered. Who I was… Before…" the boy shrugged.

Liz's fingers tightened around Chris's hand. He waited for her to speak, but she had fallen silent again.

"What do you mean? That we're like you?" Chris croaked.

An awful laughter crackled up from the thing's throat. "They succeeded, these jailers of ours," the boy's face twisted horribly, until it seemed some demon now possessed the boy. Speech seemed to come easier to it now. "But I wonder, is it enough?"

It stepped towards them then, the grin fading.

As one, Chris and Liz retreated across the padded floor, until their backs pressed against the door.

Chris raised his hands in surrender. "Please, wait, you don't have to do this."

The *Chead* paused, the hard glint in its eyes wavering. Then it shook its head. "But I do. It is my nature, isn't it?" It took another step, its eyes flickering to the one-way glass. "Besides, it's what *they* want."

Snarling, the *Chead* leapt towards them.

Without pausing to think, Chris pushed Liz away from him and stepped up to meet the creature's charge. From the corner of his eye he saw Liz stagger sideways, then the *Chead* was on him, its fist flashing for his chest. Acting on instinct, he threw up an arm, and the blow glanced from his forearm.

Chris gasped as pain jolted through his arm. Then the weight of the creature crashed into him, flinging him back into the wall. Before he could recover, the *Chead* had him by the shoulders. His stomach twisted as the long arms lifted him. Panic took him, and he kicked out with a foot, sending a desperate blow into the boy's head.

To his surprise, the *Chead* reeled back from the blow. A savage growl came from its throat as it tossed him aside. Chris bent his head and braced as the ground raced towards him. With a thud he struck, then he was rolling forward, spinning to come to his feet in one fluid movement. Straightening, he turned to face the *Chead*.

The creature stared back, the grey eyes watching him like a predator stalking its prey. Slowly it lifted an arm and wiped a trickle of blood from its lip.

His gaze flickered as he caught sight of Liz. She moved to join him, eyes flashing. "Don't do that again," she growled.

Nodding, Chris turned his attention back to the *Chead*. It seemed hesitant now. Chris was glad for its caution. On the television, he had watched *Chead* tear policemen apart, seen throats torn out and skulls shattered by a single blow. Tasers did little to slow them, and bullets only seemed to anger them unless they struck something vital.

Unarmed and trapped in the tiny room, Chris did not like their odds.

Yet somehow his blow had rattled it.

Pushing down his fear, Chris edged away from Liz. Whatever their chances, they had to try. Between them, they at least outnumbered the *Chead* two to one. They had to make the most of that advantage.

The *Chead* snarled as he moved, its head turning to follow him. From the corner of his eyes, Chris watched Liz slide sideways in the opposite direction. The *Chead* ignored her though, clearly seeing Chris as the greater threat.

Chris just hoped Liz had the strength to prove it wrong.

The *Chead's* grin returned as Chris came to a stop. A low rumble quivered in its chest. It stepped towards him, legs tensing to spring. In reply, Chris raised his fists. He slid one leg back and twisted sideways, placing himself in a defensive stance. Flashing a smile he did not feel, he gestured the creature forward.

His impudence ignited a flash of anger in the *Chead's* eyes. Adrenaline pounded in Chris's veins as it stepped in close, washing away his fear. He reacted without thought, years of training taking over. One hand swept up to deflect the blow sweeping for his face. His arm shook as the force of the blow sent him reeling, but stepping back he kept his balance, his eyes already watching for the next attack.

Another fist flashed towards him and he ducked. As he moved, his surprise grew. He had seen a blow from a *Chead* shatter a man's arm with a single blow. By all rights, his arm should have been crushed. Yet somehow he was holding his own.

The *Chead* had realised this too, and snarling it hurled itself at Chris with renewed fury. A fist flashed beneath his guard and smashed into his stomach. The breath hissed between Chris's teeth as his lungs emptied. He squeezed a half-choked groan from his chest as the *Chead* stepped in close.

Then with a shriek, Liz leapt into the fray. Bent in two and gasping, Chris caught a glimpse of her tangled hair and flashing blue eyes as she drove her foot down into the back of the *Chead's* knee.

Screaming, it collapsed beneath the blow.

TWENTY-THREE

THE SECOND LIZ SAW THE STONY GREY EYES OF THE *CHEAD*, the memories had come flooding back. For a second she had found herself back in her parent's house, in the home she had been raised in. Once it had been a safe place, a sanctuary amidst the harsh world outside.

Now though, in her memories a perpetual shadow hung over its wooden hallways, sucking out the light, the life it had once born.

In her mind, she saw again the rubble-strewn corridor, the broken floor boards and pooling blood. She saw herself turn the corner, saw the body lying in the corridor, strangely whole, where those outside had lain in pieces.

And her mother, standing over the body, her grey eyes staring.

With a scream, Liz tore herself from the memory, returning herself to the present, to the room and Chris.

And the *Chead*.

Still reeling, caught in the clutches of remembered horror, she had barely heard the conversation between Chris and the *Chead*, the revelations it offered. She already knew the truth, that some semblance of their former lives clung to the creatures.

Why else had she been spared?

She had only truly woken when Chris pushed her from the path of *Chead's* charge. Angry flames had lit her stomach, waking her from the fear, restoring her to life.

Now as she edged sideways around the *Chead*, she let that anger grow, fed it with every injustice she had ever suffered. It was her only weapon now, her only strength against the sheer ferocity of the creature standing between them. Opposite her, Chris faced the creature, drawing it away, until its back was turned to her. But before she could strike, the *Chead* leapt for Chris.

Fear chilled her stomach as blows crashed against flesh. But to her surprise, Chris did not go down. Edging closer, she saw him deflect another blow, his arms moving faster than thought, the crack of fists connecting with bone ringing from the walls.

Liz stared, mouth wide with disbelief. What she was watching was not possible. Chris was keeping pace with the violent speed of the *Chead*, matching it blow for blow, punch for punch. Her eyes could barely keep up with their frenzied movements. The air itself seemed to shake with the strength of each blow, and still Chris stood, holding his own.

What have they done to us?

Her skin tingled as the question whispered in her mind. But there was no time to contemplate the thought, no time to consider its implications. Instead, she gathered herself and slid closer, searching for an opening.

Then a blow slid beneath Chris's guard. It slammed into his stomach and drove him to his knees. The colour fled his face as the *Chead* stepped in, raising a fist to deliver the final blow.

Seeing her chance, Liz sprang forward and drove the heel of her foot into the back of the *Chead's* knee. Idly she hoped whatever changes had been wrought on the *Chead* had not removed the cluster of nerve endings located behind the kneecap.

The bloodcurdling shriek that issued from the boy's throat answered her question. The *Chead's* legs crumbled beneath the force of the blow, sending it crashing to the ground. Clenching her teeth, Liz stepped up behind it as Chris rolled away.

She swung a kick at its head. But the *Chead* was already recovering, and quick as a cobra it twisted. Hands flashed out and caught her by the leg. Before she could free herself, it stood, grey eyes glittering. A low growl came from its throat as it lifted her. Gasping, she fought to break its hold, but its hands were like iron. Knowing it was useless, Liz lashed out with a fist, and caught it on the cheek.

A shock ran up her arm as the blow connected. The fingers around her leg loosened, and suddenly she was falling. Twisting, she landed awkwardly and looked up to see the *Chead* stumbling backwards, one hand raised to its cheek.

With a growl, it straightened, and the grey eyes swept down to find her on the floor.

Liz felt her courage crumble as her eyes caught in its iron gaze. All semblance of its humanity had fled, melting in the red-hot flames of its rage. Hardly daring to breathe, she backed towards Chris, all thoughts of strategy falling away.

Snarling, it stepped after her.

"Now you've done it," Chris panted, his hand reaching for hers.

She clenched her hand around his, drawing strength from his presence, and then released him. Together they watched the *Chead* approach.

With a roar, it leapt.

Chris sprang forward, screaming his defiance. Stepping in front of Liz, he deflected the first swing of the creature's fist. But this time the force of the blow sent him reeling, and Liz had to step aside to avoid him. Then the *Chead* was on them, fists flying, lips drawn back in a snarl, its half-mad screams echoing from the mirrored glass.

A fist caught Liz in the cheek, staggering her, then the *Chead's* shoulder crashed into her chest. The breath rushed from her lungs as she hurtled backwards into the wall. Her head whipped back and struck the padding. Despite the soft surface, her vision spun from the blow. With a groan, she slid down the wall, struggling to catch her winded breath.

Across the room, Chris fought on. But he was no longer a match for the *Chead's* strength. And it was faster now, its speed and ferocity far beyond human capabilities. With contempt it knocked aside his blows. A fist crashed into his face, sending him stumbling backwards, but he refused to yield. Straightening, he launched himself back into the fray.

Desperate to aid him, Liz struggled back to her feet.

A shout drew her attention back to the fight. The *Chead* had caught Chris's fist in one hand. As she watched Chris screamed again, though this time neither of them had moved. An awful *crack* came from Chris's fist as he sank to his knees. The colour fled his face and he gave an awful groan. One handed, he struggled to regain his feet, until the *Chead's* free hand smashed into the side of his head. Chris slumped to the side then, his breathing ragged, one hand still caught in the creature's grip.

Silently, Liz pulled herself up. The *Chead's* back was turned to her, its attention focused on tearing Chris limb from limb. She flinched as another blow thudded into Chris's head. This time he made no effort to avoid the blow. A low gurgle came from his throat as the *Chead* lifted its arm, dragging him back to his feet.

Liz moved quickly, knowing she only had seconds to act. The soft floor made no noise beneath her bare feet. Without pausing to think, Liz hurled herself at the creature's back. This time she aimed high, sweeping her forearm over its shoulder. Before it could react, she pulled her arm tight against its throat and leaned back. Her feet caught the ground, giving her purchase, and she pulled harder, bending it backwards, dragging it off balance.

The *Chead* gave a strangled cry. Releasing Chris, it turned its attention on Liz. Knowing she could not match its strength or weight, Liz allowed herself to fall backwards, taking the *Chead* with her. The thud as its weight landed on her drove the breath from her lungs, but still she held on, forearm tight across its throat.

Sensing its plight, the *Chead* thrashed against her. Its legs kicked out, catching Liz in the shins. Pain lanced from her leg as something went *crack*, but no force on earth would make her let go now.

Not even death.

Long seconds passed, and the creature's struggles weakened. Its legs no longer beat against the floor, and its relentless strength no longer pressed against her as hard.

Movement came from beyond the *Chead*. Chris staggered to his feet, his face already turning purple, one eye so swollen she could barely see his hazel eye. Even so, he stumbled forward and fell to his knees beside her. He raised a fist and drove it into the *Chead's* face.

Liz felt the power of Chris's blow through the *Chead*. Its body went limp in her arms, but still she held on, wanting to be sure.

Finally satisfied, she loosened her grip, and with Chris's help, heaved the dead weight from her chest.

Then she was embracing Chris, pulling him to her, clinging desperately at his back. An awful sob built in her chest and escaped in a rush. Chris's arms tightened around her, and then he was sobbing too, his hot wet tears falling on her shoulder.

They clung to each other in silence, and let the horror wash over them.

TWENTY-FOUR

CHRIS LOOKED UP AS A DOOR CLICKED OPEN. HALT STOOD in the doorway, a triumphant grin stretching across his thin lips. His eyes feasted on the two of them, shining with a wild exaltation.

"It worked," his voice was raw with emotion. He stepped into the room, two guards following behind him before the door swung shut. "The genomes are expressing – a few at least. Muscle density factor, reaction time, agility, it's all there…"

As the man rambled, Chris struggled to pull his mind back to the present. He wrapped his arm around Liz, pulling her tight against him. A shiver went through her and he glanced down, his gaze catching in her crystal eyes.

Then she turned, facing Halt. "What have you done to us?" She croaked.

Halt drew to a stop across from them. He blinked, looking almost surprised, as though he had not expected them to speak. His smile faded as he crossed his arms. "We have enhanced you, my dear. Made you better... made you *useful*," he almost spat the last word.

Chris met the man's iron gaze. "*Why?*" He gestured to the *Chead*. "Why would you do this? Send us in here to die?"

Shaking his head, Halt moved around the room towards the unconscious *Chead*. "To see if you would survive," he answered, looking back at them. "To see if we had succeeded."

His words whispered around the room. Chris's chest contracted and he struggled to breathe. Rage boiled through his veins. He clenched his fist, but pain seared from his knuckles where the *Chead* had held him. Glancing down at his hand, he saw it was already beginning to swell.

A shiver went through him.

It would have killed me.

"You changed us," Liz was speaking again, her voice barely audible. "Did something to us... while we slept. *How?*" Her voice cracked at her final question. She trembled in his arms, though whether from rage or some other emotion, he could not tell.

Chuckling softly, Halt moved back towards them. "It was a simple matter, in the end. A little retrovirus, some genetic mapping of various species – chimpanzees, wolves, felines, eagles, and so on. Isolating the desirable genes took time, as did altering their repetition sequences to be accepted by human cells," he shrugged. "But, well, the results were worth the effort. And the best is yet to come." An awful grin spread across the doctor's face.

With Halt's words, Chris mind finally caught up with events. Revulsion twisted in his stomach as he realised the truth – that the *Chead* had not been weaker than those on the television. No, it was he and Liz who had changed.

And it was Halt who had changed them.

A scream built in Chris's chest as he looked at the doctor. An awful sense of violation wrapped around his throat. He clenched his fist again, felt the pain, but the injury was nothing to the desecration of his body. He felt defiled, like something had been taken from him, stolen by the doctor.

As the pain built in his hand, he drew back his lips in a snarl.

Halt watched them, his expression unchanged, but his hand drifted towards his watch. An awful tension hung in the air as Chris's rage gathered strength.

Then a groan came from across the room, and Halt's eyes flickered towards the *Chead*. Chris followed his gaze and saw the boy had rolled onto his side. He moaned again, then started to cough. His eyes fluttered but did not open.

"It's still alive," Halt sounded surprised. He turned back to Chris. "Kill it."

"What?" Chris blinked, staring at the doctor in disbelief.

"Kill it," Halt repeated. "That monstrosity is not worthy of this earth. Kill it, Christopher. Prove you are superior."

"No." Chris blinked, surprised by his own resolve. Releasing Liz, he faced Halt, determined to defy him. "I won't."

Halt slowly shook his head. He held up his arm. The watch flashed on his wrist, an unspoken threat. "Do not waste my time, Christopher. Kill the *Chead*, and we can move on from this unpleasant business."

A peal of laughter came from beside Chris. Turning, he saw Liz's eyes flash as she took a step towards Halt. "No, Halt. We won't. We're not your creatures, your slaves to do with as you please. Whatever you've done to us, we're still human."

Halt did not move. His eyes flickered for a second to Liz, then back to Chris. "I will give you one last chance. Kill the *Chead. Now!*"

"You're the monstrosity, Halt," Chris replied.

"Very well, Christopher." Halt looked at Liz again. "If that is your decision…"

Reaching down, he pressed his finger to the watch.

Chris closed his eyes and braced himself for the pain. Sucking in a breath, he waited for the familiar fire to encircle his throat, to sap the strength from his legs, to lock his muscles in knots of agony.

But it never came.

From his right came a high-pitched scream. Chris spun, his eyes snapping open as the breath caught in his throat. Beside him, Liz crumpled to the ground. The colour fled her face as she clutched desperately at her throat. Her feet drummed against the soft floor and a strangled scream escaped her gaping mouth.

Then she fell silent, her last gasps of air stolen away.

Chris threw himself forward, desperate to reach her, but strong arms grasped him around the waist and hauled him back. Without thinking he lashed out with his elbow, catching the guard in the face, and the hands released him. He glimpsed the man falling backwards, the other stepping towards him, but he was already at Liz's side, reaching out a hand, grabbing at her wrist.

A jolt of electricity flashed between them, and Chris was hurled backwards across the floor.

Coming to rest a few feet away, Chris groaned and struggled to sit up. Across from him, Liz writhed against the soft floor, her back arching, her mouth wide and gasping for air. Her fingers clawed at the skin of her throat, tearing at the collar's metal chain. But there would be no dislodging the steel links.

Halt stepped between them, a grim smile on his serpent lips. "Seventy-five milliamps," he shook his head. "Enough to cause severe muscle contractions, respiratory failure, death."

Behind him, Liz was as pale as a ghost, her throws of agony already growing weaker. Her mouth opened, gasping like a fish out of water. Yet somehow her crystal eyes found his. Shining with tears, they pierced him, conveying her silent command.

Don't give in!

A sob rattled up from Chris's chest as he closed his eyes, unable to watch any longer. Bowing his head, he cradled his shattered fist. Despair rose within him, threatening to over-whelm him.

"*Please!*" His sob rang from the one-way mirror.

A sudden stillness came over the room. Lying on the ground, Chris did not move, unable to look, to witness the consequence of his defiance. So long as he did not look, he could deny the truth.

Liz couldn't be gone, couldn't be dead.

But in his heart, Chris knew he had to face the truth. Blinking back tears, he sucked in a breath and lifted his head.

Liz lay where she had fallen, her limbs splayed out at random angles, the tangles of her hair caught on her face. The collar shone from her neck, the blinking red light unlit.

Staring at her broken body, a pit opened within Chris, a gulf of despair that threatened to swallow him whole. A desperate sob tore from his throat, a cry of anguish, a plea for life. Lifting himself, he began to crawl towards her. He could feel his strength failing, the last drops of energy falling from him, but with a final lung he reached out and grasped her wrist.

With barely a whisper, Liz's chest moved. A soft cough came from the fallen girl as her eyelids shifted, blinked.

"*What?*" Halt snarled.

Behind him, the door clicked again, as Doctor Fallow pushed her way into the room.

TWENTY-FIVE

"Enough, Halt," Angela almost tripped over the words as she spoke.

Halt stared back at her, his eyes wide, his surprise already turning to a wild rage. She knew she had crossed a line, defying him now. This time there were no other doctors to back her up – the others were all tending to the surviving candidates from the PERV-A strain of the virus. She shivered, thinking of the room full of candidates, their bodies ravaged by the virus. It had proven far more deadly than the B strain retrovirus the others had been subjected too.

"Excuse me?" Halt sounded almost bemused.

"I said, that's enough," Angela repeated, mustering her courage.

A few moments ago, she had been driven to act. Watching Halt's cruelty, his determination to bend the candidates to his will, had pushed her over the edge. Whatever good she hoped might come from her work, it was not worth this. It was brutal and pointless and wasteful, a display that did nothing more than serve Halt's ego.

And she could not bear to watch the girl die. Angela could not shake that feeling of kinship, could not help but see her own youthful self in the girl's eyes.

So she had acted. She had superseded Halt's controller from within the observation room, disabling the collars inside the room. As supervisor of the Praegressus Project, her watch had precedence over every other controller in the building – even Halt's.

This isn't right, the words whispered in Angela's mind as she glanced at the boy and girl. *They're just kids.*

Biting her lip, she straightened, preparing herself to face Halt's rage. "There was no point to it, Halt. They passed the test. The project is a success. But this," she waved a hand to indicate the girl, "this display is pointless. I won't allow it."

Halt shifted on his feet. A strange calm seemed to have come over him. "You won't allow it?"

Angela found herself retreating a step, though the doctor had not moved. "No," she shook her head. "I've disabled their collars."

"You forget yourself, doctor," Halt still spoke in a soft voice. "These displays of insolence… are becoming problematic."

"They are *my* candidates, Halt."

For a moment, Halt did not reply. His grey eyes studied her, sweeping across her body, cold and calculating. Angela lifted her chin, facing him down.

At last Halt nodded. He waved to the guards. "Get them up. Return them to their cell."

As the guards moved across to Christopher and Elizabeth, Halt turned back to Fallow. He stood deathly still, poised in the centre of the room as the guards shepherded the two experiments from the cells. His eyes did not blink, never left Angela's face. Finally, as the door clicked shut behind the guard, he stepped towards her.

Now Fallow found herself retreating from the rage in the man's eyes. But after two steps she found herself pressed up against the mirror, the cold glass at her back, with nowhere to look but the eyes of the doctor.

Before she could move, Halt's hand flashed out and caught her by the throat. His fingers clenched tight as she opened her mouth to scream, stealing away her voice. His lips drew back in a scowl as he leaned in.

"*How dare you?*" Halt hissed.

With a sudden, violent push, Halt slammed her head back into the glass. Stars spun across Angela's vision and her knees went weak. Pain lanced from her skull as Halt pulled her back towards him, until their faces were less than an inch apart.

"If you *ever* defy me again, I will see you in a cage with your precious candidates," Halt grated.

Red exploded across Angela's vision as he slammed her into the mirror again. Then the fingers released her, and with a muffled sob she slumped to the ground.

Halt looked down at her, open contempt in his eyes. "The experiment will continue," he said. "You will see that the final doses are administered to the candidates. Those still unconscious will remain in their comas until our research has been completed."

Darkness swept across Angela's vision, rising up to claim her. But through the creeping shadows, she heard Halt's final proclamation.

"Succeed, and I might just let you live."

TWENTY-SIX

CLANG.

Chris slumped to the ground as the cell door slid closed behind them. Liz staggered past him and toppled onto Ashley's bed. The guards had practically carried her this far. Despite coming out better than Chris in the fight, the collar had left its mark. The damage ran deep, and each inhalation brought about an awful cough and rattling to her chest.

Unfortunately, he wasn't much better.

Whatever Halt had said about success, Chris had still lacked the relentless strength of the *Chead*. When it had caught him, no amount of skill, training or mutated muscle had been enough to save him from its grasp.

Thank God for Liz, he thought, looking across at her.

She lay sprawled across the bed, her face half buried in the pillow, her back rising with each laboured breath. Every few seconds she would groan, but otherwise she lay still.

Getting to his hands and knees, Chris crawled across to Sam's bed and pulled himself up. Under the circumstances, he didn't think the others would mind if they borrowed them. Both beds were neatly made up, the covers pulled tight, the presence of their two friends wiped clean.

Minutes slipped by as he lay there, his face throbbing where the *Chead* had struck him. After a time, the clang of the outer door carried down the corridor. Idly, Chris wondered if someone had come to finish the job the *Chead* had started. There was no one else inside the prison block now. The other cells were empty, the faces that had once lined the corridor either dead or gone.

No, whoever it was had come for them.

Unable to summon the energy to move, Chris lifted an eyelid and looked out into the corridor. A woman stood outside the bars, her hands fiddling nervously with the hem of her lab coat. For a second he thought it was Fallow, before he realised she was too young, her hair blonde instead of brown. A guard stood beside the woman, looking bored.

"I'm… I'm to give you a round of antibiotics," she squeaked.

On the opposite bed, Liz did not so much as stir. Stifling a groan, Chris rolled onto his side. "Really?" he coughed. "You people are all of a sudden concerned for our wellbeing?"

The woman gave a nervous nod. "Could you, could you get to the back of the cell, please?"

Chris blinked. If he hadn't been in so much pain, he would have laughed. Instead he looked at Liz, then back at the doctor. "Sorry, lady. But I don't think we're going anywhere."

"But… but you're meant to…"

Closing his eyes, Chris lay back on the bed. "Just get it over with. Have the guard ready to press his little button, if it makes you feel better."

The woman hesitated another second, and then nodded. A buzzer sounded and the cell door slid open. The little doctor hopped into the cell, a packet of syringes held in one hand, a vial of clear liquid in the other.

Briefly, Chris contemplated the thought of resisting. After everything they'd been through, he distrusted even this harmless-looking woman. Who knew what new horror might wait in the vial. But a hollow feeling sat in his stomach, an awful, helpless weakness that sapped him of the will to resist.

After all, what was the point in fighting now? It was too late – they'd already lost, already been damaged beyond repair.

Chris slumped into his pillow and watched as the woman moved across to Liz.

"She's unconscious," she sounded surprised. "I thought… I thought the experiment was a success."

On the bed, Chris shrugged. "You'll have to ask your boss about that," he paused, his thoughts drifting. "Where are our friends? What's happening to them?"

The woman was busy preparing her syringe, and it was a moment before she answered. It wasn't until she leaned over Liz that he heard her whisper. "The others are being kept in their comas," she breathed. "To make the change easier."

Chris watched as the woman inserted the needle into Liz's back and pressed down the plunger. Then she was moving towards him, the needle disappearing into a bag marked biological waste. Another appeared as she raised the vial.

Turning away, Chris winced as the needle pinched his back. The cold tingle of the injection spread between his shoulder blades as the woman stepped back. To his relief, there was no pain, and the cold sensation quickly faded away.

Chris looked up as footsteps retreated through the cell. He watched the woman reach the door and turn back, her eyes catching in his. "I'm sorry."

Then she was gone.

Frowning, Chris shook his head, resigning himself to what-ever fresh torment had been in the injection. He was certain now it had not been antibiotics. Something in her face as she looked back, in those final words, warned him.

At least this time there was no pain.

A gurgled breath came from Liz's bed, drawing his attention back to the girl. She had rolled onto her back now, her mouth wide and gasping. Her eyes were closed, her brow creased as though she were struggling to wake. Fingers clenched at the sheets and the veins stood up against her neck.

Chris's heart lurched and a sense of urgency gripped him. Careful to protect his broken hand, he rolled from the bed and crawled across to the other set of bunks. Pulling himself up beside Liz, he reached for her as she started to thrash. A wild arm swung out, catching him in the face, and a foot struck a pole, making the bunk shake. Another awful gurgle came from her chest.

"Liz, Liz, *stop*," Chris breathed, struggling to calm her.

But with growing fear, he realised what was happening. Liz was choking, drowning in the fluid filling her lungs.

Ignoring the agony in his hand now, Chris reached out and caught Liz as another convulsion took her. He pulled her close, fighting to hold her, to turn her on her side. Desperate fists beat against him, and pain rippled up his arm as she struck his hand. Gasping, he twisted, narrowly avoiding a wild swing of her knee.

Fighting back his pain, Chris heaved, pulling Liz onto her side. As she rolled, he saw her eyes were wide now and staring, though it was clear she still lay in the grips of unconsciousness. Bloodshot veins threaded the whites of her eyes, and a trickle of blood ran from her nose, staining the white of her pillow red.

As she settled onto her side, a ragged gasp tore from her lips. Her chest rose, the gurgle fading to a whispered cough. She gulped again, wheezing in the cool air, as though still unable to get enough oxygen. Reaching out, Chris tilted her head forward slightly, memories of high school first aid returning.

Moving her upper arm, he placed her hand beneath her head, then pulled up her knees. Liz's breathing gradually eased, the gurgle slowly fading as her airways cleared.

Finally, Chris let out a long sigh, satisfied for the moment she was safe. Holding her in place, he sent out a silent thanks that Liz was so small.

Weariness swept through Chris like a wave. He looked across at Liz and smiled. Her eyes had closed again, her lips parted just a fraction, while a wisp of hair fluttered on her face with each exhalation. The sharp throb of his hand was quickly returning though, cutting through the last dredges of adrenaline. He stifled a groan of his own, eager not to disturb Liz now she had settled.

He saw her again in the padded room, thrashing on the floor, felt again the awful helplessness. He shuddered and pushed the image away.

Only Fallow's intervention had saved her, saved them both.

Fallow.

The woman's face drifted through his thoughts. She had been in this from the start, had admitted her role in the facility while they lay in the clean room.

You are the culmination of my life's work.

Was that why she had saved them, had stopped Halt in the padded room? Or was there more? Had the woman's conscience gotten to her?

Chris struggled to concentrate, but cobwebs tangled with his thoughts, and he could make no sense of the questions. His body throbbed, the ache of a hundred bruises dulling his mind. Beside him, heat radiated from Liz, banishing the cold of the cell. Distantly, he felt the pull of sleep.

His eyes fluttered open, catching a glimpse of Liz. The pained twist of her lips had faded, revealing a softness in her face, the kindness of the girl hidden within. Her breathing had quieted now, and her eyes quivered beneath her eyelids, lost in some dream.

The weight of exhaustion slowly dragged Chris's eyes shut again. He knew he should move, should return to the other bed. But the strength would not come; his last ounce of energy had fled.

Within seconds, the soft whispers of sleep claimed him.

TWENTY-SEVEN

Light burned at Liz's eyelids, dragging her back from her dreams, back to the pain. It washed over her like rain, a tingle that burned in every muscle, every fibre of her being. Gritting her teeth, she willed the agony to fade, to release her from its fiery grip.

Slowly, the pain died away, slipping from her body, until only embers remained.

Liz sucked in a breath, then suppressed a groan as the ache returned, now an icy frost spreading through her lungs. Whatever damage the collar had inflicted, it had spread to every fibre of her being. It would take more than one night to heal.

Liz froze as movement came from beside her. Cracking open an eye, she found Chris asleep beside her. For a moment she frowned, the beginnings of anger curling in her throat. Then a dim memory came to her, of water all around her, of drowning in a bottomless ocean, of fire in her chest as she breathed the salty water.

Then Chris's firm hands on her shoulders, pulling her up, dragging her to the surface. And the relief of fresh air, filling her lungs, of oxygen flooding her body.

Her anger faded, replaced by a warmth that swept away the pain. She looked at Chris, watching the soft rise and fall of his chest, the flickering of his eyelids. Silently, she remembered her fear as the *Chead* had beaten him to the ground, the terror that had risen within her. But rather than panic, it had filled her with purpose, with the need to act, to save him.

A low moan came from Chris and he wriggled beneath the thin blanket, drawing closer. She sighed as his heat washed over her, and watched as his eyes slowly cracked open.

"You know, when I said I'd give you a chance, I didn't mean it as an invite…" she teased, a playful smile tugging at her lips.

She caught him as he flinched away from her. Taking a gentle hold of his good hand, she pulled him back, drew him close, until only an inch separated them.

"Don't," she murmured, basking in the heat of Chris's body. "Don't."

His hazel eyes stared back at her, streaked with a bloodshot red, but clear and filled with… something. She leaned in, trying to make out what, and her mouth brushed against his. A jolt of energy surged through her at the touch, and then she was kissing him.

She felt Chris tensed against her, and for a second thought he would pull away.

Then his hands were in her hair, and he was kissing her back, his lips hard against hers. A tingle came from her hip as a hand gripped her. Adrenaline throbbed in her chest, spreading to swallow her. She reached out, her arms wrapping around Chris, pulling him closer, leaving no escape. Goosebumps prickled her skin as fingers slid to the small of her back.

Leaning her head back, Liz parted her lips, her tongue flicking out to taste him. The scent of him filled her nostrils as his tongue found hers, and they danced to a rhythm all of their own. Her mind fell away, drowned by the blood rushing from her racing heart. Her pain was forgotten, replaced by threads of pleasure winding through her body. Her skin was aflame, burning wherever his fingers touched.

Reaching up, she slid her fingers through his hair, pulling him deeper. A hunger filled her, a need that grew with every heartbeat. A moan slipped from her lips and she gripped him hard, desperate now.

Chris flinched in her arms and she paused, remembering his broken hand. For a moment they slowed, but their lips did not part, their tongues still touching, tasting. Liz wriggled in under his arm, her chest pounding like a drum as his good arm wrapped around her.

Liz drew back then, sucking in a breath of air. Opening her eyes, she looked at him, saw the smile tugging at his lips. She shivered, a memory rising from her past, the horror of the day before returning. A sour taste filled her mouth, the pain returning. She blinked, and a tear streaked down her cheek.

"What are we doing, Chris?" she whispered.

Chris pulled back, his eyes sad. Reaching up, he wiped away the tear, then kissed her on the forehead. "What do you mean?"

Liz shook her head. "What's the point?" she choked, closing her eyes, the darkness welling within her. "They could kill us tomorrow, mutate us beyond recognition, burn the last traces of humanity from us—"

She broke off as Chris kissed her again, quick and hard. Separating, he looked her in the eye. "We can't let them win, Liz," he whispered. "They've taken so much from us already, used us, stolen our humanity. But they can't take our spirit, our hope. It's like a flame inside me – barely a flicker now, but it keeps me going. It's mine. It's ours. And I won't let them take it."

"Haven't they already?"

Chris only smiled. "Not yet. It's like Ashley said - they're only human. They'll make mistakes." The fingers of his good hand found hers, and squeezed. "When they do, we'll be ready."

Staring into his eyes, Liz could almost bring herself to believe.

Almost.

Still, he was right. They couldn't let their captors win. For the moment, they still had each other. She would not let them take that from her too. Leaning in, Liz gave herself to the flame burning inside her. Their mouths locked and she pressed hard against him, her hands sliding beneath his shirt. A wild hunger filled her, her kisses turning ravenous. His arms went around her again, gripping her with a new fierceness. His lips left hers as he pulled away - then they were pressed against her neck, igniting flames wherever they touched.

She groaned, her neck arching backwards, her fingers tight in his hair.

His hands slid beneath her shirt, trailing across her back, tingling wherever they touched. The warmth inside her spread, and she began to tremble. Lost in her passion, she leaned in and nipped at his neck.

Liz smiled as Chris gave a little yelp. His hands continued to roam, though they had not yet gone far enough for her liking. Reaching up, she slid her fingers through the buttons of his shirt and began to undo them. Beneath, a fine layer of hair covered his chest. His skin burned beneath her fingers.

Chris's mouth found its way to the small of her throat, and with a rush of impatience she helped him with her own buttons, knowing his good hand was already occupied. His lips slid lower, his tongue darting out, tasting her, even as his hands etched invisible trails across the soft skin of her back.

Clutching hard to his arm, Liz stifled a moan as Chris paused. His fingers froze on her back, his mouth's progress coming to an abrupt halt.

Opening her eyes, Liz looked down at him. He stared up at her from between the folds of her breasts, fear sparkling in his hazel eyes. Her stomach twisted as a trickle of ice slid down her back.

"What?" she whispered.

"There's… there's something wrong… There are… lumps…" Chris replied softly.

Liz's cheeks burned, but her fear fell away. Laughing softly, she shook her head. Her hands slid through his hair, drawing him in, until his lips brushed across her.

Chris gave a low groan, then shook his head again. "No," he pulled away, "not… not those," the hackles rose on Liz's neck as he looked at her.

The heat slowly drained from Liz's face. "What?"

"On your back," Chris said, his breath harsh. "There's… something on your back."

Fear flooded Liz, and the passion in her chest spluttered and died. Sitting upright, she craned her neck, straining to see. Her movements grew frantic as she fumbled at her shirt, tugging at the collar, desperate to rid herself of it. Chris reached for her, tried to calm her, but she pushed him away. She heard fabric tear, and then the shirt came loose. Throwing it aside, she twisted her neck again and looked.

Beside her, Chris's face flushed, and his eyes flickered with desire. But she no longer cared, had eyes for only one thing now. Her naked back shone in the fluorescent lights, the lumps clear now. They bulged in the centre of her back, one on either side of her spine, midway between her arms and hips.

A pressure built in Liz's chest and escaped as a low whine, a muffled scream. An awful horror swept through her, a raging anger at the doctors, at their violation of her body.

Another shriek built, but she swallowed it down, blinking back tears.

Her eyes burned as she looked at Chris, saw the fresh tears in his eyes.

"Where does it stop?" she whispered.

TWENTY-EIGHT

Within hours, Chris found a pair of growths on his own back. Though there was no pain or discomfort, they ignited a terrible horror inside him, a building terror that threatened to overwhelm him. Whatever the doctors had done to them, it seemed they had failed after all.

They made a mistake, the words whispered through his thoughts, along with something else, a familiar word, a horror from his childhood.

Cancer.

The memory of his father's illness still lay heavy on his mind – the wasting sickness, the slow loss of strength, of life. Despite its ferocity, his father had fought back, had even won, for a time. But cancer was like a weed, always there, waiting to return. It wore you down, drew the life from you one drop at a time.

And his father, once larger than life, had been laid low.

Now as the hours ticked past, Chris watched with horror as the lumps on his back grew. It could only be cancer. Vicious and unrelenting, it would spread through their bodies, poisoning their blood, robbing them of strength, until there was nothing left but empty husks.

Lying on the bed, he held Liz in his arms, each alone in their own thoughts.

The next day, they woke to the first pangs of pain. It began as a soft twitch from the centre of his back, radiating outwards from the strange protrusions. The ache pulsed, flickering with the beat of his heart, but growing sharper with each intake of breath. Hour by hour it spread across his back, threaded its way into his chest, until it hurt just to breathe.

For Liz, it was worse. When she woke she could barely speak. Her skin had lost its colour, even the angry red marks beneath her collar had paled to white. By lunch she could no longer lie on her back. When he touched a hand to her forehead, her skin was burning hot with fever.

Each hour the lumps grew. Their skin stretched and hardened around the protrusions, darkening to purple bruises. Each bulge was unyielding to their scrutinising prods, and soon tiny black spots appeared on their surface.

When the lights flickered on the morning of the third day, Chris could hardly move from the pain. Agony wove its way through his torso, spreading out like the roots of a tree, engulfing his lungs, reducing each breath to a battle, a desperate fight for life.

The next time a guard arrived with food, Chris could no longer tell whether it was breakfast or dinner. Forcing open his eyes, he blinked hard in the light, pain lancing through his skull. The room spun and then settled into a double image of two guards. His stomach churned as two images of Liz stood over him and offered a bowl of dark looking stew. He saw her waver on her feet, and blindly took the bowl before she fell.

Sitting back, he raised a shaking spoonful of broth to his mouth, but there was no taste when he swallowed. His stomach swirled again, then he began to heave. He barely made it to the toilet. A moment later Liz was at the sink beside him.

Afterwards, Chris slid to the ground, his head throbbing in the blinding light. Liz slumped beside him, her head settling on his shoulder. For a moment the pain faded, giving in to a wave of warmth. He closed his eyes, savouring Liz's closeness, but the relief did not last long. His stomach lurched again and releasing Liz he crawled back to the toilet.

The click of the lights going out was a welcome relief.

Stomach clenched, lungs burning, head thumping, Chris crawled back to the beds. Stars danced across his vision, but he hauled himself into a bed, no longer caring who's it was. The room stank of vomit and spilt food, of unwashed bodies and blood. The scent of chlorine had long since been overwhelmed.

Caught in the clutches of fever, Chris lost all track of time. At some point he felt Liz's body beside him, though he could not recall whose bed they slept in. His fevered mind drew comfort from the heat of her presence, in the closeness of her face. Then her face warped, his own body distorting, and he forced his eyes closed.

Wild colours spun through his mind as time passed. At one point he remembered calling out, begging the guards to help them, to bring the doctors, to bring anyone. But no one came, no one responded, and he soon stopped asking for help. A short while later, he started asking for death.

In his dreams, he saw his body slowly decaying, watched his veins turn black with death, his arms begin to rot. Then he would find himself whole, riding in the passenger seat of his father's 68 Camaro, his dad driving, an infectious grin on his youthful face. A moment later he was in a hospital, the smell of bleach and beeping of machinery all around. And his father lay in a bed, his arms withered, his face lined with age. Only the smile remained the same.

Again the image faded, and Chris was back in the cell, back with the pain. Looking at his arms, he wondered what was real, what was not. One instant it was night, the next the blinding light of day, then back to black. At times he would wake, gasping for air, shivering beneath the blanket, and know in his heart he was dying.

Once, he dreamed that he was flying, that he was soaring through mountains, far from the nightmares of their prison cell.

And then he woke.

TWENTY-NINE

IT TOOK A LONG TIME FOR CHRIS TO DECIDE HE WAS NO longer dreaming. The cold air wrapped around him, sending a shiver through him, but otherwise there was no discomfort. The pain had vanished, and for a second he considered the possibility he was dead. Then a low groan came from someone nearby, and he knew he was not alone.

Squeezing open his eyes, he peered out from the shadows of his bunk bed, searching for Liz.

The first thing he realised was that they had not been alone in their fever dreams. Someone had entered the room while they slept, cleaning the mess of vomit and blood that had stained the room. Liz lay in the opposite bed, covered now by a blanket of black feathers. She shifted beneath it, then blinked across at him, raising a hand to shield her face. Her lips parted, her tongue licking her cracked lips.

"Chris?" she croaked.

"I'm here," he replied, his throat raw. A desperate thirst clutched him, and he looked across at the sink, wondering if he had the strength to reach it.

In the other bed, Liz shifted, the blanket of feathers moving with her. Dimly, Chris made to do the same, but a weight on his back pushed him down. Reaching back, the soft points of feathers brushed his hand. He shrugged, trying to dislodge the blanket, and struggled to his hands and knees.

Chris paused, a distant thought tugging at his memories. Before he could catch it, it faded into the darkness. He looked across at Liz, eyes questioning, but she had fallen silent. He clenched his fists, feeling a wrongness about himself, but unable to trace its source.

Shaking his head, Chris pushed the last of the fever dreams from his mind and rolled out of the bed onto his feet. To his shock, the weight came with him, pushing him forward. Off-balance, he crashed to the floor in a tangle of limbs and feathers.

"Chris?" Liz's voice shook.

Head spinning, Chris looked up from the floor, unable to understand what had happened. Confused, he pulled himself up, but the weight still clung to his back. Only sheer determination kept him from toppling over again. Looking at Liz, he froze at the look on her face.

Liz sat half-crouched on the bed, eyes wide. Her mouth opened and closed, but no sound came out. Her arm shook as she raised it and pointed. Shivering, he looked back, fear of the unknown rippling down his spine. But his bed was empty, the feather blanket trailing out behind him.

Chris blinked, started to turn back towards Liz, then paused. He blinked again, staring at the tawny brown feathers of his blanket. There was something wrong about the way they hung between himself and the bed, something not quite right.

Stretching out a hand, Chris tried to dislodge the blanket from his shoulders. He flinched as his hand brushed against something unexpected, something hard beneath the blanket. Withdrawing his hand, he looked at Liz, but she only sat in silent shock, her mouth still agape.

Holding his breath, Chris reached behind his neck and ran a hand down his spine.

He found the growths where they had been before, midway down his back. But they had grown now, changed, becoming long shafts that stretched out beyond his reach. A soft down of feathers covered their length, sprouting from his flesh as though they had every right to be there.

Wings.

His mind spun. He shook his head, refusing to face the truth, though they lay stretched out before his eyes. He trembled, and watched the shiver run down the wings, the tawny brown feathers quivering in the cool air.

He turned as a muffled sob came from the other bed. Liz had struggled to her feet, revealing the long black wings hanging from her back. They stretched out either side of her, each at least ten feet long, the large black feathers tangling with the sheets on the bed. Where the feathers bent, Chris glimpsed soft white down beneath, small feathers curled in upon themselves, gripping close to her flesh. The feathers shone in the overhead lights, seeming almost aflame, as though Liz was some avenging angel descended from heaven.

Wings.

Warmth spread through Chris's chest to mingle with the horror. A profound confusion gripped him; a disgust at this fresh violation, the further loss of his humanity – but also wonder, an awe for the trembling new limbs on his back.

Wings.

He looked at Liz. Her eyes were wide, glistening with tears. Her lips trembled as a shudder ran through her body. Through her wings.

For the first time he realised they were both naked. Strangely, that no longer seemed to matter. After all they had suffered, all that had been done to them, Chris's body hardly felt like his own. He felt apart from it now, separated from his nakedness.

A tear spilt down Liz's cheek, and he knew the same thoughts were filling her mind. He stepped across, struggling for balance, and drew her to him. He shivered as her arms went around his waist and her head leaned back, drawing him in.

A fire ignited in Chris's chest as their lips met. His hands slid up into her hair as her tongue darted out, sliding between his lips. The taste of her filled his mouth, and the intoxicating scent of her hair toyed with his nostrils.

After a long minute, Liz pulled back. Raising a hand to her face, she wiped away her tears. Turning, she looked at her wings, her lips twisting in thought. They hung limply from her back, feathers quivering, and he knew what she was thinking.

Sucking in a breath, Liz closed her eyes. Her face tightened, the muscles of her jaw deepening. Her brow creased, and behind her the black-feathered wings gave a twitch. Then they began to shake, lifting slightly and half opened. There they paused, as though lacking the strength for more.

Liz bit her lip, her eyes still closed, and persisted.

And bit by bit, her wings spread, until they seemed to fill the cell. Combined, they stretched more than twenty feet wide, twice the length of the beds, so that their tips poked out through the bars into the corridor.

Twenty feet of jet-black feathers, of curly white down, of a majestic, undefinable magic.

When Liz opened her eyes again, Chris saw the wonder there, the fear falling away before it.

At a nod from her, he shut his own eyes and sought to do the same. Reaching down into the depths of his consciousness, he followed the tingle that came from his back, from the newfound limbs hanging across his bed. As he concentrated, the tingle spread along his spine. The hairs stood up on his neck as new connections formed within his mind, as neurons flared into life, recognising the presence of new muscles and bone and flesh.

A tremor went through the weight on his back. There was a wrongness to that weight, an awkward presence to it, like clothes that did not quite fit. But opening his mind, he sought to accept it, to embrace it.

At last, Chris opened his eyes. A sharp crack tore the air as his wings snapped open, unfurling to fill the room. Feathers as long as his forearm brushed against the far wall, touched the bars of the cell, and he *felt it*, sensed the pressure against his feathers.

Turning, he grinned at Liz, unable to keep the wonder from his face. She grinned, laughed, opened her arms to embrace him.

Then with a deafening shriek, an alarm began to sound.

THIRTY

ANGELA STRODE AROUND THE CORNER AND STARTED towards the wide iron door at the end of the corridor. Heavy locking bars stretched across the dull metal, and a guard stood to either side, watching her approach. Each held a heavy rifle and wore the familiar trigger watches on their wrists. With a flick of their fingers, the men could activate any collar in their immediate vicinity, incapacitating any threat the prisoners within might pose.

Or at least, that was the idea.

Today, the watches had been reduced to worthless pieces of steel and glass. Just ten minutes before, Angela had entered her code to deactivate all the collars inside the facility. Halt, in his arrogance, had thought her cowed by his violence.

Instead, Angela had resolved to act.

Left alone in the padded room, fading in and out of consciousness, Angela had finally seen the true futility of her research. It had never been about a cure, or a weapon to fight the *Chead*. It had always been about *this*, this need for power, for a weapon against their enemies.

And Angela knew, threats or no, she could not allow the Praegressus project to continue.

Climbing to her feet, the weight of regret heavy on her shoulders, Angela had settled on a new path.

Now the time had come to act, and she knew she could not hesitate.

Ahead, the guards pulled back the heavy bolts, and with a screech, the iron door swung open. Angela walked past the guards without breaking stride, nodding as she went.

Inside, a hushed silence gathered over the narrow corridor as a dozen faces turned towards her. Another screech and the door swung shut, sealing her inside. Taking a breath, she started forward, careful to keep to the centre of the hall, beyond the reach of grasping arms.

Hard grey eyes followed her passage.

Tension hung like a blanket on the air as she made her way past the cells. Hate permeated the air, radiating from the dark creatures pressing up against the prison bars. There were twelve in all: six boys, six girls.

Twelve vicious killing machines, hungry for blood, for freedom.

The *Chead* watched her as she reached the corridor's end and turned back. Each had been born in the facility. Each was destined to die here. These creatures would never feel the heat of the sun, nor the cold of snow. Their eyes would never see the beauty of the mountains beyond the walls, their ears would never hear the roar of ocean waves.

Or at least, that was Halt's plan.

Each of the *Chead* wore the familiar steel collars on their neck. Each of those collars were now little more than decorative necklaces.

Standing at the end of the corridor, Angela faced the exit. The cells stretched out either side of her, the males to her left, females to her right. Something about the change accelerated the development and reproductive drive of the *Chead*. Left to their own devices, they bred like rabbits. And though the occupants of the cells appeared fully mature, the oldest was just ten years old.

Stealing herself, Angela walked back towards the exit. The grey eyes followed her, alive with intelligence, searching for an opportunity. One second, one slip, was all they needed. Several men had lost their lives by wandering too close to the bars. Angela would not make that mistake.

But she needed them to see her, to be awake.

To be ready.

As she approached the entrance, the guard by the door reached out to open it. She gazed at his face for a moment as she passed, a flicker of guilt swelling within her. But it was too late for regrets now. It was time.

As the door reached its apex, Angela looked down at her watch. It was more advanced than the others, controlled more than just the candidate's collars. As head geneticist and supervisor of the Praegressus project, she had control over many of the security protocols for the facility. That was how she had stopped Halt earlier, and what she planned to use now.

Angela pressed her finger to the touch screen.

Behind her, a buzzer began to screech, followed by the rattling of cell doors opening. Angela leapt forward as the guards looked up, confusion sweeping across their faces. They stared, eyes wide with bewilderment, as Angela stepped past them and began to run.

The screams of the dying chased her down the corridor.

ANGELA'S BREATH came in ragged gasps as she took a corner. From behind her came the roar of gunfire and the growls of the *Chead*. Overhead, lights flashed, and somewhere in the building a siren screeched. Muffled voices came from speakers at intervals down the corridors, a robotic voice asking her not to panic.

The thump of approaching boots came from ahead. She tensed as two guards raced into view, then relaxed as they sprinted past, guns held at the ready. Their eyes barely registered her, but she saw their fear. Just as well. With a dozen *Chead* loose in the building, they would be hard-pressed to survive.

A minute later she drew up outside the other prison block. She had hesitated before detouring there – only two of the seven survivors were located there. But the face of the girl had risen in her mind, and Angela knew she could not abandon her.

Fortunately, the guards had already abandoned their posts – though whether to face the *Chead* or run, she wasn't sure. The door to the cell block had been left open, and she stepped inside, shivering as her eyes swept over the rows of empty cells.

So much loss.

Angela closed her eyes, regret welling up within her. How had she been so blind? She had allowed her ambition to surpass caution, to blind her to the atrocities within the facility. Her morals, her integrity, all had been lost before her drive to succeed.

And these children had paid the price.

Moving down the corridor, Angela searched for the two she had come for. She froze when she found them, her breath catching in her throat.

She had seen them in their fever induced sleep, seen the others in their comas. She already knew the experiment had succeeded; that the homeotic genes had taken. Once stimulated, they acted like a master switch, triggering the cluster of genes embedded in the candidates' genomes. The genes corresponding to wing growth.

Angela had watched the wings grow, watched the feathers sprout like seedlings from their skin. Even so, she was not prepared for the sight that greeted her.

Elizabeth and Christopher stood in all their glory, wings spread wide, stretching out to fill the cell. They had found the ragged clothes she'd left by their beds, with the clumsy holes she'd torn in the backs. The girl's black feathers pressed against the brown of the boy's, their wings entwining in the tiny space.

Angela's heart ached with the wonder of it.

"What's happening?" Christopher demanded.

Blinking, Angela tore herself from her stupor. She shook her head, then looked down at her watch and pressed a button. The cell slid open with a dull rattle.

The two of them stood still, a wary surprise spreading across their faces.

"Come on," Angela said. "We're getting out of here. Hurry, the others should be awake by now."

Christopher's hand drifted to his neck, his fingers touching the collar. Angela shook her head and reached into her pocket. "I've deactivated them," finding the little key, she drew it out and tossed it to them. "Here, that'll unlock them. But *hurry*."

A few seconds later their collars lay discarded on the ground. Angela watched them embrace, saw the tears shining in their eyes, but she could not pause to celebrate their freedom. Apprehension nibbled at her stomach, an awful fear they would be caught.

"*Come on*," she urged again, waving them towards the door. "We need to find the others."

Their eyes widened then, their mouths opening in question, but she was already moving away. Sirens still sounded and red lights flashed in the ceiling, but there was no sign of movement as they moved out into the corridors. The guards remained preoccupied at the other end of the facility, and she hoped the other civilians would have already retreated to the safe room.

Silently she led them through the maze of the facility, to the clean room where the other survivors of the PERV-B strain had remained in their comas. She had swapped out their medication that morning, replacing the drugs with saline. They would be awake by now, and she hoped they had not wandered from the room while she detoured.

Unfortunately, the remaining PERV-A candidates were lost to her. They still lay in their comas, their bodies wracked by fever, struggling to accept the chromosomal alterations of the virus. There was nothing she could do for them now.

Ahead, the door to the clean room lay unguarded. She smiled, glad her distraction had proven so effective. With luck, they would be long gone before anyone realised they were missing. If the guards even managed to regain control of the facility. She had seen a single *Chead* tear a man to pieces. With twelve… she didn't like to think what twelve *Chead* might be capable of.

But there was no more time to think of that. Pushing open the door, Angela led the others inside.

THIRTY-ONE

LIZ STUMBLED THROUGH THE DOOR AFTER CHRIS. EVERY step was a struggle to keep upright. The new weight on her back threw her whole coordination out of sync, leaving her feeling strangely out of proportion. Even the simple act of closing her wings had taken several attempts, but she and Chris had finally managed to pull them tight against their backs. Even so, they niggled at her consciousness, an alien presence that would not go away.

The thought of freedom drove her on, the knowledge that each step carried her closer to a possible reunion with Ashley and Sam fuelling her. She sucked in a breath, joying again in the feel of her naked neck. The collar was gone, her throat free of its steel encasing. It felt like a lifetime ago since the awful contraption had trapped her. Perhaps it was.

Blinking, Liz returned her mind to the present. Looking around, she recognised it as the room they had awoken in before. The beds still lined its length, but they were empty now. The whir of machines filled the air, their tubes and wires dangling free. Her chest contracted as her eyes swept the room, searching for her friends.

A thud came from their right, and she spun, raising her fists to defend herself.

Then lowered them. Beside her Chris chuckled, as together they watched the figure sprawled on the ground struggling to sit up.

It took a few seconds for Sam to get his tangle of limbs and copper wings under control, and several more before he managed to stand. A string of curses echoed from the walls as he finally pulled himself up, red in the face, puffing like he'd run a marathon. Then her eyes drifted past Sam, and she gave a wild yelp.

Ashley strode forward, her lips twitching with suppressed humour. She moved with the same casual grace as before, her lithe legs easily finding their balance as she weaved between the empty beds. Trailing out behind her, a pair of snow-white wings shone in the overhead lights. They quivered as she moved, slowly lifting from the ground, expanding across the room.

Liz laughed again as Ashley reached her, then stepped up to draw the girl into a hug. They clung to each other for a moment, arms gripped tightly. When they finally broke apart, Ashley's eyes travelled past Liz. She raised an eyebrow at the doctor.

When Fallow did not speak, Ashley nodded and turned back to Liz. "I guess we found their weakness."

Chris shrugged. "She found us."

The distant wail of sirens prickled at Liz's ears, reminding her they were not out of danger yet. Before she could speak though, another movement came from the far side of the room. Her eyes trailed past Sam and found the remaining survivors of the Praegressus project.

Her heart sank as her eyes alighted on Richard and Jasmine. Their attitude towards the four of them did not appear to have changed in the untold weeks they'd lain unconscious. They still stood on the far side of the room, arms crossed and eyes hard with suspicion. Though it was not their faces that drew her attention. Their wings lay half-furled behind them, each sporting an array of dark emerald feathers, like those of some tropical parrot. Their eyes caught hers and she quickly looked away, unable to face their unspoken accusations, their hate that she was alive, while Joshua was gone.

Of course, she thought. *Of everyone else who could have survived, it would be Richard and Jasmine…*

Well, Richard and Jasmine, and the girl.

Standing beside them was a young girl of maybe thirteen years. Locks of grey hair tumbled around her face, where eyes wide with fear stared out at them. A button nose and freckled cheeks only served to make her look younger – how she had survived this far, Liz couldn't begin to guess. Liz shivered as the girl's eyes, one blue, the other green, found her from across the room.

Looking away, Liz cast her gaze around the room one last time, searching for the others. There had still been dozens of candidates left the last time she had been there. Now there was only the seven of them, each sporting the plain grey uniforms they'd found at the ends of their beds.

"Where are the others?" she whispered, turning to face Fallow.

Fallow looked away, head bowing. When she did not respond, Chris repeated her question. "Doctor Fallow, where are the rest of them?"

Fallow looked back, her eyes flashing. "Don't call me that. I don't deserve to be called 'doctor' after what I've done. My name is Angela." She bowed her head. "And the others did not survive. The physiological changes… they were too much for their bodies to support. Even unconscious, the accelerated wing growth was too much. Their hearts gave out from the strain."

An awful anger spread through Liz as she stepped in close to the doctor. Fallow flinched, but this time she did not look away. "How many did you kill?" Liz hissed.

Angela Fallow closed her eyes. "I've lost count," her eyes snapped open again. "But it ends here. I won't let them take you too."

Liz might have struck her if Chris had not placed a hand on her shoulder. Looking back at him, she saw the sadness in his eyes, the same sorrow from which her own rage spawned. Stepping away from Angela, she hugged Chris to her. A second later she smiled as Ashley joined them, then Sam.

"Ahem." Liz looked up at a new voice. Richard raised an eyebrow. Reaching up, he tapped his collar. "Someone care to share the key?"

Chris nodded. Reaching into his pocket he pulled out the little key Angela had given them and handed it over. The clink of the thick steel collars striking the concrete quickly followed as the five of them freed themselves.

"Are you okay there, Sam?" Chris asked as Sam finally managed to unlock the clasp of his collar.

Sam cursed beneath his breath and tossed the collar aside. "Almost," he said as a shiver went through his copper feathers.

Slowly his wings contracted. "Don't know what the idiots were thinking, putting these clunky things on our backs," he paused, eying Angela uncertainly. "Err, no offence, Doc– I mean, Angela?"

Angela shook her head, a sad smile touching her lips. "And it's alright. You have every right to complain. I would have… I would have stopped them before they gave you the injection, but I was unconscious. Then I had to wait… wait until you were conscious again."

"It's okay." Of all of them, Ashley seemed the best adapted to the new appendages. She looked over her shoulder, smiling. "I kind of like them."

"Yeah," Sam's voice was gruff, but he continued with his usual humour, "but yours are tiny. Did you have to make mine so *big?*"

Angela raised a hand to her mouth, trying to hide her smile. "It took some research of various avian species to get our specifications right. We looked at genome variations between species such as the Andean Condors and Wandering Albatross, then used them to identify genes relating to size in fragmented DNA from *Argentavis magnificens*."

"Argentavis what?" Richard growled from nearby.

"The largest known bird to have flown," Liz looked around as Jasmine spoke.

Angela nodded. "It could weigh up to two-hundred-fifty pounds. Once we'd identified all the genes related to wing surface area, we linked them with those that controlled your own sizes and weights. Thus, why yours are so... big, Samuel."

Sam glanced at Liz. "I think she's calling me fat..."

Smiling, Liz looked around the little group, a strange elation rising within her. Even with the open animosity of Jasmine and Richard, there was a connection between the seven of them now, a shared experience which could not be denied. Of all the desperate souls who had passed through this place, they alone had survived.

They alone had evolved.

And now they needed to get out.

As though reading Liz's mind, Angela turned away from the group and started towards the door. The others paused a moment to collect themselves. Feathers rustled as wings were slowly furled, and then Chris started after her, Liz close behind.

Ahead of them, Angela was stretching out a hand to open the door, when it suddenly swung inwards to meet her.

And Halt stepped into the room.

THIRTY-TWO

LIZ FROZE AS HALT TOOK A STEP INTO THE ROOM, THE others following suit behind her. Her heart plummeted into the pit of her stomach as his eyes swept the room, his confusion turning quickly to rage. Before any of them could react, they settled on Angela. He clutched a handgun in one hand, and with a snarl, he sprang.

Angela managed a scream before he was on her, his arm wrapping around her waist, spinning her against him. Pressing the gun to her head, he drew back his lips.

"What do we have here, doctor?" he snarled. Angela flinched as he shifted the gun, jabbing it into her ribs. "Have you betrayed me? Have you betrayed us all?"

Clenching her fists, Liz inhaled, tasting the scent of gunpowder on the air. Halt's gun had already been fired recently; the man posed no idle threat. She froze as his eyes turned back to them. A cold grin twisted his lips as Angela struggled in his grasp.

"*That's enough!*" he snapped.

Halt swung the gun, catching Angela in the forehead. She slumped in Halt's hands as he turned back to them. "Don't come any closer."

Liz suppressed a moan. Angela had gone limp now, her amber eyes wide and staring. Her hands swiped feebly at the arms holding her, but Halt was more than a match for the small woman. Biting her lip, Liz flashed a glance at the others. Her arms trembled, the sensation spreading through her body, down her spine, to the foreignness of her wings. A phantom ache started in her throat, the distant reminder of the collar pressing against her flesh.

I won't go back.

She flinched as her fingernails bit the palms of her hands. Drawing in a deep breath, she unclenched her hands, trying to calm herself, to find a way out of the trap. Her eyes travelled across the space separating her from Halt and Angela.

Too far.

But Chris was closer, and from the corner of her eyes, she saw him slide another step towards the doctors. If he could reach her…

No, it was still too far.

Her eyes turned back to Angela. Emotion washed over the doctor's face – fear, anger, regret. Her head sagged as her eyes closed, her whole body trembling. Then her head snapped up, and a new resolve now shone from her eyes. The fear had vanished, replaced by an implacable determination.

Liz opened her mouth to shout, but she was too late. She wasn't sure what she would have said anyway. Would she have begged Angela not to act? Or had she only wanted to thank her, for finally freeing them.

Either way, Liz never got the chance. Still clutched in Halt's arms, Angela jerked her arm and jumped, driving her weight backwards into Halt. Small as she was, the act was enough to throw Halt off balance, and cursing, he staggered backwards.

In that instant, Chris leapt, charging across the ten feet still separating them. He closed the gap in a second, his wings cracking as they beat the air, driving him on. He raised a fist and snarled as he swung it at the doctor. Another second, and it would be over.

The roar of the gun was so sudden, so deafening in the sealed room that Liz found herself stumbling backwards.

Then Chris barrelled into Halt, his fist catching the man in the face. The blow sent Halt hurtling backwards through the air. He struck the concrete with a dull thud, bounced once then smashed hard against the wall. A low groan came from him as he slumped down and lay still. The gun slid across the floor, coming to rest in a nook between the floor and the wall.

Chris landed lightly on his feet, wings still outstretched, eyes locked on the doctor. But Liz was already moving, running forward, falling to her knees beside Angela. A dark pool spread around her, the overhead lights glimmering on its scarlet surface. Her eyes were open, staring at the ceiling, her mouth wide in a silent scream. One hand still clutched at her chest, where a small red mark stained her lab coat.

Liz knelt over her, staring at the hole through blurry eyes. A low moan came from her throat as she reached out and shook the woman. She heard the soft pad of footsteps from behind her, but she took no notice.

Disbelief threaded around her mind. Whatever her crimes, Angela Fallow had been the only one in this place to show any compassion for them. Twice she had stopped Halt's torture, and in the end, she had followed her conscience, had freed them from the cells.

And now she was dead.

A terrible rage rose in Liz's chest, driving her to her feet. Spinning, she leapt at Halt, crossing the room in a single bound. She reached down and grasped him by the front of his coat, hauling him to his feet. Without effort she lifted him into the air, held him aloft, and then slammed him into the wall.

He groaned, his eyelids flickering, but did not wake. Gritting her teeth, Liz drew back a fist.

Ashley's hand caught her arm before the blow could fall. Liz half-turned, straining against the other girl, a snarl twisting her lips. Frustration built inside her and she spun, dropping Halt to the ground and swung at Ashley.

Ashley leaned back and Liz's blow found only open air. Her other hand shot out, catching Liz in the chest, pushing her back. Stumbling, Liz straightened and then leapt at her. Rage burned in her throat, filling her with a need to rend, to tear the flesh from her enemies.

"*Liz!*" Ashley screamed, raising an arm to protect herself.

The scream gave Liz pause, and she drew back. Blood pounded in her head, and a voice screamed for her to attack, but she sucked in a breath. Slowly she looked around, blinking back the red haze, and saw the fear dancing in the eyes of the others. She sucked in another mouthful of air, and faced Ashley.

"*Why?*" she asked, her voice breaking. "Why did you stop me?"

"He's not worth it," Ashley breathed. "He's not worth it, Liz. Don't let this place make you like them. Don't let it corrupt you."

Liz clenched her fists, trembling with the effort to suppress her rage. Red flashed across her vision as she turned to look down at Halt, but she fought back the impulse to reach for him.

She bowed her head. "He'll come for us," she whispered.

"They'll come for us anyway," Chris replied, placing a hand on her shoulder. "Besides, I doubt he'll be doing anything after this. They were always talking about needing results," he waved a hand at the room, "and this seems about the opposite of that."

Slowly, Liz allowed her body to relax. She looked up at Chris and nodded.

He stepped forward then, arms open, drawing her to him. They stood there in silence, holding each other, the others forgotten for a second, the nightmare around them a distant memory.

When they finally parted, Liz and Chris turned to face the others. Ashley and Sam, Richard and Jasmine, and the strange little girl stared back. Their eyes shone with emotion: hope mixed with anger, love with hate. Shivering, Liz looked at Chris.

"Let's go."

THIRTY-THREE

THE TIRED HINGES OF THE DOOR SCREECHED AS CHRIS threw himself against it. His shoulder throbbed, and his wings gave a little flap, but on the next blow the door caved. He stumbled after it, his momentum carrying him outside, where a blast of icy air caught in his wings and hurled him backwards. Pain shot from his bare feet as they stumbled on stones. Dropping to his knees, he braced himself against the howling wind, and glanced back at the others.

They filed out after him, one by one, their eyes alight with wonder. Turning, Chris looked out across a world blanketed in white. Flakes of snow swirled around them, drifting ever downwards, their intricate patterns catching in the light shining down from overhead. Clouds covered the sky, but after so long inside, it still seemed impossibly bright. Blinking back tears, Chris watched as the world opened around him.

Rocky mountains stretched up above them, sprouting like enormous trees from the slope on which they stood. Sheer escarpments of rock raced upwards, disappearing into the clouds overhead. A sheen of white covered their frozen surface, but further down the valley the snow and ice gave way to barren rock.

Around the facility there was no sign of trees or vegetation, only jagged gravel that promised to make walking difficult. They had not stopped to search for better clothing or boots, and now Chris shivered as the icy air tore through his thin clothes. A dull ache began at the back of his skull, though despite their now undoubted height above sea level, his breath came easily now.

Turning, Chris stared up the valley, his eyes trailing over the snow-covered boulders, up to where the slope disappeared into a narrow gorge. Glancing back, he studied the valley as it fell away from the facility. There was not a sliver of cover in sight. Even so, down was tempting. Down would bring them to warmer air, out of the mountains, towards civilisation. Perhaps they could find someone to help them, to protect them from the monsters that would hunt them.

But even as he considered the temptation, Chris dismissed it. They would not make it far in that direction. Lower down the clouds cleared, and their pursuers would expect them to take that route. The chase would be over before it began.

No, they needed to do the unexpected. They needed to go higher.

The others gathered behind him, huddling close, wings wrapped tight to fend off the frigid air. Turning to face them, Chris's wings extended of their own accord, curving around to encase him. The relief was instant. The cold creeping through his chest vanished.

The others watched him, wonder and fear mingling on their faces. They all knew the next few hours would decide whether they lived or died. Whatever Angela had done to distract the guards, it could not keep them busy forever. Before long, Halt would wake and the guards would come for them. Chris wanted to be far away by then.

Quickly he explained his plan, watching as Liz, Sam and Ashley nodded. Richard and Jasmine only stood in sullen silence, their faces expressionless. Beside them, the young girl hovered on the edge of the circle. So far they hadn't gotten a word from her. She huddled in close to Jasmine, a nameless, unknown quantity. Not for the first time, he wondered how she had survived.

He'd thought the other two would argue, but they nodded when he finished. "Let's go then," Richard said abruptly.

With a sigh of relief, Chris turned and began the long trek up towards the canyon. He moved as fast as the jagged gravel allowed him, wincing as each step sent a jagged bolt of pain through his feet. Silently he cursed their haste. Boots would have saved them time out in the mountains, but there was no going back now. Glancing around, he made sure the others were following and pressed on.

Half an hour passed as they made their slow way up. The wind howled around them, threatening to hurl them from the rocky slope, but they continued, wings pulled tight against their backs. Briefly Chris considered whether they should attempt to use them, but quickly dropped the thought. Conditions were not ideal for a first attempt at flight.

When they finally reached the canyon mouth, Chris paused, glancing back as the other filed up behind him. One by one they joined him in the shadow beneath the cliffs. Beyond, the canyon twisted deeper into the mountains. A river flowed along its far side, and the roaring of water echoed around them.

The hairs on his neck tingled as Chris looked back down the valley, and saw the black-garbed figures of men spilling from the building below. They gathered near the high walls, concentrating around a man in white. Blinking, Chris watched the distant figures come suddenly into focus. It was as though a film had been removed from his eyes, revealing the world around him in a detail he had never experienced. In that moment he saw them all in crystal clarity, saw the fear in their eyes as they looked at one another, the sleek black steel of their rifles, the blood and tears marking their clothes.

Between them, Halt stood with shoulders hunched, gesturing weakly with his arms. The men did not appear to have seen their little group yet, but it would only take a glance to reveal their position. Silently Chris waved for the others to get into cover, not trusting his voice, in case it carried down to the men below. Turning, he scrambled up the last few feet of the gravel slope, and into the canyon.

The others quickly joined him, scrambling over the lip one by one and dropping out of sight. They retreated behind the boulders lodged in the mouth of the pass, their eyes on Chris, waiting for him to speak.

Heart pounding in his chest, Chris slipped out from behind the boulders. Dropping low, he half-scrambled back up to the gravel lip. At the entrance to the pass, he dropped to his stomach and crawled the last few inches. Then he slowly lifted his head and peered down at the facility.

And immediately dropped back down.

THIRTY-FOUR

CHRIS SLAMMED A FIST INTO THE GRAVEL, CURSING THEIR luck.

Just a few more seconds, and we would have been clear.

He slid back down the slope to the others. Biting back his frustration, he only shook his head at their questioning looks. Below, a line of black figures were streaming their way up towards the pass, waved on from behind by the figure in white.

They had been spotted. Now all they could do was flee, and hope to outrun their pursuers.

"They've seen us," he hissed. Moving quickly past them, he began to thread his way through boulders strewn across the floor of the canyon. "Halt's with them. Let's go."

He caught a glimpse of Liz, her eyes shimmering with anger, and looked away. He could not blame her for her rage. Maybe she'd been right – maybe they should not have spared the man's life. But even with Angela lying dead at their feet, he could not bring himself to believe killing Halt in cold blood was the right thing to do.

Either way, it was too late to second guess the decision now.

Gritting his teeth against the wind howling through the canyon, Chris picked his way over the rocky ground, taking care to avoid the patches of ice. The stones were slick beneath his feet, worn smooth by the passage of floodwaters, but at least they did not hurt. Above them the canyon walls closed in, stretching up two, almost three hundred feet.

Stone ground against stone as the others followed close behind him, the rocks shifting beneath their weight. To their right the river tumbled over its stony bed, roaring as it rushed down a series of cascades, making its journey through the twisting canyon. During the Spring it would rise, filling the gorge, but in the icy winter air it remained thankfully low.

Chris's gaze carried up the valley, following the sheer walls as they twisted around and out of sight. He scanned the ground ahead, picking out a trail amidst the rock-strewn ground. He was quickly adapting to the weight of his wings. His muscles surged with a newfound energy, with the joy of freedom. Behind them the mouth of the canyon was empty, but even so he picked up the pace, springing from stone to stone with hardly a pause in between. The thought of the guards and their guns drove him on. Though they were moving at a good pace, their pursuers did not have to catch them – only get them within range of their rifles.

Redoubling his efforts, Chris felt the towering granite cliffs pressing in around him. From somewhere ahead the roar of the water grew louder. Like distant thunder it drew him on, called them deeper into the mountains. Sucking in great mouthfuls of damp air, Chris raced for the first bend in the canyon.

Boulders the size of cars littered the ground. Where the canyon narrowed they clustered in groups, almost blocking their passage. They scrambled over them one by one, slipping on the damp surfaces while the others watched, waiting for their turn.

Chris's ears tingled as a voice carried up the canyon. Acting on instinct, he grabbed Liz and pulled her behind a boulder, waving for the others to follow. An instant later the shriek of bullets tore the air, followed by the sharp crack of shattered rock. Cowering behind the boulder, they watched as a boulder where they'd been standing disintegrated beneath a hail of bullets. Hot lead tore great chunks from the stone, dotting the surface of the boulder with pock-marks.

For a moment, Chris stood frozen, terrified by the sheer display of power. In his mind he saw himself caught by the bullets, saw his flesh tear and his bones shatter. Then Liz grasped him by the shoulder and shook him back to reality. He blinked, found her crystal eyes staring at him, just a few feet away, and taken by an impulse, he pulled her close.

They kissed, hard and fast, the moment filled with a desperate passion, the thrill of a chase. A second later they pulled apart and turned to face the others. Richard raised an eyebrow, but Chris ignored him. The first bend in the canyon was close now, just a few more yards away. But the open space would leave them exposed to the guards at the base of the pass, to their unforgiving bullets.

Yet they had to move. No doubt men were already climbing towards them, growing closer with every passing minute.

"We run for it," was all Chris said before he turned and leapt from cover, unwilling to wait and see whether the others followed.

The buzz of bullets turned to a roar as he stepped into the open. Then he was racing across the open ground, stones slipping beneath his bare feet, faster than thought. With each step the shriek of bullets grew louder, the guards far below narrowing their aim. Stone chips tore his flesh as the thud of bullet impacts shook the ground beneath him. He ducked low, the hackles on his neck rising in anticipation of pain.

Then his wings were out, beating hard, driving him faster. He stumbled as he miscalculated his next jump, almost falling before recovering with a wild wave of arms. Liz bounded past, flashing him a sideways glance. But he was already up and beside her, pushing hard, lungs burning not with exhaustion, but fear. Around him he heard the gasps of the others, their desperate, unintelligible cries.

And over it all, the screech of bullets.

Then suddenly the air was clear, the cliff rising up to shield them from view. Together they drew to a stop, sucking in long mouthfuls of air, their wild eyes looking around at each other, shocked and elated, thrilled by their survival.

They did not pause for long though. They had won a respite, but they were still far from free. Ahead the canyon narrowed, the twists and turns coming closer together, and for the next thirty minutes they did not see their pursuers again. The stones grew larger around them, until only boulders remained. The giant rocks packed the gorge, the creek threading its way between them, over and under, plunging down towards the valley far below. The roar of distant water continued to grow, and the taste of the air changed, filling with moisture. In his mind, Chris pictured the stream cascading over a series of boulders, down into the canyon, and prayed it would offer them an escape.

Gathering his strength, he pressed on, drawing the others with him. The canyon floor grew steeper, winding up towards the clifftops high overhead. Their progress slowed as the way became more difficult, even backtracking where the way grew too steep, too treacherous to pass.

Striding around another bend in the canyon, Chris found his stride slowing as he took in the sight. Beside him, Liz continued her upward march, head down, eyes fixed on the ground. Around them the roar of water had turned to a deafening thunder, but it was only when he reached out and grabbed Liz by the shoulder that she looked up; that she saw where he had led them.

THIRTY-FIVE

CHRIS HAD NOT BEEN WRONG ABOUT THE WATERFALL. THREE hundred feet above their heads, a river rushed over the edge of the cliff and out into the void. Water filled the air, whirling as the booming wind caught it, turning it to a fine mist, to a light rain that fell around them, settling on their clothes and skin. At the base of the falls, the remains of the river crashed down onto a jagged pile of rocks. From there the stream wound its way down the canyon to where the seven of them stood.

Beyond the waterfall, the canyon twisted back on itself, ending in an abrupt wall of sheer rock. A pile of rubble had accumulated against the cliff opposite the waterfall, stretching up around two hundred feet. Straggly patches of vegetation sprouted from the rubble, no doubt fed by the ready source of water.

Chris closed his eyes, feeling the spray of water on his cheeks, even where they stood some four hundred feet away. It settled in his hair and trickled down his face, until he gave an angry shake of his head and wiped it away. He clenched his fists, shivering with cold and frustration.

There was no way they could climb those cliffs, no way they could reach the top.

He had led them to a dead end, to a trap. And with the guards closing in from behind, there was nowhere left to go.

Looking at the others, he saw his despair reflected in their faces. Only Ashley seemed undaunted. She moved up beside him, her eyes travelling up the canyon, to the pile of rubble. He turned, following her gaze, straining to see through the mist. A pile of jagged boulders clustered around the top of the rubble and the cliffs above them were cracked and broken. At some point the cliffs must have given way, and now a shadow stretched up from the rubble. From the distance, there was no telling for sure, but it looked like a crack they might be able to climb.

"Let's go," Ashley flashed him a smile as she strode past, taking the lead.

Chris was glad to relinquish his position. The weight of failure hung heavy on his shoulders. The others did not speak, but he could feel the eyes of Jasmine and Richard on his back. Ahead, Ashley seemed to glide across the rocks, moving with a grace Chris wished he could match. She reached the rubble mound well before the rest of them, and started to climb.

Following her, Chris only managed a few steps before the loose gravel slipped beneath his feet. He threw out an arm, grasping at the branches of a dishevelled bush, then screamed as thorns tore the skin of his palm. Cursing, he regained his balance and released the bush, only then daring to look at his hand.

Dark marks spotted his palm; the broken thorn tips embedded deep in his flesh. Blood seeped from a dozen cuts and the skin was already turning red around the marks. He swore again, but there was little he could do now. Cradling his arm, he moved after Ashley.

The mist closed in around them as they climbed, quickly soaking them to the skin. Chris shivered as a drop of water ran down his back and caught in the clustered feathers of his wings. A tingle ran up his spine as a thought came to him then. Angela's words in the clean room rang in his mind. The feathered appendages trembled in response, as though reading his thoughts.

Fly!

Chris shook his head, casting the idea back out into the void. With the wind howling through the canyon, and the cliffs pressing close, the idea was suicide.

As they neared the top of the mound, the wind picked up speed. It howled down over the cliffs to pummel at them, tearing at their wings and threatening to send them plummeting to the rocks far below. Above, the river continued its eternal plunge over the granite cliffs, filling the air with swirling clouds of water vapour.

A cry came from above. Chris looked up in time to see Ashley slip, then threw himself to the side as a rock crashed down towards him. He shouted a warning to the others as it thumped past, but thankfully they had spread out, and it tumbled harmlessly past them.

Returning to the climb, he watched Ashley recover and continue her ascent, favouring her left hand now. But she was already drawing level with the boulders ringing the crown of the slope. Picking up his pace, Chris soon joined her at the base of the boulders. Together they turned to watch as the others joined them.

Once the seven of them had gathered on the narrow ledge, they turned to face the boulders. Here Ashley took the lead again, squeezing in between two of the boulders. The way was narrow, and the extra bulk of their wings didn't help, but Chris managed to slide his way after Ashley. Ahead, the crevice came to an end at another boulder, but Ashley was already making short work of scrambling up, using the rock on either side of her to climb.

Chris waited for her to reach the top before following. The sharp pitch of the boulders and his injured hand made it difficult to find purchase. Cursing to himself, he pressed against the rocks to wedge himself in place, and then slowly began to lift himself up.

When he reached the top, Ashley was already gone. Following her wet footprints through the boulders, his optimism began to return. If they could just wedge themselves into the crack in the cliff, they might scramble their way up in the same way they had just managed. It would be a long and difficult haul – at least a hundred feet remained to be climbed, but it was something.

He stumbled as the rocks around him gave way to open ground, and he found himself in the centre of the ring of boulders. Across from him, he found Ashley with her head pressed against the cliff, fists clenched against the sheer stone. She turned as he approached, her eyes finding his.

Chris's stomach twisted as Ashley slid down the cliff wall until she sat and covered her face with her hands. Her shoulders heaved as silent sobs shook her, and tears spilt between her fingers.

Behind her the cliff stretched up towards the sky, smooth and unmarked, the shadow they had thought was a crack no more than a change in the rock, a darker shade of granite.

They were trapped.

THIRTY-SIX

LIZ PAUSED AS SHE EMERGED FROM THE BOULDERS AND found Chris and Ashley slumped against the cliff. Their faces were ashen, their eyes despondent, and she knew in that instant they were finished. Her shoulders sagged, but she moved across to Chris and placed a hand on his head. He did not look up, just stared at the barren gravel.

Crouching down, Liz pulled him to her chest. Gravel rattled as Sam appeared beside her. He squatted by Ashley, whispering softly to her, pulling her up, getting her moving again. Trapped or not, there was no time to pause, to sit and wait for death to come for them.

"I'm sorry," Chris murmured.

Liz slid her fingers through his hair and down to his chin. She turned him to face her. "This isn't your fault, Chris. You were right, this was our best chance. If we'd gone the other way, they would already have caught us. Now get up. We have to decide what to do next."

It took several tugs on Chris's arm before he gathered himself and regained his feet. By then Sam had Ashley looking more herself, though Liz suspected it was no more than a brave face. But then, that's all any of them had left now.

"So, what now?" Jasmine crossed her arms, eyes flashing as she looked around the circle. "I'm not going back."

Beside her Richard nodded.

Liz shivered, thinking of the guards creeping up the canyon towards them, of the black steel of their rifles.

No, we can't go back.

To go back now would be worse than if they'd never escaped. They had tasted freedom, rid themselves of the awful collars, breathed the fresh mountain air. And freezing though they were, with their wings drawn tight around their torsos, they were alive.

"There's nowhere left to go," Chris's voice cracked.

"Then we fight," Sam put in, his brow creased. Liz had never seen him so serious.

Around the circle, the others nodded, but Liz found herself shaking her head. Moving past them, she climbed up the closest boulder, until she was perched atop it. Looking down, she stared out over the gorge, peering through the swirling mist, seeking out their pursuers. The wind tore at her, sending her black hair flying across her face, but she ignored it.

She heard scuffling from behind her as the others climbed, but did not turn. Over the wind, she shouted back to them. "What do you think?"

Chris and the others gathered around her, and looked down over the edge.

To her surprise, Chris swallowed and retreated a step, his eyes widening. The others stood in varying states of fear, though none stood as close to the edge as Liz. To her right was the slope they had just climbed, but directly below the boulder, the gravel fell away in a sheer drop, all the way to the canyon floor two hundred feet below.

Looking down, Liz felt no fear, only a quiet resolve.

She would not go quietly back to her chains, to the cold cruelty of the doctors, to their needles and torture. She would not surrender to their bullets, to their harsh violence.

No, she would fight, she would resist, she would rage.

"You know," Ashley mused beside her. "They say birds just know. That their parents push them from the nest, and before they hit the ground, it comes to them."

"Care to go first?" Sam muttered.

Silence fell then as they stared out over the canyon, watching as the tiny specks of the guards came into view. They crawled towards them like ants, eyes searching the boulders strewn around them. But their gaze did not lift to where the seven of them stood, not yet. They were still a long way off, but they were closing quickly.

Shivering, Liz looked at the others.

They looked back, waiting.

Turning back to the edge, Liz sucked in a deep breath. Movement came from beside her as Chris stepped forward, his fingers reaching out to entwine with hers. He looked across at her, his face drained of colour. Naked fear stared from his eyes, but he smiled at her.

"Just like baby birds, right?" he tried to laugh, but it came out more as a shriek.

Liz nodded, her stomach swirling. Then she closed her eyes, and focused on the foreign appendages on her back, feeling their presence, embracing them. They were still alien to her, a violation of her body; but she needed them now, needed to embrace them as a part of her.

Concentrating, she willed them to open.

With a *crack* of unfurling feathers, the great black expanse of her wings snapped open. The others gasped, but beside her Liz sensed movement. She looked across to see the tawny brown of Chris's wings stretch out towards her own. She shivered as their wing tips met, their feathers brushing together.

Liz flashed one last look back at the others. They wore wide grins on their face now, and their eyes were alive with excitement. She grinned back, and with Chris beside her, turned to face the edge.

Together, they leapt out into the void.

THIRTY-SEVEN

CHRIS'S STOMACH LURCHED UP INTO HIS CHEST AS HE plunged from the edge. Below the ground raced up towards him at a terrifying speed, the jagged rocks looming large in his vision. Opening his mouth, he began to scream.

His wings gave a hard lurch, followed by a crack as they caught the air. Then he was soaring upwards, the wild wind catching in his twenty-foot wingspan, driving him up, up, up. His stomach twisted again, dropping sharply as the ground fell away. Chris let out another scream as he shot upwards and past the pale faces of his friends.

Concentrating, he focused on turning, beating his wings to counter the powerful drafts swirling around him, and risked a wave to those below. The others waved back, then with only a moment's hesitation, followed Chris and Liz off the cliff.

Chris swirled in the air, his wings twisting almost by a will of their own, and watched them plummet from the cluster of boulders. They dropped a dozen feet before their wings caught, halting their freefall and sending them hurtling back up into the sky. Broad grins split their faces, their eyes wild, their laughter echoing off the cliffs. In those briefest of moments, their hunters were forgotten, and there was only the joy of flight.

But it could not last. An ache had begun in the centre of his back, and already Chris could feel the strain in his chest and abdomen, the muscles pulling tight to keep his wings moving. With their broad expanse, there seemed to be no need for giant wing beats, but even the incremental adjustment of primary feathers and muscle was draining. Looking at the faces of the other, he could see the strain was beginning to affect them too.

The mist swirled around them, providing some cover from the guards below, or at least he hoped.

Sucking in a breath, Chris shouted across to the others, his words barely audible over the crack of air through their feathers. "We have to fly over the cliffs."

He had been studying the cliffs as the others gathered around them. They still towered above, their peaks tantalisingly out of reach. With the swirling winds doing their best to hinder them, it would take a massive effort to climb those last hundred feet. Glancing down, he searched again for the guards, and found them near the base of the rubble. They were looking up the rugged slope, but they still had not spotted them. Chris prayed they did not look up into the open air.

After all, who would have guessed they could fly?

Returning his attention to the cliffs, he willed himself upwards. Muscles strained and feathers shifted, and with a surge of elation he rose several feet. The others quickly followed him, their faces strained with concentration, their eyes fixed on the ledge above. It wasn't far, less than a hundred feet now, but the winds were shifting, fighting against them. And as they neared the top, the raging waters grew closer, soaking them through and stealing the last of the warmth from their bodies.

Still they pressed on, beating their wings in the thin air. Water accumulated in their feathers, weighing them down, but gritting his teeth Chris pressed on. His stomach tightened as muscles he had never used stretched and twisted, driving his wings forward, sending him upwards.

Bit by bit, the top of the cliffs drew closer.

When they were still thirty feet away, Chris risked a glance down, and swore.

The guards were staring up at them, pointing, their eyes wide and mouths open in shock. But already one was dropping to his knee, and the others quickly followed suit. Rifles were raised to shoulders and a gun barrel flashed. Almost three hundred feet above, the seven of them presented an easy target.

Without thinking, Chris's wings twisted, sending him whirling sideways, even as he screamed at the others.

"Look out!"

Then the air was alive with the screech of bullets. The others scattered like a flock of doves, flying outwards in all directions, though they strained to continue upwards. Up towards the clifftops, towards safety.

Straining for breath, Chris drove himself on, though every inch of his body was screaming. Threads of terror wrapped their way around him, but somehow he found the strength to hold on. His wings worked by instinct now, alive with the rush of desperation, driven by the need to escape.

Abruptly he found himself in clear air. One instant the whiz of bullets and howling wind was all around him, then it was gone. Looking down, he realised he had made it, that he had crossed the threshold of the cliffs. The canyon had disappeared from view, dropping away as he shot over the icy ground a few feet below, still tracking the stream upwards.

Glancing back, he watched Sam shoot up over the lip of the cliff and then dive towards the ground, quickly followed by Jasmine and Richard. They evened out about thirty feet from the ground and raced towards where Chris was pulling up and twisting to meet them. They wore wide grins on their faces, though their cheeks were red and their breath billowed out in clouds of vapour.

Chris looked past them, holding his breath, waiting for Ashley and Liz and the girl.

They appeared one by one, Liz, the girl, and finally, rising laboriously into sight, Ashley. Liz and the girl swept down towards them, but Ashley was struggling to maintain her height. Her wings were barely moving now, and her face was turning purple. She still hovered over the lip of the cliff, drifting slowly towards them, driving by sheer determination now.

Her eyes closed with sudden relief as she reached the clear air. Straightening out, her wings spread wide to catch the gentler breeze. A smile warmed her face as she looked across at them.

Then her smile faltered, her eyes widening as a shot echoed up from below. A red stain flowered in her chest and blood sprayed the air. Without a sound, Ashley's wings folded, and she plummeted to the icy ground.

THIRTY-EIGHT

ASHLEY LAY IN A TANGLED MESS OF LIMBS AND FEATHERS AND wings, her flesh torn and broken, her face buried in snow. The only signs she lived came from the slow rise and fall of her back, the low gurgling coming from her chest. She coughed, half-rolling to reveal her battered face. Blood seeped between her lips in a slow trickle, staining the snow beneath her.

She didn't move as they drew closer. Her eyes were closed, and there was little chance she could be conscious after the fall. Chris was shocked she was even alive; though he wasn't sure that was a blessing for her, or a curse. Her wings lay at awkward angles around her, and when he glanced at her legs he had to look away.

The bullet had taken her in the back and passed straight through her. Somehow it had missed her heart, but with the blood bubbling from her mouth, it appeared to have found a lung.

Another groan rattled from Ashley's chest, tearing at Chris's heart. He crossed the last of the distance between them and crouched beside her. Tears built in his eyes, but angrily he wiped them away. Reaching out, he grasped Ashley's hand and gave it a gentle squeeze.

"Ashley," he whispered as the others gathered around them. "Ashley, it's okay, we're here."

Ashley. Brave, bold, elegant. When he'd first laid eyes on her, he'd thought her fragile, a sheltered city girl incapable of standing up for herself. She had put those misconceptions to rest with her first words. And time and time again since. She had proven stronger than any of them, her will unquenchable.

And now she lay here on the side of a mountain, her blood staining the frozen earth, and there was nothing any of them could do to help her.

She was dying.

Stones crunched as Sam crouched beside him. Tears streamed down the larger boy's face. Stretching out a hand, he wiped the blood from Ashley's lips, as though the simple act might wake her, might bring her back to them. A sob tore from his chest as a fresh bubble of blood rose between her lips and burst.

He reached for her, as though to draw her into his arms, and then stopped. He crouched there with one arm outstretch, torn between his desperation to help her, and the fear he would only hurt her further.

The others stood around them in silence, each lost in their own thoughts.

Long minutes dragged by as they watched her struggle, her every breath a desperate fight for survival. They had time to spare now, though in truth all thought of escape had vanished. On the harsh mountainside, they sat by their friend and watched her life slip away.

But as minutes ticked towards an hour, Ashley still clung to life. Her body was torn and broken, her life-blood staining the snow red, but still she breathed, still she fought on.

Finally Chris knew they could wait no longer. Sucking in a breath, he stood. Tears stung his eyes as Liz joined him, sliding an arm beneath his shoulder. He looked at the others, saw the indecision in even Jasmine and Richard's eyes. They could not stand there waiting for her to die. And yet, they could not abandon her, could not let her last moments on this earth pass alone on this harsh mountainside.

He looked at the others, hating the question in their eyes. They wanted him to make a decision, though he was not quite sure when he'd become the leader. It felt strange, especially given Richard and Jasmine's animosity. But there was no time to debate it now.

"We can carry her," Chris whispered at last.

"No," Sam croaked, surprising him. The young man looked up at him, his eyes red with tears, and shook his head. "No, you can't bring her with you. She'll only slow you down."

"We can't leave her," Liz said.

Sam closed his eyes, a shudder going through him. "I know," he breathed.

Chris stared at him, a tightness growing in his stomach. "What do you want to do, Sam?"

"Go, Chris," Sam looked up at them, resolution shining from his eyes. "Go. Take the others with you. Leave, fly away, be free. I'll look after her," his voice broke as he finished, but there was iron in his words.

Looking down at Sam, Chris wondered at his courage. He opened his mouth to argue, to convince him to come with them, that they could carry her, keep her comfortable until…

"Maybe they can save her…" Sam finished.

With those five words, Chris realised they would never change Sam's mind. He meant to sacrifice himself for Ashley. He would give away his freedom, his life if there was the slightest chance she might live. Looking at her, Chris tried and failed to summon the same hope. Between the bullet and the fall, there was little left of the graceful girl he had known.

But still she fought on, her iron will unyielding. And thinking of the miracles the facility had performed on them, he wondered if Sam might be right.

At last he nodded. In his arms, Liz began to tremble, but he pulled her tight before she tried to argue further. She glanced up at him, anger burning in her eyes, but he only shook his head.

This was Sam's decision to make. His alone.

Jasmine and Richard glanced at each other, their shoulders slumped. Whatever their history with Ashley and Sam,

Chris doubted they had ever wished for this. Perhaps they would even miss his comedic presence.

"Good luck, Sam," Chris said, swallowing hard.

Sam nodded and then turned back to Ashley. With the utmost care, he slid his hands under her back and lifted her into his arms. She gave a tiny groan as she left the ground, seeming to shrink beside Sam's massive frame. Her head lifted, her eyelids fluttering, before she nestled her head into the crook of Sam's arm and grew still.

Gently, Jasmine and Richard helped tuck the shattered mess of Ashley's wings into Sam's arms. Then they stood in silence as Sam moved back towards the cliffs. His copper wings slowly spread as he walked towards the edge, his back straight, his gaze fixed straight ahead. He did not look back as he reached the edge. Without hesitating, stepped out into open air.

They stood for a moment after he had disappeared, waiting for the gunfire, praying he would reach the ground safely. But they did not go to the edge. They did not watch.

Chris didn't know about the others, but he could not bear to see Sam return to his chains.

Finally Chris wiped the tears from his eyes and faced the others. They stood shivering in the cold mountain air, their eyes red, their faces pale. Even so, they faced him, waiting.

But there was only one thing left for them to do now.

Fly.

PART TWO

THIRTY-NINE

CHRIS GASPED AS HE GRABBED AT THE LIP OF THE CLIFF AND hauled himself over the edge. Rolling clear of the hundred-foot drop, he shivered as icy fingers of air cut through the rips in his shirt. Grimacing, he looked at the red grazes on his bare feet and hands. The frozen rock had been merciless, unforgiving of the slightest mistakes. But with the wind whirling about the mountaintop, there had been no other choice.

A dull ache started to throb in the back of his head as he settled down on the rocky escarpment and looked out over the valley they had just traversed. Beyond his desolate perch, the mountains stretched out around him, their ice-capped peaks soaring up into the swirling clouds. Cliffs peeked out between the snowy blanket, their rocky faces pockmarked and broken, while in the valley below shattered rock lay embedded in the barren earth. A frozen stream carved its way through the valley, its crystal surface as clear as day from Chris's vantage point far above. The wind howled as it raced between the peaks, and the mountains echoed with the distant rumble of falling snow. Every so often he heard the sharp *crack* of breaking rock or ice, and he would flinch, expecting the bullets to follow.

Chris sat for a long time watching the valley, checking for signs of their pursuers. The broken rocks of the peak would make him all but invisible to anyone below, but even so he felt exposed on the rocky escarpment. He suppressed a shudder, imagining a black-garbed huntsman staring down the sights of his rifle, lining him up, pulling the trigger.

Closing his eyes, Chris took a breath and shoved the fear aside. He couldn't afford the luxury of panic now – none of them could. Somewhere out there, Doctor Halt and his people were hunting for them. And Halt had already shown he would do whatever it took to stop them.

Tears burned Chris's eyes as he remembered Ashley falling, saw her blood spraying the air and her broken body crumpling to the rocks. And Sam, lifting her into his arms, carrying her back to the torment they had just escaped – on the impossible hope she might be saved.

Angrily, Chris reached up and wiped away the tears before they turned to ice. Allowing his vision to clear, he looked out over the valley for a second longer. But there was no sign of movement, no hint of life amidst the desolate mountains, and breathing a sigh of relief he slid backwards out of the wind.

Retreating to the cliff he had climbed, he lowered himself over the side and began his descent. A hundred feet below, the others would be watching him from their ledge, but he did not look down. After the week-long flight through the mountains, his chest and abdomen ached constantly, and sharp pains prickled at the small of his back when he inhaled. It was almost a relief to use his arms and legs for a change.

Even so, his strength was flagging, starved away by the sparse meals of moss they had resorted to eating in their desperation. Only once in the last week had they eaten well – when Richard had spotted a fish trapped in a frozen pool. The ice had been difficult to break, and they had eaten it raw, but it had given them the strength to continue another day.

Since escaping the facility they had travelled west through the mountains, as near as they could tell. For the first few days, they had climbed higher into the mountains, up long gorges and narrow passes, until now, finally, they seemed to have reached the peak. Below, a new valley sloped down to the west, its floor falling gently away as it wound its way through the mountains. Beyond waited civilisation, the wide expanses of the Western Allied States.

Not that they knew what they'd do once they got there.

For Chris at least, one thought drove him on more than any other – to find his mother, and save her. He had not seen her since that night in San Francisco, so many countless weeks and months ago now, when police had come and spirited them away. His mother had been accused of treason – a death sentence for her and her immediate family. But that didn't mean she was gone.

It couldn't.

Gritting his teeth, Chris forced his thoughts back to the climb. The rock was slick with ice and the weight of his injuries would have slowed anyone else. But after all they had been through, the depraved experiments, the torture and imprisonment, Chris was beyond the pain now. He moved down the cliff without effort, his fingers gripping to the smallest of cracks, his toes finding the tiniest footholds. Holding his own weight no longer bothered him, the exertion of the climb was no more than a brief inconvenience. The doctors in the facility had succeeded beyond their wildest dreams.

If only it had been worth the cost.

Unbidden, a boy's face rose through the darkness of Chris's thoughts, his features distorted with agony, his limbs flailing as he thrashed on the floor of a padded room. A woman stood over him, a thin grimace on her lips, a metallic jet-injector clenched in one hand.

The image faded, only for a fresh memory to take its place. He saw again Angela Fallow's body, sprawled on the laboratory floor, blood oozing from the bullet wound in her chest. And Halt, standing over her, the gun still clutched in his fist. A well of hatred opened within Chris, fuelled by the vile, despicable things the man had done to bend them to his will.

If not for Angela, they would still be his, trapped in their cages, helpless to defend themselves against his depravity. She had freed them, opened the cells, unlocked the collars, given them back their lives.

And she had died for it.

Chris's stomach lurched suddenly as he missed his next foothold. Cursing, he scrambled for purchase, his weight falling onto his only hand-hold. The sharp rocks sliced into his fingers, and instinctively they loosened. With a shout, he fell backwards into empty space.

In that instant, time seemed to slow. His heart beat hard in his chest as he scanned the rock, spying out a fresh set of holds. Twisting in the air, his hands flashed out to catch them, even as his feet settled back into a groove in the rock. He pulled himself close to the rock face and let out a long breath.

Nice moves, Chris could almost hear Sam's voice, rich with wry humour. Swallowing, he fought back tears and continued his climb down. When he was still a dozen feet above the ledge, he released the rock and fell the rest of the way. He dropped to his knees as he landed, and then straightened to look around at the others.

Their faces were pale with cold and exhaustion, their eyes ringed by shadows. They looked at him expectantly. For close to a week they had travelled in near silence, their conversation dimmed by what they had lost, by their own private torments, and the buzz of distant helicopters. He had expected it from Jasmine and Richard – they young couple had been nothing but antagonistic since the day he'd met them.

Yet even Liz had been distant, as though the weight of everyone they'd left behind hung between them.

He looked at her now, finding her blue eyes behind the tangles of black hair. They showed the same faraway look of the past few days, and he forced himself to look away as doubts rose inside him.

Jasmine stood beside Liz with her arms crossed, her brown eyes hard and her straight black hair billowing out in the wind. Her tanned skin matched Liz's, but at five foot five she was taller than Chris's feisty cellmate. Jasmine stood shoulder to shoulder with Richard, in stark contrast to his short blond hair and pale skin. Both wore their trademark grimace, their brows creased by scowls.

Pursing his lips, Chris ignored their animosity and allowed his eyes to search for the fifth member of their little party. His stomach twisted as he found the young girl sitting on the edge of the ledge. They were not even halfway down the cliff here, and her legs dangled out over a five-hundred-foot drop. Her grey hair swirled in the breeze and while he could not see her face, he could still picture her strange multi-coloured eyes, one green, the other blue.

A shudder went through him as he turned back to the others. The girl could be no older than thirteen. He could not begin to imagine how she had survived the facility. But they were no closer to getting any answers from her. For the last week, she had remained stubbornly mute, and they still did not even know her name.

Letting out a long breath, Chris finally spoke. "There's no sign of anyone behind us," the wind howled around them, stealing away his voice. Here in the mountains it never ceased, and not for the first time he wished for more than the thin rags Angela had provided them. "It looks like we've reached the top. If we keep heading west, I think we'll start to descend now."

"Good," Jasmine said. "I'm sick of the cold."

Chris caught a flicker of irritation in Liz's eyes, but she only nodded. "Should we push on further today, or find a place to camp for the night?"

Chris glanced past them to where the sun still hung between the towering peaks. The ache in his back gave a sharp throb, the pain radiating out into his chest like the threads of a spider's web. His muscles were stiff and his stomach rumbled with hunger. Silently he wondered how much longer they could last, before their altered bodies finally reached the limits of their endurance. But there were still several hours of daylight left. They could not afford to waste them.

"Let's push on," gritting his teeth, Chris moved past them.

He paused at the edge of the ledge and glanced across at the girl. She sat in silence, her strange eyes watching him. Shaking his head, he turned away, trying not to show his discomfort. The new valley stretched away to the west, twisting past the sharp escarpment on which they were perched. The rocky spire made the perfect lookout, though for an ordinary human it would have taken long hours to climb. And when they reached the top, they would have faced only a long, treacherous climb back down.

The five of them did not have that problem.

Staring out into the distance, Chris's keen eyes picked out the distant patches of tussock grass and broken boulders scattering the slopes. Low cloud drifted here and there, but for the most part the air was clear, his view unobstructed. The valley stretched out for miles, finally ending in a distant wall of rock.

Turning his mind inwards, Chris focused on the ache in his back. A twitch ran through him, radiating out through his back, waking his body for action. Bones ached and muscles stretched as he readied himself.

Looking down at the five-hundred-foot drop, Chris tried to suppress the old tingles of fear that rose in his chest. Even after all this time, he still struggled to suppress his terror. But heights held no sway over him now, and clenching his fists he sucked in another breath.

Movement came from Chris's left, and he glanced across to see Liz step up beside him. Her eyes caught his, and she flashed him a quick grin. No more than a brief twist of her lips, shy and uncertain, but it was more emotion than she'd shown him in days. He smiled back, feeling warmth seeping back into his heart, pushing back the terrors of the last week.

Turning back to the edge, Chris closed his eyes, and stepped out into empty space.

His stomach lurched into his chest as he began to fall. Icy air roared past his ears, and opening his eyes, he saw the barren earth rushing up towards him. He turned his head as a wild scream came from beside him, and found Liz nearby, a mad joy dancing in her crystal blue eyes.

Together, they plummeted towards the rocky ground.

Grinning, Chris returned his attention to the ache in his back. His whole body burned now, the rush of adrenaline lighting up every fibre of his being. He could feel the ache spreading, tingling outwards into the foreign flesh and bone that sprouted from his back. With an eager laugh, he willed them to life.

With a sharp *crack*, his wings snapped open. His stomach lurched again as twenty-four feet of feathers caught the air, and sent him soaring into the sky. The earth fell away as the wind rustled his tawny brown feathers.

A surge of joy filled Chris's chest as he looked out over the valley floor. Boulders and cliffs flashed past, as from his right came the thump of another set of wings. He looked across as Liz fell into formation, her jet-black feathers stretching out towards his own. Warmth spread to his stomach as they touched.

From behind came the familiar crack of unfurling wings as the others followed.

FORTY

Sam groaned as the first tingle of consciousness tugged at his mind. He fought against it, clinging to the dark cloud of oblivion, desperate for its cold, numbing comfort. But slowly the light trickled in, casting out the black, dragging him back to reality, and the agony of his body.

He winced as lances of fire twisted in his muscles, and another groan tore from his lips. A low gurgle started in his chest and made its way up his throat, until the metallic taste of blood filled his mouth. Rolling onto his side, he spat it onto the concrete. He swallowed hard, and felt the cold steel collar pressing against his throat.

Lying there with his eyes closed, his memory started to return. He saw again Ashley's fall, her wondrous white wings folding in on themselves as she plummeted to the snowy ground. He remembered lifting her broken body into his arms, his whispers as he begged her to fight, to live. Then the short flight from the cliffs, his wings straining hard to keep them both aloft, the ground rising up to meet him.

And the guards waiting, their rifles held at the ready, watching their approach.

They had taken Ashley from him the moment he landed. Sam had made no effort to resist – the doctors in the facility were the only ones who could help her now. After securing Ashley, the guards had turned their attention on him. The hulking captain had stepped forward and slammed his rifle into Sam's stomach, driving the air from his lungs. As he crumpled, something hard had struck the back of his head, toppling him to the ground. Steel-capped boots had descended on him then, smashing him in the face and ribs, slamming into his back and crunching the fragile feathers of his wings.

Unable to defend himself, Sam had curled into a ball and waited for death. Finally, a blow had caught him in the side of the head, and he'd gladly given way to the darkness that rose to claim him.

Hours later he had woken in this room, to a group of hard-faced men in suits standing over him. At his first signs of movement, two guards had sprung forward and pulled him to his knees. His head still spinning from the beating, Sam had met their questions with stony silence.

Who was Angela Fallow working with?

How did she free you?

Where are they going?

His refusals to answer had been answered by fists. A blow had caught him in the forehead and sent him reeling side-ways. But as he tried to roll free of the guards, the collar around his neck had pulled him up short. Only then had he noticed the short length of chain connecting his collar to a bolt in the ground. Helpless, he had looked up in time to catch a hard boot in the side of his face.

For days now his captors had tormented him, until he no longer knew whether it was day or night. Time lost all meaning – only the presence of his tormentors mattered. Sometimes they left him alone for long hours – at others they seemed to reappear within minutes. Drifting in and out of consciousness, Sam found his senses crumbling, his sanity falling away.

Images flashed through his mind, some faster than thought, while others lingered, tormenting him. He saw Ashley standing in their cell, the familiar smile on her face, her movements lithe and graceful. Then he would see her lying still, her face a pallid grey, her eyes empty.

Other visions followed, filling his mind, tormenting him with the horrors of the past. He watched again the boy convulsing on the training field as Halt stood over him, smelt the stench of death and decay in the medical room, saw the blood staining the walls of the padded room.

Saw the blood on his hands, and his friend, lying still on the ground.

Saw the accusing stares of Jasmine and Richard.

Gritting his teeth, Sam pushed away the memories and pulled himself to his knees. He winced as the chain went taught, causing the collar to cut into his flesh. The chain was so short he could not stand – only crouch on his hands and knees. His muscles ached from disuse and a constant pain ran down his spine. A sharp twinge came from his ribs with each intake of breath. The air whistled through his broken nose, and his stomach cramped with a ravenous hunger.

Sam's heart started to race as he caught the faint click of the door handle. His left eye was so swollen he could barely see through it, but he forced his right to open and look around. The harsh light burned, but slowly the room came into focus. Other than a plain steel chair that sat just out of reach, the room was unadorned, the plain white walls and concrete marked only by his blood.

Beyond the chair, the only door stood open, as two guards pushed their way into the room. Sam watched them approach, and take up stations on either side of the chair, before turning his attention back to the doorway.

His stomach lurched as Doctor Halt stepped into the light. He shrank back as the doctor's cold grey eyes found him on the floor. Days without food or sleep had stolen away his strength, and now even the brief task of sitting up left him gasping. He sucked in a mouthful of air, and faced the doctor.

"Samuel," Halt's voice slithered through the air, "you disappoint me."

Stalking across the room, Halt lowered himself onto the chair and crossed one leg over the other. His long black pants and white lab coat were immaculate – a stark contrast to the filthy rags that covered Sam. The doctor's brow creased and his thin lips pursed as he looked down at Sam.

Looking into Halt's hard grey eyes, Sam failed to supress a shudder. There was no hint of compassion in the doctor's expression.

Finally, Halt leaned back in his chair. Tapping one finger against his elbow, he spoke. "Fallow has caused us a considerable setback, Samuel," he looked around the room, slowly shaking his head. "The President wants answers – answers we do not currently possess."

Sam bit his lip and looked away. An image flickered through his mind – of Angela Fallow sprawled on the laboratory floor, her life blood pooling around her. He tasted bile in his throat and swallowed hard.

"Samuel, you must see the folly of protecting her," Halt whispered, his voice cutting through Sam's thoughts. "The woman is dead. Just tell us who aided her, and this torment will cease. You will be moved to more comfortable facilities, provided with regular meals. Just give us what we want."

Closing his eyes, Sam almost wished he had the answers Halt wanted. But in the scant minutes they had spent in the medical room, he had never asked how Angela had freed Chris and Liz, or why. He'd been too preoccupied with other things – like why wings had suddenly sprouted from his back.

Sam looked up and forced a smile. "Look," he coughed out the word, then turned his head and spat out a gob of bloody spit. "I wish I could help you, Halt. The woman called me fat. Believe me, I'd sell her out in an instant, if I could."

A weary look passed across Halt's face. "So you say," he turned his head, staring at the grey wall, as though there was more to its plain surface than met the eye. There wasn't – Sam had spent enough time staring at the blank walls to know that. Shaking his head, Halt went on, talking almost to himself. "The survivors of the A-strain will have to suffice. They're all we have, for now."

Sam's heart lurched. "Ashley," he wheezed, his fingers clawing at the concrete. "She's not…"

Halt's lips twitched. "How quaint, that the two of you formed a bond," he waved a hand. "The girl is recovering."

Tears stung Sam's eyes as he bowed his head. He gave a low sob – one of pure relief, that Ashley lived, that his sacrifice had not been in vain. The weight of the chain around his neck grew the faintest bit lighter.

Shivering, Sam looked up at Halt, his vision blurring. "Thank you."

Halt only shook his head. "I did what was necessary," his voice was cold, "Thanks to the damage caused by Doctor Fallow, we are short on resources. The President is demanding a demonstration of our success. We will need as many healthy candidates as possible to ensure the survival of the project."

Swallowing hard, Sam looked up into Halt's eyes, and felt his sudden hope wither and die. He clenched his fists, summoning his last reserves of defiance. "I won't help you, Halt."

Doctor Halt stared at him a moment, and then slowly pulled himself to his feet. "A shame," he shook his head, a harsh smile spreading across his face. "You don't really think they will escape, do you, Samuel?"

Sam looked back up as Halt turned and moved to the door. Pulling it open, he glanced back. "If so, you are mistaken. Our hunters will have them soon. Perhaps I will have them join you in here," Halt spoke harshly as he turned to the guards who still stood on either side of the chair. "For now, I will entrust you to the care of these gentlemen. When you're ready to cooperate, do let me know."

With a swirl of his lab coat, Halt was gone. The hulking guards stepped forward as the door slammed shut behind the doctor. Grim smiles spread across their faces as they drew steel batons from their belts.

Sam looked up as the two men closed on him, the defiance withering on his tongue. He shrank away, but the chain brought him up short, leaving him crouched helpless on the ground. A low groan rose in his throat, and he fought the urge to beg for their mercy.

As one raised his baton, Sam closed his eyes, and waited for the pain to resume.

FORTY-ONE

DARKNESS PRESSED IN ALL AROUND, ENCASING HER, LOCKING her away from the light. Liz struggled against it, flailing at unseen tendrils, desperate to break free. But her hands found only empty air, and when she opened her mouth to scream, darkness poured down her throat, suffocating her cries.

An instant later the scene changed. A dull black surface formed beneath her feet, though the darkness still pressed in all around. A long, beastly howl echoed from somewhere in the pitch-black. The sound sent tingles of fear racing down her spine. She started to run, then sprint through the darkness, as scrambling footsteps came from somewhere behind her.

The howl came again, conjuring up spectres of the unseen beast. A desperate cry tore from her lips as she slipped on the smooth surface. Scrambling for purchase, Liz raced on, her mind spinning out of control, her thoughts panicked.

But however hard she ran, the footsteps behind still grew nearer, the howling louder.

Heart pounding, Liz gasped for air. She could feel the beast approaching, could sense its very presence. Fear flooded her, robbing her of strength. Her chest burned, her lungs screamed for air. Step by step, her pace slowed.

At last she could go no further. Panting, Liz drew to a stop, and great sobs tore from her throat. She turned to face the swirling darkness, and waited for the beast to appear.

The darkness boiled around her, spreading like a cloud, reaching out to touch her. She flinched and scrambled back, and with the movement the fog parted, giving way to the approaching footsteps.

Liz moaned as a woman stepped into view. Her skin was a pale white, the scarlet locks of her hair stained with darkness. Her lips were twisted with hate, and her tawny yellow eyes glowed in the pitch-black. Great white wings beat hard on her back, sending the darkness swirling out towards Liz.

Frozen with fear, Liz stood fixed in place as Ashley stepped forward. Her fingers bent in claws as she reached out and caught Liz by the shirt. In one movement, she lifted Liz into the air. A wild snarl slid from Ashley's lips as she raised a fist.

"You left me!"

With a half-muffled scream, Liz tore herself from the dream and sat bolt upright. For a moment the swirling darkness clung to her, choking her, filling her with panic. Then her gaze found the jewelled stars stretching across the night sky, and the bright glow of the half-moon, and she let out a long breath.

Clutching her chest, Liz willed her heart to slow. She shivered as she recalled Ashley's face in the dream – the pallid grey of her skin, the darkness clinging to her. Silently, she wondered whether it was an omen, whether her friend had truly passed from the light.

Was your sacrifice for nothing, Sam?

Wrapping her arms around her chest, Liz banished the thought. Her wings rustled and tightened around her, sealing in the warmth. She smiled then. The alien presence of the strange limbs faded more each day, settling into the rhythms of her body. Flight was becoming easier, her muscles slowly learning to cope with the strain, though her chest and abdomen still ached at the end of each day.

Hunger was their most pressing concern now. They had hardly eaten since escaping the facility a week ago, and the pangs of her empty stomach were quickly sapping her strength. The fish Richard had found in a frozen pool had saved them, but Liz wasn't sure whether she could last until they got lucky again.

Finally, as all thought of sleep had left her, Liz pulled herself up and moved away from the others. Her stomach gave another growl, and she placed a hand over it, willing it to silence. Tomorrow she hoped they would reach the mountain forests. There she would know where to forage for food, for berries and grubs and edible roots. In the harsh alpine tussock she was out of her depth, but the forest she knew well.

Moving across the rubble-strewn slope, Liz headed towards the distant chatter of the stream. Despite the darkness, her eyes easily made out the edges of rocks and boulders. Though the half-moon was bright, she knew such eyesight was not natural. She had spent enough time walking the countryside at night to know she should be struggling to find her way through the field of boulders. Yet now she threaded easily between them.

She could picture the stream now, its white waters cascading between the boulders. Until today, the rivers they'd passed had been frozen solid. But it seemed they had finally descended low enough to escape the ice.

Her thoughts turned to Chris as she continued across the barren ground. They had hardly spoken since the day Ashley had fallen. Almost unconsciously at first, Liz had found herself raising old walls around her heart, distancing her from the boy. Now she could feel the lonely gulf that spanned between them, and sadness touched her. She mourned for Ashley and Sam, but she did not want to lose Chris too.

A few minutes later she drew to a stop on the banks of the creek. Her feet ached from the cold, though they had slowly toughened over the last few days. Shivering, she looked down at the stream. Here the bank was only a few feet high, with piles of smooth gravel pushed up around its base. The opposite bank was maybe fifteen feet away, though the waters themselves were just a few feet wide.

Lit by the moonlight, the stream swirled over its rocky bed, the current fast and uninviting. But further upstream, Liz caught a glimpse of calm water, a pool where the creek widened. When she'd left the others, Liz had had the vague idea of splashing water on her face. But now she felt the urge to submerge herself, to allow the icy waters to wash away her nightmares.

Slipping off her shirt, Liz clenched her teeth against the mountain breeze and quickly kicked off her pants. Moving to the edge of the pool, she slid one toe into the water, and gasped as it immediately went numb. Already regretting the idea, she pressed on, her wings folded close against her back. Step by step, she moved into the pool, moaning as the water reached her knees, then waist, then chest. Finally, when Liz could barely breathe for the cold, she ducked beneath the surface.

Two minutes later Liz returned to the bank, teeth chattering, panting for breath, the oxygen sucked from her lungs by the icy waters. Goosebumps stood up along her arms and legs, and her waterlogged wings weighed heavily on her back. A shiver spread down their length, and her feathers stood on end to shake the water free. Silently Liz rushed to her clothes, desperate for their scant warmth. Another tremor went through her wings, sending a spray of water into the air.

Smiling, Liz pulled her wings tight against her back again, and slipped her shirt over her head. As it settled into place, she allowed her wings to relax again, and they extended out through the holes she'd cut in the back of her shirt. Then she scrambled into her underwear and pants, eager for their warmth. Though her skin was still damp, they at least offered some protection from the wind.

As she turned to face the water again, a rattle of stones came from overhead. She froze at the sound, before a voice called down from overhead.

"How's the water?"

FORTY-TWO

Slowly turning her head, Liz found Richard perched on the bank above her. Warmth spread to her cheeks, before her brow knitted into a furious scowl. Unsure how much he'd seen, Liz crossed her arms and raised an eyebrow, trying to hide her embarrassment.

"Enjoy the show?" she growled.

Shaking his head, Richard jumped from the rock and landed lightly beside her. He moved past, his eyes looking up at the moon. "Sorry, I didn't look," he murmured, taking a seat on a boulder beside the river. "I was just… walking."

Liz ground her teeth together, struggling to control her rising anger. A red glow flashed across her eyes as she clenched her fists. She fought the urge to pick him up and hurl him into the water. But Richard sat with his back to her, seemingly ignorant to her rage, and after a long moment she let out her breath. Even through her anger, she sensed a difference about Richard.

"What happened to him?" Richard finally murmured, still staring up at the sky. "To Joshua?"

The tide of Liz's anger retreated, as cold fingers of guilt rose to take its place. She bit her lip, the horror of her fight with the boy Joshua rushing back. She saw him again atop her, felt his fingers wrapping around her throat, the burning in her lungs. Glancing away from Richard, she reached down and picked up a stone, then tossed it across the pool. It skipped twice before landing on the other side of the stream.

"I killed him," she replied at last, "Not the doctors, or the guards. I did it."

From the corner of her eye, she saw Richard nod. "I thought so," from his tone, Liz guessed that would be the end of the conversation, but he continued, "I saw the marks on your neck, when you walked past our cell. What happened?"

Blood pounding in her ears, Liz moved across and seated herself next to the boy. They sat in silence for a while, staring at the glistening waters, as she turned the memories over in her mind. Then slowly, reluctantly, she recounted the fight. How she had struck Joshua down in the first minutes, and thought him beaten. How he had taken her by surprise, caught her and overpowered her before she could scramble free. And how she had killed him with one final, desperate blow.

Beside her, Richard said nothing as Liz spoke. When she finally finished, the silence resumed, marked only by the whisper of the river as it tumbled over its stony bed. Strangely, Liz felt a weight lifting from her chest with the confession. She had not spoken to anyone but Chris about Joshua, and even then, she had not told him the full story.

She had expected Richard to rage at her when she finished, to scream and shout, accuse her of murder. Joshua had been his cellmate, presumably his friend. But he said nothing, just sat quietly beside her, watching the water as it made its long journey through the mountains towards the distant coast.

"I'm sorry," she said at last.

Richard shrugged. "We weren't close," his eyes flashed in her direction, "After what happened last time, Jasmine and I weren't keen to bond with the newbies."

Liz swallowed at the despair in Richard's eyes. She wanted to ask more, to discover the truth behind their feud with Sam and Ashley, but the words stuck in her throat.

"We were all close in the beginning, the eight of us," Richard seemed to pluck the questions from her mind, "We were in separate cells from Ashley and Sam and the… others, but we spent time on the training field together. That was before things got bad, before people started to die."

"How long were you there for?" Liz managed to croak.

"Eight weeks before you lot showed up," he replied. "For the first three weeks, there were no deaths. Then things changed, the doctors became more urgent, pushed us harder. They started taking us away in twos…" his voice trailed off as he swallowed. "Faces began to go missing."

"And then they came for you?"

Richard nodded. "It wasn't until I ended up in that padded room with Jeremy that I realised how evil the doctors were, how perverse. We refused at first, when the voice told us to fight. But they made us, made me…" his voice broke off as he started to sob.

"You killed him," Liz murmured.

Richard did not look up. "He was my friend," his voice was filled with self-loathing, "I told them I'd rather die. But those damn collars… and then Jeremy…"

Tears streamed down Richard's face. Silently, Liz reached out a hand and squeezed his shoulder. A shiver went through him, spreading to the dark green wings that hung limply from his back.

After a long pause, Richard sucked in a breath and continued. "Jeremy refused to play their games. I'll never forget his face, when he looked at me that last time. He had a sad smile on his lips, but his eyes… there was no give in them. He shook his head, then turned and walked across to the one-way mirror. Before anyone could react, he slammed his head into the glass," Richard swallowed, his voice trembling. "He did it three times before the guards reached him. They tackled him to the ground, but by then he barely had the strength to stand. The mirror was covered in his blood. It didn't take long for the doctor to come."

Liz closed her eyes, imagining the scene, the horror. Chris had told her what had happened when his opponent in the padded room could no longer fight. A doctor had entered and given the boy a lethal injection. He had died writhing in agony.

"You didn't kill him, Richard," she whispered. "His blood is on their hands."

Richard's green eyes turned to watch her. They glinted in the moonlight, and she quickly looked away, unable to face the despair lurking in their depths. "You and Chris, you have no idea what it's like. You didn't know Joshua and William, when you were forced to fight them. It was different for us. We had faced the horrors of the facility together, suffered hand in hand against whatever those monsters threw at us. And then to stand there, to face that choice. No, I didn't kill him," Richard let out a long, shuddering breath, "but I would have. And I think he knew that."

Silence met his words. Liz stared up at the sky, unable to find an answer, to comprehend the guilt and sorrow warring within the boy beside her. Her own fight had been simple – it had been his life, or her own. Richard was right – Joshua had been a stranger to her. It should not have made her decision easier, but it did.

Finally, she spoke again, "It was the same for Ashley and Sam. You must know that? So why do you hate them?"

"Hate them?" Richard shook his head. "I don't hate them. They did what they had to too survive, just like the rest of us. No, I can't face them, because every time I look at their faces, I see Jeremy again, standing there, sacrificing his life for mine. I can't face them, because all they do is remind me what happened, of what I would have done to save my own life."

"But when Ashley fell…"

A shiver went through him then, and his voice broke as he spoke. "We were dead to each other a long time ago, Liz," he breathed. "But, in truth, I didn't have the courage to say goodbye."

On an impulse, Liz reached out and wrapped her arms around Richard. The boy crumpled at her touch, his strength failing him. She pulled him tight against her, feeling his sorrow, his silent sobs as he buried his head in her shoulder.

When Richard finally pulled away, he could not meet her eyes. "Thank you," he whispered. Slowly, he recovered his composure. "I guess, in the end, it won't matter. We'll all end up like her, one way or another."

Liz flinched at the bitterness in Richard's voice. Icy fingers wrapped around her throat, like the ghost of the collar she had once worn. Ashley's face from the dream appeared in her mind, the accusing eyes, the pallid grey fingers reaching for her. Pushing down against the rock, she stood.

"No," Liz breathed, closing her eyes, drawing in a mouthful of fresh air. She concentrated on her wings, felt them lift and stretch, until the black feathers tingled in the soft breeze. Looking down at Richard, she shook her head. "They won't catch me. They won't take me back. I'd rather die."

Richard only gave a sad smile. "Brave words, but how long will they last? How long will any of us last against them? They're after us now – Halt, the guards, the government, *everyone*. They'll come for us with everything they have. We've kept ahead of them in the mountains, but out there," he waved a hand down the valley, "in the lowlands, in the cities, that's *their* territory."

"The cities might belong to them, but the countryside is *mine*," Liz growled. Clenching her fists, she looked out over the mountains. "Out here, the government is not the power it pretends to be in the cities. The Western Allied States are huge – they cannot be everywhere, see everything. The people in the countryside tolerate them, because they have little choice, but there is no love lost for them. That's how I avoided them for so long."

Richard shrugged. "We're a little more conspicuous now. You know, with the wings and all."

Liz laughed softly. "There is that," she smiled, "But we can hide our wings. We'll find jackets or something. We can avoid the hunters, at least until the chase dies down."

"They'll follow us to the ends of the earth, Liz. We're a dark secret they want buried, especially in an election year. Even our wondrous Electors are bound to ask a few questions of the President if the truth comes out," Richard paused, "and besides, a life on the run doesn't sound like much of a life to me."

Liz shivered, remembering the long days and nights alone in the wild, the uncertainty, the fear of being caught. She had spent two years living that life, not knowing when the day would finally come that they found her. "No…" she whispered, "it's not. We need a way to fight back."

It was Richard's turn to chuckle. "Sure, let me know how that works out."

Pursuing her lips, Liz shook her head. "We'll find a way," she recalled Ashley's words from so long ago. "They're only human, Richard. They'll make a mistake."

Richard's emerald eyes found her in the darkness. "After all they've done, do you truly believe that?" he shook his head. "The things they've done to us, they're not possible Liz."

Shivering, Liz look away, the wings suddenly heavy on her back. Everything they had become, every extra ounce of strength, of agility they now possessed, was thanks to Halt and Angela and the other doctors. All seemed far beyond the realms of possibility. Liz's stomach clenched as she realised she had no response.

Silence fell then, as each drifted into the chaos of their own thoughts. Moving back to the boulder, Liz took her seat again. Together, they sat looking out over the mountains, watching as the glow of the new day slowly appeared over the distant peaks.

As the warm glow found her on the rock, Liz closed her eyes. Whatever had come before, today was a new day, and she was determined to make the most of it.

After all, who knew how many they had left?

FORTY-THREE

CHRIS SUCKED IN A BREATH, REVELLING IN THE ICY AIR filling his lungs. The wind howled around him, tugging at his lengthening hair and rustling in his feathers. His tawny brown wings stretched out on either side of him, their concave surface catching in the wind, sending him higher and higher, until the treetops were little more than specks far below.

A mile above the rugged ground, Chris watched the giant redwoods drift by. They stood in groves amongst their smaller relatives, towering above the rest of the forest, striving for glory. But their height meant nothing to Chris and Liz and the others. Their only rivals were the snow-capped mountains behind them. A cloudless sky extended around them, seeming to stretch away to infinity.

For a while, Chris allowed the others their wonder, savouring in the freedom of the open air. Just a short week ago, heights had been a terror to him, the thought of plum-meting helplessly to his death his greatest nightmare. But now he was the master of the sky, his fears caged, vanquished by the power of his wings.

Sadly, they could not remain in the open for long. Outside the jagged peaks, they were exposed in the empty sky. Though there had been little sign of pursuit in the mountains, they had heard the helicopters in the distance, and there was no doubt the government would be coming for them.

Folding his wings, Chris pulled into a dive and shot towards the distant trees. The air whistled around his ears and tore at his clothing as he gave a wild scream. Slowly, he eased his wings out a few inches, lifting his body slowly from the dive. As the trees closed, he allowed them to unfurl to their full length, and levelled out just above the canopy.

The others soon joined him, and together they drifted over the tree tops. Glancing around, Chris noticed even Jasmine wore a wild grin, her eyes alive with exhilaration. Chris allowed himself to glide lower, scanning the dense branches, searching for a way through. His chest burned and pain threaded its way down his back. He desperately needed to rest, and he doubted the others were any better off.

Spotting a gap, he headed towards it, struggling to retract his wings enough to fit through without going into freefall. Even so, he felt his descent accelerating as he aimed for the opening. Lurching in the air, a branch caught his arm, throwing him off balance. Then he was through, dropping into the open space beneath the canopy.

Looking down, he found himself still thirty feet above the ground and quickly spread his wings. His descent slowed, but he was still falling too quickly when he struck the ground. The shock of the impact took his feet out from underneath him, and he quickly rolled forward to break his fall.

Coming to a rest on his back, he picked himself up and brushed off the pine needles, hoping the others had not seen his uninspiring landing. Turning, his cheeks warmed as he found them standing nearby, watching him with amused grins on their faces.

Shaking his head, Chris flashed his best scowl. "And that, children, is how *not* to land."

Liz laughed. "Who are you calling children. Pretty sure half of us are older than you."

Chris shrugged and rolled his shoulders, trying to remove the knot that had collected in the muscles beneath his shoulder blades. His wings seemed to connect in some way to just about every muscle in his back, as well as those in his chest and abdomen. The collective strength of those muscles, along with their increased muscle density, seemed to provide the power they needed for flight.

Unfortunately, it also meant every inch of his torso burned at the end of each day's flight.

"How do we get back up?" Jasmine was looking at the canopy.

Where they stood on the forest floor, the hole in the trees was invisible. An army of tree trunks surrounded them, their red trunks straight and smooth as they stretched towards the hidden sky. Brown pine needles smothered the ground, and there was no trace of any undergrowth. Distantly, Chris recalled from biology class that chemicals from many redwood species leeched nutrients from the topsoil, preventing other plant species from colonising beneath them.

"I think we should go on foot for a while," he said at last. Their progress would be slow, but at least they would be hidden from prying eyes. "I don't think I can fly much farther without food, and it feels too exposed up there, out of the mountains."

"Well, what are we waiting for then?" Richard made a face, then turned and walked off through the trees. Jasmine followed him, the young girl silently shadowing her, leaving Liz and Chris staring after them.

Rolling his eyes, Chris flashed Liz a half-hearted grin and started after them. In truth, he was glad to relinquish the lead. He still wasn't quite sure how he'd ended up with the unofficial title of leader, but the weight of responsibility had quickly grown exhausting, and he could use the rest.

His heart warmed as Liz fell in beside him and reached out to take his hand. She flashed him a smile, her blue eyes shining with some hidden emotion. He found himself smiling back, the gesture genuine now.

"How are you feeling?" he asked.

Jasmine, Richard and the girl were pulling ahead of them, picking their way easily over the tree roots. But with Liz's warm fingers clutched around his hand, Chris felt no rush to catch up with them. Liz's sudden show of affection had stirred him from his melancholy, and he found himself thinking again of the night in the cell, when he had first fallen asleep in her bed.

Beside him, Liz shrugged. "I'm okay," she bit her lip and looked away, "I'm sorry I've been… distant."

Chris squeezed her hand and pulled her towards him. Sliding his arm around her waist, he held her close. He kissed the top of her head, breathing in the rich scent of her hair. She smiled up at him then, her head nestling in beneath his chin. They walked like that for a while, until it became too awkward to manage while avoiding the twisted roots and spider webs criss-crossing the undergrowth.

"How are your wings feeling?" he asked eventually.

At their mention, Liz's black wings lifted slightly, shivering in the air before settling back against her clothing. "Not too bad," Liz turned and winked at him. "I'm a bit lighter than you. Less work."

Laughing, Chris shook his head and bent himself to the task of keeping up with Richard. He had to admit, the boy set a cracking pace, and he was soon puffing hard in the morning air. The scent of the pine trees brought back memories of Christmas, and he found his thoughts drifting to more pleasant memories, to cold mornings beneath Christmas trees, opening presents with his mother and father.

Each lost in their own thoughts, they steadily made their way down through the foothills. Signs of life were everywhere now. Deep scars in nearby tree trunks showed where bears had marked their territory, some more than twice Chris's height. Dry pine needles crunched beneath their feet, warning the forest creatures of their approach. But Chris still caught flickers of movement from the corners of his eyes, as squirrels and mice ducked out of sight. The soft chirp of cicadas marked the end of

winter, and silently Chris wondered whether the world
had changed during the long months of their
imprisonment.

Towards sunset, the air beneath the trees filled with the buzz
of insects. The first chirps of the evening chorus soon
followed, as birds flitted through the air, darting between the
tree trunks as they chased their prey.

Without the sun or mountains for guidance, it was difficult
to judge their progress. But Chris guessed from the burning
in his thighs they'd walked several miles. It was a frustrating
pace after their rapid flight through the mountains, but
there was little they could do about it.

At least Liz had helped fill their empty stomachs. As they
walked she had collected berries and handfuls of nuts from
various trees and plants. At one point, she had even gathered a few fat white grubs from beneath the bark of a tree.
Hungry as he was, Chris had wolfed it all down without
question, though he had hesitated maybe half a second
longer with the grubs.

As darkness fell beneath the trees, they finally stopped for
the night, settling down in a shallow indentation in the
earth. It offered little in the way of protection, but it was the
best they could find beneath the trees. As they had done
every night since their escape, they set a watch, and one by
one drifted off to sleep.

A few hours later, Chris woke to a hand on his shoulder.
Blinking in the darkness, he found Liz sitting beside him, a
sly smile on her face. Before he could open his mouth, she
leaned down and pressed her lips to his. Still groggy from
sleep, he struggled to think as her fingers twisted in his hair.

Then he was kissing her back, hard and fast, his tongue darting out to taste her.

When she finally pulled away, Chris sucked in a breath. He reached out and pulled her close, his heart beating hard in his chest.

"Who's on watch?" he breathed.

"Richard," she smiled in the darkness. "He's over there. Come on," she stood, tugging at his hand.

Chris obeyed, staggering to his feet as she pulled him in the opposite direction of where Richard sat. With the thick canopy overhead, the darkness beneath the trees was complete, and even their heightened senses struggled to find a path. Still half-asleep, Chris stumbled along after Liz, barely able to keep up. But each time he slowed, she would look back, her eyes flashing in darkness, her eager smile drawing him onwards.

They managed maybe a dozen yards before Chris tripped over a tree root. Toppling forwards, he dragged Liz with him, and together they tumbled to the ground. They rolled across the soft bed of pine needles, their wings pulled tight against their backs, their laughter echoing beneath the canopy.

When they finally came to a stop, Chris found himself lying atop Liz. He stared down at her, wondering at the brightness of her sapphire eyes in the darkness, and found himself smiling again.

"Hey there," he smiled at her.

Giggling, Liz tried to wriggle free, but he refused to move, pinning her to the ground. Instead, he leaned down and kissed her. She stilled as their lips met, her hands no longer pushing him away, but wrapping around him, pulling him closer.

She let out a long breath when they parted, and laughed again. Then her wings beat suddenly against the ground, and she rolled, sending Chris toppling sideways. Before he could recover she leapt on his chest and straddled him.

"Gotcha," she laughed.

Chris grinned. Reaching up, he gently brushed a pine needle from her jet-black hair. Her eyes closed at his touch and her breath quickened. Silently, she reached up and pressed his hand to her cheek.

"Chris," she breathed.

Then she was leaning down, and her lips were pressing against his, and their hands were fumbling at their clothes. A white-hot fire swept through Chris, stealing away thought and reason, leaving only the burning of desire. Blood pounded in his ears as the buttons of his shirt gave way, and he felt the heat of Liz's hands on his chest. Need rose within him, and he fumbled at Liz's shirt. With an awkward, desperate wriggle, she pulled it over her head, leaving it tangled in the black feathers of her wings.

Chris sucked in a breath, his eyes devouring every inch of her naked body. Her crystal blue eyes shone in the darkness as she pulled him to her. Teeth nipped lightly at Chris's neck, and he moaned, wrapping his arms tight around her, feeling her naked flesh pressed against him.

Together they fell back to soft pine needles, bodies and wings entwined, the scent of the forest all around.

FORTY-FOUR

Darkness hung over the forest like a blanket, turning the pale trees to ghostly spectres. The dense canopy stretched overhead, the thick leaves and branches hiding even the brilliance of the half-moon. Not a breath of wind stirred the air, and only the far-off hoot of an owl broke the heavy silence.

Through the darkness came the soldiers – one, two, a dozen. They moved with measured steps, each movement taken with painstaking care, every man striving for silence. One wrong step, one twig broken beneath a careless boot, and they would be exposed. But these men were professionals, and they did not make mistakes.

Captain Scott's eyes scanned the shadows as he moved, seeking out the first sign of their quarry. Through the green glow of his night-vision goggles, he watched his men fan out around him, rifles held at the ready. In the darkness they were indistinguishable from one another, but all were his brothers. Each was a veteran of a dozen campaigns, with tours in foreign states as far afield as Texas and Spain.

Earlier in the day they had watched from their vantage point as their quarry emerged from the mountains and entered the dense woods below. With long range infrared sensors, they had tracked the groups slow progress through the trees, unwilling to act until the party stopped for the night and slept.

It had been a long wait, but ultimately their patience had been rewarded. Maps of the Californian mountains suggested this was one of three valleys the group could travel through. Teams were stationed at the exits to each valley, but Scott had never doubted theirs would be the one. And now it seemed his faith had been rewarded.

Aware of the enhanced nature of their prey, he had waited until well after midnight to order the final approach. The dossier he had been given suggested their prey's heightened sense of smell and hearing would warn them of the soldier's presence, but with the group asleep, he hoped to neutralise that advantage.

Shouldering his rifle, the captain edged forward as the first glow of a sleeping body came into view. He raised a hand, signalling to his men. Throughout the trees, all movement ceased. Scott waved to his two lieutenants, and together the three of them continued on. He kept the barrel of his gun trained on the sleeping figure as two more came into view. They were armed with M16 rifles loaded with 5.56mm calibre rounds. Their orders were to capture if possible – but lethal force had been authorised where necessary. Their orders came from the very top, and Scott had no intention of allowing embarrassment to fall on his superiors.

He paused when they were still a few feet away from the campsite, his eyes flickering around the clearing in sudden doubt. Through the ghostly tree trunks, he studied the three sleeping figures, and silently cursed under his breath.

Where were the other two?

On the ground, one of the bodies moved, shifting silently on a bed of pine needles. The glowing green blob lay slightly apart from the other two, and as Scott turned, he realised the figure lay slumped sideways against a tree. He smirked as he realised the boy had fallen asleep on watch. No soldier in his team would be caught performing such dereliction of duty.

Suddenly the figure straightened, sitting bolt upright against the tree. The head lifted, and Scott cursed as eyes turned to stare straight at him.

"*Go!*" he screamed through his earpiece.

FORTY-FIVE

CHRIS JERKED AWAKE AS A CRY BROKE THE NIGHT'S SILENCE. Struggling to sit up, he bit back a cry of his own as he found himself trapped in a tangle of limbs and feathers. He heard Liz curse from nearby as he tripped over a wing, before managing to get his extended limbs under control. Pulling his feathers tight against his back, he staggered to his feet.

In the darkness, he caught movement from beside him and spun. But it was only Liz, stumbling over her own wings, her eyes wide with fear as she climbed to her feet. He reached out and caught her arm, and for a moment she stilled.

Then the roar of gunfire sounded through the trees.

Together they spun towards the sound. In his sleep, Chris had lost all sense of direction, but there was no doubt in his mind that if they followed the noise, they would find the others. He glanced at Liz, finding her crystal eyes in the darkness. She nodded back, and they began to run.

Another gunshot echoed through the trees and Chris cursed under his breath. How had the hunters found them? But there was no time to ponder the question now. Ahead, he glimpsed shadows moving through the trees, the dark silhouettes of men as they closed on their campsite.

Leaping over a fallen tree, he gritted his teeth and picked up the pace. Liz landed softly beside him, her wings partly extended, her lips drawn back in a snarl. Branches cracked beneath their feet, but Chris took no notice now. The woods were alive with the sound of movement, with the crashing of heavy bodies converging in front of them.

Ahead, Chris's keen eyes made out the shadows of men standing in a circle. Without thinking, he leapt towards them. But Liz's hand flashed out and caught him by the wrist, holding him back, dragging him down behind a fallen tree. She raised a finger to her lips as Chris opened his mouth to argue, and the words died on his tongue.

Silence fell as they crouched in the darkness. Chris struggled to control his breathing, to slow the wild beating of his heart. Slowly the stupidity of their mad rush trickled through his consciousness. From the brief glimpse he'd seen, there were at least a dozen men in the forest. Each would to be armed to the teeth, and would not hesitate to kill. If not for the other shadows racing towards the campsite, Chris guessed they would have been shot already.

He glanced again at Liz, offering his silent thanks for her intervention. She nodded back, and together they lifted their heads above the fallen tree and peered out.

The circle of men Chris had glimpsed a moment before stood twenty feet away, and as they watched several more shadows moved from the surrounding trees to join them. Through the darkness, Chris could see nothing of the men's uniforms or military association, but the rifles they carried were clear enough. They held them with a professional ease, a few pointing out at the surrounding trees, while the others kept their weapons trained on the prisoners in the centre of the circle.

Richard, Jasmine, and the girl knelt between soldiers, their hands held behind their heads, eyes fixed to the ground.

Chris cursed silently to himself, wondering how the three had been taken unawares. He bit his lip as he studied the men, his heart sinking. He saw now they wore goggles over their eyes, no doubt some form of infrared technology that allowed them to see in the dark. There would be no taking them by surprise.

"What do we do?" he whispered to Liz.

"We have to save them," she replied.

Shaking his head, Chris glanced at her. "Do you really think they'd do the same for us?"

Her eyes found him in the darkness, clear and resolute. "It doesn't matter. Whether we like it or not, they're all we've got now. We can't leave them."

Chris let out a long sigh and looked away. He clenched his fingers in the dirt, struggling to think, to find some argument against Liz's words. But in his heart, he knew they were true. Friend or foe, the five of them were all that remained now of the hundreds who had suffered the horrors of the facility. For better or worse, they were bound by that experience.

"Please," he looked up as Richard's voice carried through the trees, "Please, don't do this. Don't make us go back."

Most of the men ignored the desperate plea, but one stepped in close to the prisoners. Raising his rifle, he slammed the butt into Richard's face. Richard reeled backwards from the blow, his arms wind-milling as he crashed to the dirt. He recovered quickly, and with a roar, leapt to his feet.

"Don't," the soldier spoke in a calm tone, "unless you want to sign your friends' death warrants."

Richard froze, his body taught, his fists clenched at his side. A tremor went through him as he looked at the man. A long moment past, as the shadowy men edged closer to the prisoners, guns raised. Then Richard's shoulders slumped, and he bowed his head in defeat.

"Excellent," the man nodded, then waved at the circle of soldiers, "Pack em up, boys. The other two are still out there somewhere. There's a good chance they'll be back. I want these subjects secured before they do."

Several of the soldiers lowered their weapons and leapt to do the man's bidding. Pulling handcuffs from their belts, they stepped towards Richard and the others, as the remaining soldiers covered them with their rifles.

"Now's our chance," Liz whispered.

Chris nodded, eying the space between them and the group of soldiers. Pre-occupied with their prisoners, the soldiers had taken their eyes from the surrounding trees. If Chris and Liz were quick, they could take them by surprise. Even with their goggles, the men would be at a disadvantage in the darkness, and in the confusion, Richard and the others might have a chance to slip free.

Silently, Chris gathered himself to attack.

Before he could move, a sharp crack came from behind them, and a voice growled from the darkness.

"Stop."

FORTY-SIX

Captain Scott crossed his arms as he watched his men securing the prisoners. Covered by their comrades, two stepped towards the boy, slinging their rifles over their backs as they moved. They grabbed the boy by each arm and forced them behind his back. The half-folded wings that sprouted from the small of his back made the task difficult, and the boy clearly had no intention of making things easier.

"Please," the boy begged as a third soldier stepped forward with the handcuffs. "You don't know what you're doing. What they'll do to us."

Stepping forward, Scott stared down at the boy, reading the terror in his eyes. The prisoner tried to flinch away, but his men held him tight, looking to their captain in question.

Scott shook his head. His fist flashed out, catching the prisoner in the face. He reeled backwards, and only the men holding his arms kept him from falling.

"*Silence*," Scott growled, "By the law of our land, you should be dead. You were offered mercy, offered a chance at redemption. But you threw it all away," he raised his fist again, his anger catching light.

Before the blow could fall, a blood curdling howl echoed through the trees. He froze, staring at the prisoner for a second, and then whirled to face the forest. The darkness was absolute, but with the night vision goggles any heat signatures approaching their position would be obvious.

There was nothing.

His men shifted nervously around him as they scanned their surrounds, weapons at the ready. Scott took a step towards the trees, unslinging his rifle as he moved. Beyond the circle of his men, the forest was empty.

Shaking his head, he cast one last glance at the pitch-black trees, and then started to bark fresh orders to secure the prisoners. Before he could finish the command, an audible *thud* came from behind him.

And then someone began to scream.

Scott spun, raising his rifle to fire, already cursing his decision not to execute the prisoners. Whatever their orders, he should have trusted his instincts. He had seen *Chead* in action, glimpsed the aftermath of their slaughter inside the facility. However pathetic the three teenagers seemed, they were far too dangerous to hold.

But as he turned, he realised the three prisoners were still kneeling on the ground where he had left them. Making a decision, he pointed his rifle, but before he could fire the glowing outline of a man staggered into his line of sight.

The man reached out a hand, fumbling at his vest, and then collapsed soundlessly to the ground.

As he went down, another figure moved within the circle of his men. Even in the strange glow of his night vision goggles, Scott knew it was not one of his men. That it was not even entirely human.

He stumbled backwards as the *Chead* leapt, its feral growl filling the darkness. Movement came from overhead, and then ethereal green figures were falling from the trees, landing amongst his men with cat-like grace.

And the night erupted in chaos.

The roar of gunfire snapped Scott from the beginnings of panic. He lifted his rifle and took aim at the silhouette stalking towards him, but before he could squeeze the trigger it dove behind the glowing bodies of his men. Cursing, Scott spun, barking orders as he searched for a fresh target.

"Men, form up on me! They're in the trees!"

His orders fell on deaf ears as pandemonium swallowed up the disciplined order of his team. They stumbled back from the onslaught of the superhuman creatures, their formation shattered. The *Chead* darted amongst them like wolves in a henhouse, rending and tearing as they went. To his left a soldier reeled backwards, his high-pitched scream dying away as a fountain of green sprouted from his chest.

Scott fired as the *Chead* leapt from the soldier's lifeless body. The bullets shrieked as they tore through a nearby tree trunk, but the creature was already gone, its powerful legs sending it soaring through the air. It landed with a thump on another of his men, driving him to the ground with a sharp *crack*.

Flashes of gunfire lit Scott's night vision, blinding him for a moment. Turning his face away, he shouted again over clamour, his fear rising as years of iron discipline melted away.

"Men, on me, *goddammit*!" he hurled himself to the side as a body flew past where he had been standing. It crashed to the ground a few feet away and did not move.

Rolling across the pine needles, he rolled back to his feet. All around him, green figures blundered between the trees, all semblance of order lost. In the chaos, the prisoners had vanished, either killed or fled, but he no longer cared. Survival was his only goal now.

Glancing around, Scott realised he had drifted from the circle in which his men had been standing. He now found himself away amongst the trees, on the edges of the desperate battle between his men and the *Chead*.

Heart pounding, the captain gripped his rifle tight and weighed his options. Though the chatter of gunfire still sounded, it was clear from where he stood the battle was lost. The *Chead* were too fast, too powerful to combat in close quarters, especially in the darkness. The moment it took his men to distinguish between friend and foe was all the creatures needed.

No, this was a lost cause now. His men were as good as dead.

Closing his eyes, Scott forced himself to turn away. Shame rose in his throat as he started to run, to flee the chaos. The screams of dying men chased after him, rising up through the howls of the *Chead*, piercing him to his soul. A voice inside screamed for him to turn back, to stand alongside his men, to die a soldier's death.

But his terror was greater still, and he raced through the darkness, desperate to escape the slaughter.

Scott froze as a sudden silence fell over the forest. He glanced back in the direction of the battle, suddenly hesitant. Had they succeeded after all? Had they done the impossible, and fought off the *Chead?* But he heard no triumphant cries, no wild shouts, no sound at all, in fact.

Swallowing, he looked around at the forest. It seemed deathly still now, without so much as the chirp of a cricket to break the silence. A shiver went through him, and then he was running again, a pure, unadulterated horror gripping him.

He ran for what felt like hours, stumbling over roots and crashing into the pale shadows of tree trunks. He ran without thought of where he was going, only of what came behind, of the death that stalked him through the darkness.

Finally, lungs burning, body aching, he found he could run no more. He staggered to a stop, shoulders heaving, one arm clutching at a tree trunk for support. Bending in two, he gasped in a lungful of air, struggling to catch his breath. In his desperate flight, he had lost all track of time, all sense of direction, but he must have traversed several miles by now.

Straightening, he let out a long breath and looked around. Somehow in his race through the forest he had kept hold of his rifle and night vision goggles. He studied his backtrail for a moment, searching for a hint of movement, for the tell-tale glow of warm bodies. But the forest remained empty, and nodding to himself, he turned away.

And froze as an ethereal green figure emerged from the trees ahead of him.

Soft laughter whispered through the trees as the *Chead* stepped towards him. Through the glow of his goggles, Scott watched a vicious grin twist its features. Out of sheer instinct, the captain raised his rifle, but the *Chead* was faster still. With brutal ease, it leapt forward, tore the weapon from his grasp, and hurled it into the trees.

Before Scott could move, iron fingers gripped him by the throat and lifted him into the air. The *Chead* stared up at him, its eyes bright in the glow of his goggles.

"*Human*," the creature spoke in a guttural growl.

Scott gasped feebly in its hold, mouth wide, struggling for breath. He kicked out at the creature, slammed his fists into its arms, anything to break its hold. His lungs burned and darkness swirled at the edges of his vision, but nothing he did seemed to touch the creature.

As his vision began to fade, he remembered, finally, the EPIRB on his vest. It would bring help, send the helicopter straight to his location. With the last of his strength, he slammed his fist into the button on his shoulder. The EPIRB gave a low beep, and then fell silent.

A smile tugged at his lips as he looked down at the creature. His lungs screamed for air and a dull pounding drummed on the back of his skull, but help was on its way.

"*You will not own us*," the *Chead's* teeth flashed.

Scott opened his mouth to scream as the grip around his throat tightened. Stars flashed across his vision as the creature's fist slammed into his head. Darkness loomed, threatening to swallow him.

No! he screamed in the silence of his thoughts as the *Chead* raised its fist again.

And then everything went black.

FORTY-SEVEN

"*GO, GO, GO!*" CHRIS SHOUTED OVER THE GUNFIRE.

He darted under the flailing arm of a soldier and leapt towards Richard and Jasmine. The young girl was already on her feet, but the other two were slower to react. They still knelt on the ground, mouths wide, staring at the horror unfolding around them.

But there was no time to contemplate the fate of the soldiers. Springing forward, Chris grabbed Richard by the shirt collar and hauled him to his feet. Beside him, Liz did the same with Jasmine, and then they were moving again, pressing on through the dying men and howling *Chead*.

An instant later they were clear and amongst the trees, leaving the chatter of gunshots and blood-curdling screams behind. Chris glanced around as they raced through the forest, catching glimpses of the others as they stumbled over unseen obstacles. They made no effort to mask their passage. If the *Chead* had wanted them dead, they would already be in the ground.

Instead, the creatures had saved them.

Chris swallowed as he ran, remembering the *Chead's* sudden appearance beside them. The creature had frozen them with a look, its cold grey eyes stealing away their voices. Silently, it had lifted a finger to its lips and shook its head. Then it was gone.

A few seconds later, the screaming had started.

Now as Chris fled, questions raced through his mind, one after another. Who were these *Chead?* Where had they come from? Why were the creatures helping them?

But there was no time to stop and wait for answers. Despite the *Chead* having the element of surprise, the soldiers were well-trained and well-armed. And if they prevailed, he doubted they would still be in the mood to take prisoners.

Leaping over a fallen log, Chris ran on, silently cursing their slow pace. They needed to get airborne, to take to the skies and leave the soldiers and the *Chead* far behind. Glancing up, he searched the canopy for a hole, for any gap in the branches that might allow them to escape. But the trees stretched out overhead, unbroken.

They ran for over an hour before they finally reached a clearing. By then the sounds of gunfire and the screams of the dying had fallen away, and the first rays of the morning sun were streaming through the canopy. It appeared out of nowhere – one moment they were racing through the trees, the forest floor still cast in shadows; the next there was sunlight all around, and they were stumbling to a stop, staring in amazement.

Long grass stretched out for a hundred feet from where they stood, sloping gently down towards the west. The others quickly drew up around him, shoulders heaving as they caught their breath, their wings already stretching out towards the light. They still stood near the edge of the tree-line, but looking out across the grass, Chris realised they were not alone in the clearing.

A herd of goats stood amongst the long grass, their white coats glistening in the sun. Their heads were raised, their beady eyes turning to stare at the intruders. Sleek black horns twisted from their heads and blades of grass hung from their mouths as they chewed absently. A kid danced amongst the adults, ignorant to the threat the humans posed, though some of the adults were already turning away.

Yet as the herd started to move towards the opposite side of the clearing, an angry roar filled the air. And suddenly the goats were no longer running away, but towards them. Eyes wild and voices raised in high-pitched screams, they bolted towards Chris and the others, fleeing the unseen noise. A swirling wind raced after them, bending the grass beneath it, tearing leaves and branches from the trees around the clearing.

"Get down!" Chris heard someone shout as a dark shadow fell across the clearing.

Without pausing to think, Chris obeyed, hurling himself down into the long grass. He caught a glimpse of the others following, then a goat leapt past, obscuring his vision.

Looking up, he saw the dark shadow of a helicopter pass by, blades whirling, sun glinting from its metallic body.

An instant later it was gone, disappearing in the direction of their camp. The angry buzz of its blades faded away, but now the reek of gasoline lingered over the clearing, staining the air.

Chris waited a moment in the long grass, listening in case it turned back, before pulling himself to his feet. Standing in the open, he felt his heart pounding hard in his chest. He clenched his fists, struggling to control his fear, to fight back the panic. But he could not control the shaking of his body, the trembling of his legs as the horrors of the night crashed down on him.

Movement came from his right, and he turned to find Liz standing beside him. Their eyes met, and then they were embracing, and Chris felt her shuddering with the same terror that swirled within him. They clung together for a long minute before breaking apart.

Taking a breath, Chris finally managed to control his fear. He looked at the others. "Are you okay?"

Richard and Jasmine stared back, their hair frazzled and faces marked by dirt where they had fallen in the darkness. Otherwise, they looked no worse for wear from their brief period in captivity. The young girl sat in the grass behind them, her grey wings hanging limply from her back as she stared at the ground. Richard and Jasmine stood with their arms folded. Richard kept his expression carefully blank as he nodded, but Chris could see the fear behind his eyes.

Beside Richard, Jasmine's brow creased in anger. "We're fine," she snapped as she stepped towards him, "but where the hell were you two?"

Chris blinked, almost stepped back from the force of her fury. "What?"

"Where were you?" Jasmine hissed, jabbing her finger at them like a knife, "When the soldiers came, when we woke with guns in our faces. *Where were you?*" she all but screeched the last words.

She broke off as Richard stepped up and placed a hand on her shoulder. "Jas, don't," he breathed, looking across at Chris as he spoke, "I saw them go off. I was on watch," he bowed his head. "It was my fault. I was so tired, I must have fallen asleep."

Chris's stomach wrenched at Richard's words, and across the clearing Jasmine twisted away from him. She thrust her hands into his chest, sending him stumbling backwards. "*You fell asleep?*"

Jasmine stepped forward and shoved Richard again. The boy made no move to defend himself, only bowed his head before her rage. Shrieking, Jasmine swung a fist at his face, catching him in the cheek. The blow sent him reeling, and tripping over his own feet, Richard fell to the ground.

Before Jasmine could land any more blows, Liz leapt forward and caught her by the arm. "Jasmine, *stop!*"

A low growl came from Jasmine's throat as she turned on Liz, fist raised. Quick as a cat, Liz caught her other wrist as well. "Don't," she snapped, looking Jasmine in the eye. "It's not his fault. We should have come back earlier, taken over the watch from him. We were careless, foolish even. We should have guessed they'd be waiting for us to appear, to leave the safety of the mountains. We could spend all day debating who's fault this is, but there's no time. That helicopter could be back any minute."

Chris swallowed. Liz was right – there was no way of knowing whether the men in the helicopter knew what had happened to the soldiers, but it would not take them long to find out. Then they would lock the area down, trap them in the forest while their soldiers closed in from all around.

"We have to risk it," Liz spoke again, "we have to fly. If we stay low to the trees, we'll be difficult to pick out. But we need to get clear of this forest, and fast. The whole place is going to become a battle ground when they see what the *Chead* did to their men."

"How?" Richard asked softly as he picked himself up from the ground. Ignoring the glare Jasmine shot him, he looked up at the sky, "There's no cliffs to jump off around here, in case you hadn't noticed."

Chris looked across the clearing, studying the gently sloping grass, and the trees rising up on the far side. "I think we can do it," he answered, "If we run hard across the clearing, I think we'll be able to get enough lift to take off. Just like a kite."

He flashed the others a grim smile. Without waiting for an answer, he started to run. Darting across the damp grass, he spread his wings and picked up his pace. The air cracked as twenty-four feet of tawny brown feathers beat down. Muscles tensed along his torso as the wind caught. The soft grass bent beneath his feet, warm to the touch.

Gritting his teeth, Chris watched the trees on the far side of the clearing rapidly approaching. When there were only a few feet remaining, he sucked in a breath and sprang. His auburn wings beat down hard, and his stomach lurched as he lifted higher. He grinned as the earth fell away, then banked quickly to avoid the trees rushing towards him. Soaring around the circumference of the paddock, he watched the others follow him.

Then the five of them were airborne, and without pausing to think, Chris shot up above the treetops. He cast a glance back in the direction the helicopter had taken, but there was no sign of it. Even so, it could not have gone far. Shifting his wings, he headed in the opposite direction, down the valley towards the distant Californian plains. Wings cracked as Liz settled in beside him, her eyes fixed straight ahead.

A broad valley stretched out around them, the redwoods covering its floor like a carpet. But to either side low cliffs hemmed them in, stretching down to the mouth of the valley, where the last of the hills gave way to the grassy floodplains.

Chris scanned the cliffs as they flew, searching for the shadow of a cave, but there was nothing. Casting a glance back, he could still see no sign of the helicopter, but over the roar of the wind, he heard the whine of an engine again now, drawing closer.

Ahead, the cliffs bent away to the right as the valley altered course slightly. Straining his wings, Chris shot for the cliff-face to the right, where the curve in the rock would hide them from the helicopter farther up the valley. Beside him, Liz's black wings were a blur, beating hard to keep her above the treetops. They were so close Chris could have reached out and touched the pine needles.

He let out a long sigh as they passed around the curve of the cliffs and out of view. But he knew the respite would not last long. Ahead, the cliffs ended abruptly, as below the forest spilled out onto the Californian plains, before finally giving way to the grasses of the prairies. Beyond, brown fields stretched out as far as the eye could see. Sheep and cattle dotted the fields, but the open land offered little to hide them from the prowling eyes of the chopper.

He looked across as he heard Liz shout, and saw her bank to the right. Her hand rose, waving them to follow, and then she was soaring across the last of the trees. Chris turned and chased after her, his eyes travelling out over the land beyond. Far across the plains, a small mountain rose towards the sky, alone amidst the endless flat. Liz was making straight for it.

Seeing her plan, Chris increased his pace, his wings beating hard to catch her. The crack of feathers striking air came from behind as the others followed. Below the last of the forest gave way to dry grass, and their shadows flashed across the fields, their wings stretched wide to either side of them. Ahead the mountain grew larger, extending five hundred feet above the surrounding prairies. Scraggly trees covered its steep sides, though he doubted they would offer much cover. He hoped Liz knew what she was doing.

The mountain stood at least two miles from where the valley ended. Flying hard, they raced to close the gap, ever aware of the mounting buzz of the helicopter.

When they were still a few hundred feet away, the thud of whirling blades turned suddenly to a roar. Ahead, Liz folded her wings and plummeted from the sky. Chris dived after her, pulling his wings tight against his back, spiralling down towards the plains below. Less than a hundred feet from the ground Liz's snapped back wings open. The air cracked as they caught, halting her fall. Without looking back, she shot towards the mountain.

Levelling out, Chris gave in to his fear and glanced back. The chopper had emerged from the mouth of the valley. It hovered above the last stretch of trees, a dark shadow staining the open sky. So far it did not seem to have spotted them. Filling his lungs, Chris pressed on.

The mountain rose up before them, a dark wart on the endless prairies. Liz banked as she reached its rocky edge, flying horizontal to its slopes until she disappeared around the far side of the mountain.

One by one, they followed her.

Chris breathed a sigh of relief as the shadow of the mountain fell across his wings, hiding him from view. He started to slow, expecting Liz to pull up, before he realised she was still flying hard around the mountainside. His chest burned, and a sharp cramp had begun in the small of back, but Liz wasn't giving them any time to argue. Groaning, he followed her, the aches of their week-long flight through the mountains pounding in every inch of his body. Mutated physiology or not, they desperately needed food and rest.

Slowly, Liz drifted closer to the mountainside, the beat of her wings slowing as she neared its rocky slopes. The scraggly trees grew taller on this side of the mountain, offering at least a little cover from prying eyes. And ahead,

Chris noticed a sharp split in the mountainside, as though some giant had carved a piece of rock from the steep slopes.

Chris frowned as he realised Liz was making straight for the shadows of the crease, as though she had known it was there all along. Staring ahead, he blinked as shapes took form within the shadows. A cluster of buildings clung to the side of the mountainside, all but invisible in the gloom of the valley. Thick vines and creepers clung to the aluminium roofs and wooden walls, and it was clear the buildings had been abandoned long go. Even so, the sight of civilisation sent a tingle of renewed energy through Chris, and he raced to catch up with Liz.

A few minutes later, he touched down in the broken courtyard between the buildings. His wings shook with the effort, and he stumbled slightly as his legs took his weight. Folding his wings, he groaned at the ache spreading up his back. He kneaded the side of his head, feeling the first tingles of a migraine beginning.

Liz had landed a full minute before him, and was already moving towards the largest of the buildings. Before he could call out, she pushed through the broken door and disappeared inside. Exhausted, Chris shook his head and chased after her, leaving the others to catch their breath outside.

Moving to the doorway, he paused on the threshold and looked down the empty corridor. Dust covered the floor, untouched except where Liz had left light footprints leading down the hall. A dark stain marked the floorboards at the end of the hall, and an untouched silence clung to the shadows. Taking a step inside, Chris found himself wondering why the occupants had left this place.

His ears twitched as he sensed movement from deeper inside the building.

"Liz?" he called.

When she did not answer, Chris swore softly under his breath, and started along the corridor. Apprehension growing in his chest, he followed Liz's footprints through the dusty rooms.

He found her in what must have once been the lounge. She stood in the empty room, her back turned and head bowed, wings half spread behind her. Her shoulders shook with silent tears, and her black hair hung limp around her neck.

Chris quickly crossed the wooden floor and placed a hand on her shoulder. A tremor went through her at his touch, and a single sob tore from her throat. The first prickles of fear touched Chris as she turned, her blue eyes finding his.

"Liz, what is this place, Liz?" he whispered.

Tears streaked her cheeks as she looked up. "Home."

FORTY-EIGHT

Sam winced as the steel door clicked open. A sharp sob tore from his mouth, and an involuntary shudder ran through his body as he scrambled backwards. The collar snapped tight around his throat, halting his retreat, and a desperate moan rattled from his chest.

Every muscle, every bone in his body ached. Even the sleek copper feathers of his wings were twisted and broken. They lay scattered around the room like fallen leaves, torn from his flesh when his captors grew tired of beating his body. No matter how hard he tried to escape the pain now, it was always there.

Even in his dreams he could not escape its touch.

And now his tormentors had returned for more.

Clenching his fists against the concrete, Sam clung to the last traces of his sanity, as the soft pad of footsteps drew closer. He waited for the tell-tale squeal of the chair as someone sat, but it did not come. Another tremor went through him and he squeezed his eyes shut.

"Good morning, Samuel." Sam jumped as Halt's voice broke the silence.

Tears stung his eyes as he finally looked up. Halt stood over him once more, arms folded, his cold grey eyes staring down. Sam had lost all track of time since he'd last seen the doctor. His torture had been left to others.

A distant flutter of anger rose in Sam, little more than a spark of the rage that had once fuelled him. And looking into Halt's cold, remorseless eyes, even that fell away, leaving only unchecked terror. His shoulders slumped and tears spit down his cheeks. Another sob tore from his throat.

"Please," he choked, all trace of defiance stripped away. "Please, no more, I can't…"

Sam flinched as Halt shifted, but the doctor only crouched beside him, a grim smile on his pale face. Stretching out an arm, Halt patted him gently on the shoulder.

"My dear Samuel," he whispered, almost pleasantly, "It pains me to see you suffer so. You are one of our chosen, one of the few deemed worthy of this gift. Do you not wish to be free again?"

Huddled on the floor, with Halt's warm hand on his shoulder, Sam barely registered the doctor's words. But the last few syllables clung to him, piercing the fog of his shattered body, pulling him up from the darkness.

Free again…

Standing, Halt retreated across the room and lowered himself into the iron chair. Entwining his fingers, he looked down at Sam. "I have an offer for you, Samuel," he said.

Deep within him, Sam heard a voice shouting, telling him to fight, to resist the man's words. In his soul, he knew anything Halt offered would be a trap, a ploy to lure him into some fresh torment. Even so, Sam clung to them like a drowning man, desperate for a lifeline against the torments of his cell.

"Please," he croaked, bowing his head, "I'll do anything. Just, no more, *please!*"

Halt chuckled as he climbed to his feet. "That is good to hear, Samuel," behind him the door clicked open as two guards entered. Halt nodded at them and waved to Samuel, "Unlock the chain."

Sam shrank against the concrete as the men approached. Both had their rifles slung over their shoulders and the hated batons clipped to their belts. But they made no move to use them. Instead, one produced a key and unlocked the bolt that kept the chain fixed into the ground. Lifting the chain, he offered it to Halt.

Trembling on the floor, Sam did not move as Halt took the chain and gave it a tug.

"Stand, Samuel," Halt ordered softly, "Join me. There is someone who would like to see you."

Goosebumps ran down Sam's arms as the words slithered through his consciousness. Pulling himself to his feet, he allowed Halt to lead him out of the stark concrete room and into the long corridors of the facility. His bones creaked as he moved, and his muscles ached with the long days spent huddling on the ground. He stumbled after Halt, each step an agony, the weight of his half-folded wings heavy on his back. From behind him came the thud of boots as the guards followed, their rifles held at the ready now.

The trip did not take long. A few quick turns down the brightly lit corridors, and Halt drew to a stop again. He released the chain that connected to Sam's collar and nodded at the door, "I will give you some time to get reacquainted."

Sam shuddered as he eyed the steel panelled door, his sluggish mind struggling to comprehend what game Halt was playing. He glanced at the doctor, unable to believe this could truly be happening. Surely it was a trap, some cruel trick to shatter the last traces of his sanity.

But there was no turning back now. Swallowing his fear, his heart thudding hard in his chest, Sam reached out and twisted the door handle. As the door swung open, he stepped inside. His eyes swept the room beyond, taking in the white washed walls and grey linoleum floor. The room was empty except for a single hospital bed. But it was the girl lying in the bed that drew his attention.

Ashley lay with her eyes closed, the damp tangles of her scarlet hair swirling out across the pillows. She wore plain green hospital scrubs, the short sleeves and low collar revealing the full extent of her injuries. Purple bruises marked her face and arms, and red abrasions streaked her pale skin, bound now by stitches. Needle marks dotted her arms, and tubes and wires encased her elegant body, stretching back to the host of machines sitting at the head of the bed. Her pale white wings hung limply around her, tangled with the thin sheets that covered half her body. A familiar steel collar shone around Ashley's throat, and handcuffs bound her arms to the metal rails running horizontal along the hospital bed.

Relief swept through Sam as he saw her chest rise. His heart lurched, his breath catching in his throat. In an instant he had crossed the room.

"*Ashley*," he breathed.

Ashley's eyelids fluttered at the sound. A crease marked her forehead as her eyes opened, her tawny yellow irises shining in the bright light. They widened when she found him standing over her.

"Oh, *Sam*," she whispered, "What have they done to you?"

Sam only shook his head. Carefully taking a seat on the side of the bed, he reached out and took one of her hands.

"It was worth it," he said softly, "You're alive, Ashley. *You're alive*."

He could hardly believe what he was seeing. In the countless days of torment, in his darkest hours, he had long since convinced himself she was gone, that he had sacrificed himself for nothing. But now here she was, alive and breathing, staring at him with those haunting amber eyes, and it was all he could do not to crumble with the joy in his heart.

Alive.

"What did you do, Sam?" Ashley's whispered, her voice barely audible over the beeping machines.

Sam attempted a laugh, but a sharp pain pierced his chest, and it turned into a groan. He shook his head. "What I had to do. What needed to be done, to save you."

Ashley closed her eyes a moment, pain flickering across her face. Her fingers squeezed his hand, and then released him. "You shouldn't have done this, Sam," she whispered, and he saw tears glistening in her eyes. "I wanted you to be free."

Reaching out, Sam wiped away the tear that streaked her cheek. "Sorry, Ash," he smiled, "but you know I make poor decisions when you're not around."

Colour spread to Ashley's cheeks as she shook her head again. "Sam…"

Grinning, Sam leaned forward and pressed his lips to hers, cutting off whatever she had been about to say. He felt her tense for a second, then she was returning the kiss, tilting back her head, drawing him in. A warm tingle spread through Sam as her tongue darted out to dance with his, and the taste of her filled him. Reaching up, he ran a hand through her hair, drawing her deeper. The pain of his body melted, giving way to his passion.

Then a click came from the door, and they pulled quickly apart, turning to see who had entered.

A dark smile twisted Halt's lips as he walked across the room. He ignored them as he drew up on the other side of Ashely's bed. Standing for a moment, he studied the host of machines connected to Ashley, nodding slowly to himself.

"It looks like she will recover," he said at last, "With the proper care, of course."

"What do you want, Halt?" Ashley croaked.

"From you, my dear?" his eyes flickered towards her. "Nothing. At least, not until you have recovered. For now, it is Samuel we need."

Looking into Halt's eyes, Sam felt the agony of his tortured body come rushing back. The awful helplessness he'd felt for the past days returned. Ashley's fingers tightened around his hand, and there was a glimmer of fear in her eyes now.

"Thanks to the unfortunate actions of Doctor Fallow, we now find ourselves short of candidates who survived the change," Halt continued. "The PERV-A viral strain your group received has proven far less… lethal than alternative strains," he pursed his lips, "Of those who received the PERV-B strain, only two remain intact."

Sam clenched a fist around the sidebar of Ashley's bed. "How many have you killed Halt?"

Ignoring the question, Halt lowered himself into the chair on the opposite side of the bed and looked across at them. "Due to our shortage of viable candidates, I have decided to forgive your past… transgressions," his lips twisted into a scowl. "We cannot afford to terminate successful candidates, however vexing their actions."

Taking a long, shuddering breath, Sam stared down at Halt, silently cursing the man's cruelty. *Now* they could not afford to terminate candidates? For long weeks and months, he had watched children marched from the prison block, never to return. He had stood in a padded room, and been forced to choose his own life over his friend's. Closing his eyes, Sam saw Jake's face staring up at him, his eyes pleading.

The breath caught in his throat and he quickly pushed away the memory. "What do you want, Halt?" he echoed Ashley's earlier question. He summoned as much defiance as he could muster, but even to his own ears, the words lacked conviction.

"If we are to convince the President and his Directors to continue funding for the Praegressus Project, we must give them results. Every successful candidate we present to the public, is a greater demonstration of the project's viability."

Shivering, Sam thought back to the prisoner block, to the lines of staring faces. All gone now, all dead but for the seven of them, and the two unnamed candidates who had survived the other strain of the virus. His stomach twisted at the horror, at the spectre of death that hung over their lives, the weight of the loss.

And now Halt wanted Sam to help him continue his monstrous project.

"No," Sam gritted his teeth, "I'd rather die."

Halt let out a long breath and shook his head. He turned to look at Ashley, his smile fading. "Such a disappointment." The words were barely a whisper, but they sent a rush of fear through Sam.

Before either of them could react, Halt's hand flashed out and caught Ashley by the wrist.

Sam began to rise from the bed, his lips curling back in a snarl. He clenched his fists, ready to put an end to the monstrous doctor once and for all. Even in his weakened state, he was sure he could snap the man's neck before the guards arrived to stop him.

"Stop," Halt's command echoed around the room, freezing Sam in place. He nodded to the watch on his wrist, reminding Sam of the collar around his neck. "That's quite far enough. Sit down, Samuel."

Looking into Halt's eyes, Sam knew he was beaten. Slowly, he lowered himself back into place on Ashley's bed.

Halt nodded and turned back to Ashley. A cold smile lit his face as he raised Ashley's hand. Her forehead wrinkled with pain at the movement.

"She is still quite weak, Samuel," Halt whispered. "With the drugs and antibiotics running through her system, any ordinary human would be in a coma. As it is, they have rendered her no stronger than a child."

At that, Halt grasped Ashley's hand and with deliberate slowness, started to bend back one of her fingers. A low groan came from Ashely as she tried to pull away, but the handcuffs held her in place. His anger rising, Sam shifted, but Halt lifted his arm, flashing the controller on his wrist.

"Fallow's commands have been overridden. So unless you both want an unpleasant shock, I suggest you sit, Samuel. I doubt her body is strong enough to survive the collar's touch."

Clenching his fists, a terrible fear rose within Sam. Ashley lay in the bed, her eyes shining with tears, her jaw locked in pain. Halt still held her finger, bending it backwards to the limits of ordinary movement. Glancing at Ashley, Sam saw the fear on her face, but as their eyes met, she slowly shook her head.

Closing his eyes, Sam let out a long, rattling breath and settled back on the bed.

"Very good," Halt whispered. "But it is too little, too late. You are a slow learner, Samuel, and so another lesson must be given."

Sam's eyes snapped open as he heard something go *crack*. Beside him, Ashley threw back her head and screamed. She thrashed in the bed, her movements weak and restrained by the handcuffs, her face contorted in agony. Her feet kicked out, as though fighting off some unseen enemy. Sam reached for her, but her cuffed hands threw him back as she screamed again.

On the other side of the bed, Halt still held Ashley's hand in an iron grasp. Sam's eyes trailed down her arm, to where one finger was now bent backwards at an awful angle.

"You bast–"

Without taking his eyes from Sam, Halt jerked his hand. Another *crack* echoed through the room. Ashley shrieked, her free hand clawing at the metal bar, powerless to escape. Her screams died away and her eyes started to roll back in her skull. Before she could lose consciousness, Halt tugged at her broken finger, and the focus returned to her eyes. A low whimper came from her throat as her desperate eyes found Sam, begging him to save her.

"Move an inch, Samuel, and I'll break another one," Halt growled.

Ashley lay taught as a wire, her hair a tangled mess around her face, her good hand clenched tight around Sam's wrist now.

"Please," Sam whispered, biting back tears. This was worse than the cells, worse than the collars, worse than his silent beatings in the white-washed room. "Please, stop. I'll do whatever you want."

The smile on Halt's face spread. "Very good, Samuel," he whispered. "I always had faith you would come through for us." Looking down at Ashley, he released her hand.

Tears streaked Ashley's face as she bit back a sob. Sam's heart warmed at the defiance in her eyes, but they both knew there was no resisting this man. He had proven time and again his cruelty knew no bounds, that no one was beyond his power.

"Tomorrow, we will be moving you both to our complex in San Francisco," Halt continued. "You, Samuel, will join the survivors of the A strain. They are still uncomfortable in their abilities. You will show them what they are capable of. Then, in a week, the three of you will be presented to the public. You will become the new face of the government's fight against the *Chead*. You will be the shining light the public will look to for hope. Do you understand?"

Sam nodded, not trusting his voice to speak.

"Good," Halt's gaze flickered to Ashley. "So long as you cooperate, Ashley will receive the best of treatment. And one day soon, I hope she will join you. For now though, her wellbeing is in your hands, Samuel. Fail us, and I will make you watch as I break every bone in her little body."

At that, Halt reached down and caught another of Ashley's fingers. With a hard jerk of his wrist, he twisted it back, shattering the bone in one swift, violent jerk.

FORTY-NINE

Closing her eyes, Liz listened to the silence of the house around her. Darkness stretched through the empty rooms, the night hiding the walls and ceilings she knew so well. Beneath the reek of mildew and dust, the familiar smells of home remained. Gone were the voices, the life she had once lived, but the shell still endured, and with it, the memories.

Somewhere outside, a cricket chirped, and she could hear the soft breathing of the others as they slept nearby. Richard and Jasmine lay on opposite sides of the lounge. Jasmine had not spoken since the clearing, but she and the young girl seemed to have bonded. The enigmatic thirteen-year-old lay curled up next to Jasmine, her eyelids flickering gently with some dream. Chris was somewhere outside, keeping watch while the others rested. They were taking no chances now, not after what had happened the night before.

They had spent the day huddled inside the house, listening for the tell-tale buzz of the chopper, praying its search would not reach their lonely mountain. The shadow of the valley and wooden walls would not shield them from a persistent search, but at least they were hidden from casual observers. The dark contraption would have to come close to find them, and they would hear its approach long before then.

In the long hours, they had explored the house. Liz had helped retrieve what remained of her parents' clothing. Most was motheaten and covered in mildew, but it was still far better than what remained of the rags they'd escaped in. There were also several pairs of shoes, and heavy jackets they could wear to cover their wings.

When the shadows of nightfall fell across the plains beyond the mountain, the group had finally allowed themselves to relax. Richard had ventured out into the trees around the ranch, returning an hour later with a turkey, its neck broken and dangling from a bloody hand. In the meantime, Liz and the others had gorged themselves on oranges and half-green apples hanging from the trees around the ranch.

It was dark by then, and Richard had set about lighting a fire in the long dead woodstove. He had been silent since the incident in the forest, and Liz could sense the weight hanging on his shoulders. Whether it was the remembered terror of his capture, or the guilt at having fallen asleep while on watch, Liz could not tell. But she could do nothing to help him – the burden of her own memories hung over her now, rising up from a past she had thought long buried.

She had thanked him for the meat though. The turkey had been old and tough, probably one of the birds her father had once kept, but to her half-starved stomach it had seemed a banquet. Her hunger satisfied, her strength had quickly started to return.

Now, in the darkness of night, she finally felt strong enough to face her past. Memories of her parents drifted through her mind – of them sitting around the woodstove that stood in the centre of the kitchen, the taste of her mother's rabbit stew, of the long days manning the fields surrounding their solitary mountain peak.

Her parents and the other workers had tended to the flocks of sheep and cattle grazing on the prairies around the mountain, often spending cold nights sleeping in the fields when work took them to the furthest pastures. Though little of the profits went to her family, it was an honest living, and they had been happy here.

But now the ranch had been abandoned, the land left untended, the buildings allowed to succumb to nature's encroachment. She wasn't surprised. It would have been hard to convince the bravest of workers to return here after what had happened.

Letting out a long breath, Liz climbed to her feet. She felt a desperate need for company, to escape the lonely whispers of this place. Her cheeks flushed as she recalled the night before, of Chris's hands around her, his lips on her neck, his flesh pressed hard against hers. A shiver went through her as she moved through the darkness. Following the old, familiar hallways, she made her way outside.

It took a long time to find him. Only when a stray root tripped her and sent her sprawling to the ground, did she hear a soft call from overhead. Looking up, she realised he was sitting on the tin roof. He smiled down, and waved for her to join him.

Without a decent runup, flight was out of the question. But taking a hold of the steel drainage pipe, Liz quickly pulled herself up the way she had done so many times before. She strode across the roof, careful to follow the rows of nails that marked the support beam, and lowered herself down next to Chris.

"Couldn't sleep?" he asked. His arm wrapped around her waist and pulled her close.

Liz nodded and looked out into the darkness. The clouds had gathered late in the afternoon, and now the sky was solid black, the moon and stars hidden away. Even so, her eyes could still make out the distant fields, still saw the tell-tale movement of the grass as the wind blew across the plain. The branches of the trees rustled around them as the breeze raised goosebumps across her skin. Shivering, she wriggled in closer to Chris, hoping to steal some of his warmth.

He smiled, and his wings lifted, stretching out to enfold them both in his auburn feathers. Liz settled in beneath his arm, basking in the heat of his body. They were silent for a while then, content to share the quiet beauty of the night, and the comfort of each other's presence.

"What happened here, Liz?" Chris whispered at last. "Where did everyone go?"

Liz shuddered, and Chris tightened his grip around her, his fingers giving her arm a reassuring squeeze. She took a long time to gather her thoughts, to face the darkness of the past, but Chris waited patiently, his mouth shut, silent.

"They're dead," she said finally.

Chris nodded. "The *Chead*?"

Letting out a breath, Liz recounted her story. "It seems so long ago now. I had just gotten back for the summer, had caught the bus all the way from San Francisco. My parents lived here with the farmhands that helped them out in the fields. They managed the land all around this rock."

Beside her, Chris stared out into the darkness. "Your family owned it all?"

Liz snorted. "Of course not. Before the American War, it was Flores land. But after…" she shrugged. "Like most rural families, my grandfather fell into debt after the war. He was forced to sell off his holdings to settle his obligations. We were lucky the landholder was happy for our family to stay on as managers."

She waited for Chris to comment, but he said nothing. Nodding, she turned her thoughts back to the night everything had changed. "I got in late that day. It was almost dark, but I was excited to see my parents and friends. The workers were practically family. I was daydreaming as I walked up. At first, I didn't notice the silence…"

Chris's arms tightened around her. She looked up to find his hazel eyes watching her, soft in the darkness. Biting her lip, Liz summoned her courage and continued. "The farmhands were scattered around the courtyard – some whole, others in pieces. But there was no sign of my parents."

She broke off again as tears brimmed in her eyes. Angrily, she wiped them away. Her fists clenched, but she forced them to relax, to breathe. "I didn't think. I ran into the house, screaming their names. Inside, everything was torn and broken. At the end of the corridor I could see blood on the floor. It was only then that I stopped, that reason caught up to me. But by then it was too late. I couldn't stop myself, I had to see, had to know," she broke off, a sob tearing from her chest.

Strong arms held her close as she struggled to control her grief.

"Your parents?" Chris whispered.

Liz shuddered again, and slowly shook her head. She bit her lip, determined to continue, to speak the words she had never dared voice aloud. "My father," she croaked. "He lay in the hallway, his blood…." she shook her head, "But my mum… my mum stood over him, her head down, her shoulders shaking. And her eyes… her eyes were *grey*, Chris," she choked on the last words.

Burying her head in Chris's shoulder, she waited for him to reply, unsure how he would respond. But he said nothing, only held her tight. When she finally looked up, there were tears in his eyes. Leaning down, he kissed her gently on the forehead.

"I'm sorry," he whispered.

They said nothing for a long time then, just sat together, staring out into the darkness. The wind began to pick up strength, shaking the branches of the trees hanging over the roof. Liz shivered, pulling her own wings closer to her back as she nestled in next to Chris. Her head lay on his chest, and she could hear the steady thud of his heart beneath her. Reaching out a hand, she entwined her fingers with his.

"What happened next, Liz?"

She sucked in a breath, her thoughts drifting back, remembering the cold grey eyes staring from her mother's face. There had been nothing left of her crystal blue gaze, of the gentle kindness she offered to all she met. But as they'd found Liz, there had been a flicker of recognition, of *something* other than animalistic hunger.

"She left," Liz whispered. "I never understood why. I stood in that corridor for a full minute, too scared to move a muscle. But she just stood there, staring. Then, she seemed to come alive. She walked past me like I wasn't even there. I never saw her again."

She didn't add that it had been three days before anyone showed up, when the landowner finally reported a shipment of goods from the farm as missing. Those three days were little more than a haze for Liz. Her mind had receded, and succumbing to shock she had crumpled to the hallway floor. Hours later some form of awareness had returned, and she had found herself covered in blood. Finding her father's dead eyes watching her, she had screamed and fled into the forest.

After that, she could remember only flashes – of her standing in a shower, the blood streaming down the drain. Then standing over a shallow grave, her father lying amidst the dirt. The taste of vomit in her mouth, and the reek of death.

It wasn't until the police arrived that some form of sanity had finally returned. She had told them what had happened, watched as the SWAT team entered the forest, listened to their brief reassurances. But later, as she sat shivering in the back of a wagon, she had heard the policemen talking. They did not believe her story, that the *Chead* had spared her.

As they began to discuss where to take her, Liz's senses had come crashing back. With them came memories of the warnings, of the disappearances. She had slipped silently away into the woods then, and never looked back.

Now, on the roof with Chris, Liz could hardly believe she had returned. An awful loneliness rose within her, a desperate grief for her parents and the life she had once lived. Sobbing, she clung to Chris, lost in the terror of her past, in the madness that had swallowed her existence.

FIFTY

CHRIS WATCHED AS THE FIRST LIGHT OF THE MORNING SUN lit the distant horizon. It began as a soft glow far in the distance, still hidden by the curve of the earth, but quickly rising into view. Sunlight shone across the plains, turning the fields of grass to gold, and revealing the black and white dots of sheep and cattle. He closed his eyes as the first rays reached them on the rooftop, basking in their warmth.

Turning his head, he watched Liz where she was curled up beside him. One of his wings lay draped across her like a blanket, and she clutched it in her fingers, a soft smile touching her lips. Her own wings had relaxed with sleep, and now hung limply behind her.

His mind drifted, recalling again the story she had told him. He shivered, unable to comprehend the shock, the horror of witnessing her mother change. He bit back a sob as he thought of his own mother, and wondered at her fate.

Where are you, mum?

He still clung to the hope she was alive, that the government had spared her from execution, or delayed her sentence. He couldn't bring himself to face the alternative, that she might be gone, that he might be alone.

If she was gone, he didn't know how he would go on.

Grimacing, Chris forced his thoughts to more practical matters. They were a long way from safe yet. They had found a temporarily asylum on Liz's ranch, but it was only a matter of time before the search reached the lonely mountain. Today, tomorrow maybe, but no longer than that. Once the helicopter found the dead soldiers, and realised the escapees had breached their cordon, the hunters would come for them. They had to be far away by then.

But with the wide plains stretching out to the west, they would be spotted in minutes if they flew.

Chris stifled a yawn and rose to his feet, struggling to free his wing from Liz's unconscious grip before tucking them against his back. Liz stirred with the movement, her eyelids flickering briefly, before settling back into sleep. Crouching down, he gently lifted her into his arms.

Letting her great black wings trail beneath her, he moved to the side of the roof and jumped. His own wings snapped out as they fell, catching him and slowing his descent. He landed with a soft thud of bare feet on dirt and retracted his wings. Idly, he wondered again at the strange new appendages, at how quickly they had all adapted to their presence. Though he still tripped over their bulk occasionally, each day they became more a part of him.

He found Jasmine and Richard in the living area. Richard stood by the window, looking out over the plains. He glanced up as Chris entered, then resumed his silent vigil. Jasmine was in the adjoining kitchen, silently licking her fingers. A guilty look flashed across her face when she saw him, and she quickly looked away. Glancing at the countertop, Chris saw the remains of the turkey had been picked clean. His stomach gave a sharp rumble at the sight.

Shaking his head, Chris crossed the room. The young girl lay asleep beside the long dead fireplace, her grey wings pulled tight around her. He lay Liz gently beside her. To his surprise, the young girl gave a soft murmur, and her arms stretched out to embrace Liz.

Chris smiled at the sight, warmth spreading through his chest. Whatever pain Liz might be feeling, she had the rest of them now – even this strange little girl, it seemed.

He looked back at Jasmine and Richard, feeling the heavy tension that hung over the room. Yesterday, little had been said of the ambush in the forest. They had all been too exhausted, still in shock after what had happened, what they'd witnessed. Jasmine hid it well, but he could see her fear, concealed behind the anger. The encounter with the soldiers had scared her to the core.

"Good morning," he offered softly.

Richard turned away from the window. "You didn't wake us, for the watch?"

Chris let out a long breath and shook his head. "I couldn't sleep anyway. I thought you could use the rest."

Jasmine snorted as she walked out of the kitchen. "Yeah, right. Not because you were worried *he* might fall asleep again."

Richard bowed his head and looked away, but she moved towards him, a fire burning in her eyes.

Quickly stepping into her path, Chris raised his hands. "It's not his fault, Jasmine."

"No?" her brown eyes glared at him, her emerald wings trembling on her back, "What about you and Liz then? Wandering off into the forest, leaving us to be caught. I guess we know how things stand between us, don't we?"

"How things stand?" Chris stepped forward, until only an inch separated them, "How things stand is the two of you have never been anything but antagonistic to us. And why? Because we were forced to fight your friends? Because we were jailed with Ashley and Sam?"

Jasmine refused to back down. Her eyes were like daggers as she looked up at Chris. "They killed our *friends*," she snapped.

"And you didn't?" Richard's voice interrupted their exchange. He stepped forward, face hard now. "You made the same decision, Jasmine. Or else Chelsea would be here instead of you, wouldn't she?"

Air hissed between Jasmine's teeth as her face paled. "Don't you *dare* bring her into this!"

"*Stop!*" Chris growled, cutting over the two of them. He glanced at Liz, and was relieved to see she still slept. He went on in a softer tone. "Stop this, both of you. We've all been forced to do things we regret. We went through that hell together, in case you'd forgotten. But we're all that's left now. We're all any of us has. We have to find a way to work together."

Jasmine took a long breath as she looked at Chris. She opened her mouth to speak, but her voice cracked, and suddenly she seemed to shrink. Shaking her head, she turned away. "You don't understand," she shuddered. "When they caught us... when we were kneeling there on the ground. I've never been so afraid, knowing they were taking us back, that there was nothing I could do to stop it from happening."

"Jasmine..." Richard's voice was soft as he stepped towards her.

"*Don't!*" Jasmine shrank away. "Just... don't, Richard."

"It wasn't his fault, Jasmine," Chris repeated his words. "You saw how many there were, the weapons they had. They would have shot us down if we'd tried to run. I don't think it would have mattered in the end, whether Richard was awake or not."

A strained silence fell across the room then. Chris shivered as a cold breeze drifted in from the front door. He moved across to the kitchen and attempted to scavenge a scrap of meat from the turkey carcass.

"What happened in the forest, Chris?" it was Richard who spoke, but when he looked up he saw Jasmine shifting closer too.

Giving up on the turkey, he picked up a loose apple and took a bite. The image of the *Chead* falling from the trees flickered through his mind, punctuated by the screams of the soldiers. His stomach twisted and he tossed the apple back onto the bench.

"The truth? I don't know. We were watching you from the trees, talking about how to free you," he eyed Jasmine pointedly at that. "But before we could act, the *Chead* appeared. I didn't even hear them approach. One stepped between us and the soldiers, while the others melted into the trees. A few minutes later, the screaming started."

Jasmine shuddered as she wrapped her arms around her chest. "Why would they help us?"

Chris shrugged. He had been asking himself the same question ever since their appearance. That, and where they had come from, what they had been doing in the forest in the first place. He started to speak, to voice his own questions, when a movement came from the doorway.

As one, the three of them spun towards the doorway

FIFTY-ONE

"Well... what do we have... here?"

For a second, time seemed to slow. As Chris spun, he glimpsed the figure in the doorway, heard the voice, but he was already moving. Stepping forward, he placed himself between the intruder and the sleeping girls, raising his fists in defiance. His lips drew back in a snarl, but inside a desperate fear wrapped around his chest, draining away his strength.

The *Chead* reclined in the doorway, arms crossed, its features twisted with amusement. Long black hair hung around its face, but there was no missing the familiar grey eyes. The orange jumpsuit it wore was torn and stained, the sleeves ripped clean off at the shoulders. Sleek, powerful muscles rippled along its arms as it stepped into the room. It looked to be around Chris's own eighteen years, though there was no telling with the *Chead*. Its sickly-sweet scent reached Chris's nostrils as it looked around, its very presence a threat.

Chris's stomach lurched as he realised he knew the creature. It was the same *Chead* from the facility, the same one he and Liz had fought – and spared. He swallowed as its eyes fixed on him. He tensed, preparing himself.

The *Chead* smiled. "Come now," the words seemed almost hesitant, but there was no mistaking their strength, "if we wished you dead… we would have left you to… the soldiers."

"Stay where you are," Chris bared his teeth, his wings snapping open, "Don't come any closer."

The *Chead's* grey eyes lingered on his wings as it took another step. "Curious…" its voice grated. Lifting a hand, it reached out to touch his wing. Chris took an involuntary step backwards, and the *Chead* laughed.

Swallowing his fear, Chris growled. "Get out."

The *Chead's* face went blank as its cold eyes drilled into him. Chris shuddered, but forced himself to stand strong. He could sense the others behind him, hovering close, and drew strength from their presence.

"You're outnumbered," he breathed. "Leave, *now!*"

A sly grin spread across the *Chead's* lips as it began to cackle. Movement came from around them, as the other creatures Chris had glimpsed in the forest filed in from the hallway. Unable to control his fear, Chris retreated into the centre of the room, until he collided with Richard. The *Chead* spread out around the room, forcing the three of them back towards the fireplace. Looking around, Chris counted eight pairs of grey eyes watching them.

The first *Chead* moved forward, until it stood face to face with Chris. He flinched as it reached out and stroked the feathers of his wings, but there was nowhere left to retreat now.

"Curious," it repeated, its words smoother now. It looked at him. "So… I was not wrong."

Chris took a long breath, struggling to control his panic. "What do you want, *Chead?*"

"So… impatient," a broad grin split its face as the grey eyes travelled past him, to where Liz still lay asleep. Absently, Chris wondered whether the girl would sleep through a hurricane. "We are not yet… all present."

It started to step past him, but Chris moved to intercept it, anger taking light in his chest. Whatever these creatures were here for, he wasn't about to let them harm Liz. Not without a fight.

Before he could take two steps, two *Chead* leapt forward from the circle and caught him by the arms. Grunting with effort, they hauled him back as he fought to break free. A soft smile on its lips, the first *Chead* strode past, moving across to where Liz and the young girl lay by the fireplace.

"The other… one," it turned and grinned at Chris, its stilted voice touched by humour, "my… champions."

Chris was about to reply when a movement came from the floor. Before anyone could react, Liz leapt from the ground and tackled the *Chead* from behind. Her weight sent it stumbling forward as she wrapped an arm tight around its throat.

As the *Chead* fought to regain its balance, Liz spread her wings and beat them hard. Still off-balance, the *Chead* lost its footing and was dragged backwards, as Liz lifted its full weight off the ground. She landed in the corner, and turned to face the remaining *Chead*.

"*Back!*" she snarled, teeth bared.

The other *Chead* exchanged uneasy glances. Then the creature in Liz's grip twisted, and its elbow flashed back into her face. A harsh *crack* echoed through the room as the blow staggered her. With a violent jerk, the *Chead* tore itself free and sprang free.

Chris tensed against the *Chead* holding him, preparing to fight, to defend Liz against the creatures.

But the first *Chead* only laughed. Shaking its head, it turned its back on Liz and stalked across to Chris.

"The girl is… spirited," its teeth showed as its lips curled back, "She is… yours?"

Shrieking, Liz launched herself across the room. Quick as a minx, the *Chead* spun. Parrying a wild blow from Liz, its hand flashed out and caught her by the wrist. A low rumble sounded in Liz's chest as she swung her other arm, but the *Chead* easily caught the blow. Grinning, it stared down at her. Liz looked back helplessly, both fists trapped in its iron grasp.

Then her knee flashed up, straight into the *Chead's* crotch. The *thump* as the blow landed made even Chris wince, and the *Chead* folded like grass before the wind.

"My name is Liz," she growled, staring down at the gasping figure, "and I belong to *no one.*"

The *Chead* chuckled as it straightened. "Such fire..." it bowed its head, "my... apologies."

"*Artemis!*" Chris jumped as a new voice shrieked from the corner of the room.

Every face in the room turned as a ball of grey hair and feathers barrelled past, and leapt at the first *Chead*. The *Chead* stumbled backwards, surprise showing on its face, but at the last second the young girl pulled up short. The wild grin fell from her face as her jaw fell open.

"Oh..." she gulped, and retreated a step.

The *Chead* stared at her, its brow creased in confusion. The girl took another step back, then turned and hurled herself at Jasmine. Jasmine staggered as the tiny girl wrapped her arms around her leg. Righting herself, Jasmine looked around the room, eyes wide with shock. Then she reached down and put her arms around the trembling girl.

The first *Chead* had not moved during the exchange. It stood staring at the girl, its grey eyes suddenly hesitant, as though perplexed. Finally it looked back at Chris and raised an eyebrow. "Strange..." its nostrils flared, "strange... company, you keep."

Shaking his head, Chris moved between Jasmine and the *Chead*. A feral anger rose in his chest as his patience snapped, giving way to steely resolve. He took a step forward, until he stood face to face with the *Chead*, and stared into its icy eyes.

"What are you doing here?" he growled. "Why did you save us from the soldiers?"

He clenched his fists, bracing himself for a fight. He could guess now where these *Chead* had come from. They had to have been prisoners of the facility. They must have escaped at the same time as Chris and the others. But that still did not explain their appearance in the woods.

The smile fell from the *Chead's* lips at Chris's words. The grey eyes stared back at him, unreadable.

Then the *Chead* shrugged. "A debt…. was owed," the creature shifted, licking its lips, "You spared… Hecate's life. You suffered… for me."

Its grey eyes flickered towards Liz as it spoke, and Chris saw again the scene in the padded room, saw Liz writhing in agony, the shock collar flashing around her neck. He shuddered and his hand drifted unconsciously to his throat. But the steel chains were long gone, and angrily he pushed the memory away.

"Your name is Hecate?" he asked, the angry words dying in his throat.

The *Chead* smiled, a dull laughter rattling in its throat. "You thought... we would call each other… *Chead?*"

The whisper of laughter came from the other *Chead*, reminding Chris of their presence. A shiver ran through him at the inhuman quality to the laughter. Though they looked like ordinary teenagers, there was no doubting the absence of humanity in their grey stares.

He turned his eyes back to the first *Chead*. "Thank you, Hecate," he paused, unsure how to continue. "How are you here? How did you escape the facility?"

"The woman... released us," its eyes flashed, the grin turning feral, "The fun we had... before we left."

Chris blanked. Finally, they knew how Angela Fallow had distracted the guards long enough to free them. She had unleashed the captive *Chead* on the facility. He shuddered at the slaughter they would have left behind them, and wondered how anyone had survived to come after them. But then, a well-placed bullet would still stop a *Chead* in its tracks, and in the long corridors of the facility, the guards would have eventually overwhelmed the creatures.

"How did you find us?" Liz asked.

"After... our brothers and sisters... began to fall, we left." The *Chead* eyed them with a grin. "You fly slow... sleep too much. And your stench... was not hard to track."

Chris wrinkled his nose, trying to ignore the cloying sweetness the *Chead* carried with them. It filled the room, overpowering, though he had never heard it mentioned in the news reports about the *Chead*. He guessed an enhanced sense of smell was yet another alteration he could chalk up to Halt and Fallow's meddling.

But sense of smell aside, he knew there had to be more to *Chead's* actions than Hecate was letting on. Folding his arms, he shook his head. "You did not follow us all this way, save us from those soldiers, just to say thank you."

The *Chead* smiled again. "You are... correct," its teeth flashed as its grin widened, "We came to see... if you would join us."

"Join you in what?" Liz asked softly.

Hecate turned to look at her. "In the war... to come."

Chris blinked. "The war to come?"

"For all our existence… we have suffered," the *Chead's* eyes flashed. "Beaten. Tortured. Murdered. We were born into captivity… destined to die there. But now we are free… and we will make our tormentors pay."

"You want to fight the government?" Liz breathed.

"The government?" the *Chead's* head bent to the side, "It is humanity… that made us suffer… It is humanity… that must pay with its blood."

Chris blinked, and behind them Richard snorted. "All of humanity?" Richard asked, his voice rich with sarcasm. He stepped up beside them, suddenly bold. "There's eight of you. The government has thousands of soldiers. And there are millions of people in the Western Allied States."

The *Chead* shifted, turning to face the taller boy. "Their soldiers are *nothing*," it growled. "The *Chead* are *legion*."

Though Chris could make no sense of Hecate's words, he felt himself grow cold. Ice trickled down his back as he looked at the unyielding figure of the *Chead*, imagining an army of such creatures. Then he shook his head and dismissed the image. The facility could not have contained an army. Hecate was clearly deranged, driven mad by the long years of imprisonment.

Beside him, Richard laughed. Before any of them could react, Hecate sprang forward and caught him by the shirt. Growling, the *Chead* hauled Richard into the air. Richard swore as his feet left the ground, and then lashed out with a fist. The blow caught the *Chead* square in the face and sent it staggering backwards.

Richard stumbled as Hecate released him, his wings flaring out to steady him.

"Some legion," Richard spat. He looked around the room, defiant, a wild anger in his eyes. "Maybe you're not a match for us, after all."

Hecate straightened, but made no move towards Richard. Instead, it turned back to Chris. "Consider my offer," the *Chead* grated out the words, "are you with us... or with *them*?"

Closing his eyes, Chris shook his head. Pity swelled inside him, a sadness for the hate and torment that had shaped these creatures. Despite their brutality, despite the slaughter and destruction that followed their awakening, he sensed a depth to the *Chead*. There was more to them than the feral creatures he had seen on the television.

They were more human than anyone realised.

Yet Hecate and these others, born within the cold walls of the facility, had never been given the chance to discover that humanity. The vile cruelty of Doctor Halt had shaped them, moulded them with hate and fear, allowing nothing else to grow.

"I'm sorry, Hecate," he addressed the *Chead*, "we cannot help you. Doctor Halt and the ones who supported him are our enemy. Not humanity. After all, we are human ourselves."

Now it was the *Chead's* turn to laugh. "So you think... but will *they*?"

FIFTY-TWO

Liz let out a long breath as the last *Chead* slipped through the doorway. Heart still pounding, she moved to the window and watched as eight shadows slid from the house into the surrounding trees. For a long time she stood watching the woods, waiting to see if they would return. But the only movement came from the wiry branches swaying in the morning breeze, and finally she turned back to the others.

Richard and Jasmine still stood in the centre of the room, their faces pale. The girl clung to Jasmine's leg, the occasional tremor of her wings belaying her fear. As Liz moved away from the window, Chris stepped back in from the hallway and looked at her.

"They're gone?"

She nodded, and he crossed the room and pulled her into his arms. Holding him tight, Liz struggled to relax, to cast aside her fear. But now, with the heat of the moment gone, it clung to her, spreading until her whole body was trembling. Her breath rattled in her chest as she closed her eyes, and saw again the boy's grey eyes staring down at her.

After a few moments, the terror began to pass, and she loosened her grip on Chris. Their eyes met as they parted, and she nodded at Chris's unspoken question.

"I'm okay," she looked at the others. "What about you, Richard, Jasmine?"

"I'm fine," Richard shook his head, "they're not so terrifying in person."

Taking a breath, Jasmine stepped away from him, taking the girl with her. A hurt look spread across Richard's face and his shoulders slumped, but Liz ignored him. Jasmine would get over what had happened in the forest eventually. They all would.

Beside her, Chris chuckled softly. "They're terrifying enough for me," shaking his head, his eyes settled on the young girl still clutching at Jasmine's trousers. He crossed the room and knelt beside her. "Hey there."

The girl whimpered and shrank back as Chris offered his hand. Her wings rose to hide her face, the grey feathers shivering with her fear. Chris let out a long sigh and looked up at them, eyebrows raised.

"Any ideas?" he asked. "This is getting a little ridiculous."

Liz rolled her eyes and shook her head in amusement. She looked across at Jasmine. "How about you boys go out back and pick some fruit. Give us girls some time to talk."

Richard and Chris shared an awkward look, before doing what she said. Liz watched them go, and then turned to face Jasmine. Jasmine stared straight back at her, her eyes hard and arms folded defensively.

Letting out a long sigh, Liz attempted a smile. Ignoring Jasmine's frosty glare, she strode across and lowered herself to the wooden floor. Crossing her legs, she nodded to Jasmine, indicating she should do the same. The taller girl hesitated, then with a snort she joined Liz on the ground. Sitting cross-legged, she watched with bemusement as the younger girl crawled into her lap and hid her face beneath her wings again.

Liz smiled, and even the corner of Jasmine's lips tugged upwards. Scooting forward on her bottom, Liz reached out a hand and rested it gently on the girl's wings. A shudder went through them, her terror obvious. Silently, Liz began to stroke the girl's feathers, waiting for the trembling to stop.

When the girl finally seemed to have calmed, Liz spoke in her friendliest voice. "Hello again," she paused, struggling to find the words she needed. "I thought it was about time us girls had some alone time. Richard and Chris have gone to find us some breakfast, and those creatures aren't coming back. You're safe, you can talk to us."

Somewhat to her surprise, the girl's wings retracted, revealing her pale, tear-streaked face. She blinked up at Liz, then turned to look around the room. Liz withdrew her hand and sat up straight, waiting to see what the girl would do. The mismatched blue and green eyes swept the room once, then again, before she was apparently satisfied they were alone. With a quick burst of movement, she scrambled from Jasmine's lap and sat beside them, crossing her legs in a mimic of the older girls.

Jasmine and Liz shared a glance, before turning back to the girl.

"My name is Liz, and this is Jasmine," Liz spoke again, then, "You can speak?"

The girl nodded silently, her eyes flicking between the two of them.

"Can you tell us your name?" Jasmine asked now, leaning in, a friendly smile on her lips.

The girl swallowed, looked around the room again, then nodded. "My name is… Mira," she whispered.

Grinning at her success, Liz carefully held out her hand. "It's nice to meet you, Mira."

Mira stared at her hand, her eyes wide, as though unsure what to do with it. After a minute Liz gave up and retrieved her hand. Ignoring the awkward moment, she pressed on. "Where do you come from, Mira?"

The girl blinked. "Come… from?" she looked from Liz to Jasmine, "I don't know…"

Mira's lips quivered and tears gathered in her eyes. Jasmine let out an impatient sigh. Seeing her frustration, Liz spoke quickly, before the other girl drove Mira back into her shell.

"It's okay, Mira. Maybe we can help you," she moved forward and put an arm around the young girl.

The girl shuddered, and with a violent shove pushed Liz away from her. Liz gasped at the girl's strength. She fell backwards onto the wooden floor as the girl leapt to her feet, her eyes flashing with grief and anger.

"*It's not okay!*" Mira screeched, the words tumbling from her now, "He's gone! They took me away and now he's gone and there's no one left to look after him!"

Jasmine and Liz stared up at the girl. Her wings had spread with the angry words, and her shoulders shook with every harsh intake of breath. Slowly, Liz drew herself to her feet. Jasmine rose to stand beside her. She glimpsed movement in the hallway, but raised her hand, signalling for the boys to stay out of it.

"Mira," she said softly. "Who's gone? Who took you away?"

"Artemis," Mira's voice trembled. "Artemis is gone. That man in the white coat took me away from him. He left Artemis there to die!"

"What man?" Jasmine asked.

"Who is Artemis?" Liz questioned at the same time.

"The man you call Halt," Mira answered Jasmine's question. A shudder went through Mira as she spoke the name, and her feathers stood on end.

"And Artemis?" Liz repeated.

"Artemis… he's… he's my father."

FIFTY-THREE

"Your father? Why would your father look like a *Chead*?" Liz muttered, half to herself. How could the girl mistaken the *Chead*, Hecate, for her father?

But her words had driven Mira back inside her shell. Silently cursing herself, Liz stepped towards her, but now Mira retreated across the room. Reaching the corner, she crumped to the ground and curled into a ball on the wooden floor. Harsh sobs tore from her throat as the grey wings rose to cover her again.

To Liz's surprise, Jasmine moved across and crouched beside Mira. Wrapping the girl in her arms, Jasmine glared up at Liz. "Well done," she hissed. "And I thought I was the blunt one."

Guilt welled in Liz's chest but as she stepped towards them, a low growl came from the girl. Liz froze, her heart inexplicably beginning to race. She took a quick step back again. She had felt the girl's potency just a moment earlier, and despite her own strength, one look at the girl's mismatched eyes was enough for her to back away.

Movement came from the hallway, and the boys stepped quietly into the room. They had found an old potato sack somewhere and filled it with fruit from the trees behind the house. Her stomach growled at the sight.

"You did well," Chris said softly as he joined them, offering her an apple. He grinned. "Well, better than me anyway."

Liz took the apple with a smile and pulled him to her. Her fear fell away as his arms went around her, and for a second she closed her eyes, letting the worries of the world recede. But even in Chris's strong embrace, she could not quite banish her dread.

She knew it was not just the girl, but everything that had happened since their escape. The soldiers, the helicopter, the *Chead*. It felt as though things were spinning out of control, like they were racing towards some awful fate, over which they had no control.

When they finally separated, Liz kissed Chris lightly on the cheek before facing the room. Mira seemed to have recovered somewhat, but her lips remained tightly shut, and no amount of prodding would get her talking again.

Moving to the window, Liz looked out through the dust streaked glass. Her stomach clenched as she realised that with the boys back inside, there was no one keeping watch. She cursed under her breath as she stared out the window, her heart suddenly racing.

Outside, the cluster of buildings remained unchanged, untouched by movement. The midday sun beat down across the iron roofs, harsh and unforgiving despite the cold winds blowing down from the mountains. The relentless heat was a grim reality of life on the prairies. Her parents and their farmhands had worked the early mornings and late evenings to avoid the scorching sun, taking siesta through from midday and into the afternoon. But even with those precautions, heatstroke and dehydration was common.

Liz stood for a long time at the window, her eyes searching the shadows. Her stomach twisted with unease, refusing to be quelled by the silence outside. It swirled and shrank, and a wave of nausea rose in her throat. Prickles of fear spread down her spine as she finally turned back to the others.

"I think we should get out of here," she announced, surprising even herself.

The others stared back. Richard frowned and Jasmine snorted. Even Mira took a moment to look up. Only Chris seemed to take her seriously.

"What?" he asked.

Crossing the room, Liz looked around the little group, her urgency growing. "I think we should get out of here, right now."

Jasmine pulled herself to her feet, one hand still resting in Mira's grey hair. "It's got to be a hundred and forty outside," she argued. "I don't know about you, but I'd like to keep my skin intact."

"What's wrong, Liz?" Chris ignored the others, his eyes fixed on hers.

Liz shook her head. "I'm not sure. It just doesn't feel right, staying here. Not after the *Chead*..."

"They were pretty quick to take off, Liz," Richard replied. "I don't think they're coming back."

"I know," Liz murmured. She bit her lip. "But I still don't like it. If they could find us so easily, how long before the soldiers do the same. And what if the *Chead* were followed here?"

As she spoke the words, the sense of urgency exploded in her chest, like sparks catching in leaf litter. In her mind, she saw soldiers creeping through the forests around the house, rifles held at the ready. Suppressing a shriek, she reached out and grabbed Chris by the wrist.

"They could have led Halt's people right to us," she said.

Chris stared back, his hazel eyes dark in the shadows of the room. Then he was nodding, spinning to face the others, the words tumbling from his mouth. "Liz is right," he said, already moving. "If they're tracking the *Chead*, Hecate might have led them right to our doorstep."

Sweeping up the heavy jacket he had claimed as his own, Chris looked around the room. Liz's sense of urgency was spreading now, as the others realised the truth of her words. Richard moved into the kitchen and collected the potato sack of fruit, while Jasmine swept up the bundle of jackets they had piled in the corner. She tossed one to Richard as he emerged from the kitchen, before offering one to Liz.

Then they were moving towards the doorway. Richard took the lead, the potato sack slung over one shoulder and jacket bundled under one arm. Jasmine came after him, leading Mira by the hand, while Liz and Chris took the rear.

Liz paused in the doorway, turning to cast a final glance back over the living room. She swallowed as grief rose in her throat. Even empty, without furniture or family, this was still her home. Her two years on the run had not changed that. This was where she had taken her first steps, where her father had taught her to tie a lasso. It was where she had been loved, where she had been safe. It was the last connection to her past, to her mother and father and friends.

She turned away as tears blurred her vision. Something tore inside her as she moved down the corridor after the others, as though something precious and fragile had shattered. She held her breath, struggling to hold back the tears, and rushed out the front door into the courtyard.

"Where do we go?" Richard asked as she emerged into the sunlight.

Liz swallowed. "Into the forest," she croaked. "Up the mountain to the edge of the treeline. We can make better time moving at the edge of trees, but we'll still be under cover."

Richard nodded and started off into the woods. Together, they worked their way into the scrub and started up the mountain, using the low-lying trees as cover. Thick branches twisted overhead, pressing in on them and making movement difficult. But they would shield them from the air, if there was anyone watching.

Liz had made the climb many times as a child, but she was older now, no longer small enough to slip easily between the dense branches. Small, sharp stones covered the steep slope, making her grateful for the boots they had scavenged from her house. She grasped at tree trunks as her feet slipped on the loose stones, clambering upwards, fear driving her on.

Within minutes they were all panting, even their newfound strength and endurance struggling with the steep mountainside. The unstable slope required time and patience, but their frantic rush to clear the ranch left no room for caution. So despite their exhaustion, they pressed on, ever upwards through the dense trees.

It took them an hour to reach the treeline.

They were just in time.

Gasping for breath, Liz lowered herself to the rocky scree as the others collapsed around her. The mountain stretched up another hundred feet to the summit, but from here the slopes were barren of life. She looked back at the trees, past the scraggly branches reaching out towards them, searching the valley below for a last glimpse of her home.

For a second, everything was quiet. Below, the brown fields stretched out from the mountain, the tiny specks of cows and sheep moving slowly over the flat surface, while the grey lines of empty rivers wound their way across the plains. Amidst the trees below, she glimpsed the dull gleam of a metal roof, but otherwise the ranch was hidden from view.

Then movement on the horizon drew her gaze. An ugly black speck marred the endless blue sky, far off in the distance. But as she watched it grew, and with it came a far-off rumbling. In seconds it had doubled, then tripled in size, a menacing presence racing towards their little mountain sanctuary.

Sunlight glinted off steel as the jetfighter banked, its speed slowing as two dark shapes disconnected from its underbelly. They shot across the sky, leaving long white streaks of cloud behind them. The shriek of the jet engine rose to a roar, its angry voice echoing from the slopes around them, all but deafening.

Liz rose quickly to her feet, but there was no time to run, to take flight. Only to stare as death raced towards them. Beside her, Jasmine screamed and tripped on the loose gravel. Richard caught her before she fell, and she clung to him, their eyes fixed on the approaching missiles, their animosity forgotten.

The ground shook as the missiles struck, slamming into the slope far beneath them. A scream built in Liz's throat as she watched a blossom of flame rise from the side of the mountain. She caught a glimpse of an iron roof flung high into the air, of wooden boards disintegrating, then Chris was there. He pulled her to him, wrapping her in his arms, drawing her away from the sight. But even turned away she could still see the image in her mind, see the flames consuming everything she had ever known. She could feel the heat on her back, even from where they stood high above, and hear the wild howls of the flames.

Sobbing, she buried her head in Chris's shoulder. For a long while, they stood together like that, unable to move. Eventually she heard the others stirring, and felt Chris preparing to pull away. She hugged him harder for a second, and then released him. Turning to stare down the slope, she watched the flames licking the hillside, spreading through the forest, consuming all they touched.

And silently, she turned away.

FIFTY-FOUR

SAM SUCKED IN A BREATH AS HE WALKED ACROSS THE OPEN hall, the wooden boards creaking softly beneath his boots. His body felt fresh, all but recovered from the relentless beatings. Even after everything he'd witnessed over the past few months, he was still shocked by how quickly he had healed. Within a day, the dark bruises and swelling around his eye had begun to fade. Yet another boon of their genetic manipulation, he guessed.

Even so, his heart was heavy. He had not seen Ashley since the day he'd watched Halt torture her. He had expected to see her when they shifted him to San Francisco, but he had been alone in the prison van. With his collar chained to the floor, he had spent the long journey with nothing but the roar of the engine and the stench of gasoline for company. The road had been old and rutted, and he had been bounced around like a sack of old potatoes. The air had quickly grown hot and suffocating, the steel walls burning with the heat of the sun.

Sam had suffered the journey without complaint though, thankful to at least be free of his empty prison cell, of the relentless torture.

Now as he strode across the hall, his body healed, with fresh clothes on his back, he could almost imagine himself free. Almost – if not for the unrelenting pressure of the collar around his neck.

He kept his wings pressed tight against his back as he moved. Like the rest of his injuries, they were healing nicely, and he now felt at ease with the strange appendages. Distantly he recalled the difficulty he'd had even standing when his wings first appeared. It would have been embarrassing, if he'd not been so preoccupied with escape.

Armed with the memory, he knew he should have viewed the spectacle taking place in the centre of the hall with more compassion. But he could not help but grin as he watched the antics of the boy and girl he had come to meet.

They clung desperately to one another as they staggered across the wooden floor, their long black wings hanging behind them like dead weights. Their mouths were wide open, panting as they struggled to remain upright. Every so often one would shriek and topple to the ground. They seemed to lack any control over their wings, which would shift position almost spontaneously, throwing them off balance just when they seemed to find their feet.

The girl sported long blonde hair and plain brown eyes, and stood at least a foot shorter than Sam's own six foot five. Her features were sharp and pronounced, and dark bruises spotted her pale skin. She seemed to have the better control over her faculties, though it was a close match.

The boy's dark skin and athletic build stood out in stark contrast to his partner. Even half-stooped-over by the weight of his wings, the boy was an equal of Sam's height. The only feature that matched between the two were the brown eyes and black wings – and even those differed vastly in size.

Neither had noticed Sam's approach, and when he finally drew to a stop beside them he was forced to clap his hands to get their attention. Their eyes widened when they looked up and found him standing beside them. Then they promptly toppled onto their backsides.

Sam laughed, and then quickly masked it with a cough. Shaking his head, he raised an eyebrow. "That was graceful."

The boy scowled up at him. "I'd like to see you do any better."

Sam smiled. With a sharp *crack*, his wings snapped open, the copper feathers spreading out to shade the two teenagers from the overhead lights. Their mouths dropped to the floor and the colour fled their faces.

As Sam slowly contracted his wings, the girl stuttered. "How… how did you do that?"

Sam laughed as he offered her a hand. Pulling the girl to her feet, he held her steady and smiled. "What's your name?"

The girl hesitated. "Francesca," she mumbled finally, then waved at the boy who was still finding his feet. "This is Paul. You look familiar. Who are you?"

"My name is Sam. We were probably neighbours in the facility. It seems we belong to the rather exclusive group of unfortunate souls lucky enough to have survived that nightmare," he paused, "but the two of you look like you just woke up."

The two shared a glance. "The last thing we remember was the injections in our cell, and passing out from the pain," Francesca took a breath, her face paling, "Next thing we know, we're in some prison van. And there was just the two of us. Well, us two, and the girl."

Sam's heart skipped a beat. "What girl?"

"Didn't get a name," Paul finally found his feet, "She looked pretty beaten up. Big bandages around her chest and things."

Sucking in a lungful of air, Sam struggled to contain his excitement. "Describe her."

"Ahhh," Francesca bit her lip. "Skinny girl, pale skin, red hair?"

Sam closed his eyes, a smile tugging at his lips.

Ashley.

"You know her?" he heard Paul ask.

Sam nodded as he looked back at them. "Did she say anything?"

"Not much," Francesca offered. "Like we said, she was pretty beaten up. She just warned us about... well, these," she gestured to her wings with a shrug.

"Yes, you do seem to be having some problems," he smirked. "You looked like new-born foals, stumbling around like that."

Paul scowled. He crossed his arms defiantly, but the effect was somewhat diminished as his wings shifted suddenly, throwing him back off balance.

Sam chuckled as the boy stumbled sideways into Francesca. "Halt wasn't kidding when he said you might need some help."

The two exchanged a glance as they steadied themselves. "Halt sent you?" Francesca asked.

The smile fell from Sam's lips as he nodded. He eyed them both, weighing them up. They were vaguely familiar, though he could not recall any particular time he had seen them in the facility. Both looked fit and well-toned, in good shape considering the time they had spent in the coma. The girl looked like she could have been a cheerleader in her former life – her long blonde hair and pale skin certainly matched the stereotype. In contrast, the boy could easily have been a line-backer in a college football team.

But who were they really? And could he trust them?"

"I'm here to teach you how to use those," Sam said at last, deciding to withhold judgement for the moment, "to show you what you're capable of."

"What we're capable of?" Paul frowned.

"Yes," without warning, Sam sprang forward and grabbed the boy by the shirt. With one hand, he lifted him from the ground.

Paul gasped, his eyes bulging as he stared down at Sam. "What—"

He broke off as Sam released him. He landed easily on his feet, but the weight of his wings pulled him off balance again, and he crashed back to the wooden floor. He stared up at Sam, eyes wide, mouth hanging open.

"How did you do that?" Francesca whispered finally. "He must weigh 250 pounds, at least."

Grinning, Sam offered Paul a hand. When the boy was back on his feet, he glanced between the two of them. "Oh, that's just the tip of the iceberg, kidos."

FIFTY-FIVE

CHRIS SIGHED AS HE LOWERED HIMSELF INTO THE PLASTIC chair. His legs ached from the long march across the mountain slopes, and his arms and face throbbed where sunburn had started to set in. His pale skin had darkened over the days since their escape, but it was no match for the scorching rays of the midday sun.

Closing his eyes, he leaned back in the seat and rested his head against the cold brick wall behind him. Not for the first time in the last few hours, he sent up silent thanks for Liz's quick thinking. If not for her, they would have been caught in the inferno that had swallowed the ranch. Whether the missiles had been meant for the *Chead* or themselves, they would probably never know. But it didn't matter now – it was clear their pursuers were after blood.

Afterwards, Liz had led them around the mountain in silence. Her movements had been stiff, almost robotic, and his attempts to reach her had fallen on deaf ears. Chris and the others had been little better. Chris could barely comprehend the display of power they had witnessed, how close to death they had come. And so they had followed Liz across the mountain slopes without complaint.

An hour later, Liz had finally turned and started down the side of the mountain. Chris and the others breathed sighs of relief as they re-entered the trees. Before the wiry branches closed over them, Chris had caught a brief glance of the plains below. The brown fields still stretched out in all directions, but here the thin line of a road cut away from the mountain. It led off towards the western horizon, where a cluster of distant buildings hovered beneath a shimmering haze.

They descended rapidly through the trees, struggling to keep up with Liz. She leapt between patches of bare earth, landing on roots and grabbing branches, barely pausing to recover her balance. Chris and the others followed as best they could, even their newfound agility struggling to keep pace with the silent girl.

When they reached the bottom, Liz had glanced briefly at the sky, and then stepped out into the open. She moved without hesitation, striding determinedly out into the long brown grass. As she walked, she pulled on the jacket she had taken from the house, hiding her wings beneath the denim fabric. Even folded tight against her back, they still left a bulge beneath the jacket, but Chris hoped it would fool the casual observer. He and the others quickly followed suit.

They had already weighed the risks of taking flight, and dismissed the idea. During the day, it would be suicide. A bunch of winged teenagers were bound to be spotted, even in the sparsely populated countryside. At least on the ground, they might pass as ordinary people, and be overlooked by the governments spotters. And while the long grass offered little cover, it was better than nothing.

They had walked for an hour through the open paddocks, keeping parallel to the road, before Liz paused suddenly and looked back. She squinted, her gaze travelling past Chris and down the road to where it twisted around the mountain. Chris followed her gaze and saw a cloud of dust approaching. The clatter of iron hooves and the hard thud of wheels reached them a second later.

He shared a glance with the others, and then ducked down into the long grass. Waiting in the meagre cover, Chris watched the dust cloud closely. It quickly grew larger, though from the sounds that reached them, he knew it was not a car. A few minutes later, he saw the horses take shape amidst the cloud, followed by a cart on steel rimmed wheels. A man sat on the bench up front, reins held in one hand as he urged the horses onwards.

Letting out a sigh of relief, Chris had settled down in the grass to watch the wagon pass by. But as it neared, movement came from away to his right as Liz lifted herself from the ground. He swore as she walked towards the road, waving at the man with the reins.

A shout came from the road and the clatter of hooves started to slow. Glancing around, Chris had searched for the others, but the long grass hid them from view. He swore again, then pulled himself up and started after Liz.

"Woah!" the driver's voice carried across the field as the wagon drew to a stop.

Liz was already on the road, grinning up at the driver. Chris stumbled after her, Jasmine, Richard and Mira emerging from the grass around him.

"Hey there, little missy," Chris noted a southern twang to the man's accent as he spoke. "Whatcha doing all the way out here?"

"We've come down from the Huerta property," Liz replied easily. "The landowner's kids are visiting. My sister and I wanted to show them the town while they're here."

The wagon driver looked up and noticed the rest of them for the first time. His eyes slid over Jasmine and Richard without concern. But his brow hardened as his gaze settled on Chris and Mira, taking in their pale skin and short-cropped hair. Chris stared back, surprised at the sudden hostility in the man's eyes.

"The Huerta's is a long way off," his tone had turned gruff. "Don't see ya folks around here a lot. Ya walk the whole way?"

Liz nodded, displaying her best smile. "Camped under the stars last night. Shoulda seen the city slicker's eyes when they saw them."

The man laughed at that, and after another moment's hesitation, he nodded. "Righto. Let it not be said old Ronaldo forgot his manners. Jump in the back, folks. You can ride up here with me, missy."

Laughing, Liz had joined him, while the others climbed warily into the hay stacked high in the back of the wagon.

A few hours later, after a bumpy ride that left Chris's backside aching, the cart had finally rumbled into the town. The driver pulled over in the main street to let them out before waving goodbye. He was heading to a property further down the highway, but he gave them directions to the only motel in town.

Once he'd driven off, Liz had promptly ignored his instructions and led them down a side street. As they wound their way through the town, Chris could not help but stare at the world in which he now found himself. It was as though they had stepped backwards through time. He glimpsed the occasional old car or truck parked in the streets, their paint long since faded away and their bodies speckled with rust. But it seemed most of residents made do with wagons and horses. They lined the streets, waiting outside the old buildings as their owners came and went.

Taking in the spectacle, Chris half-expected men in cowboy hats to stumble from the local pub and start a gunfight in the street. But with the sun creeping towards the distant horizon, the roads were quiet, and most people avoided the strangers passing through their midst.

Only when Liz drew up outside the bus station had Chris finally guessed her intentions. Before he had a chance to stop her, she walked up to the lady standing behind the only ticket booth. Pulling a thin black wallet from her pocket, she handed over a wad of bills, and then returned soon after clutching a bundle of tickets in her hand.

"Where did you get that?" Richard asked, nodding at the wallet.

Liz only shrugged, her eyes hard, expressionless. "We needed it more than him."

Chris swallowed. Ignoring the others, he stepped in close to her. She flinched back from him, but he grabbed her before she could move, and wrapped her into his arms. She resisted for just a second, stiffening and trying to pull away. But he refused to release her, and all of a sudden, she crumpled in his arms.

"It's okay," he whispered. He drew her quietly away from the ticket booth, where the woman still stood watching them.

Liz was shaking in his arms, her hot tears soaking into his shoulder, harsh sobs tearing from her throat. Unable to find the words to comfort her, to make everything okay, Chris did the only thing he could. He held her in silence, and waited for her grief to pass.

Slowly the tears had faded away, her shaking lessening. When she finally pulled away, her eyes were wet, but with a gentle smile she leaned forward and kissed him on the cheek.

"Thank you," she whispered.

Chris smiled. "For what?"

But she only shook her head. Taking a breath, she looked across at the others, who waited nearby. Richard and Jasmine still stood apart from one another, the wounds not quite healed. Mira had wandered off amongst the rows of plastic chairs, her hands in her pockets as she eyed the tiny food stand opposite the ticket booth.

Looking back to Liz, Chris reached up and wiped a tear from her cheek. "So, where are we going, Liz?"

Liz's lips tightened. "San Francisco," she looked around defiantly as she spoke, as though daring them to object. "I'm tired of running, of hiding. Sooner or later, they're going to kill us. Or worse, catch us and take us back. We have to find a way to fight back, to put an end to this once and for all."

"And going to the capital is how we do that?" Richard scowled. "That sounds like suicide to me. You can count me out."

Chris's stomach twisted. "Are you sure about this, Liz?"

Pursing her lips, she nodded. Her eyes locked with Richard's. "You were right, that night in the mountains, Richard. Living on the run, never knowing when the hunters will finally catch up, it's not a life at all. Trust me, I've lived it. We have to find a better way."

Jasmine had been unusually silent, but she stepped forward then. "There's hundreds of street cameras, police, informants. How do we avoid them?"

Liz shrugged. "We keep our heads down, stick to the crowds. San Francisco is a city of millions. However hard they try, they can't keep them all in line," she paused, her eyes sweeping over them. "Besides, they've got our families. If they're still alive, we can't turn our backs on them."

That last point had marked the end of any further argument. The discussion carried on for a few more minutes, but the thought of finding where their parents were, of possibly rescuing them, had taken the fight from Richard and Jasmine. Even Mira had returned from her wandering, asking whether they could find Artemis as well.

Now, as Chris settled back in the bus station chair, he smiled at the thought of the five of them taking the bus. It was genius of Liz, really. With the wide-open plains, they could not fly during the day, and at night they would have no way of telling which direction they were heading in. The bus would have no such problems. And better yet – it was the last thing Halt and his hunters would expect. After all, who would take the bus, when they could fly?

The only problem was the wait. For the last two hours, the five of them had tried lying in various positions on the rows of plastic seats, struggling to get comfortable. The bus was already an hour late, and there was still no sign of its arrival.

He hoped it would be in better condition than the other vehicles they'd seen in town, but from the state of the bus station, it wasn't looking good. A corrugated iron roof stretched overhead, still radiating the heat of the day, but there were no walls to keep out the wind. The ticket booth was even smaller than their prison cells in the facility. The lady behind the glass had her feet up on the bench, and was reading from a book titled *Wild*.

Opposite the booth stood the food cart. From the pictures on its side, it offered an array of burgers and hotdogs. None looked particularly appetising, but the faint scent of food still made Chris's stomach rumble. Unfortunately, there was not enough cash left in the stolen wallet for hot food, and they were forced to make do with the fruit in their bag.

A television flickered on the wall of the ticket booth, facing the row of a seats in which they sat. Glancing at the screen, Chris frowned as the image went black. A second later a new image shifted into focus. It showed a man standing on a steel podium, facing a crowd of journalists. The man wore a dark red tie and his short grey hair was slicked flat against his skull.

He held his shoulders straight as he looked out over the crowd. Prominent cheekbones gave his face a harsh look in the glow of the overhead lights. His hazel eyes fixed on the camera as he waited for the reporters to settle.

Chris stared at the screen, his heart starting to pound, as a sense of premonition tingled in the back of his mind. Swallowing, he glanced at the others. The man's face was one they all knew. In fact, it was impossible to forget.

The man standing on the podium was the President of the Western Allied States.

FIFTY-SIX

"Ladies and gentlemen," the President began, his voice smooth, his tone sombre. "I am here today with news on our recent troubles."

As he spoke, the President stared straight into the camera, his eyes seeming to reach through the television itself. Chris shivered, glancing around to see if the others were watching. The volume was low, but his ears had no trouble picking up the words.

"As you know, we have recently stepped up our domestic counter insurgency efforts. Acting on intelligence provided by the Director of Domestic Affairs, numerous rebel groups and their foreign benefactors have been apprehended in recent months."

"Mr President!" a woman's voice carried through the speakers as a reporter stepped forward. Two men in suits moved to intercept her, but the President waved them down, and nodded for the woman to continue. "Could you provide some indication of the sources used to identify these groups?"

"I'm afraid that's classified," the President stared down his nose at the woman, "but I assure you, both myself and your Electors have scrutinised the source and can testify to its legitimacy. There can be no doubt, these are dangerous persons – both to our individual security, and the safety of our nation."

The President paused then, waiting to see whether the woman would interrupt again, before continuing. "We have brought the full force of our laws down on individuals associated with these groups. Enhanced interrogation methods have allowed us to identify ringleaders, and collapse networks of foreign spies who work to undermine our sovereignty. Those found guilty of treason have been executed, while their families and close associates have been detained and sentenced to follow them."

The others were all staring at the television by now. This was the first news they'd heard about their abductions, and how their disappearance had been presented to the public. It seemed Doctor Halt had been telling the truth when he'd said their families were accused of treason.

Chris's stomach twisted at the mention of execution. He felt a hand on his arm, and glanced up to see Liz watching him. He attempted a smile, but the effort was a miserable failure. Silently he turned his head back to the television.

On the screen, the President was still speaking. "While we are confident our actions have discouraged further resistance by these groups, there has been an unfortunate setback," he paused, and Chris's heart lurched as he realised what was coming. "Several associates of these traitors recently escaped from a secure facility in the Californian mountains. While we had hoped to quickly reacquire these individuals, to date they have evaded our militaries best efforts to bring them to justice. Our soldiers have suffered several casualties due to their actions. Unfortunately, we believe they may have now reached civilian populations."

The President broke off as the mob of reporters started to shout questions. Across the bottom of the screen, four faces flashed into view. Chris swallowed as he saw his own face staring back at him, alongside mugshots of Liz, Richard and Jasmine. Strangely, Mira's face was missing, and again he wondered about the girl's strange past.

He looked up at the woman in the ticket booth, and the man working the food stand, but neither were paying any attention to the broadcast. He looked around at the others, wondering what they should do. Liz shook her head, her lips pursed tight, and nodded back to the screen.

The reporters had quieted now, allowing the President to continue. "As I said, these four individuals are considered armed and highly dangerous. They should not be approached under any circumstances. The parents of each were apprehended for their involvement with rebel activities, and were sentenced to death for high crimes against the state. Their sentences were scheduled for the December executions, and carried out as part of the New Year's Eve celebrations. Unfortunately, this only makes these individuals more dangerous – they have nothing left to lose."

On the screen, the President's mouth continued to move, but Chris could no longer hear the words. Blood pounded in his ears as he stared at the screen, drowning out all other sound. An awful pain lanced through his chest, as though someone had just driven a knife into his heart. He gasped, struggling suddenly for breath, as the pain swept out to consume him. Inside, he could feel something breaking, something shattering into a thousand pieces. A low moan built in his throat, as from some great distance he heard Liz's voice, calling his name.

Almost in a trance, Chris turned to stare at her. Liz spoke again, her lips moving, her eyes watering with unspilt tears, but no sound reached Chris's ears. She leaned forward, her arms wrapping around his chest, pulling him to her, but still Chris felt nothing. An empty void had opened inside him, stretching out to swallow him whole.

His stomach swirled and a sick nausea rose in his throat. Pushing Liz away, he staggered to his feet. He felt a desperate need to scream, to shout and shriek and rage, to lash out until the world felt his pain. Then an image of his mother rose in his mind, her eyes warm and lips curled in a smile, and despair swept away his fury.

Silently, Chris sank back onto the twisted plastic seat, and buried his head in his hands.

FIFTY-SEVEN

LIZ WINCED AS THE BUS LURCHED OVER ANOTHER POTHOLE, sending her bouncing towards the roof. The engine roared as they raced down the gravel road, its maintenance long forgotten by a government intent on expanding their own wealth. A massive network of railroads criss-crossed the prairies, carrying harvests from distant properties to the cities and their shipping ports, but for the locals, the bus was their only option for transportation. No one Liz knew had the money to afford the passenger train, let alone a car.

Now, some eight hours into the bus ride, Liz was still struggling to sleep. When they'd first boarded, the bus was already packed, and they had been forced to stand for the first few hours. The bus stopped and started constantly to pick up and drop off passengers though, and slowly they edged further down the aisle in the hope of finding seats.

Even with the fall of darkness, the heat in the bus was suffocating. The breeze from the open windows barely reached them in the aisles, and by the time a seat opened beside Liz, her head was swimming.

Unfortunately, Liz knew from experience the cramped seats were little better than standing. The old benches were meant to fit two passengers, but the cramped conditions meant three people squeezed onto each seat. This left Liz perched half in the aisle, still far from the cool breeze coming through the windows. To make matters worse, she could feel the muscles of her wings beginning to cramp beneath her jacket, and when she leaned back against them, a sharp ache quickly developed in her back.

Finally, the two large women in the seats beside her rose and shuffled their way off the bus. Liz quickly moved across to take the window seat, allowing the others to figure out who would take the two remaining spaces. Mira and Jasmine soon slid in beside her, while Richard and Chris stayed standing.

Her heart twisted as she looked up at Chris. He had not spoken since the news broadcast. His eyes had taken on a haunted look, and his skin was a pallid grey mixed with the red of his sunburn. She desperately wanted to pull him into her arms, to hold him and love him until he was whole again.

She had tried to comfort him, the way he had comforted her just a few hours earlier. But Chris had been as stiff as a board, his eyes blank, void of emotion. He had pushed her away and boarded the bus without looking back.

Now, closing her eyes, Liz prayed he would be okay. They had to stick together, had to be strong if they were to survive. They were alone now – truly alone, the five of them against the world.

Mira seemed to be the only one of them capable of sleeping through the hellish bus ride. She nestled between Liz and Jasmine, curled up on the seat with her knees tucked up to her chin. Glimpsing a tangle of feathers hanging out from beneath her purple jacket, Liz carefully reached down at tucked them back out of sight. She smiled, realising it was one of her mother's favourites. She had often worn it when the winter storms rolled in, bringing with them the howling wind and drenching rains.

But the memory only brought back the image of her home, of the last connection she had to her parents, disintegrating in the flames. She turned away, struggling to banish the image, lest she fall back into an abyss of her own.

"They didn't have her picture up," Jasmine's voice whispered from the darkness.

Liz looked across at her. The bus was full, but most of those sitting appeared to have nodded off. Even the people standing looked asleep on their feet, their eyes closed and heads leaning against arms clenched around steel polls. Only Chris and Richard remained awake, their eyes staring vacantly into space.

"It's strange, isn't it?" Liz replied finally. She eyed the girl carefully. Since the incident in the forest, and with the *Chead* after, something had changed with Jasmine. Maybe she had become less antagonistic, less distant. It was difficult to tell. "And she thought the *Chead* was her father."

"*And* she was taken by Halt himself," Jasmine added her eyes alight. "Halt wasn't involved with any other abductions, as far as I heard."

Liz frowned at the new information. She bit her lip, trying to make sense of what they knew about Mira, but the answers refused to come. They fell silent as the bus pulled to a stop in front of a tiny shack, and a new passenger stumbled aboard. The man leaned against a pole and closed his eyes, apparently well used to the torture of the night bus.

As the bus's engine roared once more, Liz changed the subject. "Do you really think… do you believe what the President said?"

"He had no reason to lie," Jasmine replied quietly.

After a moment's hesitation, Liz reached out and squeezed Jasmine's shoulder. She could hear the grief in the girl's voice, the unspoken sorrow. They had all been so focused on staying alive, on surviving the horrors of the past weeks and months, that the fate of their parents had become a distant worry. Now it seemed that distance had crumbled, giving way to harsh reality.

She looked away after a while, and stared out into the darkness outside the bus. Clouds had rolled in with the evening, and now the sky was dark, the open plains hidden beneath the blanket of night. In the faint light of the bus's headlights, Liz saw her reflection in the clouded glass. Her hair was a wild tangle, her eyes hard, her brow creased by frown lines.

She stared at the face, so different from the girl she had once been. Even before she had been taken, her life after the loss of her parents had been harsh. It had taken its toll. She had become hard, unforgiving in her desire to survive. It was a fate she would not wish on anyone.

"I hope it was quick," she turned back as Jasmine spoke. Tears streamed down the other girl's face as she continued, "I hope they didn't suffer."

Liz looked at the girl, surprised by her strength. She remembered then how she had reacted in the forest, when the soldiers had captured them. While Richard had begged, Jasmine had been silent, offering only a frosty glare to the circle of soldiers. And now, after hearing the fate of her parents, it seemed like she was coping better than anyone.

"What did they do, your parents?" Liz asked suddenly, sensing a need in Jasmine to talk, to remember.

The other girl fell silent, and for a moment Liz thought she'd misread Jasmine's thoughts. She was starting to turn away, preparing herself for another attempt at sleep, when Jasmine finally spoke.

"They were managers in a rural meat packing plant," Jasmine's voice barely rose above a whisper, "They didn't even put up a fight. We were sitting around the table, just starting dinner, when the SWAT team kicked down the door. They told us we were under arrest, cuffed our hands behind our backs before we could even think of resisting. Then they led mum and dad out of the room, and pulled a black hood over my head. A few minutes later, I heard a woman's voice speaking, then something cold pinched my neck. That's the last thing I remember, before I woke up in the facility."

Liz shivered at the simplicity of Jasmine's story. The passiveness with which her parents had surrendered only served to highlight the absurdity of their charges. Surely traitors would fight, would resist capture to their dying breath.

"I'm sorry," she breathed.

"Don't," Jasmine cut in. She looked away, staring into the darkness of the bus. "I don't need your false pity, Liz. We both know we've only stuck together this long because it's our best chance of survival."

Liz blinked at the harsh tone to Jasmine's voice. She fell silent, turning over the other girl's words, wondering whether they were true. She was right, in a way. There had been little love lost between them in the past, though she had thought that might be changing.

"You're wrong," she said at last. When Jasmine didn't turn around, she continued, "We're in this together because, whatever you may think, we're family now. The five of us are all we have left."

"Yeah, right," Jasmine hissed, struggling to keep her voice under control. She looked at Liz then, her eyes hard. "In the forest, if the *Chead* hadn't come, you would have left us for dead."

"No," Liz cut her off, "If the *Chead* hadn't come, we would have found a way to save you."

Jasmine snorted, but she didn't reply. Liz sighed as the silence stretched out between them. Glancing down, she watched Mira sleeping, thinking idly that at least one of them was enjoying the ride. She reached out and stroked the girl's soft grey hair, wondering again at the mystery surrounding her.

"Whatever you think, we *are* family, Jasmine," she said at last. "Maybe this is just about survival for you, our little group. But it's not for me, and it's not for Chris."

"I guess we'll see," Jasmine replied.

Liz nodded. Her gaze turned back to the aisle, where Chris stood with his head leaning against a steel pole. His eyes were closed, though she doubted he was sleeping.

"I'm worried about him," she said suddenly, not caring whether Jasmine listened or not. "I don't know what's going to happen when we reach San Francisco, what he'll do."

"Probably something stupid," Jasmine said wryly.

"I'm serious," Liz growled. "I'm afraid he'll do something reckless, something that will get him killed. I'm afraid I'm going to lose him."

"Maybe," Jasmine's breath whispered on the air, "and maybe he'd be right to do it. I mean, what's our alternative? Our parents are dead. We're wanted fugitives. And you haven't exactly been forthcoming with ideas to bring down the government. Maybe reckless is what we need," she paused. "Besides, I'd rather go down fighting, than go back to being a slave."

Jasmine's hand drifted to her throat, to the soft flesh where her collar had once rested. Liz found herself shivering as she remembered the awful devices, the agony as electricity lit every nerve in her body on fire. Even so, she shook her head.

"It doesn't need to come to that," she argued. "Not if we're smart, if we lay low. Our parents wouldn't have wanted us to throw away our lives."

Soft laughter came from the darkness. "Lay low? We're heading into the very heart of the government's power," her eyes flashed as she looked at Liz. "No, Liz. If we did what our parents wanted, we would have never left those mountains."

Liz fell silent at that, unable to find an answer to Jasmine's words. Closing her eyes, she turned them over in her mind, wondering if they were true, what her parents would have thought of her now. What would they want her to do now?

She smiled as she recalled a time when she was young, when bandits had come to their lands and started stealing livestock. Her mother and father had gathered up the farm hands and started handing out rifles. They had ridden off at dawn, and returned by dusk, the missing livestock in tow.

"You're wrong, Jasmine," she said at last. "They would want us to fight back."

FIFTY-EIGHT

CHRIS STAGGERED AS HE STEPPED OFF THE BUS, HIS LEGS almost giving way beneath him. The trip had passed by in a blur of anger and grief, the long hours trickling away with every lurching mile. The journey had extended through the night and most of the next day. Now, almost twenty-four hours after they'd first stepped aboard the steel contraption, they had finally reached San Francisco.

Blinking in the fading light, Chris looked around at his surroundings. They were on the edge of downtown San Francisco, somewhere amidst the cramped jumble of buildings that was the National Bus Station. People crowded the footpaths and asphalt, racing between the lumbering buses, struggling to find their way through the packed space.

Since the end of the American War, the population of San Francisco had exploded, and available land had quickly dried up. With expansion in their downtown location all but impossible, the National Bus Service had been forced to cram the last twenty years of growth into the eighty-year-old station. Now the facility was bursting at the seams. Their bus had taken an hour just to manoeuvre its way through the queues of buses waiting outside.

Chris sucked in a breath as he watched the crowd, unable to summon the energy to care about the bodies pressing in around him. Without checking to see whether the others followed, he moved off through the station. A dull emptiness swelled within him, a lonely gulf that sucked away all emotion, leaving him alone, stranded amidst his sorrow.

Threading his way through the garbage littering the footpath, Chris scanned the crowds, searching for an exit. Concrete walls surrounded the boarding area in a U shape, with a narrow entranceway for the buses on the opposite side of the station. But there were numerous doorways through which passengers could enter and exit. Spotting one nearby, Chris headed for it, wrinkling his nose as he stepped over a puddle of liquid that smelled distinctly of urine.

The doorway led him indoors, where the press of people was even denser. Without fans or air conditioning, the heat inside was stifling, even compared to the hellish nightmare that had been the bus ride. His frustration building, Chris shoved his way through the crowd and made his way towards a glowing blue sign that read 'exit'.

Outside, the crowds thinned a little, though the sidewalks were still a mess of human refuse. But before he could go further, a hand grabbed him by the arm, and a voice called his name.

"Chris…" Liz looked up at him as he turned, pain shining from her crystal blue eyes.

Chris paused for a moment, looking down at the girl, searching for the emotions she'd once ignited within him. The pit in his chest twisted, and something flickered inside him. Then it was gone. He shuddered as the sense of loss spread. In its place was a desire to run, to escape.

Shrugging off Liz, Chris turned away from her. He heard her call out, but through the noise of the crowd, her words were unrecognisable. His feet carried him quickly down the sidewalk, away from the others, away from his grief.

Around the station, a host of makeshift market stalls had been erected on the sidewalk, though many were beginning to pack away their wares for the night. Steel braziers burned on the street corners, hotdogs and hamburger patties charring on the blackened grills. Beggars sat beneath their piles of rags, squeezing in between the host of humanity around them. Some held out their hands in silent beseechment, but most just sat staring into space, their eyes devoid of hope, of life.

Chris moved on in silence, head down, refusing to meet the eyes of those he encountered. A woman tried to step into his path, pushing some jewelled necklaces at him, but he quickly shoved his way past. The woman staggered backwards into an overflowing garbage can. Her screams of abuse carried after him, but Chris was too consumed to hear her rage.

His own anger was far greater.

As he made his way through the tangled streets, darkness slowly fell over the city. He left behind the bustling marketplace, moving onto quieter sidewalks, and darker streets. The only pedestrians around now went quickly about their business, eager to be home. This was not a safe neighbour-hood, and with nightfall only the boldest of citizens would dare to be out.

Footsteps came from behind Chris as the others struggled to keep pace with him. Soft voices called after him, but still he did not turn back. Overhead, the streetlights flickered on, but with half of their bulbs broken, they did little to illuminate the darkness.

"*Chris!*" Liz's voice was insistent now. "Chris stop! We need to get off the streets before–"

Liz broke off as a scream echoed down the road. Chris paused midstride, the high-pitched shriek cutting through his thoughts, lifting him momentarily from his spiral of despair. He looked up as it came again, recognisably female now.

A need rose in Chris's chest – a need to act, to fight, to do *something*. His mother was dead, publicly executed as part of some sick New Year's celebration, and he had been power-less to stop it.

But he was powerless no longer.

Fists clenched, Chris began to run.

He leapt over a pile of garbage, his keen eyes scanning the sidewalk ahead, picking a path through the refuse. Ahead, he glimpsed the dark shadow of an alleyway. The scream came again, echoing out from the darkness of the alley, and he turned towards it.

As he came around the corner, he took in the scene without breaking stride. In the shadows, a young girl lay sprawled on the ground, her eyes wide with terror, staring at the two men standing over her. A gash marked her forehead, and her long brown hair lay in tangles across her face. Her coat was torn, its copper buttons lying scattered on the concrete around her.

Her eyes looked up as Chris appeared, her mouth opening to scream again. Before she could speak, one of the men stepped forward and slammed a boot into her stomach. She crumpled beneath the blow, gasping against the filthy concrete.

A low growl rose from Chris' chest as he stepped towards the men. His boot brushed against a can as he moved, sending it rattling across the ground. The men spun at the sound, their eyes finding Chris in the shadows.

Chris hesitated as he saw the police badges shining on their chest, and the blue uniform stretched over their muscular frames. One held a baton casually in his hand, and both wore guns holstered on their belts.

The one who had kicked the girl rested a hand on his gun and growled. "You'd best turn around, kid."

The other moved towards the girl as the speaker stared Chris down. Chris bit his lip, weighing up the distance between himself and the man. Less than ten feet separated them – he could cross that distance in a second. He looked back at the man, and smiled.

The policeman's eyes widened as Chris leapt. His hand tensed, hesitating just a second, before he began to pull the weapon from its holster. But to Chris, the man could have been moving in slow motion. By the time the gun slid free, Chris had already closed the distance. With casual ease, he reached out and caught the man by the wrist.

His foes' eyes widened as he struggled to break Chris's hold, his teeth flashing in the light of a distant streetlamp. But he quickly found he was no match for Chris's mutated strength. Grinning, Chris started to squeeze. A satisfying *crack* came from the man's wrist, and the gun dropped uselessly to the ground.

A flicker of movement came from the corner of Chris's eyes, and turning he saw the other policemen drawing his gun. Tensing, Chris grasped the first man by the collar, lifted him over his head, and hurled him at the other officer. The man flew through the air, his arms wind-milling, and landed on his colleague with an audible thud.

Chris strode towards them, watching as they tripped over themselves trying to get back to their feet. He grinned as he saw the terror in their eyes. Gone were his days of running away, of hiding and sulking while his tormentors enjoyed their privileged lives. The President was right about one thing – he had nothing left to lose now. He would act, would watch the government and all its members burn if he could.

The second man still had his gun, and he pointed it at Chris from the ground. Chris sprang to the side as the barrel flashed, and heard the crack as lead struck the brick wall behind him. He scowled as the man fired again, leaping to the side, then dove forward and kicked out at the gun. It flashed one last time before his boot sent it flying sideways into the wall.

A sharp pain came from Chris's arm and for a second he reeled back. Then a flash of red passed across his eyes, and the pain faded. A boiling rage rose inside him as his breath came in ragged gasps. The man whose wrist he'd broken was on his feet again, swinging his baton with his good arm.

Snarling, Chris reached up and caught the baton mid-swing. The man's face paled, but Chris gave him no time to retreat. Grabbing his arm in an iron grip, Chris dragged him forward into a crunching headbutt. The man staggered beneath the blow, but Chris wasn't finished with him. Grasping his arm, he swung the man around, and hurled him head first into the wall.

A sickening crunch came from the man's skull on impact. Sliding down the wall, he lay unmoving on the ground, a dark stain marking the bricks where he'd struck.

Ecstasy swept through Chris as he turned on the remaining policeman. Rage boiled through his veins, numbing the pain in his arm. He took a step forward, watching with satisfaction as sheer terror lit his victim's face. Then he leapt.

The policeman raised his hands in front of his face in a desperate effort to fend him off. But he was like grass before the wind to Chris, and he crumpled beneath Chris's fist. As he fell, Chris landed on his chest, his weight driving the breath from the man's lungs. His mouth gaped wide, desperate for air, as Chris threw back his head and laughed.

A wild joy swept through Chris as he slammed another blow into the policeman's face. The cop's head snapped back from the force of the impact, bouncing into the concrete. His eyes rolled into his skull and a low groan rattled in his chest, but Chris no longer cared. He lashed out again, his knuckles cracking as they slammed into flesh, the sound of blows echoing down the alleyway.

By the time Liz and Richard pulled Chris away, he was covered in blood. Red rage drowned his thoughts, and hissed as they grabbed him, struggling to break free. Twisting, he lashed out at the others, but Richard and Liz held him tight, their strength more than a match for his own, and finally the fight began to drain from him. The red faded from his vision and his heart-beat slowed.

Chris slumped in their arms, gasping as the pain returned. Agony shot from his arm, pins and needles radiating down to his hand. But it was still nothing to the ache in his heart, the agony of his loss.

A sob built in his chest, persistent, undeniable. It tore from his lips as the first hot tears spilled down his face. He cried out as Liz pulled him to her, burying his head in her shoulder, holding her tight, as though his life depended on it. A fear rose inside him, that if she let him go, he would slip away, would lose himself in the depths of his despair.

"What are we doing, Liz?" the words rose from somewhere inside of him, "It's all out of control."

He felt a shiver go through her as she pulled him closer. But she did not answer, and they stood together in silence, amidst the long shadows of the alleyway.

Closing his eyes, Chris gave in to his grief. He let it wash through him, to ebb and flow with the pain of his body. He embraced it, accepted it. Slowly, the tension went from him, the mad chaos that had taken hold falling away. And through it, he sent up an offering, a thought, a final farewell to the woman who had raised him.

Mum, I love you.

FIFTY-NINE

SAM DUCKED AS PAUL'S FIST FLASHED FOR HIS FACE, THEN backpedalled as the smaller boy chased after him, giving Francesca time to regain her feet. He shook his head as the boy stumbled. Paul recovered quickly, but the second it took allowed Sam to leap clear, his copper wings beating slightly to carry him across the hall.

He watched as Paul and Francesca gathered themselves and came after him. They moved with more confidence now, already growing used to the alien weight of their wings, though they were still far from perfect. Unlike Sam and the others, they were taking longer to adjust. Their wing movements were still stiff and robotic, their responses delayed, as though the connection between mind and wing was not quite complete.

They stalked towards Sam now, faces grim as they watched for a hint of his next attack. Grinning, Sam let them come. It had been days since their first meeting, but the two had proven slow learners. He had been wondering whether the lack of immediate danger might be slowing their progress. After all, it had been the rush of adrenaline, the desperate need to escape, that had driven Sam and the others to leap from the cliffs and fly.

So Sam had decided a change of tack was needed.

As Paul stepped into range, Sam tensed and sprang at the younger boy. Paul's eyes widened, but Sam was on him in an instant, his wingtip swinging out to catch the boy in the face. He felt a satisfying thud and grinned as Paul stumbled back clutching his nose.

Growling, Francesca stepped in to take Paul's place. Her sudden charge caught Sam by surprise, and he staggered sideways as her fist crashed into his ribs. Wincing, he retreated a step, silently admiring her strength. Whatever problems they had with their wings, there was nothing wrong with their other enhancements.

Sam scowled as the girl came at him again. Twisting sideways, he reached out and caught her by the wrist. Francesca yelped as he used her momentum to fling her over his shoulder and across the room.

He grinned as the girl hurtled through the air, arms raised to break her fall. Then her black wings shot outwards, catching in the air and slowing her descent. Francesca yelped in surprise, then dropped lightly to the ground. Blinking, wings still half-spread, she turned to stare at Sam, eyes wide.

"Very good," Sam grunted, "Now show me what you've got."

Ignoring her still gaping face, Sam leapt high into the air, his wings snapping out as he moved. With one powerful stroke he crossed the hall, and drove his booted foot into the girl's midriff. The blow sent her bouncing across the wooden floor until she came to rest near the far wall. Wheezing, she tried to right herself, her mouth wide and gasping.

An angry growl came from behind Sam, and he spun in time to block a savage blow from Paul. His fist crashed into Sam's wrist and sent a shock juddering down his arm. Grimacing, Sam retreated, twisting to avoid another wild swing from Paul. Then his knee flashed up and caught the other boy in the stomach, stopping him in his tracks.

They drew back a step then, pausing to weigh each other up. Sam had to admit, the two were good fighters, but that was no surprise. They had to be, to have survived this long. If not for his own skill and greater experience with his wings and strength, Sam doubted he could have taken them both. As it was, he was enjoying the chance to vent his frustration.

As Paul came at him again, Sam tensed, readying himself for the next attack. It came in a rush of flashing fists and elbows, but Sam blocked each of them calmly, and then leapt forward and grasped Paul by the shirt. Pivoting on his hip, Sam turned and hurled the boy across the room in the same manner he had Francesca.

Unfortunately, Paul's wings did not come to his rescue. He rose in an arc, and then crashed down into the wooden floor with a hard thud. Shaking his head, Sam watched the boy stagger to his feet, his lips drawn back with rage.

"You need to stop thinking, and *act*," Sam hissed as he leapt, slamming a fist into Paul's stomach to send him reeling backwards.

Pale-faced and gasping, the younger boy struggled to recover. He raised his fists and deflected another blow from Sam. Then he was charging forward, his arms grasping Sam around the midriff and tackling him to the ground. The breath exploded from Sam's lungs as he landed on his back.

Rolling on the ground, Sam sent Paul stumbling backwards with a sweep of his wings. They beat again as he leapt into the air, carrying him out of range.

Landing lightly, Sam struggled to regain his breath as he berated himself for lowering his guard. Across the room, Francesca had re-joined Paul. They stood together, waiting for him to make the next move. Gritting his teeth, Sam flashed an unconvincing grin and stepped towards them.

It was their turn to watch him come now, both suddenly looking confident in their abilities. It seemed he might have been right, that the rush of adrenaline was what they needed to help their minds gel with the alterations to their bodies.

They attacked together as he stepped within range, Paul half a step ahead of Francesca. Working in concert, they forced Sam to a standstill, then back a step, and another. Sam reeled as a blow struck him in the face, followed immediately by a kick to the hip. Anger flared in his chest, and growling, he allowed it free reign. It swept out to engulf him, sending fresh energy to his limbs.

For a second, Sam's head spun, and his vision flashed red. Heart pounding in his chest, he twisted as Paul came at him again. Lashing out, he caught the boy by the throat and hauled him into the air. Blood pounded in his head as he watched the boy kick feebly in his grasp, hardly feeling the blows as Paul struggled to free himself.

Blood pounded in his ears as elation swept through him. Dimly he heard a voice scream, and turning he raised an arm to fend off a blow from Francesca. She stumbled sideways as he struck her, but quickly righted herself and came at him again. Snarling, he hurled the boy aside and faced her, his delight turning to rage at her defiance.

Fear flashed in her eyes and he grinned. She stumbled backwards, but it was too late now. He leapt forward, reaching out to catch the arm she raised to defend herself. In a single movement, he hoisted her above his head and hurled her at the wall.

The girl's wings flared open in a desperate attempt to stop herself, but this time her momentum was too great, and she struck the wooden wall with a hard thud. She fell to the ground in a tangle of limbs and feathers. A low moan came from her throat as she struggled to rise.

Sam clenched his fists, revelling in his power, feeling the throb of anger within him. Smiling, he stepped towards the girl. She was still straining to right herself. Reaching down, he grasped her by the hair and hauled her up. Her brown eyes flickered up to stare at him, filled with a helpless terror.

Sam paused, a whisper of doubt cutting through his scarlet rage. For a second, another image imposed itself over the girl's face – of a boy, his face bloodied and bruised, on the ground, gasping for breath. He saw the boy struggling to stand, to regain his feet and continue to fight, but unable to find the strength.

And he saw the blood covering his hands, the bruises on his knuckles.

Jake.

Releasing Francesca, Sam staggered backwards as his friend's face rose his memories. Guilt swelled inside him, sweeping away the rage, and the red faded from his vision. A low whine came from his throat as he sank to his knees.

He glanced around, his heart racing as he found Paul on his knees nearby, clutching at his bruised throat, gasping for breath. And Francesca, stumbling to her feet, her legs unsteady as she looked across at him. In his chest, the guilt turned suddenly to fear.

"What the *hell* was that?" Francesca gasped.

Before Sam could answer, a slow clapping carried across the open hall. They turned as one, and stared as Halt walked slowly across the wooden boards. He wore a smile on his thin lips as he looked at them.

"Well done, Samuel," he breathed, his eyes shining. "It looks like we're almost ready."

SIXTY

L<small>IZ SHIFTED NERVOUSLY ON HER FEET AS SHE LISTENED TO</small> Daniella stutter through her story. The girl had been speaking for five minutes already, the words tumbling from her in a rush as she told her mother the story of her rescue. The older woman stood beside the girl, her eyes wide and face pale as she watched them – the five intruders on her doorstep.

After the confrontation in the alleyway, Liz had soon realised Chris had been shot. Though the wound was hardly bleeding, Chris had quickly gone into shock. As he started to shake, Liz had lowered him to the ground and then emptied the last few apples from their potato sack. She used it to bind his arm, but looking around at the filthy alleyway, she knew it would need further attention, and soon.

It was then the girl Chris had rescued had reminded them of her existence. Staggering to her feet, she had introduced herself in a wavering voice as Daniella. She looked around twenty years of age, and though still terrified, she had managed to stammer her thanks, before Chris's bullet wound caught her attention.

To Liz's surprise, instead of terrifying the girl, the sight of Chris's injury seemed to galvanise Daniella. Pulling herself together, she insisted they come with her to her mother's apartment. She had been heading there late from the train station when the policemen had offered to escort her home.

Despite her reluctance, Liz and the others had had little choice but to accept Daniella's offer. While some of the colour had returned to Chris's face, the risk of his wound becoming infected was too great out in the street. It needed to be cleaned, at the very least, and there was no way they could take him to hospital.

Now Daniella was finally wrapping up her story, finishing with how Chris had been shot and how he needed help. As she fell silent, her mother's eyes turned back to the group. Liz's cheeks grew hot as the woman's gaze fixed on her. She suddenly found herself uncomfortably aware of the filthy state of her clothes, and that it had been a long time since her dip in the mountain river. The five of them were well used to their own stench, but she winced at what the woman must think. Gritting her teeth, she readied herself for the woman's rejection.

All of a sudden, Daniella's mother clapped her hands. "Thank you, children," she all but shrieked. Her words trailed off as she continued to stare. Her eyes drifted to Chris, who Liz supported over her shoulder, and finally seemed to take in the blood-stained bandage. The woman blinked. "You're injured."

"Yes, mum, I told you!" Daniella said.

That seemed to finally snap the woman out of her trance. She flicked another glance at her daughter, then without speaking, crossed the room and drew Chris and Liz into a gentle hug. "Oh, thank you, thank you so much," her voice was warm as she released them. She looked at Chris. "We'd better take a look at that, hadn't we?"

Chris nodded silently, his lips drawn tight. The tension fled from Liz as the woman moved to a cupboard in the wall of the apartment. She closed her eyes, relieved at the thought of an adult taking control of the situation. The constant tension of their flight had drained her, and she wanted nothing more than to sleep for the next week, and let someone else worry about their problems.

"Take a seat," Daniella's mother gestured to the couch as she rifled around the closet. "Don't worry about the mess. I can't *believe* this. Now where is that first-aid kit. It's not much, you should really see a doctor, go to the hospital or something... but I suppose you can't really do that, can you? What is this city coming too, policemen assaulting ordinary citizens, it's like we're out on the *farms* or something. My name is Danny, by the way. Short for Daniella, but went and gave that name to my daughter, didn't I?"

Anger flared in Liz's stomach at Danny's casual insult about the farms, but she pushed it down with an inward shake of her head. While the police in her local village had technically worked for the government, they had generally been valued members of the community. They had certainly never gone around trying to rape young girls.

Dismissing her anger, she led Chris across to the couch, and let out a sigh of relief as they sank onto the soft cushions. She winced as she glanced back and saw the dirt staining the white fabric.

"Ah ha!" Danny emerged from the closet holding a red pouch decorated with a white cross. She moved across the living room, stepping around the coffee table, and took a seat on Chris's other side.

She seemed to have regained her composure now, and quickly threw herself into the task of patching Chris up. Idly, Liz wondered how much good the little first aid kit could do for a bullet wound, but there was no doubt the wound needed to be cleaned.

Beside her, Chris winced as the woman began to unwrap his makeshift bandage. Liz smiled, and reached out to take his good hand. His fingers clenched around her hand, and his hazel eyes glanced at her. She flashed him her best smile. "Don't be a baby."

Before Chris could respond, Daniella crossed the room and lowered herself onto the coffee table in front of them. She flashed Liz a scowl before reaching out and patting Chris's knee. "It's okay," she said warmly. "Mum will patch you up."

Chris nodded his thanks and returned her smile. Liz suppressed a growl, reminding herself of the trauma the girl had just experienced. She was only reaching out to Chris to show her thanks. But she could not help but feel a twinge of jealously at the way Chris smiled back at her.

Beside them, Danny hissed as the last layer of bandage came away, revealing the jagged tear the bullet had left in

Chris's arm. Blood had congealed around the wound, while black dirt spotted the red where grime had worked its way into the wound. Muttering to herself, Danny turned to rummage in her first-aid kit.

She came up a second later with a bottle of rubbing alcohol. Chris's eyes widened, and Liz gave his hand a quick squeeze. As she did, she flashed a look at Richard, hoping he caught its meaning. If the pain became too great, they might have to hold Chris down.

"Hey," Chris grumbled. "I saw that. Don't get any ideas, you two. I'll be good," with that he leaned back into the couch and silently offered his arm to Danny.

Chris flinched as Danny brushed the alcohol soaked cloth across his wound, but Liz held his hand tight and he steadied. A low whimper came from his throat as Danny began cleaning out the dirt.

"You big wuss," Liz whispered in Chris's ear, then smiled as he turned to look at her.

Ignoring Daniella's presence on the coffee table, and her hand still on Chris's knee, Liz leaned in and kissed Chris hard on the lips. Her heart fluttered as he melted beneath her, relaxing into the couch as she pressed herself against him. She heard a snort of indignation and a thud as Daniella stood and stamped away. She felt a twinge of guilt – the girl had only been trying to help – but at least she had distracted Chris from the pain.

Liz pulled back after a long moment. "That help?"

Chris gave a wry grin and nodded. Raising her hand, she stroked his cheek, feeling the soft hairs of his unshaved jaw brushing across her skin. Chris closed his eyes, relaxing at her touch, though Liz knew well the agony of rubbing alcohol on exposed flesh.

A few minutes later, Chris let out a long sigh as Danny announced she was done. "Looks like the bullet passed straight through," the woman chattered as she started to apply antiseptic cream. "Definitely should be seen by a doctor though. I hate to think what might happen if it became infected. You could lose your arm! Oh I don't know, such a mess, I wish we could do more for you. You look like such nice kids. Where are you from?" she looked around the room as she spoke, taking in the state of their clothes and filthy faces. "It looks like you've come a long way?"

Liz nodded, thinking quickly. "We came down from Seattle. Just finished school and heard there might be work here. Our bus broke down on the way though – took days to get here, by the time they sent a replacement and all that."

The woman nodded. "Oh dear. Well, I'm not sure about the work – I'm just a lowly office lady – but why don't you help yourselves to the bathroom? Clean yourselves up and spend the night. Really, it's the least we can do!"

"Yes, stay," Daniella seemed to have recovered from her earlier dismay. She stood in the doorway to what looked like the kitchen, arms folded as she watched them.

Glancing at the others, Liz hesitated. She knew they should leave, that there were soldiers out hunting for them, and a price on their heads. Staying meant risking the lives of Danny and Daniella, or possibly alerting the two to their status as fugitives. But even as she thought of refusing, she felt the constant ache of her body, the utter exhaustion from the bus ride and the strain of the long days on the run weighing on her. They were all at the end of their endurance, near the point of collapse.

And the thought of a hot shower was all but irresistible.

SIXTY-ONE

LIZ CLOSED HER EYES AS THE HOT WATER RAINED DOWN OVER her face, basking in its heat. It engulfed her head, muffling the distant sounds she could hear from the neighbouring apartments. The water filled her nose too, washing away the stench of her body. The loss of sensation came as a welcome relief, as she realised suddenly how stressed she had become, strained by the constant barrage of her senses.

She shivered, wondering then how long she could take it, whether the human mind was designed for so much input. Or would the sensory overload one day grow too much, the barrage of sights and smells and sound too much for her mind to process. What would happen to her then?

Sucking in a breath through the running water, Liz pushed the thought away.

Live in the moment, she thought to herself.

She savoured the heat of the water running off her naked skin. It ran over her head and through her long hair, dripped from her shoulders, down to her matted feathers. How long had it been since her last hot shower? Certainly not in the facility, where they had been lucky if the guards remembered to feed them, let alone take them to the showers. Nor while she'd been on the run. There'd been no chance of that, not while she had moved from rural village to town, never knowing when her next meal might come, let alone a bath.

No, it had been at the boarding school her parents had sent her too. Much as she had hated the place, hated being the only rural girl amidst the ranks of rich kids from the city, she could not deny the place had its luxuries. Though her parents' ranch had had hot water, it had been heated by the fireplace, so it was only available during the winter. And only then if you were one of the first to rise in the mornings.

Which as a teenager, meant there had been as much chance of her getting a hot shower, as her finding the cure for cancer.

Rubbing her hands over her skin, Liz watched the dead skin flake away. Dirt, skin and blood dripped to the tiled floor as she scrubbed her body clean. There it swirled with the gathering water, and disappeared down the drain. She watched it go, strangely entranced. Silently, she wished she could wash away darkness inside her the same way, that she could turn back the clock to before all this happened.

Liz jumped as someone knocked on the door and she heard a voice call out to her. "Liz?"

She smiled as she recognised Chris's hesitant tone. Silently she slipped out of the shower and moved across the bathroom, her wings clenched tight against her back to keep them from dripping. Standing behind the door, she pulled it open, reached one hand out into the corridor, and pulled Chris inside.

His eyes widened as he saw her standing naked, her hair and skin wet from the shower, her wings slowly spreading out behind her. She laughed as his cheeks reddened, secretly pleased at the effect she had on him. Though he still wore his filthy clothes, she stepped in close, until their faces were just an inch apart. Wrapping her arms around his waist, she pulled him into a kiss, taking care not to bump his injured arm.

As their lips met, she felt him stiffen against her. Then he was kissing her back, his lips hard against hers, his tongue darting between her lips. She moaned as his good hand slid up to her breast. Biting his lip, she began to undress him, tugging him towards the shower as she did so. Before they went any further, she wanted him *clean*.

Dragging him beneath the hot water, she pulled him to her, her heart racing as his naked chest brushed against her. Her skin tingled as his good hand slid up her back, to where her wings stretched out behind her. They brushed against her feathers, sending ripples of pleasure down the length of the alien limbs. Then his fingers continued on, and they were in her hair, pulling her lips to his, and he was kissing her hard, pushing her back against the wall of the shower.

Giggling, Liz slid sideways away from him. Snatching up the soap, she tossed it to Chris. "Soap first. Before you get that wound dirty again. We'll bandage it up afterwards."

Chris laughed, his eyes burning with desire. But with a wry smile he obeyed. She watched the dirt and dried blood run from him with the same curiosity she had felt before. Even now, amidst the heat of their passion, she could feel the pain radiating from Chris. It rose from his core, sharp and demanding, with a strength that threatened to consume them all. He had been so reckless since the news report, as though he no longer cared what happened to him. Boarding the bus, walking through the dangerous neighbourhoods of San Francisco, it was all so different from the Chris she knew, the Chris that would fight to the death for the ones he loved, but never think of putting them in danger.

Thankfully, he seemed more himself now, more like the Chris that had suffered and escaped the facility alongside her. The pain still shone from his eyes, a sharp, more recent reflection of her own, but it seemed contained now, under control. Silently, she prayed she was right.

Chris gave a low growl as he scrubbed the last patch of dirt from his skin and tossed the soap aside. He looked across at her, his hazel eyes almost feral as he drank her in. Liz smiled, basking in his gaze as she crossed her arms and raised an eyebrow.

"Well, what are you waiting for?" she placed her arms on her hips. "I'm all yours…"

Eyes dancing, Chris stepped forward, and pulled her to him…

When Liz finally moved from the shower, she was panting hard. Warmth spread from her stomach, seeping outwards to fill her, lighting every nerve in her body afire. She smiled as Chris followed her out, his fingers sketching out a trail along her waterlogged feathers. Closing her eyes, she trembled with his touch, still surprised at the sensitivity of her strange new limbs. Idly she wondered if Daniella or Danny had noticed the lumps beneath their jackets. She supposed they hadn't – otherwise who knew what they would have done.

Pulling two towels from the rack, she handed one to Chris before starting to dry herself. Watching Chris from the corner of her eye, she smiled as he struggled to dry himself with one hand. She was surprised how little it had slowed him. In fact, the bleeding already seemed to have stopped. Even so, she knew from her time working with animals on the farm that it should be stitched. Unfortunately, hospital grade stitching did not come in your standard first-aid kit.

Still, at least his wound was now clean and dry, and they could bandage it when they returned to the living room.

As they dried themselves, they spread their wings in the tiled bathroom, letting their damp feathers bask in the overhead heating lamp. Their feathers stood on end, and every so often a shiver would go through them, sending out a fine spray of water.

Afterwards they pulled on the clean clothes Daniella's mother had given them. Her husband was apparently away on business – he was a translator of some sort – and she suggested it was a good opportunity to get rid of his old clothes. Looking at the fine shirts, Liz lamented the need to tear holes in the back to fit their wings. Even on her, the shirts would not fit over their feathery bulk.

Once they were dressed, Liz eyed her old jacket with distaste. Her wings were enjoying their freedom – being cramped under the jacket did not agree with them. And now she was clean, she could smell the reek of sweat and dirt coming from the heavy denim. But unless they wanted to terrify their friendly hosts, it seemed they had little choice. Reluctantly, they pulled on the jackets before sliding out the door.

Warmth touched Liz's cheeks as she found Jasmine, Richard and Mira waiting in the hallway outside. Her mouth dropped open and she flashed a glance back at Chris. "You didn't mention they were outside!"

Chris's cheeks were beet-red, but Jasmine cut in before he could respond. "It got a little awkward in the living room," she glanced at the others and shrugged, "Guess I'm next."

She disappeared into the bathroom before Richard or Mira could argue. Richard bowed his head, his lips curling downwards as he tucked his hands into his pockets.

Taken by a sudden empathy, Liz reached across and squeezed his arm. Richard looked across at her, his eyes shining in the light of the hallway. No words passed between them, but after a moment Richard nodded and looked away.

Stepping back, Liz took Chris's hand and led him back towards the living room. She frowned at the other's lack of courtesy – and foresight. Someone should have stayed with Daniella and her mother, if only to ensure they were safe. As they moved down the corridor, she heard voices speaking, and recognised the faint whine of the television. The floorboards squeaked beneath their feet to announce their approach, and the voices suddenly broke off.

The door clicked as she pushed it open and moved back into the living room. She hadn't really taken it in earlier, but now her eyes passed slowly over the room. The apartment was plain and rundown, but still displayed far more wealth than her parents could ever have hoped for. Steel bolts held the front door closed directly opposite them, while to their left was the door to the kitchen. To their right was the square dining room table, and beyond that the white fabric couch and flat screen television. Past the television, a broad window looked out over the city, at the distant skyscrapers and steep hills of San Francisco.

To her surprise, the television was dark, though she was sure she had heard it just a moment earlier. Daniella was still sitting on the couch, but her mother was standing, already starting towards them.

"How was your shower?" Danny smiled.

Liz's ears twitched at the tone of her voice. Had it been slightly higher than before? She closed her eyes, weariness settling around her shoulders like a cloak. Forcing a smile, she nodded at Danny, dismissing her worry as exhaustion.

"Wonderful, thank you," Chris said beside her. She glanced across and saw him smiling, apparently at ease. "Just what we needed after that bus ride."

Danny nodded absently as Daniella lifted herself from the couch and moved across to them. Reaching out, she tugged at the sleeve of Chris's jacket. "You're wearing your jacket. Wasn't what I picked for you… more comfortable?"

"Leave him alone, Daniella," Danny said sharply. Liz jerked her head up as the woman strode across and pulled Daniella away. "They'll wear what they want."

Daniella scowled as she pulled herself free. "They don't *have* too," she retorted.

Danny folded her arms and stared down at Daniella. The girl held her ground for a moment, then with a grunt, she turned and pushed past Liz, disappearing down the hallway. Shaking her head, Danny looked back at them and flashed a smile. "Would you like some coffee, dears?"

Exhausted as she was, Liz wanted nothing more than to sleep. Coffee was the last thing she needed. But the woman was already moving away, muttering about boiling water as she disappeared through the door to the kitchen. Liz glanced at Chris, but he only shook his head. She noticed his face was pale, and taking his arm they moved across to the couch.

Reaching across the coffee table, Liz picked up the first aid kit. Carefully rolling up the sleeve of Chris's jacket, she applied a fresh layer of antibacterial cream to Chris's wound. She was surprised by how fresh it looked already. She had been right earlier – the bleeding had stopped, and was it her imagination, or did it look smaller? Shaking her head, she dismissed the absurd thought, and started applying a bandage to Chris's arm.

Jasmine appeared as Liz was finishing up the bandage. Her skin was red from scrubbing and her black hair hung damp around her face, but she looked cleaner than Liz had ever seen her. She still wore the jacket from earlier, and Liz wriggled on the couch, reminded of the damp feathers slowly dripping water down her back.

She smiled as Jasmine approached the couch, noticing the girl was looking relaxed. "Good shower?"

Jasmine smiled back. "I could barely bring myself to get out. Where's Daniella and her mother?"

"Daniella is down the hall somewhere," Liz replied. "Her mother is making coffee."

Jasmine wrinkled her nose. "I hope its decaf. Who's taking first watch?"

"I think Richard still owes us one there," Liz replied softly.

She watched Jasmine's face darken, but Liz had decided in the hallway the feud between the two had gone on long enough. Richard had made a mistake, and he would have to live with it. But if they were to survive, the five of them needed to get along.

"You have to forgive him sometime, you know," she whispered.

Jasmine looked up at that. Her eyes softened for a second, before her jaw clamped tight. "Do I?" she growled. "And why is that?"

Liz did not back down. "Because you love him," she replied. "Because he's family."

"I…" Jasmine closed her eyes suddenly, her shoulders slumping. She dropped to the couch beside them and drew her knees up to her chest. "They almost caught us. Because of him."

"Yes," Liz shrugged, "But in the end, we're just kids, Jasmine. We're not soldiers, we're not trained for this, whatever mutations they managed to cram into our DNA."

Jasmine lowered her eyes at that, but did not respond. Liz smiled, hoping she had gotten through to the girl. Then she leaned back into the crook of Chris's good arm and closed her eyes. Basking in his warmth, they waited in silence for Richard and Mira to return.

Mira was the next to appear. She moved silently across the room and quickly climbed up onto Jasmine's lap. Liz smiled inwardly as Jasmine rolled her eyes at her. She was beginning to suspect the other girl enjoyed Mira's affections more than she let on. Eventually Richard emerged too, still drying his hair with a towel as he looked around the room.

He paused beside the couch and looked around again, his forehead creased. "Where's Daniella and her mother?"

Liz blinked, struggling to look around, her mind foggy with sleep. She shook her head, suddenly realising Richard was right. Daniella's mother still had not returned with the coffee. What was taking the woman so long?

Just as she was struggling to sit up, Danny finally appeared in the doorway of the kitchen. She paused there, a steaming mug in each hand. Then she moved across the room and placed the mugs on the coffee table.

"Everyone clean? Good, good, I'm so glad, must be a relief after that trip. Where did you say you came from again? Seattle right? Such a long, long way," she paused, looking at Jasmine and Richard. "More coffee?"

Before either could speak, she turned and raced back into the kitchen.

Shaking her head, Liz struggled to muster her thoughts, and decided the coffee might not be a bad idea after all. Much as she'd like to sleep, and leave their worries for the morning, they needed to figure out a plan. Reaching across the table, she lifted the mug and took a long gulp of the hot liquid.

Beside her, Chris groaned and sat up, blinking sleep from his eyes. He spotted the other mug and swept it up before anyone else could claim it.

Liz sighed as the hot liquid warmed her chest. Though winter was behind them, the nights were still icy, and the house felt cold after the heat of the shower. The others remained where they were, Richard standing, Jasmine and Mira curled up on the couch beside her.

"That was… strange," Richard remarked, his eyes fixed on the kitchen doorway.

Taking another sip of her coffee, Liz's mind finally began to tick over again. She frowned, thinking of the voices she'd heard earlier, how she'd been sure the television had been on. Idly, Liz realised Danny must have switched it off when she'd heard them coming.

"Danny switched the television off, before we came in…" she mumbled her thoughts out loud.

Richard looked around. "What?"

"They were watching the television, while we were getting clean. I heard it. But they switched it off when they heard us coming."

Frowning, Richard reached down and picked up the remote from the coffee table. They all turned to stare as the television flickered into life. The speakers started to blare, but Richard quickly hit the mute button. The five of them stared as a man appeared on the screen, pointing to a map of the Western Allied States, and the rainclouds approaching San Francisco.

But that was not what drew their attention.

A banner ran along the bottom of the screen, bright red with white text that spelled out 'wanted for treason'. Beneath the writing, four faces stared from the screen. Liz's stomach twisted as she stared at her own face, an awful fear clamping around her chest.

Richard flicked off the television and turned back to them. "We have to get out of here."

And then the lights went out.

SIXTY-TWO

CHRIS THREW HIMSELF TO THE FLOOR AS THE DOOR TO THE apartment shattered inwards. He heard a thud as something skittered across the floor, then a blinding flash of light and sound exploded through the room. A scream came from his right as red lines streaked across his vision. Rolling to the side, he screamed at the others, but over the ringing in his ears, Chris couldn't even hear his own voice.

Blinking in the darkness, Chris struggled to regain his night vision. Pain came from his arm, but he pushed it aside, fear sweeping through his chest. Scrambling on his hands and knees, he looked up as he heard the thud of boots on tiles. White lights danced across his vision, but through them he saw shadows moving through the darkness.

They're here!

"Get away from the door!" he called a warning as he rolled behind the couch.

As another thud came from the doorway, he began to crawl towards the window, praying the others would have the same thought. The apartment was on the fifth floor – if they could break the glass and jump, the hunters would not be able to follow them.

His heart leapt as he heard glass shatter, and straining his eyes, he tried to see who had made it to the window first. Red streaks still flashed across his vision, but they were already fading, giving way to darkness. The room slowly came into focus, every inch easily visible in the dim light from outside.

He smiled at their hunters' mistake. With their altered senses, the darkness was no hindrance to them. Now, even with night vision goggles, the soldiers would be at a disadvantage. Crawling out from the cover of the couch, he looked back at the window, expecting to see Liz or one of the others already there.

Instead, he froze as the hulking figures of two soldiers stepped through the broken window. Sleek black night vision goggles covered their eyes and they held heavy rifles at the ready. Glass cracked beneath their boots as they fanned out.

How? They were five stories up, how could the soldiers have gotten in through the window?

Chris quickly backpedalled behind the couch, but this time he was too late. As he ducked out of sight he saw the men turn towards him and raise their weapons. Gunfire crackled through the room, and Chris hurled himself to the ground, bracing himself for the bullets. He knew the flimsy sofa would offer no resistance against hot lead.

To his surprise, the pain did not come. A series of heavy *thunks* came from the sofa, as muzzle flashes lit the room. Pulling himself up, Chris glanced over the edge of the cushions, and then dropped back down with a curse. Half a dozen darts had embedded themselves in the fabric. So the hunters weren't here for blood – they wanted to take the five of them alive.

Over my dead body, Chris thought grimly.

Reaching up, Chris tore off his jacket and flexed his wings. He gathered himself, listening for the tell-tale crunch of heavy boots on broken glass. Before he could move, he sensed movement beside him, and turned in time to see Liz scramble around the edge of the couch. Her wings were already out, her sleek black feathers blending in with the shadows.

The tread of a boot carried to their ears. He smiled, pleased by the caution their hunters were showing. These men were clearly wary of them. Chris just hoped they lived up to their reputation.

A roar sounded from the other end of the room, and glancing around the corner of the couch, Chris watched Richard and Jasmine charge at the soldiers by the window. Wings out, lips drawn back in wild snarls, they attacked like avenging angels descended from heaven. The soldiers moved with painful slowness, unable to match the speed of their winged prey. In a second Richard was on them, Jasmine just one step behind.

The first of the two yelled out as Richard tore the rifle from his grasp and hurled it at his face. Leaping to his feet, Chris moved to join them, but movement near the door drew his attention. Silhouettes strode through the darkness, fanning out from the doorway, already raising their weapons to take aim.

Knowing they had Richard and Jasmine in their sights, Chris did not hesitate. Roaring, he dived at the nearest figure, catching him off guard and hurling him backwards. The others turned at the sound, momentarily distracted, and then Liz launched herself into their midst.

The five silhouettes staggered back from her fury as one went down in a pile of feathers and fists. A second later Liz sprang back up, already moving towards her next target. The soldier she'd struck did not get back up.

One of the men turned to point his weapon at Liz, but Chris was on him in an instant. He only had one good arm to work with, but in close quarters, that was all he needed. Balling his fist, he slammed it into the soldier's chest. Even with body armour, Chris heard the distinct *crack* of breaking ribs. As the man gasped and sank to his knees, Chris spun on his heel and drove his boot into the side of the man's head.

He moved on as the man dropped to the ground, his keen eyes searching the darkness for another victim. Chaos had spread through the soldiers, the fury of Liz's attack scattering them across the room. Muffled thuds came from the window as Richard and Jasmine finished off the hunters there, while only two soldiers were left standing on Chris's side of the room. Grinning, he stalked towards them.

But now the shock of their attack had worn off, and the soldiers were regaining their senses. More men swept into the room, charging through the doorway in a stream of bodies. Chris swore as rifles pointed in their direction, and he dove towards the dining table. Liz was already ahead of him, and she hurled it on its side as they dove behind it. The crack of steel darts on wood echoed through the room as the soldiers opened fire.

Heart racing, Chris crouched behind the table with Liz and waited for the firing to stop. He prayed Richard and Jasmine had not been caught in the cross-fire. He had not seen what had happened to Mira, but he hoped the girl had found cover somewhere.

Silence fell as the gunfire ceased. Chris glanced around the corner of the table in time to see Jasmine and Richard make a break for the window. The path was clear now, the men that had crashed through lying slumped on the ground. Jasmine was in the lead, her long legs carrying her across the room before the soldiers near the door could take aim. Her wings spread as she neared the open window.

Movement came from beyond the curtains as the silhouette of a soldier stepped through, rifle already raised. Caught midstride, Jasmine had no time to react as the barrel flashed. But beside her, Richard was already moving, shoving her aside. An instant later, half a dozen darts sprouted from his chest.

His eyes widened as he stumbled, then with a roar he threw himself at the man in the window. The soldier staggered sideways as a blow caught him in the temple, but two more were already stepping forward to take his place.

And Richard was slowing now. Another dart sprouted from his chest as he staggered backwards from the men, still shielding Jasmine with his body as they retreated behind the sofa.

The soft squeak of a floorboard reminded Chris of the soldiers near the door. He glanced at Liz, and found her crystal blue eyes watching him in the darkness. He swallowed, and flashed a smile that did not reach his eyes.

"I'll take the ones on the right. You get the left," he whispered.

Liz nodded, and gripping the edge of the wooden table, she hurled it across the room. The intruders had spread out as they moved to encircle their hiding place, but a group near the door still stood close together. They lifted their guns as Liz moved, but it was already too late. The dark mass of the table crashed into them, crushing them against the far wall.

Then Chris was charging at the soldiers, taking advantage of their momentary shock to cross the distance separating them. But they were ready for him this time. Two already had their rifles at their shoulders, and the barrels flashed as Chris reached the first of the intruders. He felt a sharp pinch in his side as he leapt and drove his foot into a man's face.

The force of his kick sent the man flying back into his comrades. Swearing, Chris reached down and tore the dart from his side. Tensing his fist, he quickly tested his strength, but he couldn't feel any difference. A dull ache came from his wounded arm, but otherwise the bullet wound had not slowed him. He chalked that up to some increased resistance, and then hurled himself at his next victim.

In the cramped quarters of the apartment, the men struggled to bring their bulky rifles to bear on the winged teenagers. Guns flashed, but with Chris and Liz amidst their ranks, they were just as likely to hit each other as their prey.

Wings flaring, Chris leapt at another man, driving both feet into his sternum and hurling him across the room. Beside him, Liz crashed into another man, driving her shoulder straight into his chest. The force of the impact sent the man staggering into the soldier alongside him, and the two went down in a pile of limbs.

But even as the soldiers fell around them, more poured in through the door and window. On the other side of the room, Chris caught glimpses of Jasmine laying into the men around her. Richard crouched at her feet, head bent, his wings limp, and the beginnings of despair clutched at Chris's throat. Outnumbered and surrounded, there was no escape now.

A sharp pain came from his back, and Chris spun to wrench the weapon from the soldier's arms. Clubbing the man over the head with the heavy rifle, he turned again and hurled it into another soldier. The force behind the projectile sent the man crashing to the ground.

A scream came from Liz and he turned in time to see her go down under a pile of soldiers. A second later she was up again, hurling the soldiers from her, scattering them like leaves before the wind. Chris moved towards her, and staggered as his leg went numb. His vision whirled and his stomach wrenched as a wave of nausea swept through him.

Another soldier came at him, gun raised to finish him off. Straightening, he twisted as the gun flashed, but too slow. As the dart caught him in the shoulder, he grasped the barrel of the gun and tried to wrench it from the soldier's grip. To his surprise, the man held on, and the barrel flashed again, sending a dart straight into Chris's chest.

The strength fled his legs and suddenly Chris found himself on his knees. An eerie calm settled over him as he looked up at the soldier, watching the bright flash as the rifle sent another dart into his flesh. This time he did not feel the pain as it struck. A great weariness settled around his shoulders as he swayed.

"Liz," he breathed, watching her across the room.

He looked down at his chest, at the darts protruding from his flesh. He fought to reach up, to tear them out, but his arms refused to obey. They hung limp at his side, dead weights as the soldier drove his boot into his stomach.

"*Chris!*" he heard Liz's voice from a distance.

He struggled to keep his eyes open, to find her in the growing shadows. But the darkness rose up to swallow him, and he fell away into oblivion.

SIXTY-THREE

"*CHRIS!*" LIZ SCREAMED AS SHE SAW HIM GO DOWN.

Hurling aside a soldier, she leapt over the bodies scattered across the floor and charged at the man standing over Chris. He looked up as she closed on him, even managed to lift his rifle, before her fist caught him in the face. The force of the blow sent his head whiplashing backwards and he crumpled without a sound.

But she had turned her back on the other soldiers now, and two raised their guns and opened fire. Her wings cracked open, the long black feathers brushing aside the darts. But she still felt a pinch from her shoulder as one got through. Gritting her teeth, she crouched and hauled Chris up, and then stumbled away from the door.

She heard the click of guns being reloaded, and ahead she saw Jasmine stumble. The girl still stood over Richard, half a dozen bodies scattered around her. Liz felt a surge of hope, that maybe they could carry the boys to the window, that they might still escape. Then she saw the tips of the darts protruding from Jasmine's shoulder and arms, saw her wings beginning to slump, and the hope withered in her chest.

Lowering Chris to the floor beside Richard, Liz drew back her teeth and snarled. Beyond Jasmine, more men poured through the window. Past the shattered glass, a steel cable lead across to a neighbouring building, where a dozen men still waited to join the fight. Ignoring them, she moved to stand beside Jasmine.

Hissing, Jasmine gathered herself and leapt at a cluster of men, scattering them with her fury. Teeth clenched, Liz followed after her. But already it was clear the darts were having an effect. Even as she joined the other girl, she could see Jasmine slowing, her blows now lacking power. She watched her tear a weapon from a soldier and slam it into his stomach – but a moment later the man straightened and drawing a baton from his belt, he leapt forward to re-join the fight.

Jasmine staggered as the steel baton caught her in the side of the head. She retreated a step as Liz sprang between them and sent the soldier reeling with a blow to the head. This time he did not get back up. Side by side, they retreated to where Richard and Chris lay.

"Go, Liz," Jasmine panted, "Get out of here, before they get you too."

Liz shook her head and reached out to steady Jasmine as the girl stumbled. Glancing sideways, Liz forced a smile. "I told you, we're family. And we're not finished yet."

Baring her teeth, she tore into another intruder as Jasmine slumped to her knees. As her fist crashed into his face, she felt a sharp pinch from her backside. Swearing, she caught the soldier by the shoulder and spun towards the hunters creeping towards them from the door. In one fluid movement, she hurled the man into their midst.

She grinned as the men scattered, then swore as her leg suddenly went numb. She clenched her fists, fighting back the weakness, as soldiers closed in around them. They must have been running short of ammunition, because they hesitated before firing, waiting to see whether she would collapse.

Liz swayed on her feet. She glanced across at Jasmine, and her heart clenched as she saw the girl collapsed over Richard. Swallowing, she faced the circle of soldiers, alone now against a dozen men. She sucked in a breath, and then stepped towards the nearest man.

Crack.

A gun roared, and another dart tore into Liz's side. She staggered, the numbness spreading, but she took another step. Gunshots sounded again, and she felt two more stabs of pain from her back. By then she had reached the man, and stretching out an arm she clawed at his weapon. But he only retreated a step, before slamming the butt of his rifle into her face.

Light flashed across Liz's vision as the blow struck, driving her to her knees. She looked up at the man, cursing her weakness, struggling to regain her feet. But the tranquiliser pumping through her veins was too much for her now, and with agonising slowness, she toppled backwards to the ground.

The soldier smiled down at her. Reaching for a radio strapped to his shoulder, he spoke into the black microphone. "Targets neutralised. We're ready for you, boss."

Liz's stomach clenched and tears stung her eyes as she looked up at the man. Despair wrapped around her throat and she found herself begging. "Please, just kill us. Don't let him take us back."

Grinning, the man drew back his boot and drove it into her face. The blow slammed her head back into the floor. She tasted blood in her mouth as the man lifted his foot again and hammered the steel-capped boot into her side. The force of the blow lifted her from the ground and sent her sprawling across the ground.

Laying on her side, she listened as the man's footsteps retreated. Staring at the open door, she struggled to sit up. But her limbs refused to obey, and she found she could no longer even blink her eyes.

Around the room, the soldiers were reaching up to pull the night vision goggles from their faces. An instant later, the lights flickered back on, filling the room with blinding white. Pain stabbed through Liz's eyes, and she willed them to close, without success.

A moment later, footsteps came from the hallway outside. A man appeared in the doorway, wearing a familiar white lab coat. Liz's stomach clenched as she looked up at his face, and felt the last traces of courage crumble within her.

Halt wore a cold smile as he crossed the room. He stood over her and folded his arms. "Well done, Commander. They are all present?"

Before the soldiers could respond, a wild shriek erupted from the corridor. Mira tore into view, grey wings flashing as she emerged from her hiding place and shot straight at Halt. He staggered backwards as the girl crashed into his chest, her unnatural strength knocking him back.

Liz's heart fluttered as Mira tore at Halt's face, her lips drawn back in an animalistic snarl. Around the room, the soldiers retreated from her fury. Hope tingled in Liz's chest as she found herself hoping Mira would tear Halt's head from his shoulders.

Then Halt straightened, and his arm shot out to catch Mira by the throat. Liz's heart lurched in sudden fear, before she reminded herself Mira's augmented strength was more than a match for an ordinary human's. She would snap Halt's arm like a twig.

Mira squirmed in Halt's grasp, then lifted her hands and brought them down on Halt's elbow. Liz watched, waiting for the sharp crack of breaking bone, for Halt's scream and for Mira to slip free.

Instead, Halt smiled. Snarling, he lifted Mira higher, even as she kicked and tore at him. Then with casual ease, he hurled her head first into the wall. Mira shrieked as she struck, and then slumped unmoving to the ground.

Turning back to the commander, Halt shook his head. "I suggest you secure the subjects properly, *Commander*. We wouldn't want any more… incidents," he looked around the room, eyes sweeping the shattered remains of the apartment. "When you're done, take care of the woman and her daughter. They did a great service to this country, reporting the fugitives. But we can't have any witnesses of this... unfortunate incident."

As he spoke, Halt turned and looked down at Liz, the smile still frozen on his thin lips.

And his cold grey eyes pierced her.

SIXTY-FOUR

AGONY PULLED CHRIS BACK FROM THE DARKNESS, DRAGGING him slowly to wakefulness. He made to sit up, but flopped sideways as he found his arms fastened behind his back with steel cuffs. A sharp ache came from the wound in his arm and he bit back a cry. Rolling onto his side, he clenched his teeth, swallowing the pain, before forcing his eyes to open.

His heart sank as the room shifted into focus. The first thing he saw was a wall of thick wire mesh. A quick glance around confirmed his suspicions – he was lying in a cage. Apparently, someone had decided handcuffs were not enough to hold them.

He allowed his eyes to roam across the rest of the room, and breathed a sigh of relief as he found the others lying nearby. They had each been given a cage of their own. He spotted Liz lying unconscious on the floor of the next cage, her wings hanging limply around her. Richard, Jasmine and Mira were on her other side, while half a dozen empty cages stood to his left.

Chris struggled to sit up, cursing the steel cuffs holding his hands fastened behind his back. His wings shifted behind him, stretching out to help steady him. In the narrow confines of the cage he had little room to manoeuvre, but he finally managed to get to his knees.

A moan came from Liz's cage, and he scooted across to the wire and peered through. A purple bruise darkened Liz's forehead, but otherwise she seemed unharmed. He breathed a sigh of relief as her eyes fluttered open.

"Chris," she murmured.

Before he could warn her, she tried to sit up, and promptly fell on her face. A string of curses rolled off the concrete walls as Chris suppressed his laughter. Movement came from the cages beyond her as the others woke.

Trying a second time, Liz managed to rock back on her haunches. Her blue eyes focused on him and she shot him a look. "You never saw that," she looked around then, taking in the row of cages and plain concrete walls. "Where are we? Trying to recreate our first date, Chris?" her tone was light, but he could hear the fear behind her attempt at humour.

Chris looked away, blinking back sudden tears. He strained his wrists against the cuffs, but as pain shot through his arm, he realised it was hopeless. With them locked behind his back, he could leverage the full extent of his strength against them.

"I don't know, Liz," he said finally. He bowed his head. "I'm sorry, this is all my fault."

His voice cracked as guilt swept through him. What had he been thinking, rushing off the way he had? They'd had no business in that alleyway. If not for his stupidity, he would never have been injured, and they would never have found themselves in Daniella's apartment.

"Don't be stupid, Chris," Liz leaned her head against the wire and closed her eyes. "You couldn't have known Daniella and her mother would betray us. And besides, do you really think I would have just stood there while those policemen attacked her? You were just a step ahead of the rest of us."

"I was reckless," Chris argued. "I rushed in without thinking, without caring what happened. If I'd been more careful, had listened to you, none of this would have happened."

"Maybe," Liz shrugged, "They had guns though, Chris. If you hadn't acted so quickly, we would never have gotten close to them. How's your arm?"

"It's a bit sore. Not as bad as last night though," he replied.

Liz smiled, but before she could respond, the door on the opposite wall clicked and swung open. Three men stepped through wearing the familiar blue uniform of the guards at the facility. Chris's heart sank.

No, we can't be back.

His worst suspicions seemed to be confirmed as Doctor Halt followed the guards inside. He wore the same white lab coat and sleek black pants as the last time Chris had seen him. A thin smile on his lips, Halt strode towards them, letting the door slam shut behind him.

"Awake at last, I see," his voice was cold as he walked down the row of cages, surveying each of them in turn. Chris noticed Jasmine, Mira and Richard were sitting up now, their eyes plastered to the ground, unwilling to meet Halt's gaze.

Reaching the end of the row, Halt turned and marched back, stopping finally in front of the guards.

"All still in one piece, it seems," he clenched his arms behind his back, "Fallow's little escapade did not prove so disastrous after all. We'll call it as an unplanned test run, I suppose. The President and his Directors will certainly be pleased with the results."

Chris stared up at the man, struggling to shake off the clutches of despair. But crouched on the ground, his arms bound behind his back and the wire mesh hemming him in, he could not summon the energy to fight back.

"This isn't the end, Halt," Liz growled from her cage. She struggled to sit up straight, her wings flailing against the wire.

Halt stepped up to her cage, the smile falling from his lips. "You're wrong, Elizabeth Flores. This is very much the end. The President will soon approve the extra funding I need to continue the Praegressus project. Once I have finalised matters here in San Francisco, I will have you shipped back to our primary facility. There I will watch you torn apart, piece by delicate piece, and use what we find to perfect our recombinant DNA. You and your little friends will be consigned to the pages of history; remembered as nothing more than stepping stones in our path to evolutionary perfection."

Chris shuddered and looked away. There was an almost fanatical rage in Halt's grey eyes as he glared down at Liz.

But shaking her head, Liz laughed in the face of Halt's fury. "I know what you are, Halt," she replied. "I saw what you did, before I passed out. You're *Chead!*"

Chris gaped at Liz's accusation. He stared at Halt, watching for some reaction. The doctor's grey eyes hardened and his posture seemed to stiffen. He slowly shook his head. "You had best keep such notions to yourself, Elizabeth. Or I may decide to dissect you right here in San Francisco."

Liz snorted. "Go ahead. I'd rather die than go back to that place."

A long silence stretched out as the two locked eyes. Finally Halt shook his head and smiled. "As invigorating as this conversation is, I am needed elsewhere. When I return, I will introduce you each to fresh new collars – and a lesson in etiquette to go with them. For now, you'll have to make do with the company of these men here. I'm afraid they're quite new, but they'll ensure you don't have any mishaps."

With that, Halt turned and walked from the room. The three guards edged forward to take his place, their weapons held loosely against their chests. Their eyes flickered over the rows of cages, lingering on Liz and her outstretched wings. While Chris had tucked his wings tightly against his back, hers extended across her cage, their black feathers shining in the overhead lights.

All the fight seemed to have fled Liz with Halt's dismissal. She sat with her head bowed and shoulders slumped, unaware of the guard's attention, until one of them spoke. "You think they're real?"

Another of the men laughed. "You heard the doctor – they're experiments," the man stepped closer to the cage as he spoke, and raising his rifle, slammed the butt into the mesh.

The wire of Liz's cage rattled with the impact, and Liz glanced up, her eyes widening. The guard laughed again as her wings lifted slightly from the ground. He turned back to the other two. "Look pretty real to me!"

The others stepped closer, peering through the wires at the dark feathers filling the cage. The cages were only ten feet wide, while at their full extend Liz's wings spread more than twenty, leaving them pressed up against the wire. Chris could hardly blame the men for their curiosity, though it made him sick to his stomach, to see Liz treated like a caged animal.

"You think she can actually fly?" another of the guards muttered.

"Of course she can fly," the first replied "You think these people are *stupid* or something? Why would they give her wings if she couldn't use em?"

"Piss off," Liz snapped suddenly. Crouched on the ground, she retreated to the back of the cage.

Outside, the guards looked at each other and then burst into laughter.

"Feisty, isn't she?" the first guard grinned as he leaned against the wire. "What's your name again, pretty girl? Elizabeth, wasn't it?

Liz pursed her lips and looked away.

"Leave her alone," Chris growled from his cage, but the men ignored him.

"Let's take a closer look, shall we boys?" the man who appeared to be the ring leader suggested.

The others paused at that, sharing a glance. "Don't think that's a good idea, James. The doctor seemed pretty keen on keeping them where they are."

James only laughed. "Who's going to know? Look at her, she's tiny! And her hands are cuffed behind her back. You think we can't take her?"

The second guard fell silent, as the third shrugged. "Can't hurt. You heard the doctor. He's gonna put her down when he gets back anyway. Give us something to tell the boys at the pub about, at least."

That was enough for the first guard. He reached down and removed a set of keys from his belt and turned back to Liz's cage. Heart thudding in his chest, Chris scrambled to get his legs beneath him, and finally managed to haul himself to his feet. Stumbling forward, he threw himself against the wire to catch the men's attention. His wings stretched out, slamming against the steel.

The men paused and turned to stare at him.

"Leave her alone," Chris growled. "If you touch her, I swear I'll kill you all."

The men glanced at one another, momentarily frozen by the ferocity of Chris's gaze. Then the man called James grinned, glancing down the row of cages. "What do you know, they've all got wings, boys," turning his back on Chris he stepped up to the door of Liz's cage, "This one's still the prettiest though."

Chris swore and threw himself against the wire again, but the men ignored him now. Inside her cage, Liz crouched on the ground, still struggling to find her feet. Gritting his teeth, Chris strained against his cuffs, ignoring the agony that lanced down his arm. The cold steel sliced into his skin, but did not give. With his arms locked behind his back, he could not exert enough force to break them.

He watched on, helpless, as James unlocked Liz's cage. The other two stood back, as the door swung open, their rifles trained on Liz. Rage flashed in her eyes as she gathered herself, obviously ready to launch herself at the men, guns or no.

James paused in the doorway, studying her closely. Smiling, he raised his hand and pointed at Chris. "I wouldn't, my dear. Alex, Oliver, shoot the boy if she tries anything."

Inside her cage, Liz's shoulders slumped. James laughed again and stepped into the cage, ignoring the string of curses Chris hurled in his direction. Reaching down, he grabbed a fistful of Liz's hair and dragged her to her feet. Her screams echoed through the room as he hauled her from the cage. Her wings cracked the air, slamming into the wire mesh, but with her hands pinned behind her back, she had no means to defend herself.

Chris stared, helpless, as the guard shoved Liz into the middle of the room. She stumbled forward, a gasp tearing from her throat as he released her. Eyes wide, she spun, her wings fanning out to fill the room. Her skin had paled, the dark bruise on her forehead standing out in stark relief. Rage shone from her eyes as she faced the ring of men.

A low growl rattled from her throat as one of the men reached out and grabbed a handful of her feathers. She spun towards him as he tore a fistful of black feather loose. He held them up in triumph. "They're real boys!" he laughed as he looked at Liz. "You don't mind if I take a souvenir? Don't think you'll be needing them, where the doctor is taking you."

Liz stalked towards him, but James stepped in quickly behind her. Before Liz could turn, he slammed the butt of his rifle into the back of Liz's head. She staggered at the blow, losing her balance and crashing to the floor in the tangle of feathers. Without her arms, she could do nothing to break her fall. Before she could recover, James drove his boot into the small of her back, pinning her to the concrete.

Grinning, he looked at the others. "Who's first?"

SIXTY-FIVE

SAM STOOD SILENTLY IN THE SHADOWS OF THE STAGE, looking out over the crowd that had gathered beyond the podium. They stood in silence, staring up at the figures on the stage, waiting for the announcement. The press stood at the front, their cameras pointed up at them, red lights flashing as they prepared to broadcast to the nation.

Swallowing, Sam glanced at Paul and Francesca. They stood to either side of him, their faces tight with fear, their eyes lingering on the man standing beside Halt. A dozen black-suited bodyguards ringed the two men, their hard eyes scanning the crowd. They were clearly taking no chances.

Not with the life of the President of the Western Allied States.

Whispers spread through the crowd as the President squared his shoulders and stepped into view. Striding across to the podium, he looked out over the gathered faces. He moved with a regal grace, with the air of a man used to power. Not surprising, after the long decades he had served as President.

Gently placing one hand on the smooth mahogany of the podium, he waved to the crowd. The whispers died to sudden silence, as every person present looked up with expectation. Even the sharp clicking of cameras died away. It had been a long time since the President had spoken in such a public setting. Usually he spoke from his office, or to private press conferences. Now the whole nation was waiting with baited breath to see what he had to say.

"My fellow citizens of the Western Allied States," he began, his smooth voice carrying out over the crowd. "Thank you for joining me here today. I know recent times have been hard. I appreciate your courage today, to stand with me here and defy the threats of local terrorists and foreign states against our proud nation."

He fell silent, his eyes sweeping the crowd, as though he were speaking to each and every one of them. "But I have come here today to tell you the dark days are numbered, that a solution is at hand."

Whispers spread through the crowd as heads turned to one another. Then the President spread his hands, and silence fell once more. On the stage, Halt stepped from the shadows and approached the podium.

"My people have been working on a solution to combat the menace of the *Chead*," the President continued. "Though our enemies abroad would see us fall to the chaos they have seeded, their efforts will only make us stronger. The terror they seek to spread will only unite us in our effort to defeat them. And now we have an answer to their monstrosities, a beacon of hope to light our way."

He paused, letting his words sink in, the anticipation build. Then he continued. "Our scientists have taken inspiration from the evil of the Chead. They have studied their physiology, identified their weaknesses, and developed a response."

Sam let out a long breath. That was their cue. He glanced at the others, hesitating on the brink. It was not too late to turn back, to flee the stage and deny Halt and the President their victory. But even as he tensed, an image of Ashley flashed across his vision, of her strapped to the bed, and Halt standing over her.

The fight fled him, and he hesitated no longer.

The crowd stilled as Sam stepped into the light. He could sense Paul and Francesca at his shoulders, but he kept his eyes fixed on Halt, on the triumphant grin on the doctor's face. His heart sank, but there was no going back. Slowly, he strode to the front of the stage, and looked out over the mass of humanity gathered for their presentation.

They were on Fisherman's Wharf, gathered around a makeshift stage at Pier 39. The crowd stretched out along the waterfront in either direction, as far as the eye could see. A stillness came over them as they looked up at the three teenagers standing alongside the President, their foreheads creasing in sudden confusion.

The President raised a hand. "Ladies and gentlemen, I give you the future."

At the President's words, Sam closed his eyes and bowed his head.

Forgive me.

With a sharp crack, his wings snapped open, and the great expanse of copper feathers spread to fill the stage. Behind him he heard the whisper of feathers as the others followed suit. Opening his eyes, he looked out again at the crowd.

A thousand faces stared up at him. Mouths hung open and eyes bulged at the impossibility of what they were witnessing. Not a soul moved. Not a voice spoke. The silence was absolute, stretching over the crowded streets like a blanket.

Then the whispers began, quietly at first, then in a rush, as though a dam had been broken. As one, the reporters began to shout questions. Cameras flashed and the crowd jostled forward, desperate for a closer look.

On the stage, Sam bowed his head, struggling to hold back tears. The collar pressed tighter around his throat, and shivering, he silently retracted his wings. Glancing at Halt, he saw the exaltation on the doctor's face, as he basked in the triumph of the moment. He closed his eyes again, unable to face the shame welling up within him, the sense of helplessness.

What have I done?

SIXTY-SIX

"*Liz!*" Chris cried.

His chest constricted as he heard the others screaming from the neighbouring cages. He threw himself at the wire mesh, felt the cold steel cutting into his face, and stumbled sideways. His wings beat the air, keeping him upright, tearing at his steel confines, desperate to escape. But nothing he did made a difference. Heart racing in his chest, he watched the nightmare unfolding outside his cage.

Liz lay pinned beneath the guard's boot, her hands still cuffed behind her back, her wings beating weakly against the cold concrete. She kicked out with her feet, but the other guards stood out of range and only laughed. Then one drew back his boot and drove it into her side. The blow folded Liz in two as the breath was driven from her lungs.

In his cage, Chris cursed the men, threatening bloody murder, but they continued to ignore him, intent on their victim. On the ground, Liz shrieked as James crouched over her and grabbed a handful of her hair. Jerking back her head, he forced her to look at him.

"You be good now, Elizabeth," he sat back on his haunches and nodded at the cages, "or an accident's going to happen to one of your buddies there."

Liz only growled and strained against her cuffs. Her wings swung out, catching James in the ribs toppling him to the floor. He cursed as he landed on his backside. Cursing, another of the guards stepped forward and stamped on Liz's wing. Liz arched her back as he ground her feathers into the concrete, a silent scream tearing from her throat.

Regaining his feet, James dusted himself off and scowled down at Liz. He drove his boot into Liz's side again, smiling with satisfaction as Liz gasped into the concrete.

"Please," Liz's voice quivered. "*Just leave us alone!*"

The grin on James's face grew as he crouched beside her again, but Chris felt a touch of premonition at Liz's words. He frowned, leaning against the wire, peering out at the tangle of bodies. Liz lay stiff against the concrete, her wings retracted protectively against her back now. She did not move as James reached out and stroked the black feathers, speaking softly. "Just be a good girl, and we'll put you back in one piece."

The hackles stood on Chris's neck as the guard brushed the hair from Liz's face. A scream built in his throat, a desperate cry of anger, or untold rage. He strained against the cuffs, the steel cutting into his wrists. Pain streaked from his bullet wound, but he didn't care, hardly noticed.

In the centre of the room, Liz had gone deathly still. Smiling, the guard bent down, reaching for her…

As his hands brushed across her skin, a blood curdling scream filled the room, so loud it sent Chris staggering backwards. It went on and on, tearing at his ear drums. Unable to cover his ears, Chris sank to his knees, and watched as the men went reeling.

As quickly as it had begun, the scream cut off. The guards blinked, and James cursed as he stepped towards Liz. Before he could reach her, a sound like nails on a chalkboard rent the air, followed by the sound of steel chains striking concrete.

A feral growl rose from where Liz lay huddled on the ground. A shudder went through her feathers, her black wings stretching out to cover her. Then Liz was crouched on all fours, her hands suddenly free, her black hair pasted across her face. Her eyes flashed in the glow of the overhead lights, falling on the three guards standing over her, tainted by some indescribable hatred.

Chris staggered back from the wire of his cage. The breath caught in his throat and he struggled to breathe, to comprehend what he was seeing. His stomach twisted and he shook his head, clenching his eyes closed.

But when he opened them again, nothing had changed.

Liz still crouched on the ground, her lips drawn back in a snarl, her wings tensed behind her. And her eyes… gone was the crystal blue he knew so well.

In their place was the cold grey eyes of the *Chead*.

The guards stumbled backwards, their mouths wide, fumbling for their weapons. Before they could so much as scream, Liz sprang.

The first man collapsed as Liz collided with his chest and bore him to the ground. He managed half a shriek before Liz's fingers flashed out and caught him in the throat. Blood sprayed the air, cutting off his screams, as a low gurgling started in his chest. He gaped, eyes wide as blood filled his lungs. Laughing, Liz leapt at her next victim.

The second guard almost managed to raise his rifle before Liz was on him. Tearing the weapon from his terrified hands, she hurled it aside and reached out to catch him by the neck. His mouth widened, but he could not even scream as she slammed him backwards into the wall. A sickening crunch came from his skull, and his eyes rolled up into the back of his skull.

Tossing the man aside, Liz stepped over the lifeless body, her grey eyes tracking James as he stumbled across the room. He screamed, fumbling for his rifle, but she was already on him. He staggered backwards as she stripped it from his hands, until his back pressed up against Chris's cage.

"No, please, no, *don't!*" he shrieked the last word as Liz charged.

He raised his arms to protect himself, but Liz's hands flashed out to catch him by both wrists. With a sickening wrench, she tore her arms apart.

Chris blanked and forced himself to look away. But he could not block out the sounds of rending flesh and breaking bones. His stomach churned as James screamed and started to beg. Another thud came, followed by another scream, and wild laughter filled the room.

When the guard finally fell silent, Chris could hardly bring himself to look. Sucking in a breath, he turned to face the slaughter.

Liz stood outside his cage, her clothes covered with blood, even the black feathers of her outstretched wings stained by it. Her shoulders rose and fell in a rhythmic fashion, as her cold grey eyes studied him. Her lips drew back in a snarl as he moved, and slowly she reached out a hand to the wire. Gripping it between her fingers, she began to squeeze.

Chris swallowed as the steel wires bent before her strength. He retreated backwards until his back pressed against the rear of the cage. Fear wrapped its way around his stomach as he stared at Liz, searching for the girl he loved, begging for this all to be a nightmare.

But there was no sign of blue in Liz's eyes, and snarling she threw herself at the wire. The steel rattled and bent beneath the impact, but did not give. Chris strained against his handcuffs, as the others screamed at him from the other cages. Blood pounded in his ears, muffling their words, but it didn't matter. The handcuffs refused to give.

He looked up at Liz as she attacked the wire again. He recognised the madness in her eyes. It was more than just the cold grey of the *Chead*. In the facility, Chris had proven he could match the *Chead's* strength. But he could still remember the fury that had come over the *Chead* at the end of their fight. And with that fury came a renewed strength, a fresh power that had left Chris begging for mercy.

He saw that rage in Liz's eyes now. She would tear him limb from limb.

Unless he could reach her.

"Liz," he breathed. Summoning his courage, he stepped towards her. "Liz, please, it's me, Chris. Please, come back to me."

He flinched as Liz roared and threw herself at the wall of the cage. His heart pounded hard against his ribs as the steel poles supporting the corners of the cage bent beneath the force of the impact.

"Liz, *stop!*" Chris screamed as she attacked again.

But his words fell on deaf ears, and he retreated to the corner, watching as the poles slowly bent towards him. He glimpsed the others standing in the nearby cages, watching now in terrified silence, desperate not to draw Liz's attention.

Despair rising in his chest, Chris slumped to the floor. He couldn't stand to lose Liz, not like this, not now. She alone had drawn him back from the brink, from the gulf of despair into which he had fallen. If he lost Liz too, he didn't know how he would go on.

He looked up into her grey eyes, watching her throw herself against the wire, still not quite believing what he was seeing.

How could this happen?

Finally he had to look away, to close his eyes and wait for the end to come. But to his surprise, a sudden silence fell over the room. Looking up, he found Liz still standing outside his cage, her grey eyes staring. Then they blinked, and her chest swelled as she sucked in a great, shuddering breath.

For a long while, she stood still, fists clenched at her side. Chris stared into her eyes, searching for a trace of her crystal blue, hardly daring to breathe. Time stretched out, long seconds uncounted.

Then Liz shook her head, and her grey eyes blinked as she retreated a step. Her head twisted, her gaze sweeping the room, seeming to take in the devastation for the first time. A shudder went through her as she lifted her head, her nostrils flaring.

A low growl came from her throat as she turned and stared at the door. Her shoulders rose as she drew in another breath. She shook her head, snarling at the bodies lying scattered around her.

"Liz," Chris whispered, desperate to reach her.

She whirled at his voice, eyes wide, flashing with sudden fear.

Then she spun back to the door, and fled.

SIXTY-SEVEN

THE *CHEAD* ROARED AS A BULLET GRAZED HER SHOULDER. Then she was amongst the men with their puny weapons, tearing and rending, and they were falling back before her rage. Their screams sent a warm thrill through her veins, but they quickly fell silent. She stood amidst their bodies, the taste of blood strong in her mouth, as she searched for fresh victims.

Alone.

Growling, the *Chead* moved on. Turning a corner, she found the woman she had missed, staggering away down the corridor. Rage spread through her veins as she leapt, bearing the woman to the floor. The woman's screams cut off as the *Chead's* fingers tore through her throat.

Straightening, the *Chead* scanned the corridor, searching for movement. Blood stained the walls, but none had escaped her vengeance. Lifting her head, she tasted the air, seeking out the strange smell. It called to her, alien but familiar.

Desire tingled in her veins as she breathed it in. Turning, she moved towards it.

The *Chead* moved down the long corridors on silent feet, her senses reaching out, searching for signs of life. But there were no more sounds, no hint of movement. The stark white corridors were empty, the group she had slaughtered perhaps the only occupants.

Turn back, the *Chead* hesitated as a girl whispered in her mind. Then, snarling, she pushed the voice aside and continued after the scent. It filled the air, growing stronger with every step, rich and sweet and irresistible. Her pace quickened, desire mingling with rage, muting the need to rend and tear.

Long minutes later, the *Chead* found her way barred by a steel door. She paused outside. Lifting her head, she breathed deeply, tasting the scent she tracked. It hung heavy around the door. There could be no doubt. The source was beyond.

Clenching her fists, the *Chead* charged. Again and again she hurled herself at the door, feeling it bend and shift with each blow, rattled by her power. She sensed movement beyond, and redoubled her efforts, determined not to let the source of the scent escape her.

Stop, the voice came again, but she ignored it.

Roaring, the *Chead* drove herself against the door a final time. Steel hinges shrieked and with a crash it buckled inwards, collapsing to the ground beyond. Triumph quickened the *Chead's* racing heart, and teeth bared, she stepped inside.

SIXTY-EIGHT

CHRIS SAGGED AGAINST THE WALL OF HIS CAGE AS LIZ FLED through the door. His shoulders slumped and he slid to the concrete. Closing his eyes, he sucked in a deep, shuddering breath.

What the hell was that?

His mind was still reeling, struggling to comprehend what he'd witnessed. But there was no denying it – Liz had changed, succumbed to the relentless rage of the *Chead*. The vile guards had never stood a chance. And neither had he.

"Chris?" Richard's voice came nearby.

Chris opened his eyes and looked through the wire at the others. They huddled in their cages, wide eyes staring back at him, faces pale with shock. Richard had found his feet, but Jasmine and Mira still sat on the floors of their cages, their faces lined with exhaustion. He could feel the same fatigue throbbing in his muscles, and he found his mind drifting.

What did they use in those tranquilisers?

Shaking his head, he fought against his weariness. "What did you say, Richard?"

Richard was looking out at the room, his eyes lingering on the bloody slaughter Liz had left behind. Blood and limbs and bodies lay scattered across the floor, barely recognisable as the three men that had stood there a few minutes earlier.

"We have to get out of here," Richard said grimly. "Can you get out?"

Chris took a second to assess the damage Liz had inflicted on his cage. The poles had bent, but not broken, and the thick wire still hemmed him in on all sides. Grimly, he shook his head.

Then he saw a glimmer of metal amidst the bloody mess on the floor outside his cage. He scrambled forward eagerly. "The keys," he said.

Twisting, he tried to reach them through the wire mesh. But with his hands cuffed together, he couldn't manoeuvre enough to reach them. He looked up at Richard and Jasmine, despair welling in his chest.

"I can't reach them," he said.

Jasmine snorted. "You clearly haven't watched enough television."

So saying, Jasmine lay down on her back on the floor of her cage. With her arms still cuffed behind her, she stretched them down until her hands rested behind her knees. Then, lifting her legs, she bent her knees and strained until the handcuffs passed beneath her feet.

Climbing to her feet, she waved her hands in front of her in triumph.

"Now you," she grinned.

Chris, Richard and Mira quickly repeated the procedure. When Chris looked back up, Jasmine was staring down at her hands, her forehead creased. Veins stood out along her arms as she strained. With her hands in front of her, she could now bring the full force of her strength to bare. Slowly, the chains of her handcuffs buckled, until with a violent jerk, they snapped apart.

Looking up, Jasmine grimaced. "These people have under-estimated us for the last time. Come on, Chris, get the keys."

Chris nodded. Gritting his teeth, he tensed his arms and pulled them apart. Pain streaked down his wounded arm, but he resisted it, determined not to let the others down. A second later the steel gave way with a sharp shriek. Dropping to his knees, he reached a hand through the wire links and lifted the keys from the bloody floor.

Within minutes the four of them were standing outside the cages, looking around at the carnage their friend had left behind. The keys had also unlocked the broken remains of the handcuffs, although it had taken time to find the right key amidst the bulging chain.

Staring at the slaughter, Chris forced himself to avert his eyes. Looking at the others, he saw the questions in their expressions, the same ones whirring through his own mind. Why had Liz changed? And were they destined to follow her? Would they all one by one turn into monsters?

Shuddering, he pushed away the thought. "We'd better get out of here. Liz can't have gone far."

Richard frowned. "Chris…" he lowered his head and looked away, "Chris, Liz is gone. You saw her eyes. Whatever that was, I don't think she's coming back from it. We can't waste our time looking for her. Halt could be back any minute."

Chris stared back, the first embers of rage catching in his chest. "How can you say that?" he growled. "After everything we've been through, how can you even think about leaving her?"

"I don't like it any better than you do," Richard met Chris's eyes for just a moment, long enough for him to see the sorrow there, "but we have to be realistic. She turned, Chris. She's *Chead* now. She's gone."

"No." Chris stepped in close and grabbed Richard by the arm. "She's not. She's still in there. You saw her, she had the chance to kill me, but she didn't. I'm not leaving her."

Richard pulled his arm free and turned to Jasmine. "Jasmine…" he started, then stopped, still unsure of himself with her, "Jas, tell him we have to go."

Chris looked across at Jasmine, pleading silently for her help. He was so tired, his strength at its end. He couldn't do this without them.

Jasmine's eyes flickered from Chris and back to Richard, a frown twisting her lips. Finally she let out a long breath, and stepped up beside them. Her eyes fixed on Richard as she drew him into her arms.

Richard's eyes widened at her sudden show of affection, but a second later his arms went around her, and they stood for a second in silence. Finally, Jasmine pulled away again and looked up at Richard.

"Thank you, Rich," she smiled. "You took a bullet for me, back in the apartment."

"Well, they were darts, but…" Richard trailed off as Jasmine placed a finger on his lips.

Then she turned back to Chris, her eyes resolute. "And so did Liz. I told her to run, to leave us behind. She could have gotten free, but she chose to stay and fight for us," she looked back at Richard, "If our positions were reversed now, she wouldn't leave, Rich. We're family, we have to help her."

The two of them stood staring at each other for a long moment, before Richard closed his eyes and nodded.

Just then, a low whimper came from Mira. Chris turned and staggered backwards as she sprang at him. Her wings beat the air, carrying her past as Chris leapt out of her path. But she was not aiming for him. With another beat of her wings, she disappeared through the open door.

Chris swore, and no longer hesitating, he started after her. He heard footsteps and muttered curses as the others followed, but outside Mira was already racing down the long corridor. Sucking in a breath, Chris sprinted after her, desperate to catch the girl before she got them all killed.

At the end of the corridor, Mira took a sharp turn to the right. Chris picked up the pace, afraid of losing her, as his eyes scanned the path ahead. A trail of bloody footprints led in the direction they were heading, and silently he prayed Mira did not encounter Liz before they caught her.

Turning the corner, his stride faltered as he found a fresh scene of slaughter. But Mira was already halfway down the corridor, sprinting hard on her short legs, her grey wings beating sporadically to hurry her along. Panting, Chris leapt after her.

Two men lay slumped one over the other halfway down the hallway, their blood making the floor slick beneath his feet. A rifle lay on the floor nearby, while another had been embedded in the plasterboard wall.

Ahead, Mira vaulted around another bend. Chris barrelled around the corner after her. She was still fifty feet ahead, but he was closing fast. The hushed voices of the others chased after him as he glanced around, expecting guards or doctors to appear. But the hallways remained empty, and he guessed Liz had killed those men before they had a chance to sound the alarms.

Slowly he closed the gap with Mira, until only a few feet separated them. But as he reached out to catch her, Mira's wings beat down and sent her soaring forward out of reach. Swearing, Chris tried to do the same, and crashed to the ground as the length of his wings struck the walls on either side. The narrow corridors were perfect for her smaller wingspan, but it left his all but useless. Climbing back to his feet, he chased after her again.

The game of cat and mouse ended as Mira abruptly drew to a stop. Chris's arms windmilled and he staggered sideway into the wall to avoid smashing the girl from her feet.

Coming to a stop, he quickly reached out and grabbed Mira by the arm.

As the others drew up behind him, he straightened, finally paying attention to where Mira had led them. The first thing he noticed was the bloody footprints – fainter now, but there was no doubt in his mind they had been left by Liz. Then his eyes travelled a few feet further down the corridor, to where a steel door lay crumpled on the ground.

His stomach twisted and he glanced sideways at Mira. She stood beside him, staring through the broken doorway, her shoulders rising and falling with each shallow breath. Her wings shuddered on her back, and her whole body was coiled tight as a spring.

"Where have you brought us, Mira?" Chris whispered.

Her strange eyes looked up at him, their green and blue irises shining. "Artemis."

SIXTY-NINE

Eyes closed, Liz rose from the darkness, following the soft whispers of an ancient voice. Tendrils of madness wrapped around her, threatening to pull her back down, but the voice was urgent, insistent. It lifted her from the haze, pulling her into the light, returning her to reality.

She shuddered as sensation suddenly returned. A scream built in her throat but she swallowed it down. Blinking, she looked around, biting back a sob as memory of the *Chead* flashed through her mind. Trapped in her own body, she had witnessed the creature's slaughter, helpless to intervene, a silent witness to its madness.

When the men had grabbed her, when she had realised their intent, a wild fury had taken her. Laying on the ground, helpless and threatened, she had felt a pressure build within her. As they reached for her, that pressure had snapped, and the rage had swept her away. Powerless against it, Liz had closed her eyes and succumbed.

When they opened again, it had been the *Chead* staring out.

The steel handcuffs had given way like paper before her power, and her tormentors quickly followed suit. She could still remember the ecstasy, the wild joy of the slaughter, the pleasure she'd taken ripping the guards limb from limb. But now the memory made her sick, and tasting bile in her throat she rolled onto her side and threw up.

Her arms shook as she finally sat up. A memory flickered through her mind, and she recalled the voice that had called her back. Blinking, she looked around the room, and finally noticed the man sitting beside her.

They were on a narrow hospital bed in some kind of infirmary. She could not quite recall how she'd come there, only that the *Chead* had followed a scent, that she had been drawn through the facility by it. Looking at the man, there was no doubt he had been the source.

He sat watching her, an old man out of time. His face was lined, the skin hanging from his arms in heavy folds. His skin was ghostly pale and he wore a plain white shirt to match, stained with age. A rattling came from his chest as he sucked in a breath. Only his hair had remained untouched by the years. Its long black strands hung across his face, out of place on his ancient body. The cold grey eyes of the *Chead* stared from the wrinkled face.

"Welcome, my child," the old *Chead* whispered, a smile touching his lips. "I have been waiting for you."

As he spoke, a dam seemed to shatter within Liz, and she felt all the horror, the terror and anger, the devastation of the past week come crashing down on her. She suddenly found herself sobbing, overwhelmed by the emotions boiling within her. Then frail arms were wrapping around her, and shuddering, she buried her head in the *Chead's* chest, and cried until she thought she would surely drown in them.

The ancient *Chead* said nothing, only held her, his soft hands stroking her hair and wings.

Time passed. Nestled in his lap, Liz could almost imagine herself a child again, wrapped in the warm embrace of her parents. Closing her eyes, she breathed in his scent, the strange sweetness that marked the *Chead*. Only now, with him, it no longer seemed threatening.

They waited in silence, staring across at the broken door.

Liz sat up straight as Chris stumbled through the doorway, her heart lurching in her chest. His eyes widened as they swept the room and found her on the hospital bed, sitting beside the ancient *Chead*. She closed her eyes, expecting to see his face twist with the horror of what she'd done. Blood covered her clothes and wings and hair, forming a gruesome paste she feared might never come out. Biting back a sob, she waited for his anger.

A soft hand brushed across her cheek, lifting her chin, pulling her up. Her eyes fluttered open and found Chris beside her, arms open to embrace her. "Liz," he breathed, his voice filled with wonder. "Your eyes, they're blue."

With a half-choked cry, Liz threw herself into Chris's arms. His hands went around her back, stroking her wings, even as her arms wrapped around his back. His shirt slipped up and she felt the warmth of his flesh beneath her fingers. Desire flickered within her…

Then Chris was screaming, stumbling back from her, his face twisted with pain. He staggered across the room, crashing into another hospital bed and crumpling to the floor. Mouth open, Liz stepped after him, reached out to help him.

A wrinkled hand caught her wrist and pulled her back. "Stop, child," the *Chead's* voice whispered, "You'll only hurt him further. It will pass."

Liz stilled, staring in horror as Chris writhed on the ground, his hands clawing at his back. His wings slammed into the hospital bed and sent it crashing to the floor. A sound came from the doorway, and Liz looked up to see Mira, Richard and Jasmine staring in. She swallowed.

What have I done?

On the floor, Chris's movements slowed. He panted softly in the quiet, his eyes clenched shut, as he fought some unknown battle, some unspeakable pain.

Finally he stilled, and his eyes flickered open again. Liz groaned as she looked into his bloodshot eyes, desperate to go to him, but the *Chead* still held her back. Slowly, Chris picked himself off the floor, his limbs trembling with the effort.

"What…" he croaked, his voice trailing off. Grimacing, he tried again, "What is going on, Liz?"

Tears filled Liz's eyes as she shook her head. "I don't know."

She turned as the *Chead* released her wrist, looking up into the ancient face. The grey eyes stared back at her, filled with a soft compassion. "I am sorry, my child. Sometimes, the change has… unpredictable outcomes."

"*Artemis!*" Mira's shriek echoed through the room as the girl shot through the open door, apparently willing to wait outside no longer.

Leaping across the room, she threw herself into the old *Chead's* arms. The *Chead* chuckled as he stumbled backwards and sat down hard on the hospital bed. "Mira," his voice was warm as he addressed the girl, "My child, what has he done to you?"

Mira froze on his lap, suddenly uncertain. Liz watch the girl look away, saw the tears gathering in her eyes. "It was that man, Doctor Halt," she murmured. "He gave me some injection."

"Ah tsk my child, don't cry. You are still my child, my little Mira," the old *Chead* pulled the girl into a hug as he spoke.

Irritation prickled Liz's stomach, fuelled by her gnawing fear. "*What do you mean, unpredictable outcomes?*" she all but shrieked, interrupting the reunion.

The old *Chead* looked up, the smile falling from his face. "The *Chead* virus is complex. Of the genes it integrates into its hosts DNA, many are never activated and remain dormant. Nematocysts are rarely triggered during the change."

"Nematocysts?" Liz croaked.

"Stinger cells, found in marine jellyfish. The virus has incorporated them into your skin cells. When disturbed, they respond by delivering a sting. The neurotoxin they deliver can be fatal with long exposures, although some of us have developed a resistance."

Liz's skin tingled and the hackles on her neck stood on end. She shook her head, shrinking backwards against the bed. Instinctively she reached out and clenched the sheet between her fingers. "No," she whispered. "We're not… how can… *I'm not Chead!*"

Her voice rose to a shriek and she staggered away from the old *Chead*. Her eyes swept the room, seeking out some escape from the waking nightmare. For the first time, she took in her surroundings. Hospital beds lined the room, most empty, but a few had plastic curtains drawn around them. She guessed they were also empty though from their lack of response. A television was bolted onto the far wall, but otherwise the room was unadorned.

"My child…" Artemis said.

Liz's head whipped around as the old *Chead* stepped towards her. "*Stop saying that!*"

Artemis only smiled. "It is the truth, my child. You are all children to me, for I am Artemis, first of the *Chead*, father to all who have come since."

SEVENTY

CHRIS'S MIND WAS REELING AS A HEAVY SILENCE FELL OVER the infirmary. His body still throbbed from Liz's sting, a burning pain radiating out from the small of his back. But with Artemis's words, his thoughts were suddenly occupied with more pressing questions. He found himself staring at the *Chead*, studying his weathered face, as though somewhere in his wrinkles was the explanation for his words.

But there could be no explanation, no logical reasoning out of his proclamation. It simply wasn't possible. If this creature was the first of its kind, the first *Chead* to exist, it meant...

He shook his head. "That's not possible."

The old *Chead* stepped towards him, his grey eyes glistening. "And why is that, my child?"

Richard approached, his fists clenched. "Because no one knows where the *Chead* came from," he said.

The ancient eyes turned to the taller boy. "A lie. We were created here, within these very walls, at the glorious heart of the Western Allied States."

There was bitterness in the *Chead's* words as he turned away. Artemis made his slow way across the room, his movements weary, and lowered himself onto the bed. The grey eyes looked at them again, passing over each of them in turn.

"Who are you, Artemis?" Chris whispered.

The ancient eyes found his. "Once I was Dean Chester of Salt Lake City, Utah, born to Mary and John Chester, immigrants to the United States from South Africa. Once I was like you, young and filled with innocence. As a child, I watched my proud nation elect a half-mad oligarch to President, and witnessed first-hand the disintegration of the nation I had come to call home. And before my eighteenth birthday, I watched the forces of the Western Allied States gun down my family, and take the children of Salt Lake City as prisoners of war."

Silence fell across the room as they stared at the old man. Chris swallowed, his mind spinning as he struggled to grasp the implications of the creature's words. He frowned as he realised the dates did not add up. The American War had ended in 2030, twenty years ago, but the *Chead* looked at least eighty years old.

Before he could question him, Artemis continued. "We were brought back to San Francisco, to this very building. It was then we learned how desperate the Western Allied States were becoming. Though they had the backing of Canada and Mexico, they remained outmatched by the forces of the United States. They were desperate for something, anything to change the course of the war," he paused and took a heavy breath. "They were working on a virus, one that would turn their troops into unstoppable killing machines, that would allow a soldier to run for days on end, to tear ordinary men to pieces, and shrug off bullet wounds like scratches."

"No," Liz whispered, shrinking back from the old man. "No, the *Chead*... my people, we have suffered for *decades*. The government, they couldn't, they wouldn't..." her words trailed off as tears shone in her eyes.

Chris started towards her, his own heart twisting with the horror of the *Chead's* words. Then he froze, the remembered pain giving him pause. Her fingers had touched him like fire, sending burning waves rippling through his body, setting his every nerve ending aflame. He had lost himself in the agony, though it had only been the briefest of touches.

Artemis stepped up in Chris's place, his voice soft. "My child," opening his arms, he drew Liz into his embrace.

"How?" Chris croaked, seeing his hands gripping the bare skin of Liz's arms.

"As I said, some of us have developed a resistance," Artemis replied softly.

Beside Chris, Richard cast a nervous glance at the door. "Chris, we need to get out of here."

Chris could sense his agitation, but he shook his head. Everything the old *Chead* said, every fresh revelation, only raised more questions. Questions that demanded answers. "What happened to the other children?"

Artemis closed his eyes. "For years, we suffered here. There were hundreds, maybe thousands of us at first. But we were nothing to them. Uneducated country hicks that had no place in their world. Children and teenagers, boys and girls, they all died horribly, their bodies warped by terrible mutations. For the longest time, all I could hear when I closed my eyes were their screams."

"When my turn finally came, I fought them, and when that failed, pleaded for them to just kill me. Death would have been preferable to the things I had witnessed. But there was no resisting them, no escape, and I received my injection, just as all the others had before me."

"But you survived," Chris breathed.

The old *Chead* nodded. "Ay, I survived. By then they knew they were close to a viable solution. Even then, I thought I was lost. All I remember from that time is the pain, the awful fever that gripped my body. Then there was just red, only a burning rage that consumed everything I was, everything I had ever been. There was only the *Chead*."

Chris shuddered, his eyes flickering to Liz and back. "But it did not last?" he asked. "You remembered yourself, who you were?"

"Yes," Artemis grimaced. "I don't know how long I was lost, but eventually I began to find my way back through the rage, to resurface. It was then they realised they had succeeded, had turned me into their perfect weapon. Only, my mind had returned too late – they had won the war by other means."

"Washington, DC," Chris said, remembering pictures of the smouldering ruin. The surprise detonation of a ground based nuclear warhead had decimated the leadership of the United States, as well as millions of civilians. In the ensuing chaos, the forces of the Western Allied States had gained the foothold they had needed, and shattered the backbone of the USA.

"*So why did they do this to us?*" Liz shrieked as she pushed herself away from the old *Chead*. "Why would they unleash those monsters on their own people? The war was *won!*"

"Fear," Artemis replied.

"Fear?" Jasmine questioned, speaking for the first time. "What do you mean, fear?"

"After the war, it was only a matter of time before people started questioning the government. Especially your rural communities, whose youth had been conscripted and their wealth decimated by taxation. The government needed a new enemy to fight, a demon for the populace to hate."

"So they created one," Richard growled, his arms crossed, fingers clenched around his arms.

"So it would seem," Artemis replied. "The *Chead* gave them the excuse they needed to alter laws, to send the army into unruly communities, to impose curfews and hunt out foreign 'traitors'. They gave your people a monster to fear, while your leaders quietly stole your freedom."

As Artemis fell silent, Chris asked the question that had plagued him since he'd watched Liz's eyes turn grey. "But none of this explains why Liz changed, why you think we're your children. We were created by the government, but we're not *Chead*. A doctor named Angela Fallow created the virus that changed us."

A dry, rasping laugh came from the old *Chead*. "No, my child. I have seen many variations of the *Chead* over the years. I have heard those here speak of your Fallow, of the young doctor they thought might finally perfect their virus. By then, the Directors had restricted knowledge of our origin to a select few. But that did not prevent them manipulating young minds into continuing their work," he bent his head and smiled. "The wings are new, but at our core, we remain the same."

"What were they trying to perfect?" Chris pressed, as Richard shifted nervously alongside him.

Artemis spread his arms, gesturing to his wrinkled skin. "Surely you have noticed, my child, that I do not look well for a forty year old. That, and our habit of losing control and tearing innocent bystanders apart."

"Chris," Richard hissed through clenched teeth. "That's enough. There'll be time for questions later. We need to get out of here."

Jasmine nodded her agreement and Chris swallowed his next question. He turned back to Artemis. "Let's go, we're getting you out of here."

Artemis smiled. "But what about your friend? You can't leave her behind."

Turning, he nodded at the far corner of the room, where plastic green curtains had been drawn around one of the beds. Chris frowned, glancing back at Artemis a second, unsure of the man's meaning. Then, stomach clenched, breath held, he moved across the room. Hands trembling, he reached up, and pulled the curtains open.

SEVENTY-ONE

THE BREATH CAUGHT IN LIZ'S THROAT AS SHE STARED AT THE bed Chris had just revealed. Time seemed to slow, and all noise fell away. She took a trembling step towards the bed, then another, past Chris as he stared in disbelief, beyond the curtains, to where her friend waited.

Ashley lay on her side, her eyes closed, red hair spread across the white pillow, her white wings hanging half-folded behind her. Her shoulders rose and fell with each gentle breath as she murmured softly in her sleep. Her skin was ghostly pale, the last traces of purple bruises still marking her arms and face. A steel collar shone around her throat, and an IV bag hung from the wall beside her bed, a thin tube stretching out to deliver the contents through a stent in her arm.

"Ashley," she whispered.

Taking care not to touch skin, Liz reached out and placed a hand on Ashley's shoulder. She shook her gently, and watched as the girl's eyes flickered. She caught a glimpse of her tawny yellow eyes, before they drifted close again.

She looked back as Artemis spoke. "They have her drugged."

Growling, Liz gently pulled the tube from Ashley's arm. She looked down at the girl, unable to believe her eyes, to trust Ashley was really here. Last she'd seen her, Ashley had been a broken mess, her chest torn open by the bullet, her wings shattered by the fall. Yet here she was, still sporting a bandage around her chest, but whole, alive.

Liz shook her head, counting the days. Had it been a week, or two since their escape? Somewhere in the chaos she had lost track, but however long it had been, this should not have been possible.

"Guys, save the reunion for later, we need to get out *now*," Richard spoke from behind them.

"She's still unconscious," Chris replied. "And what about the collar?"

"Try the keys," Richard hissed, insistent now. "And we can carry her. But it's been too long. Sooner or later, someone is going to stumble onto those bodies and sound the alarm."

Beside her, Chris came alive. He nodded and produced a set of keys from his pocket. He started to flick through the ring, searching for a key that might match, glancing at Artemis as he worked. "We can bring them all down with your story, Artemis. Once people find out the truth, it's only a matter of time before the whole government crumbles. Will you come with us?"

Artemis smiled. "My child, I have spent twenty years locked in this prison. My body is failing me, and I have been confined to this infirmary for months. But I would like to take my final breaths in fresh air. Of course, I will come."

Chris grinned as the collar around Ashley's neck clicked open with the third key he tried. Then the smile fell from his lips. "What about Sam?" he looked at Artemis again. "What about our other friend?"

"I have scented others here, since she arrived. But I have never seen them," Artemis replied. As he spoke he lifted his head, his nostrils flaring. "And they are not within the building now."

Liz swore, her heart sinking. What would Halt do to Sam, when he discovered Ashley gone? But they could not leave her here, to suffer whatever torments Halt had in store.

The smile had fallen from Chris's lips, but he shifted into action at another prompting from Richard. Reaching down, he slid his hands under Ashley's back and gently lifted her into his arms. He staggered forward a step, struggling with her weight.

"*Chris*, your arm!" Liz hissed, stepping towards him.

"I'm fine," Chris grated through clenched teeth, his face pained. "It's okay, I can do it. It'll be slow, but I don't want to hurt her anyway."

"Don't be stupid, Chris," Richard stepped towards him. "Let me take her."

Chris shook his head. "No, she's our friend, I'll take her. You should go ahead with Artemis. We need to get him to safety. Once he talks, its all over. This place, the Praegressus Project, everything."

Richard hesitated, glancing at Jasmine before facing them again. "She's our friend too, Chris. I won't leave her, not again," he drew himself up. "We're in this together, all of us."

Chris smiled. "I know. But he needs to be our priority. If you can get him clear, nothing else will matter. Do you know a way out, Artemis?"

The old *Chead* nodded and Chris smiled. "Good, tell me."

After Artemis had repeated the directions they needed to reach the exit elevators twice, Chris finally nodded. "Okay, I've got it. You guys had better get out of here then," he paused, his eyes wavering. "If anything goes wrong, meet us at Daniella's apartment. It's the last place they'd expect us to go."

As the others moved off, Liz turned and looked at Chris. He started to speak, but she cut him off. "If you think I'm leaving you, you can think again," she paused, the smile fading from her face. "I'm sorry, Chris, that I hurt you."

He shook his head. "It's not your fault."

Yet she could see the hurt in the tightness of his face, the distress in his eyes. Silently, feared things might never be the same between them again. But there was no time to linger on the thought.

Turning towards the door, Liz nodded. "Let's go."

SEVENTY-TWO

"I want to see her, Halt," Sam growled as he settled into the back of the limousine.

Halt stared back from the opposite seat, his grey eyes hardening. Beside Sam, Paul and Francesca shifted nervously, their mouths clenched shut. Swallowing, Sam felt the cold metal of his collar press against his throat. But this time he would not back down.

"Is that so?" Halt whispered, his tone threatening.

"I've done what you asked," Sam replied. "I've taught them to use their wings. I've shown myself to the public, gotten you your funding," his shoulders slumped and nausea swelled in his stomach, "Please, I just want to see her, to know she's okay."

He was begging now, but he no longer cared. He had to know it had been worth it, that he had not sacrificed his integrity, had not betrayed everything he believed for nothing.

Turning, Halt stared out the window at the passing crowds. His face was impassive, his eyes unreadable. Only his voice when he spoke betrayed his excitement. "The President is impressed," he looked back at them, a smile warming his lips. "I will have all the funding I could ever need. You have done well, Samuel. I will reward your good behaviour. When we return, I will grant you an hour with the girl."

"Thank you, Halt," Sam croaked, bowing his head. He closed his eyes, already picturing Ashley, already imagining her in his arms again. She was alive, and he would see her soon. It had all been worth it.

Or had it?

His joy curdled as he thought of the countless lives he had sentenced to the horrors of the facility, of the sons and daughters who would now vanish into the Californian mountains, never to return. How many more would die now, because of him?

And what would happen once the Praegressus Project succeeded? Once they perfected their virus, and turned it loose on their soldiers?

The drive back to San Francisco seemed to take an age. The four of them sat in silence for the rest of the journey, Halt in his triumph, Sam and the others lost in their own personal nightmares. When the car finally pulled to a stop, Sam could hardly wait to escape the stifling compartment. But he sat patiently with the others, waiting for Halt's command. Like mutts on a leash, they knew the consequences of disobedience.

Once outside, Halt called for them to follow, and one by one they filed out of the limousine. To Sam's surprise, they were not in the grim basement carpark where they had been picked up earlier. Instead, they found themselves on the sidewalk outside a massive marble courthouse. They were at the base of a broad staircase leading up to the building, where a large revolving door waited between thick stone pillars.

Sam glanced at Halt. "I thought we were going back to your facility."

Halt smiled. "We are."

Without waiting for a response, he started up the staircase, gesturing for them to follow. Sam glanced at the others, but they kept their lips shut tight. There had been a strained truce between them since the incident in the training hall, and Sam quickly looked away again.

Clenching his fists, he started after Halt. He still didn't know what had happened that day, what had driven him to attack them with such ferocity. One second he'd been enjoying the chance to stretch his wings and test his new strength, the next he'd found himself pounding the two teenagers into the ground. He shuddered at the memory, and the nightmares it conjured.

At the top of the stairs, Halt paused and waited for them to catch up before continuing through the revolving door. Inside, a tall-ceilinged entrance hall stretched out before them. Marble pillars towered to either side of them. Overhead, the domed ceiling had been decorated with a mosaic mural depicting the story of the American War. Down the length of the hall, brave WAS soldiers were shown fighting off the villainous forces of the United States, while at the end a mushroom cloud sprouted from the ruins of the once-famous Whitehouse.

The hall was mostly open space, but around its edges wooden benches lined the walls. On the benches, men and woman in expensive suits waited in silence, their rigid postures and gold embossed wristwatches belying their importance. At the far end, several reception desks stood in front of a row of elevator doors.

Straightening his shoulders, Halt strode towards the desks, waving them after him. Together, they made their slow way across the hall.

Sam scowled as the men and woman on the benches looked up and saw their approach. His wings shifted uncomfortably – he had pulled them tight against his back, but they were still evident to anyone that looked. And just a few hours earlier his face had been plastered all over national television. Within seconds, every eye in the hall was transfixed on Sam, Paul and Francesca.

Whispers rose around them, as their audience turned to one another. "Is that? It can't be! It's them… look at those feathers!"

His cheeks warming, Sam closed his ears to the sounds and stared straight ahead. It was easy to tell what Halt was doing. He wore an arrogant smile as he strode across the room, basking in the attention. This was his moment, his victory, and he was making sure everybody knew it. In his white lab coat, there could hardly have been a greater contrast between the doctor and the rich men and women around them – and yet there was no mistaking who held the power here.

The woman behind the reception desk stood as they approached, her eyes flicking nervously between Halt and his slaves. "Welcome... Doctor Halt," she faltered, then smiled, "Congratulations on your announcement."

Halt smiled. "Thank you, Janet. We'll be needing the elevator to the subterranean department."

"Of course, Doctor."

As the receptionist turned to her computer, a whirring sound came from one of the elevators. The numbers above the door started to flash, but Halt had already turned away, and was now languishing against the desk, the smug grin still on his lips.

Sam's eyes widened as the steel doors to the elevator slid open and a girl stepped out. An old man, a young girl, and a boy followed after her, then froze as they looked around. They hesitated only a second, before silently starting to creep away from the elevators.

Sam could only stare as Richard and Jasmine slid around the far end of the receptionist's desk. His heart pounded in his chest as he glanced at Halt, wondering how the doctor had not noticed them. Breath held, he clenched his fists against the desk, and silently screamed for them to move faster.

They made it another two steps before Halt finally looked up.

SEVENTY-THREE

"*ARTEMIS*," HALT HISSED. "WHAT ARE YOU DOING OUT OF your cage, old man?"

A hushed silence fell over the hall as all eyes turned to look at the group huddled around the far side of the receptionist's desk. Richard and Jasmine stood frozen in terror, their wings half-spread, staring across at Halt and Sam. Behind them, the old man straightened and stepped past them.

"Doctor Halt, it's been a long time," the old man's voice was hushed with age.

Halt brushed past Sam and strode towards the old man, a scowl darkening his face. "You thought you'd just walk out the front door, did you? Thought you'd finally *do* something," he shook his head, "I should have killed you years ago."

"Death would have been preferable to the life you allowed me," the old man took another step, closing the distance between himself and Halt. "To watching you slaughter my children."

Behind the old man, Jasmine was struggling with the young girl from the first facility. She was snarling across at Halt, her grey wings flapping in Jasmine's face as she struggled to break her hold. But the old man Halt had called Artemis only had eyes for the doctor.

"I will happily oblige, *Chead*," Halt growled. As he spoke, his hand flashed out and caught the old man by the throat.

Artemis's eyes widened as he fought to break Halt's hold. "*How?*" he croaked the word.

Smiling, Halt lifted him into the air. "A little experiment of my own. Did you not notice my eyes?"

With that he tossed the old man casually aside. He went crashing into the heavy metal desk with a thud and slumped to the floor. Halt followed him, hauling the old man back up.

"I thought I'd finally deciphered the *Chead's* developmental issues," Halt spoke in a casual tone as he smashed a fist into the old man's face. Beyond him, Jasmine, Richard and the young girl could only look on in shock. "Unfortunately, I was wrong."

He slammed the old man back into the desk, and grinned as his victim groaned. "But your sweet Mira will soon show me the answer. Do you like her pretty wings? She is something else now, *Chead* no longer. And soon, when the virus is perfected, I will follow her."

Halt laughed as he yanked the old man back into the air. "But you, Artemis, you are obsolete."

At that, Halt wrapped both hands around the old man's neck and twisted sharply. A loud *crack* echoed down the hall. The old man went suddenly limp, his eyes fluttering closed. Smiling, Halt tossed him aside like a ragdoll and then turned to look at the others.

"*No!*" across the hall, the young girl screamed and tore herself lose from Jasmine's arms.

Sobbing, she threw herself on Artemis's broken body, her wings spreading out to enfold the old man. Her body shook as she buried her head in his chest, her sobs echoing out across the hall.

A bemused smile played across Halt's lips as he turned to look at Sam and his companions. He nodded across at the winged intruders. "My patience for our guests' insolence grows thin. Take care of them."

Sam hesitated, glancing from Richard and Jasmine and back to Halt. Behind him, Paul and Francesca took a reluctant step forward, their eyes wary. The collar seemed to constrict around Sam's throat as he swallowed, reminding him of Halt's unspoken threat.

He looked again at Jasmine and Richard. There was no love lost between the three of them, not now, not since they'd faced the final test in the facility. Since that day, there had been blood on all their hands, a shared guilt, a common hatred.

Even so, he had no wish to fight them.

Seeing Sam's hesitation, Halt raised his wrist, flashing the watch on his arm. "Do it. I can still kill your girlfriend from here, Samuel. Don't reverse all your good work now."

Sam gritted his teeth and nodded. He stepped up beside Paul and Francesca, squaring off against the two intruders. Jasmine and Richard shared a reluctant glance, their emerald wings spreading out to either side.

"Give up, Richard, Jasmine," Sam called across to them. "You're out numbered. We don't want to hurt you."

Richard stared back, contempt in his eyes. "Give up?" he asked. "What have they done to you, Sam? How can you stand there and ask us to go back? You know what they'll do to us."

Sam ran a hand through his long hair, struggling to keep the pain from his face. He knew the truth of Richard's words, but he could not turn back now. He had come too far now.

"So be it," he breathed.

To either side of him, Paul and Francesca started forward, and growling, Sam leapt. His wings beat down hard, carrying him into the air and straight for Richard. But with a snarl, Jasmine bounded forward to intercept him. He staggered as her fist caught him in the ribs and sent him reeling, the fury of her onslaught catching him unawares.

On his other side, Richard charged in, but Paul and Francesca threw themselves into the fray, diverting Richard's attention away from Sam. The three of them went down in a rush of flailing limbs and feathers.

Sam swore as Jasmine's wingtip flashed out and caught him in the face. Lurching back, he raised his fists and gathered himself, narrowing his eyes as she came at him again. He tensed as she stepped within range, but before he could attack she leapt into the air, and her foot flashed out to slam into his collar bone.

"*Traitor!*" Jasmine shrieked.

Sam finally managed to duck her blow, and then drove forward. Catching Jasmine around the midriff, he hurled her backwards. She spun, her wings beating hard to break her fall. Smiling, she lifted into the air. Adrenaline thudding in his skull, Sam stretched his wings and leapt after her.

Above, Jasmine rose to the ceiling, her emerald wings shining in the fluorescent lights, and then dropped like a stone towards him. The move caught him by surprise, and her boot slammed into his face with a crunch. He crashed back to the floor, the impact driving the breath from his lungs. Gasping for air, he struggled to sit up.

A scream came from overhead, and through sheer instinct Sam rolled to the side. Jasmine struck the ground where he had lain with a harsh *crack*. Porcelain chips sliced the air as the force of her attack shattered the tiles.

Recovering, Sam rolled to his feet as she straightened. Spinning, his wings flashed out and caught Jasmine square in the face. Taken unawares, she staggered, and he saw his opening.

Sam lunged forward, his fist flashing out to catch Jasmine in the shoulder. His arm shook with the force behind the blow, and it sent the smaller girl stumbling backwards. But she wasn't about to go down so easily. Growling, she bared her teeth and straightened, but Sam was already on her, his boot flashing out to catch her in the stomach.

Jasmine gasped as the blow connected and she slumped to her knees. Seeing his opening, Sam clasped both hands together, and as Jasmine tried to regain her feet, brought them down on her head.

At the last second she looked up, but there was no time to avoid his attack. The force of the blow drove her face first into the tiles. Her wings thrashed as she collapsed, forcing Sam to leap clear. When he looked back, she was struggling to stand. But as he watched, her eyes rolled back in her skull, and she toppled back to the ground.

Panting softly, Sam stood over her. An awful guilt ate at his stomach as her eyes flickered open. A low moan came from her throat as she looked up at him, her brown eyes half-glazed.

"Please, Sam," she coughed. "Don't make me go back. Kill me, but don't make me go back."

Sam shivered as he looked down at her, his heart clenched in a vice. His breath caught in his throat, and images rose from his memory. Looking down at Jasmine, listening to her beg, he saw again the padded room, saw the pain in Jake's eyes, as Sam chose his own life over his friend's.

And he knew he could not do it again.

Letting out a long breath, he shook his head. "I can't do this."

He turned away from Jasmine then, closing his ears to her pleas. Looking out across the hall, he saw Richard pinned against the far wall, desperately trying to hold off Paul and Francesca. The young girl still crouched over Artemis, sobbing into his chest, her grey wings drooped across the ground. Halt was standing over her, a dark scowl on his face.

As Halt reached down and lifted the girl into the air, Sam stepped towards him.

"Halt!" he growled. "Leave her alone."

SEVENTY-FOUR

CHRIS STUMBLED AS ASHLEY'S WEIGHT SHIFTED IN HIS ARMS, and pain flashed from his bullet wound. He gritted his teeth, but the pain wasn't half as bad as the night before. It was clear now the virus had changed more than just their muscles, done more than give them wings. It was the only explanation for Ashley's miraculous recovery. Before they'd left the infirmary, Liz had checked the wound beneath her bandages – it was almost healed.

A whimper came from Ashley and Chris slowed his pace. He took the opportunity to catch his breath, as he glanced ahead at Liz.

She strode down the long corridor, following the directions Artemis had given, her shoulders rigid. Chris swallowed, fighting the need to go to her, to spin her around and tell her everything would be okay. Remembered pain flared across his skin and he turned his eyes to the floor.

In his arms, Ashley moved again. He glanced down as her eyes fluttered open, a frown creasing her brow. "Chris?"

His heart fluttered at her words. A smile spread across his face as he drew to a stop. Ashley wiggled in his arms, lifting her head to look around. "Liz?"

Liz grinned as she turned back. "In the flesh," she stepped forward, and then paused, her shoulders falling.

Ashley closed her eyes with a groan. "Argh, I feel like I've been hit in the head with a brick."

"Chris probably bumped it on the way out of the infirmary," Liz commented wryly.

Chris laughed. "Please, I was careful. And besides, I've been shot, so join the club, Ash."

Ashley raised an eyebrow. "Pretty sure I joined that club first," she grinned. "But put me down if you're that much of a baby. I think I can walk."

Grinning, Chris carefully put Ashley on her feet. She swayed slightly, and he offered her his good arm. "Easy there."

Nodding, Ashley panted softly as she straightened. Her snowy wings hung behind her, flexing slightly with each breath. Her fingers gave Chris's arm a squeeze and he smiled back at her.

Then her eyes shifted to Liz. "What, no hug for an old friend?"

The smile fell from Liz's face and she quickly looked away. But Chris had caught the shimmer of tears. Ashley looked at him quizzically as Liz started off again, but Chris only shook his head. "It's a long story. It can wait. Come on."

They started off again, moving slowly still to allow Ashley time to recover. She was still uneasy on her feet, no doubt the result of the drugs lingering in her blood stream. But that she was standing at all, just a few weeks since being shot from the sky, was a miracle in itself.

"What are you guys doing here?" Ashley asked softly as they walked. "What madness made you come back here?"

In the lead, Liz snorted. "Blame Chris," she replied, apparently having recovered some of her humour. She looked back. "He was distracted by a pretty girl. Got us all caught."

"Sounds about right," Ashley laughed.

"It wasn't *that* bad," Chris half-heartedly defended himself. He shifted Ashley's weight on his shoulder, and continued after Liz.

"Hmm, let's see. You got shot," Liz counted off his failings. "Got us caught and locked away. Is there something I'm forgetting?"

"Hey, we found Ashley, didn't we?"

Liz snorted again and Ashley laughed. They drifted into silence as they made their way down the long corridors. No one appeared to stop them. There was not another living soul in sight, and Chris remembered what Artemis had said about the operations being moved. He guessed their new headquarters had been the facility they'd escaped from in the mountains.

Idly, he wondered where they were now, where such a place could be hidden amongst the packed buildings of San Francisco. The facility was massive, and there had not been a single window in sight. The weight of the concrete walls and ceilings pressed in around him. His wings twitched, and a longing for the escape of open skies rose within him.

Soon.

Chris breathed out a sigh of relief as they turned the final corner and found steel elevator doors waiting for them. Artemis's directions had been perfect – but from here on, the way forward was a mystery. Artemis had never been beyond the elevators. He had lived his entire adult life within these concrete walls, never allowed to see the sun, to feel the breeze on his skin. The thought of such an existence almost brought Chris to tears.

Liz strode into the elevator as Chris and Ashley staggered after her. Ashley was taking more of her own weight now, and she disengaged herself from Chris as they stepped inside and leaned back against the wall. Moving to the control panel, Liz pressed the button for the lobby.

"Hope there's no one home," she murmured.

To their surprise, the elevated shuddered and began to move upwards. Chris glanced at the others, sharing in their disbelief.

We're underground, he realised.

"Where's Sam?" Ashley said suddenly.

Chris bowed his head. "We don't know."

Ashley's eyes shone, but she nodded.

"We'll find him, Ashley," Liz said as the elevator lurched to a stop.

They looked around as the doors slid opened, readying themselves for whatever lay without. But nothing could have prepared them for what they saw.

A massive hall spread out before them, lined columns stretching up to the domed ceiling high above. A row of reception desks stood in front of the elevators, where three women were huddling in fear. Beyond, pure chaos had engulfed the gallery. Men and women stumbled across the tiled floor, rushing for the revolving door at the far end, while in the centre of the open space, five winged figures fought in a blur of sound and movement.

A flash of green and copper feathers came from overhead as Sam soared upwards to clash with Jasmine, only for a sharp kick of her boot to send him crashing back to the ground. Then a shriek drew their attention to where Richard stood wrestling with two newcomers. Chris stared as Richard leapt into the air, his wings beating hard, only for the boy to jump on his back. Black wings tore the air as he dragged Richard back down. They crashed into the tiles and rolled across the ground. Richard was up first, but the girl was on him before he could recover, sending him staggering back towards the far wall.

And in the centre of it all, Halt.

The doctor stood with arms folded, a calm smile twisting his thin lips. His grey eyes watched the scene with detached interest, as though this was no more than a game to him. The body of Artemis lay at his feet, his neck twisted at an awful angle. Mira crouched over the old *Chead*, weeping into his chest. As Chris watched, Halt reached down and pulled her from the body.

Hauling Mira up by her hair, Halt held her in front of his face. "Ah, my little Mira," he laughed as she tried to break free, but her strength was no match for the doctor's.

Liz was right, Chris thought as he stepped from the elevator. He had not had time to think about Liz's accusation back in the cages, but here was the evidence. Mira had more strength in one arm than an ordinary man. Halt shouldn't have stood a chance.

Chris slid towards the reception desks, Ashley and Liz following close behind as they sought to understand what was happening. Ashley was moving without aid now, and some of her old sharpness had returned to her eyes. They crouched together behind the desks as the women fled into the elevator, and shared a glance.

"Halt!" a familiar voice echoed through the hall. "Leave her alone."

Chris peered over the desktop and watched Sam striding across the hall, his copper wings spread, his face filled with rage.

Halt stared for a second, seemingly taken aback by Sam's pronouncement. But his surprise did not last long. Scowling, he tossed Mira aside and then he reached down to press a finger to the watch on his wrist.

A collective scream carried through the hall as Sam and the two winged strangers crumpled, their hands clutched desperately at their necks. Face dark with rage, Halt strode across to their incapacitated friend. Lifting his boot, he drove it into Sam's side, sending him sliding across the tiles.

"How dare you defy me!" Halt's rage echoed from the ceiling as Sam clawed at the tiles, his body still convulsing. Caught in the clutches of the shock collar, Sam could do nothing to defend himself.

On the other side of the hall, Richard stood over the boy and girl he had been fighting, blinking in surprise. A smile tugged at his lips as his gaze travelled across the hall and found Chris and the others. But Chris was already moving, racing towards Halt. He leapt past Mira as she staggered to her feet, gesturing for her to stay back. This had gone on long enough. It was time they rid themselves of the vile doctor. And this time, he wasn't going to let anyone get in his way.

Chris was still a few feet away when Halt looked up and saw him coming. He drove a final kick into Sam's chest before turning to face the greater threat, his grey eyes flashing with rage. A wild grin spread across his lips as Chris leapt.

At the last second, Halt twisted away, and his fist flashed out to catch Chris in the stomach. The breath exploded between Chris's teeth as he staggered back. But he straightened quickly and went for the doctor again.

Now Halt leapt at him, and through sheer instinct Chris turned, shifting himself from the doctor's path. As Halt barrelled past, Chris flicked out with his foot and caught the doctor square in the stomach. Halt crumpled beneath the blow, and grinning Chris stepped in to finish him.

An awful growl rattled up from Halt's throat as he straightened suddenly. Before Chris could jump back, a fist caught him in the side of the head. He reeled away as stars flashed across his vision. Staggering, he felt the strength flee his limbs. Then a second blow caught him in the chin and hurled him backwards.

Chris gasped as he crashed down on the hard tiles. Bones creaking, he struggled to sit up, before a heavy boot crashed down on his chest. He collapsed back to the ground, ears ringing as his head struck.

With a blood curdling scream, Liz appeared from nowhere and slammed into Halt. Wings flashing, the force of her attack lifted Halt off the ground and sent him hurtling through the air. Heart pounding, Chris struggled to sit up, to find the strength to help Liz.

But she didn't need it.

Liz stood a few feet away, her lips drawn back in a snarl, wings extended, fingers clenched like claws. As the doctor staggered back to his feet, she sprang, her hand flashing out to catch him by the throat. With inhuman strength, she hauled him above her head and held him there.

Halt growled as he struggled in her grasp. Then his eyes bulged, and a short, sharp shriek rattled up from his throat. Liz's eyes flashed blue and grey as she lifted him higher, watching as his feet kicked helplessly at empty air. His flesh paled and veins bulged in his forehead, his skin turning an angry red where Liz held him.

Chris shuddered as Halt began to moan, the low, pitiful sound of a dying animal. He couldn't imagine the pain, the pure agony sweeping through the doctor's body. He had only felt Liz's touch for an instant, but it had been enough to take his feet out from under him. This... this could only be infinitely worse.

Purple lines spread up Halt's neck, radiating out from Liz's touch. His struggles weakened, the whites of his eyes now stained red. A low whine hissed from his mouth, but Chris could see the life fleeing his body, suffocated by Liz's touch.

Then he was still.

With a casual shrug of her shoulders, Liz tossed Halt's lifeless body aside.

Chris swallowed as she turned towards him. Grey speckled eyes stared down at him, and for a moment he wondered who was looking out – Liz, or the *Chead*. Then she blinked, and the grey faded away, the blue swelling to replace it.

She shuddered as her shoulders sagged. Chris found his feet and stepped towards her, and then froze as memory of her touch returned.

Hurt flashed across Liz's face as she saw him hesitate.

Without speaking, she turned away.

SEVENTY-FIVE

A DAGGER TWISTED IN LIZ'S CHEST AS SHE SAW THE FEAR flash across Chris's face. She sucked in a breath, fighting back the sting of tears, and turned away from him. Across the hall, she saw Ashley and Sam embracing one another. The collar that had been around Sam's neck lay on the ground beside them, the key she had passed Ashley earlier still in the lock. Beside them, Jasmine had staggered to her feet. Mira huddled under her arm, her cheeks streaked by tears.

Pushing aside her pain, Liz moved to join them. She heard Chris's footsteps as he followed her, but did not look back. In that moment, she could not face him, though all she wanted was to bury her head in his shoulder. Glancing down at her hands, despair rose in her chest, threatening to drown her. Would anyone ever hold her again?

Artemis was dead, and with him the hope they'd had of exposing the government's corruption. No one would believe them without proof, without the *Chead* that had witnessed it all, the supposed monster who spoke like a human. No, the secret had died with Artemis.

But against all chances, they had found Sam and Ashley, had rescued them from the clutches of the government. They just had to make it through the front door, and they were free. The last of the crowd had fled through the revolving door, leaving them alone in the hall.

Her eyes drifted beyond their little group, and found Richard still on the far side of the hall near the elevators. He was crouched over the strangers he'd been fighting, trying to remove their collars. Sam and Ashely were too preoccupied in their reunion to have noticed, but wearily she moved towards Sam's collar to retrieve the key.

Before she could reach it, a bell dinged from the direction of the elevators. Looking up, she saw the metal doors slide open. A woman stepped into view. Her gaze swept the hall, and lifting her arm she pointed at them. Men stepped from the elevator behind her, lifting their rifles to take aim.

Then there was no more time for thought.

On the far side of the hall, Richard looked up as the first of the men stepped from the elevator. His eyes turned towards Liz, and she saw the fear that flashed across his face. Their eyes met, and Liz saw the fear fall away from him. He nodded across at her, and turned away.

"*No!*" Liz screamed.

But it too late; Richard was too far away. He was closer to the elevators, already cut off from the exit by the men and their heavy guns. Straightening, he spread his wings and roared. The guards swung round at the sound, and Richard charged.

The others turned as the first gunshot rang out. Still several feet from the men, Richard lurched as the bullet took him in the shoulder, but he did not slow. He ploughed into the first man, baring him to the ground as he tore the weapon from his grasp.

He was up again a second later, already charging at the next guard. A gun roared again, and blood blossomed from Richard's chest. He stumbled, almost went down, before reaching out and smashing another man off his feet.

Then he spun, his eyes meeting theirs from across the hall. "*Go!*"

Another gunshot tore through the room, and then they were sprinting for the door, half-dragging Jasmine with them, even as she pleaded for them to go back, to leave her behind.

Boom. Boom. Boom.

Liz winced with each gunshot, but she did not look back. Every step she expected hot lead to tear through her body, for a hail of bullets to bring them all down. They raced towards the exit, wings spread and beating hard, half-sprint-ing, half-flying.

They shoved Jasmine through first as they reached the revolving door, and crammed Ashley and Mira in after her. Chris and Sam followed, as Liz cast one final look back.

Richard was still on his feet, swaying as he looked around at the ring of guards. His wings slumped to either side of him, torn and broken by bullets, and blood stained his shirt. He staggered for a second and then straightened, his green eyes looking up to catch Liz's gaze. A smile tugged at his lips as he lifted his arm.

Liz turned away as the roar of gunfire filled the hall.

EPILOGUE

HECATE DREW TO A STOP AT THE EDGE OF THE EMPTY stream and looked back, checking the others were close. They trickled in one by one, picking their slow way across the plains. The harsh sun beat down from overhead, burning at their pale skin, even as the orange globe dropped towards the distant peaks. Their shadows cast long silhouettes across the grass.

As the seven *Chead* drew up around them, Hecate's thoughts drifted back to the strangers they'd left behind. In his mind's eye, he saw again the explosion that had erupted from the side of the mountain, engulfing the buildings in which the group had been hiding. Out on the empty plains, Hecate had watched the flames, waiting to see whether anything had survived.

But there had only been the flickering of the flames, and as dusk fell, he had finally turned away.

Now, days later, Hecate still felt the pang of regret.

Such a waste.

The boy and girl had been talented, strong. The *Chead* could have used their strength. Still it didn't matter now.

For days they had raced across the grasslands, their powerful legs carrying them easily across the flat ground, following a distant scent. They had rarely stopped to sleep, and ate as they moved, slaughtering chickens and other livestock when their hunger demanded it. They revelled in their freedom, in the touch of the breeze over their skin, the sun on their faces.

Though they had been born within the facility, each of them possessed a rugged endurance, an ability to run for endless days and nights. Their imprisonment had not lessened them – the doctors had been sure to keep them healthy and fit, the better for their experiments.

Now, Hecate could sense the wind changing, carrying with it fresh traces of the scent they followed. A delicious sweetness filled the air, familiar and at once alien. It was close now, its source at hand.

The others smelt it too. They shifted around him, faces lifted to breathe it in. They growled and Hecate nodded. Tensing his legs, he leapt down onto the streambed.

Starting upriver, he listened to the crunch of gravel as the others followed. His eyes scanned the riverbed ahead, searching for the source, but finding only plain grey stones. There was no water in sight, only the empty bed of what had once been a great river. Perhaps as Spring set in, the snow on the distant peaks would melt, and return the waters to the dried-out river.

But for today, the river remained dead.

Ahead, Hecate's keen eyes alighted on a dark shadow amidst the stones. Drawing to a stop, he allowed the others to gather around him. His lips twitched as he looked down at the entrance to the cave. The worn bedrock around the entrance suggested the river had once plunged underground here, falling down to depths unknown. Now though, with the waters gone, the entrance to the cave stood open.

The sweet scent of the *Chead* hung thick in the air.

Grinning, Hecate dropped down into the darkness.

Here ends book 1 of the Evolution Gene
Continue the adventure with:
Havoc

NOTE FROM THE AUTHOR

Sorry, I know, I'm awful. I hope you guys didn't get toooo attached to Richard, because I'm afraid unlike Ashley, he won't be coming back. Mutated muscle density and regenerative abilities or not, he ain't bulletproof! Feel free to vent your frustration in a review though, maybe even let me know who your favourite characters are so we don't have any more accidents…

FOLLOW AARON HODGES

Join Aaron Hodges on his Patreon for exclusive sneak peeks into his current works in progress and **a free digital copy of all upcoming novels!**

https://www.patreon.com/aaronhodgesauthor

OR

Join his newsletter to r**eceive TWO FREE novels and a short story!**

https://aaronhodgesauthor.com/newsletter

ALSO BY AARON HODGES

Book 1: Warbringer

Book 2: Wrath of the Forgotten

Book 3: Age of Gods

Book 4: Dreams of Fury

The Alfurian Chronicles

Book 1: Defiant

Book 2: Guardian

Made in the USA
Monee, IL
05 December 2021

84011271R00284